desperate measures

Books by Elle Casey

CONTEMPORARY URBAN FANTASY

War of the Fae (10-book series)
Ten Things You Should Know About Dragons
(short story, The Dragon Chronicles)
My Vampire Summer
Aces High

DYSTOPIAN

Apocalypsis (4-book series)

SCIENCE FICTION

Drifters' Alliance (ongoing series)
Winner Takes All (short story prequel to Drifters' Alliance,
Dark Beyond the Stars Anthology)
The Ivory Tower (short story standalone, Beyond the Stars: A
Planet Too Far Anthology)

ROMANCE

By Degrees
Rebel Wheels (3-book series)
Just One Night (romantic serial)
Just One Week
Love in New York (3-book series)
Shine Not Burn (2-book series)
Bourbon Street Boys (4-book series)
Desperate Measures
Mismatched

ROMANTIC SUSPENSE

*All the Glory: How Jason Bradley Went from
Hero to Zero in Ten Seconds Flat*
Don't Make Me Beautiful
Wrecked (2-book series)

PARANORMAL

Duality (2-book series)
Monkey Business (short story)
Dreampath (short story standalone, The
Telepath Chronicles)
Pocket Full of Sunshine (short story & screenplay)

desperate measures

ELLE CASEY

Elle Casey

PO Box 14367

N Palm Beach, FL 33408

Website: www.ElleCasey.com
Email: info@ellecasey.com

ISBN/EAN-13: 978-1-93945570-3

Second Edition

DEDICATION

To Grace Rainforth

1

aimee

AIMEE SAT AT THE TABLE with her checkbook in front of
her and her ancient laptop open to the page that showed her bank
account balance. Tears rose up and threatened to spill over onto
the cheap, faux leather cover that encased the little pieces of paper
that were supposed to pay her debts. Only, these particular pieces
of paper that said, 'Pay to the Order of' weren't going to be paying
anyone for anything, anytime soon – seeing as how the balance
glaring out at her from the computer screen was glowing red.

"Crap and double crap," she whispered to herself. She looked
over at the houseplant dying on the windowsill and said, "How
am I supposed to buy groceries with no money? Pay the mortgage? Get gas?" She dropped her head into her hands, letting her
pen fall to the table with a clatter. *How did my life get so screwed up?*
she wondered, for the hundredth time in the past few months.

She pushed her chair out and stood up, reluctantly heading over
to the telephone. By some miracle it was still working, even though
she hadn't paid the bill in two months. She was saving her mea-
ger cell phone minutes for emergencies, relying on this landline to
communicate with the outside world. She dialed the number that

literally made her sick to her stomach as she thought about who it would connect her to. *Him.* The person upon whose feet she wanted to and could fairly lay all the blame for her current sorry situation.

"Hello, *Parsons, Kenrick, and Glad, Attorneys at Law,* how may I direct your call?" said the cheerful, professional voice on the other end.

"May I speak with Jack Parsons, please? This is Aimee."

"Oh," said the voice, abruptly. And then, "Hi, Aimee," in a softer tone laced with pity. "Hold on a sec, okay?"

"Sure, Lucy. Thanks."

Aimee thought about all the years she'd known Lucy, the dependable receptionist at her husband's law firm. She wondered how much Lucy had known about Aimee's husband and his assistant, Tiffany, and she speculated about all the things Lucy *hadn't* said to her. Aimee didn't believe Lucy was as clueless as she acted, but she tried to remind herself that Lucy had children to support and really needed her job. She couldn't be expected to tell Aimee any of the firm's dirty little secrets, even if they did involve Aimee's husband.

The line clicked and Jack Parsons came on the line. "Jack. What do you want?"

"Hello to you too, Jack." Aimee hated her meek tone but didn't have the guts to change it. She wished she could sound more angry, but something always stopped her. She wrote it off to years of her mother telling her that manners were what separated us from monkeys.

"I don't have time to play games, Aimee. What do you want this time?"

She hardened her heart to his disregard. "I need you to pay me my temporary support. You're three weeks late now. I can't pay my bills ... I can't even pay for food at this point."

"You need to get a job. You know that. I've told you several times."

"Listen, Jack, you know I've been trying. No one is hiring right now, especially someone without a college degree who's been a housewife for the past ten years. I have no current work experience! I can't even get a job cleaning houses, for chrissakes."

"You don't need to curse at me."

"Whatever. I don't have time for your self-righteous bullcrap. You filed for this divorce. I need to come pick up a check. When will it be ready?"

"I'm busy right now. Heading out for depositions. You can come by on Monday."

"That's three days from now!" she cried desperately. The couch cushions had long ago given up the last few coins they held. And if it hadn't been for him emptying out their savings accounts behind her back, she wouldn't be where she was right now – poorer than she'd ever been in her entire life. Even as a teenager, she'd always paid her bills on time with money she'd earned and saved.

"Not my problem," he said callously. "Maybe if you'd tried harder to get a job two months ago, you wouldn't be in this situation."

Aimee gripped the phone so hard, it was a miracle it didn't break in half. "Oh yeah?! Well, maybe you shouldn't have cheated on me and slept with your practically-teenage, bubble-headed assistant! Ever thought of that?!"

The only answer she received was the sound of a dead line. She didn't even know if he'd heard that last bit – and that only made her angrier, because that was the piece he really needed to hear. She wished she could cram it down his throat. With a golf club.

Her eyes lit up. *Golf clubs!* He had put his favorite set in the garage the other day when he'd run out of room in the trunk of his Aston Martin. She remembered seeing it propped up in the corner near the water heater when she'd gone out to find the mop earlier.

She put the phone down on the counter and ran to the three-car garage, flicking on the light absently while her eyes scanned the hyper-organized space, looking for the dark blue hulking figure of her almost-ex's well-maintained, top of the line set. He called these golf clubs his babies. She remembered bitterly what he'd said when she saw the credit card balance and the ridiculous charges for the various drivers and irons.

"I have to spend my money on *something*," he'd said. "You aren't getting pregnant, so if I can't have a kid, these new clubs will be my babies." He'd poured himself another martini and laughed at his own cruel joke, as Aimee struggled not to wad up the credit card bill and throw it in his face. Instead, she'd calmly filed it away, as she was expected to.

Stupid, stupid, stupid. I was such a frigging welcome mat for him – always letting him wipe his feet off on me. Frigging jerk.

Her eyes lit up as they spied the leather bag that held Jack's babies. He'd spent over thirty grand on them a year ago. That was just before he'd started boinking his assistant, Tiffany. Aimee's upper lip raised in a silent snarl, just thinking the name. *Tiffany*. He'd stopped golfing so much after he started 'working late' and going on 'weekend work retreats'. And after Tiffany had gotten pregnant? Well, these golf-club-babies had taken to hanging out in Aimee's garage more often than not.

Apparently, Tiffany's garage was too full to fit his clubs in. Too full of the new SUV Jack had bought her and all the baby gifts he and his friends had started collecting. Jack and Tiffany were having a boy, so there were a lot of things to buy, of course. And there would be no money left over for spousal support or food for an unemployed soon-to-be ex-wife. Aimee knew that short of a huge court battle, she wasn't going to be able to depend on any financial support from him. She tried not to scream at the unfairness of it all, focusing instead on doing what needed to be done.

She walked over and grabbed the bag, wrestling it across the empty garage and into the house. She dragged it to the living room and dropped it heavily in the middle of the floor. She didn't have to worry about hitting any furniture on her way, since most of it was gone now. Her ex was fond of making unannounced runs over to her house when she wasn't home to steal furniture, paintings, and the knick-knacks they'd collected during their marriage, to bring back to his new girlfriend's place. Aimee had heard from a neighbor that Jack actually brought Tiffany along when he came sometimes, which meant that the slutty husband-stealer had been walking through Aimee's house as if it were a department store, picking out all the items she wanted to furnish her house with

- the new townhouse that Jack had bought with their marital savings and put in Tiffany's name.

Aimee had finally gotten wise to his deceit and had taken her favorite things and locked them in the trunk of her car. So far, he hadn't figured that out. Not for the first time, she wished she had a friend who would take some things for her, to keep them out of Tiffany's hands; but all of the people she had thought were her friends, were actually just wives of her husband's friends. Once he'd declared his undying love for Tiffany, they'd all flocked to her like flies on crap.

Aimee left the room to retrieve her camera from her purse. She needed to get a shot of the golf clubs while there was still some good light in the front room.

Twenty minutes later, she had four nice pictures of the clubs, the bag, and all the little gloves and balls and tees and whatnot that had been in the pockets, loaded up onto the Internet and advertised on Craigslist. She rubbed her hands together, waiting for the emails to start flooding in.

The first one came within five minutes.

IS THIS FOR REAL? YOU'RE REALLY SELLING THESE OR IS THIS A SCAM?

She smiled, more than a little maliciously, her conscience only nagging her a little. She typed out her response:

YES IT'S FOR REAL, AND NO, IT'S NOT A SCAM. MAKE ME AN OFFER.

While she waited for the disbeliever to email her back, another email came in. And then another. "Thank goodness for golf nuts," she said to her houseplant, as she replied to each message in turn. All but one sender wondered if she were off her rocker, so she started just cutting and pasting a standard response.

She felt something on her leg and reached down automatically to pet the cat that wasn't there. He hadn't been there for months. She was pretty sure he'd died of a broken heart after Jack had left and refused to take him along. Tiffany was allergic to cats, plus there had been the future baby to think of. Chauncey was never Aimee's cat – Jack had bought him one day fifteen years ago on a whim – but she missed his company anyway. She wished she could get a new pet, but was worried about how she would feed it. The houseplant was going to have to fit the bill for companionship for now.

She focused on the last email that had come through – this one different in tone than the others – from someone named 'Elizabeth @ Channing Burkes'.

I HAVE A CLIENT WHO WOULD BE INTEREST-ED. WOULD YOU TAKE TEN THOUSAND FOR THE SET?

"Whoa!" Aimee shouted out into the empty kitchen. She knew the clubs were worth nearly three times that, especially since they were hardly used and a few were custom made, but she had never expected to get anything near this amount. She narrowed her eyes. "You'd better not be scamming me, you turd."

She started typing:

YES. BUT NO CHECKS AND NO WIRING OF FUNDS FROM NIGERIA. AND IF YOU'RE A LAW-YER, YOU CAN FORGET IT.

The houseplant sat there, almost as if staring at her ... admonishing her. "What?" she said, looking at it and trying again not to feel guilty. "He's the one who left and took all our money, not leaving me anything to support myself with. What else am I supposed to do? I already sold my wedding ring and engagement ring – which was a quarter the size of Tiffany's by the way – and all the silver and china."

The houseplant just sat there. Being a plant.

Aimee rolled her eyes. "He'll have me committed if he ever catch-es me talking to you, you know." She refused, for that reason, to further defend her decision to sell the clubs and not to any lawyers. Lawyers were bad guys in her book. In her experience, all they did was take and take and take ... and then walked all over anyone who was stupid enough to have given them anything. Just like Jack.

The email inbox beeped at her, telling her a new message was there from Elizabeth.

NO, I'M NOT A LAWYER. I'M AN ACCOUNTANT. I'M HAPPY TO BRING YOU CASH. I'VE ALREADY SPOKEN WITH MY CLIENT AND RECEIVED HIS APPROVAL. WHERE WOULD YOU LIKE TO MEET?

Aimee hemmed and hawed. *Where? Where? Where?* She looked at the plant again. "Where should I meet her? I don't think letting anyone come here is a good idea." She was a single woman, alone, and desperate. That would be obvious to anyone seeing how sparsely the place was furnished now and how crappy Aimee herself looked. Jack was almost fond of saying how much she'd let herself go. He, on the other hand, looked as if he'd just stepped off the cover of a men's fitness magazine. All the weight he'd gained during their marriage had melted off once he'd started staying at the office late. *Funny, how that worked.*

Before she could come up with a suitable answer, another email from Elizabeth came through.

I'M GOING TO A BOOK CLUB MEETING TONIGHT. YOU COULD MEET ME IN THE BOOKSTORE PARKING LOT IF YOU'D LIKE.

"Hmmm, bookstore. That sounds safe and anonymous."
Aimee quickly responded:

THAT SOUNDS GOOD. SEND ME THE ADDRESS AND TIME AND I'LL MEET YOU THERE. REMEMBER, CASH ONLY. NO HUNDREDS.

She felt a little like a thief, the way she was talking, but she worried that someone was going to pass her a bunch of counterfeit money and leave her minus the only thing she had left of value in her house, other than her car - which she couldn't afford to sell and be without transportation.

Another message popped up.

I DON'T MEAN TO BE RUDE, BUT I NEED TO TELL YOU THAT I CANNOT PURCHASE STO-LEN MERCHANDISE. DO YOU HAVE PROOFS OF PURCHASE?

Aimee's face colored, but she quickly pushed aside any misgivings about the ownership of the clubs – since technically Jack was still her husband, and he'd already taken more than that in value of her stuff – and typed:

THEY ARE NOT STOLEN. THEY ARE MY HUS-BAND'S. I WILL BRING THE RECEIPTS. I JUST DON'T WANT ANY COUNTERFEIT MONEY. SOR-RY IF THAT WAS WEIRD.

Aimee had kept the receipts as directed by Jack, who was really anal about financial records. He insisted that she tape all of their receipts onto pieces of paper and then file the papers in binders, while also simultaneously entering the amounts into the accounting software they kept for personal expenses. So when their accountant came each year, he could be left alone in a room with all the binders and the computer to do his work uninterrupted. Jack didn't want to pay a single red cent more to the accountant than he needed to, so he used her free labor to do most of the job all year long, allowing the tax preparation to be done in record time, especially taking into account their considerable household expenses. Golf club community living didn't come cheaply, nor did Jack's expensive habits.

The response email came with a beep.

VERY GOOD. I'VE ATTACHED A MAP WITH DIRECTIONS AND INFORMATION ABOUT THE WOMEN'S BOOK CLUB MEETING, IN CASE YOU WANT TO JOIN US. IT'S A NEW GROUP AND WE NEED MORE MEMBERS.

Aimee clicked on the attachment and saw that the bookstore was close and that the book club had just finished a book she had read last week. It would only take about ten minutes to get there. She was a serious book lover, but hadn't been to that bookstore in months. Unable to afford new novels anymore, she was at the library two times a week, trading in the already read for the unread. She'd even gone so far as to trade in all the books she'd collected over the years to get credits at the local used bookstore. She'd burned through those in two months.

Aimee thought about the idea of gathering with a group of women to discuss stories they'd read and was definitely intrigued. She didn't have any friends to talk to. *It might be nice to have something to think about other than desperation, for a change.* She looked at the houseplant and frowned, trying to remember how much gas she had left in her car. She smiled as she realized that soon, she'd have ten thousand bucks and would be able to fill up her tank and maybe even buy a new book as a treat. The rest of the cash she'd hide away for emergencies. Like food. Her stomach growled, reminding her that it hadn't been fed yet today. She quickly typed out her response,

I'LL SEE YOU AT SEVEN. AND I WILL PROBABLY STAY FOR THE MEETING. SOUNDS FUN! THANKS FOR THE INVITATION.

She clicked over to the ad she'd placed and removed it, sending out a mass email to all the people who had responded, over fifty in less than thirty minutes, telling them the clubs were sold. Once she heard the zooming sound that told her the email had gone out, she shut her computer off and went to her bedroom, looking for something to wear that might be suitable for an evening of talking about romance and true love. *Bah. As if that even exists.*

2

kiki

$\mathcal{K}$IKI REACHED INTO HER CAVERNOUS closet, shoving her rarely used anymore conservative khaki pants and button-down shirts aside, to grab her favorite Jimmy Choo thigh-high black suede boots. She sat down on her bed, pulling them up slowly, enjoying the feel of the soft, high-quality material sliding across her skin. She was letting her legs go bare underneath because she could – they were long, thin, and bronzed to perfection, with just the right amount of muscle tone. There was no need to cover them up with uncomfortable pantyhose or tights. She did wear a pair of small footies to keep her feet from sweating, though. She hated sweaty feet and this was Florida, after all.

She looked at her diamond-encrusted platinum watch, happy to see that she had plenty of time to drop by the bookstore for a new romance novel and a cup of coffee, before visiting a friend in the hospital and then going to work. She stood up next to her bed, pulling the edges of her short, stretchy miniskirt down. It had ridden up to reveal her purple lace panties. This skirt was definitely not the sitting down type; but it didn't matter, because where she worked, she wouldn't be sitting. Not in the beginning anyway, and not without an extra payday.

She grabbed her black Dooney & Bourke satchel that managed to match just about anything she wore, and headed out the door. Seconds later she was sliding into the mint-condition, numbers-matching, '69 Camaro that rested in her tiny townhouse garage, when it wasn't menacing the streets of Orlando with its awesomeness.

She'd bought the car as a piece of junk five years ago from an old granny who'd had it parked in a barn out of town for forty years, using tips she'd earned at work over the years to have it restored. She didn't do any of the work herself – she had nails that needed to stay pretty – but her mechanic was a genius. The only parts that weren't original were the air-conditioning, the stereo, and the alarm system that she'd had him put in. A girl could only do so much roughing-it, and Orlando's humidity is legendary.

She put the key into the ignition and turned the engine over, reveling in the heavy rumble of the muscle car's engine that surrounded her, smiling as she thought about her destination. The bookstore was one of her favorite places to hang out. Anybody who knew her at work would probably laugh at that and think it was a joke. Kiki was a different person there on purpose. It was a mask she put on, separating what she had chosen to do to accomplish her goals from who she really was as a person.

She slowly backed the car out of the garage and into the street. She grabbed the chrome and black gear shift and flexed her bicep, pulling it down two notches with heavy clunking sounds. She felt the corresponding response from the massive engine trying to surge the car forward as it adjusted itself into Drive. Three hundred and seventy-five horses were ready to take Kiki wherever she wanted to go, and fast. The tip of her boot barely lifted off the brake and touched the accelerator before she was off, on the hunt for her next escape – into the land of romance and chick lit where her brain lived when it wasn't playing the game of life with a bunch of people who she, for the most part, couldn't care less about.

Kiki arrived at the bookstore in fifteen minutes, beating her former record by a full three. She'd gotten green lights the entire way there, and that never happened. *Must be my lucky day*, she thought, as she switched the engine off, smiling at her good fortune. She looked at the clock on her dashboard and realized she had at least ninety minutes before she had to leave for the hospital. She wasn't relishing that trip one bit, but it had to be done. At least there would be some time to get lost in a book for a while, first.

Kiki got out of the car and pulled her skirt down to cover her exposed underwear once again, mindless of the stares sent her way by every single person close enough to see her.

Everything about Kiki screamed 'look at me' – from her car, to her clothes, to her natural, stunning beauty. She didn't do it on purpose; it's just who she was. She used to cover up her inner-Kiki when she was younger and going to college, but once she reached thirty, there didn't seem to be any point. It didn't help make friends anyway, so what did it matter?

Kiki walked with long strides toward the bookstore with plans to head straight for the romance novel section, her high heels not slowing her down one bit. She was just about to grab the large brass handle of the front door to pull it open, when a flier taped to the front of it caught her attention.

WOMEN'S ROMANCE READER / BOOK LOVER MEETING TONIGHT! JOIN US FOR COFFEE AND BOOKS AT 7:00 P.M. NEW MEMBERS WELCOME.

Kiki stood there, reading and re-reading it, wondering what it was all about. A quick self-evaluation told her she was a book lover and that romance and chick lit were her favorite genres. Even when she strayed from time to time into thrillers or fantasy, she always came back to women's fiction. Maybe it would be fun to join a few other girls who felt the same way she did about books.

She shook the thoughts away, sending them out of her head as quickly as they had come. She didn't make friends, and she didn't join clubs. The first part wasn't really her choice; and the second part, not joining clubs, was a choice made for her in the past by others. Every time she joined one, whether it was academic or socially-based, they all ended in the same way – with girls hating her and guys wanting her. It was a disaster she'd learned to avoid years ago.

Kiki pulled the door open, stepping back as she prepared to enter, and accidentally bumped into someone behind her. She spun around quickly, her hand still on the door. "Oh, sorry! I didn't see you there." She realized a second later that her heel had landed on an uneven surface and her face blanched. "Oh *shit*, did I step on your toe?" It didn't take much with these heels and her very tall stature to cause some serious damage to unprotected toes. She was thin, but her well-muscled frame brought her in at about a hundred and thirty pounds, and when most of her weight was focused on a half-inch square of spiked heel, one wrong step could leave one hell of a bruise.

"Oh, no, not at all. That was my golf club you stepped on."

Kiki raised an eyebrow at the woman who was now standing in front of her, making a quick appraisal: housewife, about thirty years old, ten pounds overweight, in bad need of a style makeover, eager, friendly face, and looking like a crazy person carrying a golf club into the bookstore.

"Are you going to go beat some books to death?" asked Kiki.

"What?" asked the girl, confusion written all over her face as she stood there in her too-tight jeans and flowing, flowered chiffon top.

"With the golf club? In your hand?" Kiki gestured with her chin at the object and started to wonder if this girl might be a little batty.

The girl looked down at the hand that was holding the club, understanding finally dawning across her face a half-second later. "Oooh!" she said smiling and then giggling. "Yeah! I mean, no! Of course not. I would never beat a book to death. Now, an ex-husband? ... That's a different story." Then she stopped talking immediately and frowned guiltily, as if she'd said too much.

Kiki smiled. "I know the feeling." She pulled the door open more fully, inviting the woman to go in before her.

The girl tilted her head to the side, an expression of disbelief on her face. "You're divorced?"

"No."

"I was gonna say," said the girl, shaking her head, moving to go inside.

"What's that supposed to mean?" asked Kiki, following her in and wondering if she should feel offended.

The girl rolled her eyes, turning around in the foyer to look at Kiki fully again. "Oh, shit, I'm sorry. That sounded so rude. I'm a jerk. I just meant that if someone as beautiful as you can get dumped, there's absolutely no hope for someone like me."

Kiki smiled, humorlessly. She hated hearing about how beautiful she was all the time. "Beauty isn't all it's cracked up to be, believe me. Besides. You're pretty."

"Uh-huh," said the girl, not sounding at all convinced. "Well, anyway, sorry if I said something to offend you. I'm a little nervous right now." She went to grab the second door to open it and enter the retail floor area of the store.

"Nervous about your upcoming golf game? Or the murder of your ex?"

The girl laughed and then started whispering, "Neither. I'm going to a book club meeting. I've never been to one before. Are you a member?" She pulled open the second door and stepped through, standing in the entrance where it was usually as quiet as a library.

"No. I'm just here to buy a book," said Kiki, whispering too.

"Oh. Okay. Well, nice meeting you ... sorry, I didn't ask your name yet."

"It's Kiki."

"Okay, well, nice meeting you, Kiki. My name's Aimee, by the way. Love your boots." She smiled big and then walked away, going to the front desk. Kiki went in the opposite direction, to the women's fiction section. She couldn't help but look back after a couple steps and smile at the girl who for some strange reason had brought a golf club into the bookstore to attend a romance lovers' book club meeting.

3

elizabeth

$\mathcal{E}$LIZABETH WAS NERVOUS. SHE HATED carrying this kind of cash around with her, especially when it wasn't her cash to lose. She hadn't been able to think of anyplace safer than a bookstore to meet. It was second only to a church, but since she didn't go to services regularly, she felt a little guilty about using its sanctuary to exchange used goods in an under-the-table type fashion.

Her eyes cast about the store, trying to guess the identity of the seller of the golf clubs. She'd positioned herself in the romance section so she could see the entrance easily. She watched as two people stood outside the front doors, talking. One of them was really tall and the other one short. She couldn't tell if they were together or not, but they entered at the same time. One of them, the shorter one, was carrying a golf club. *That has to be her.* Elizabeth watched as the two women split up, one going to the front desk and the other coming straight in her direction.

Elizabeth didn't want to be caught spying, so she grabbed a book off the shelf and acted liked she was interested in reading it. She paid no attention to the cover as she flipped the book over, ignoring the words on the back in favor of trying to get a peek at the girl headed her way.

She was tall and wearing those kind of sexy boots that went way, way up, leaving only a bit of thigh showing. The reason any of her leg was visible at all was because she had a micro-mini on; otherwise, if she'd been wearing a skirt like Elizabeth normally wore, there would have been no skin showing, the skirt hiding what little thigh might have been exposed. Elizabeth smoothed her hand down her pants self-consciously when she saw how high this other girl's skirt was riding. The woman looked like a hooker in that outfit. The hot pink skin-tight top and short leather jacket completed the ensemble perfectly. Elizabeth wondered what a prostitute was doing in the bookstore. *Is this the newest place to pick up men? Why is she coming into the romance section? To get pointers?*

The prostitute stopped at the bookshelf right next to Elizabeth and began scanning the shelves. Elizabeth stepped over a bit to give her room to browse. She felt stuck. This woman was standing right there where Elizabeth had pulled the book from, making it impossible for her to put it back without having to ask her to move.

Crap. I need to get out of here. Elizabeth was becoming more anxious by the second. She needed to get over to the girl with the golf club in her hand, before she ended up in the book club meeting with it, forcing Elizabeth to make explanations she'd rather not. She looked at the cover of the book she was holding in her hand to figure out where to put it back, since the books in this section were alphabetized by author last name. She nearly choked when she realized she'd pulled an erotic romance off the shelf, whose title and cover left very little to the imagination.

Elizabeth's conscience wouldn't allow her to just shove the book back anywhere. She hated it when people did that, since it made it so hard for someone else to find later. Plus it made extra work for the employees, which wasn't right. She took a deep breath and said, "Excuse me," reaching over to put the book back in its place.

The girl in the mini-skirt raised her eyebrow as she took in the title. She looked at Elizabeth and asked, "Is it any good?"

Elizabeth didn't respond for a moment, only realizing after a split-second that the woman was speaking to her. "Um, excuse me?"

"I said, is that book any good? The one you were just holding in your hand. *'Hot Beef Injection'*."

"Oh, God, no ... what? Um ... I don't know," stuttered Elizabeth, humiliated that she'd been caught with that book in her hand, her face going beet red above the collar that was buttoned all the way up under her business suit. She'd come directly from work.

"Is it no, you didn't like it? Or no, you don't know because you haven't read it yet?"

"What?" asked Elizabeth, ready at any moment to go into full panic mode. This woman was asking her questions about a book she'd no sooner buy and read than she would the latest auto-biography written by a serial killer.

The girl pulled the book off the shelf and held it out to Elizabeth. "Did ... you ... like ... this ... book?"

Elizabeth's eyes nearly bugged out of her head as she anxiously and quickly pushed the book away from her. "Put it away!" she whispered. "Before someone sees you!"

The girl smiled. "Sees me what? Holding a book? That's what people do in bookstores."

Elizabeth rolled her eyes and stepped away to give herself some breathing space. "Not those kinds of books. Not me."

The girl shrugged. "Well, someone must. Otherwise, they wouldn't be in here." She looked down and flipped the book over to read the back, smiling at something she saw there.

Elizabeth figured she knew exactly what kind of people read those kinds of books. She stepped to the side as if she were going to leave. The voice of the girl stopped her.

"Do you have any suggestions? Something ... not so sexy, maybe?"

"What do you mean by that?" asked Elizabeth, slightly offended that this hooker person would think she was somehow only knowledgeable about non-sexy books. She'd read plenty of hot romances in her time. That's how she knew she'd really missed

out in the sex department in her own love affairs. None of her relationships had ever been anything like the ones she read about.

"Nothing personal. I can see you don't read the erotic stuff,
since you're embarrassed about it. And you're standing here in
women's fiction. That tells me you must like the genre. So? Do
you have any recommendations?" The girl stood there, practically insisting that Elizabeth answer her.

The book lover in Elizabeth won out. She couldn't help but talk
about books with someone else who wanted to. This was totally
different than trying to force bookish conversation on someone at
work who really wasn't interested in the things Elizabeth found
exciting.

Elizabeth stepped toward the girl, smiling tentatively and
speaking in quiet tones. "Well, actually, there's this great book I
just read, that we're going to discuss at the book meeting that's
starting in about five minutes." She turned and grabbed a book
off the shelf, handing it to the tall girl. "Have you read this one
yet?"

The girl smiled. "Yes, actually, I read that one when it came out
in hardcover. I couldn't wait for the paperback."

Elizabeth was pleasantly surprised to hear that. She was guilty
herself of paying way too much for a hardcover because she
didn't want to wait. "Did you like it?"

"Loved it. Except for the end. It kind of pissed me off, the way
it seemed like it was hurried a bit."

Elizabeth's face lit up. "I know! I totally agree!" She shook her
head. "Sometimes I wonder what authors are thinking when they
do stuff like that."

The girl smiled back at her, saying nothing.

"Well, if you want, we're having this book club meeting, and
we'd love to have you come by. If you're not too busy." Elizabeth
was excited to have not just one new member, but possibly two
coming to the meeting. *Who cares if they're a hooker and a nut walking around with a golf club. Book lovers are book lovers.*

She'd started the group just a few weeks prior, but so far had
only gotten two other women to join, and only one of them was as

nuts about books as she was – and this lady was nearly a hundred years old from the looks of her and not always able to hear everything that was being discussed. At this point, Elizabeth would be delighted to even have a hooker join them, so long as she loved books too.

The girl shrugged. "I don't know. Maybe next time. I have somewhere I need to be."

Elizabeth's face fell. "Oh. Okay. Maybe next time, then. We meet every other week here at seven. Feel free to come anytime. There are no dues or anything. You can call the bookstore, and they'll tell you what book we're reading."

"Thanks. I might do that."

Elizabeth returned her smile. "Okay. I have to go. I'm meeting someone before we start. My name's Elizabeth, by the way." She held her hand out.

"Kiki." The girl took her hand in a firm grip and shook it.

Elizabeth had expected a limp fish, not the business-like grasp she received. She smiled at the incongruity. Kiki wasn't exactly what Elizabeth had assumed she'd be like, based on what she was wearing, but it was refreshing to be wrong in a good way like that. She hurriedly put the book that she'd suggested to Kiki back on the shelf and walked off, intent on finding the girl with the golf club. It was time to do her back-alley dealing and get rid of this lump of cash that was in her bag. Then she'd be able to move on to more interesting things – like talking about true love and wine and chocolate.

She sighed as she made her way to the front desk, wishing life could really be about that stuff instead of clients and spreadsheets and tax forms and endless calculations of debits and credits on balance sheets that meant nothing to her personally. This pitiful book club was the only thing keeping her from going totally insane.

4

aimee

IMEE LEFT THE FRONT DESK, toting the golf club and ignoring the curious stares of the customers and employees standing
around, as she headed for the area in the corner of the store she had
been told was set aside for the book club meeting. It was billed by
the employee she'd talked to as a small space, closed off by glass
walls, with couches inside and easy access to the bathroom.

She got halfway across the store before she was approached by
a matronly-looking lady wearing a conservative brown business
suit, her hair up in a severe bun at the back of her head. Aimee had
noticed the old-school 'do in profile, when the woman looked right
and then left quickly, as if she were nervous about something.

"Hello," said the woman. "Are you ... here to sell some golf
clubs, by any chance?"

Aimee smiled, holding out her free hand awkwardly as she
battled the purse that was threatening to fall off her shoulder at
any second. "Hi! Yes, that's me. I'm Aimee."

Elizabeth took her hand, shaking it softly, smiling back perfunctorily. "I'm Elizabeth. Do you want to do this in the parking
lot? You can move the clubs to my trunk that way. Before the

meeting." She paused, searching Aimee's face. "Are you coming to the meeting?"

"Yes, I am. Wouldn't miss it for the world." Aimee knew she was more excited than she probably should be – it was just a book club for gosh sakes – but it was the first fun thing she'd done in a long time, and it wasn't costing her anything except a little gas money, so that was just the guilt-free bonus she needed. She was happy without even figuring in the unloading of Jack's babies for ten thousand dollars.

"Good. I'm parked at the end of the row, farthest from the door. In the blue Buick."

"I have a green Toyota. I'll drive my car over closer to yours. The bag is heavy."

Aimee walked out, followed by Elizabeth. They each went to their cars, and Aimee brought hers over to park next to Elizabeth's, squeezing her way into a spot that was right next to one of those loud, man-cars with a gaudy orange paint job and a double black stripe down the center.

Once there, she opened her trunk and pulled the bag out to stand it up at the back of the car.

Elizabeth went into her Buick and pulled out a leather portfolio that was sitting on her front passenger seat.

Aimee noticed that it appeared to have a checklist inside, neatly clipped to the inner hard surface of the folder.

"Okay," said Elizabeth, "let's do a quick inventory."

Aimee raised her eyebrows in question, but said, "Oookaaaay. No problem."

Elizabeth must have sensed her reticence because she explained, "I am buying these for a client. I have to be sure everything is here. I don't want to have to reimburse him out of my own pocket if anything is missing."

Aimee felt bad for some reason she wasn't even certain of, so she said, "Oh, don't worry about it; I totally understand. Go ahead. Tell me what's on the list."

Elizabeth nodded and immediately got down to business, calling out club types and different item names as they had been listed in the advertisement, while Aimee searched through the bag and pulled one thing out at a time, allowing Elizabeth to inspect it and check it off her list.

When they were finally done five minutes later, and Aimee had showed her the receipts, Elizabeth put the closed folder under her arm and grabbed the bag by one of its handles, getting ready to lift it up and put it into her waiting trunk.

"Here ... let me help you with that. It's super heavy," said Aimee, as she stooped to grab the bag at another spot.

Elizabeth chose that exact moment to bend over too, causing both of their heads to come together with a loud clunk, sending both of them falling backwards onto their butts.

The golf clubs and the heavy bag holding them went down with a crash, landing on the bag's side halfway out into the driving area of the row they were parked in.

"*Owowowowow!*" yelled Aimee, sitting up instantly and grabbing her head. "Oh, *boy*, that hurt like a *mother!*"

Elizabeth's only response was to sit up with a quick hiss of breath, her face showing the supreme control she was exercising over the pain.

Aimee's attention was pulled away from her rapidly forming headache by the loud footsteps she heard coming over at a hurried pace, the click, click, clicking of boot heels on the surface telling her who it was before Aimee actually saw her.

"Wow, are you guys okay?" said a female voice. "That was an epic head crack. It was like watching the Three Stooges, live on stage. Only with two stooges, not three."

Aimee turned her head to look at the girl who had approached and stopped practically above her – Kiki. From her vantage point, Aimee could see right up her skirt. "Nice panties, Kiki," she said, not thinking before opening her mouth.

Kiki grinned. "Thanks. Victoria's Secret."

"Oh, I love that place," said Aimee, talking in a dreamy voice.

"You guys know each other?" asked Elizabeth.

Aimee noticed Elizabeth casually reaching up to check her purse, feeling the strap across her chest. Aimee wondered if she should feel offended that it seemed like Elizabeth was worried about getting her purse stolen. She looked up at Kiki to see if she noticed or if she was offended.

"We met today, as we were coming in," explained Kiki. "It's not every day you see a person going into a bookstore with a golf club in hand. I thought she was going to beat someone in there to death."

Aimee smiled. "Yeah. It's my conversation starter. Never fails."

Elizabeth smiled, loosening her grasp on her bag.

Kiki held her hand out for Aimee to grab. "Come on. Get up. That ground is super dirty."

Aimee took her hand and used it to leverage herself into a standing position. Then she held her hand out to Elizabeth at the exact same time as Kiki did. They all smiled, as Elizabeth took both their hands and stood up. She spent the next few seconds brushing off her rear end and legs, then feeling the sides of her hair to make sure none of it had escaped the confines of her bun.

"So," said Elizabeth when she was finished.

"So," said Aimee, looking at the other girls, feeling a little awkward.

"Do you guys need help here, or what?" asked Kiki.

"Yes," they both answered in unison, causing more grins to erupt from the group.

Kiki took charge. "You guys get the ends. I'll help you balance it, Aimee."

Aimee followed her orders, carefully measuring the force she had to use to lift it against the strength she felt coming from Elizabeth, and in no time they had the monstrous thing loaded into her trunk. Aimee watched with satisfaction as the weight of the clubs caused the Buick's back end to go down a little. *Bye bye, Jack's babies.*

Elizabeth reached into her purse and pulled out a manila envelope wrapped around stacks of bills.

"Whoa. This is like a serious deal going down here, isn't it?" asked Kiki, a slight smile on her face.

"Yes. Very hush, hush. But it's not drugs or anything illegal," assured Aimee. She went to shove it in her purse, but Kiki put her hand on her arm to stop her.

"Aren't you going to count it?" she asked.

"No. I trust her."

Kiki looked at her, confused. "I thought you guys just met."

"We did," said Aimee, not understanding what Kiki was getting at.

Kiki rolled her eyes. "Count the money."

Aimee felt her face getting red. "That's okay, really. I don't need to."

Elizabeth nodded her head. "No, Aimee, you should. Go ahead. I counted it three times, but you should make sure."

Aimee felt herself starting to sweat. "No, I'm okay. We have a meeting anyway."

Kiki crossed her arms. "Why don't you want to count it? Now I'm curious, so you have to tell me. I can be very annoying when I don't get my way."

Aimee looked at Kiki, visions of an Amazon warrior flashing across her mind's eye. Kiki could be pretty intimidating when she wanted to be, apparently. "I just ... I don't want to be rude, I guess."

Kiki snapped her fingers and then held out her hand, palm up. "Hand it over, Rover."

Aimee looked at Elizabeth, noticing that she merely raised her eyebrows at Kiki's command, saying nothing to disagree with it. Aimee only thought about Kiki taking her money and running away with it for half a second before she handed the bundle over to her. She glanced down at Kiki's boots and decided that she had a pretty fair chance of catching Kiki, even if she did decide to take off, since Aimee herself was wearing her very well-worn ballet flats. Kiki's legs might be a mile long, but she couldn't possibly go very fast with those heels on.

Kiki reached into the bag, pulling out the four stacks of bills. She flipped through them almost as fast as the bank's counting machine at Aimee's favorite branch. She liked the people at that bank because they didn't know her husband, and she didn't feel like she was suffering under anyone's scrutiny when she walked in to deposit what turned out many times to be rubber checks that he'd write on purpose, just to make her life miserable.

"Wow, you're good at that," said Elizabeth, her mouth turned down in a frown of respect.

"I count a lot of bills every night," she offered, without further explanation.

"Do you work at a bank?" asked Aimee.

Kiki raised one eyebrow at her. "No." She shoved the money back in the envelope. "If you're looking for ten Gs twenty, it's all there." She handed the envelope back to Aimee.

"A casino?" asked Aimee.

"No," said Kiki, still looking at Elizabeth.

Elizabeth frowned. "No, that's not right. You made a mistake."

Kiki shrugged. "No, I didn't. See for yourself." She stood there, arms folded, waiting to see what Elizabeth would do, the toe of her boot tapping lightly on the asphalt.

Elizabeth held out her hand. "Do you mind, Aimee? I'm pretty sure I counted correctly."

"Sure, go ahead," said Aimee, mystified. She wasn't exactly certain what was going on. Kiki had said 'ten geez twenty'. *What does that mean? And why is Elizabeth upset about it?*

Elizabeth counted the money again, much slower than Kiki had, and then looked up when she was done, taking a twenty dollar bill out of one of the stacks. "You're absolutely right." Her expression and voice said she couldn't believe it. "How could I possibly have made that mistake?"

"What mistake?" asked Aimee.

Elizabeth handed her the envelope, minus the twenty-dollar bill. "I had miscounted somehow. I was giving you an extra twenty dollars."

Then it hit her. Aimee smacked herself on the forehead. "Ooohhhh ... ten *Gs* twenty, not ten *geez* twenty! Now I get it."

The other two looked at her like she was nuts.

She shook her head. "Never mind. I'm a space cadet. We're all good." She shoved the envelope into her bag. "Want to go inside now? Book club?" She looked hopefully at the two women in front of her. This was the most interaction she'd had with another woman in months – other than the cashier at the grocery store – and it felt great. She didn't want it to end yet.

Elizabeth turned and slammed the trunk down on her car and pressed a button on her keychain, locking everything and turning on a car alarm. "I'm ready."

Aimee turned to Kiki. "Are you coming?"

Kiki hesitated, looking from Aimee to Elizabeth and then over at the front door of the store. "Mmmm, I don't know. I really have to go see a friend." She bit her lip self-consciously, making her seem suddenly more innocent to Aimee – maybe even a little shy.

"Can your friend wait an hour?" asked Elizabeth, clearing her throat and smoothing down the front of her suit pants.

Kiki thought about it for a second and then shrugged her shoulders. "Why not? I guess it would be okay for just an hour."

Aimee smiled, noticing that Elizabeth also looked happy. "Okay, then, let's go!" She shut her own trunk and pushed her button to lock and alarm her doors, gripping her purse to her ribs hard as she made her way back to the store with the others. Inside that bag was the only money she was probably going to see for the next few months, so she couldn't afford to get mugged in the parking lot. She felt safe here, though, with Kiki and Elizabeth. They were a couple of unlikely friends, but it worked for her just fine.

5

kiki

THE THREE WOMEN MADE THEIR way through the parking lot and back to the bookstore. Kiki said nothing, mulling over her situation with curiosity. She was more than a little surprised at herself that she had agreed to go to a book club meeting with two women she had just met. But something about them was growing on her.

First there was Aimee, walking around like a loon with that golf club, happily clueless, and obviously in need of female companionship. Kiki was willing to bet that Aimee had just been shafted by her husband. Probably a guy she'd been with for while, from the looks of her wardrobe and weight. In Kiki's experience, women who were dating tended to dress more in the current style and went to the gym more often than Aimee was obviously going.

Then there was Elizabeth. She was more of a mystery. Kiki noticed her smoothing her hair and suit a lot, making sure there were no wrinkles and no stray wisps escaping that crazy librarian bun she had practically stapled to her head, there were so many pins in it. Her hair looked healthy, though, and possibly pretty long. Kiki wondered what it would look like down and loose. Her own hair was her pride and joy, thick, long and able to take

ELLE CASEY

a curl so easily. She loved messing around with it, but it was always more fun to do someone else's hair – especially when it was a makeover-type situation. Both of these girls needed serious redos as far as Kiki was concerned.

They reached the glassed-off room used for the book club meeting to find one woman already there. Kiki schooled the expression on her face to remain calm, but she was pretty sure she was looking at one of the oldest human beings on the planet. She had to be at least a hundred. Maybe more. She looked like a raisin, and she had a bag with a string of yarn coming out of it that was feeding the bootie she was knitting in her hands. The yarn was the ugliest green color she'd ever seen.

"Well, hello, girls," said the old lady. "I was starting to wonder if I was going to be talking to myself about the book this week." She chuckled as her fingers kept moving, the sounds of knitting needles making clicking and sliding sounds of metal on metal.

"Hello, Betty," said Elizabeth. "I'm so sorry we're late. We got hung up in the parking lot."

Betty waved her off with her knitting, jabbing it in the air one time before starting to move the needles again. "Don't worry about it. I have plenty to keep me busy. You don't get as old as I am by worrying about every little thing and being impatient."

"And how old would that be?" asked Kiki, sitting down next to the old woman while holding onto her skirt bottom so it wouldn't ride up, dropping her satchel on the ground next to her chair. She turned her legs sideways so she wouldn't flash her underwear at Elizabeth who was sitting down across from her.

The old woman smiled. "Sassy. I like it. I'll be ninety-seven this month."

"Oh, my goodness," said Aimee, smiling and taking a seat on the other side of Betty. "That's wonderful. What's your secret?"

"Sex, drugs, and rock and roll," answered Betty, without missing a beat.

Kiki burst out laughing, unable to help herself. She looked at Betty, and they shared a smile. Kiki knew right away, Betty was someone she could get along with.

Kiki looked over at Elizabeth and saw that her cheeks had a little color in them now and she was no longer looking at Betty; instead, she was busying herself with getting things out of her purse. Out came a paperback of the book they would be discussing and a leather portfolio binder. Finally, she pulled a very expensive-looking silver pen from the outside pocket.

"I took the liberty of structuring some questions that we could discuss as a jumping-off point. Some were suggested on a few websites I visited, and others were some I just came up with after reading the book." Elizabeth looked up at everyone sitting in the room. "If that's okay with all of you."

Aimee looked at the door and out into the bookstore beyond, before asking, "Is there anyone else coming? Maybe we should wait."

"Don't bother," said Betty. "I talked to Ethel. She fell down two days ago and still has a sore hip. She's not coming."

Elizabeth smiled apologetically. "The group is still pretty new. It's taking us a while to get off the ground."

Kiki knew she should just get up and walk out – get the hospital trip over with and then go to work, even though it was still early. But the expression on Elizabeth's face stopped her. She looked so sad for a second. Kiki didn't want to be the one to make her feel any worse.

"I'm not worried about small groups. Go ahead with your questions if you want. I'm ready." Kiki looked at the other two and they seemed to be in agreement.

Aimee put her purse behind her in the chair and leaned over with her hands clasped in her lap, looking attentively at Elizabeth. Betty just nodded her head, her attention focused on the bootie in front of her.

Elizabeth smiled, tapping her pen on her list. "Okay, then. First, I have this question: 'This book had a contemporary setting in a big city. How do you think that influenced the characters and the decisions they made in the story?'"

Betty was the first one to speak up, and Kiki was more than a little surprised at how insightful her comment was. Aimee jumped in, eager to agree and then expand on what Betty had said. Elizabeth put her pad down on the table and laid the pen on top, joining in to discuss a counter-point that instantly got the conversation up to a very lively level. Kiki felt herself drawn in, unable to just observe anymore.

Ninety minutes later, Kiki looked down at her watch and gasped, shocked that she'd stayed that long. "Oh, shit. Sorry ladies, but I have to go." She stood up and quickly pushed down her skirt.

Three sets of eyes followed her progress up. Aimee was the first one to speak. "Oh. Okay. Well, I'm glad you decided to stay."

Kiki smiled. "Me too."

"You'll come to our next meeting, I hope?" said Elizabeth.

"You'd better. Without you, we'll all just be agreeing with each other the whole time, and that's boring," said Betty, finishing up the second bootie she'd started somewhere in the middle of the debate on the finer points of using love triangles in romances.

"I'll be back. As long as you guys will be."

All the heads around the table were nodding like bobble dolls. "Good," said Kiki. And she meant it. "See you in two weeks then? Seven o'clock?"

"Yes. Exactly. Why don't you give me your email address? I'll send you a reminder," suggested Elizabeth, handing over her portfolio and pen so Kiki could write it down. "I'll send a group email out and then you guys will have each other's addresses too."

Kiki took the paper and pen from her and wrote down her full name and email address, adding her cell phone number, just in case. "You can also text me if there are any sudden changes. I put my cell on there too." She handed the paper over to Aimee.

Kiki grabbed her satchel and threw it over her shoulder. "Okay. I'm out of here. I'll see you girls in a couple weeks."

Aimee stood up, putting the folder and pen down on the table in a hurry so she could come over to Kiki. Kiki found herself bending over automatically to be grabbed into an enthusiastic hug. She reached around awkwardly to pat Aimee on the back. "Uh, thanks. That's ... nice."

Aimee stepped back. "Sorry. I'm a hugger."

Kiki smiled. "Don't worry about it. I like hugs as much as the next girl."

Elizabeth stood and held out her hand.

Kiki took it and shook it firmly.

Betty waved her knitting at Kiki. "See you later, sweetie."

"Bye, Betty," said Kiki. She left the circle of women and went out the glass door. She looked back and saw that they were all gathering their things to leave too. It made her feel good for some reason to know that they weren't going to continue the meeting without her.

As she walked out to her car, the bright orange Camaro parked next to Aimee's Toyota, she smiled at how strange it was that she'd enjoyed herself so much. A book club wasn't her normal type of club to hang out in. And Betty wasn't even from the same generation. And the other two? Well, they were from different worlds entirely. But none of it mattered. She'd had a good time and hadn't laughed so hard or felt so free to just relax and talk about something that interested her in ... well, she couldn't remember how long it had been.

She wondered, as she drove her car over to the hospital, if she'd ever had a good time like the one she'd had just now. Sure, she had friends. One of them was currently hospitalized after having been mugged recently. And she talked plenty when she was at work. But it wasn't the same. Everywhere else, she had to watch herself, guard her words, be the person everyone expected her to be. With Aimee, Elizabeth, and Betty, she hadn't felt that way at all. It was as if they wanted to hear what she had to say, and then thought about it after she'd said it. She liked the feeling that her words had value to someone other than herself.

She pulled into the hospital parking lot and steeled herself for this visit with her friend, pushing aside the warm feelings she felt growing for her new friends. The ugliness she had to deal with now would only taint it unfairly, and she didn't want that to happen. This new, budding friendship, that had just fallen into her lap without effort, was something special. She just knew it.

6

elizabeth

ELIZABETH DROVE BACK TO HER office after leaving the bookstore. She wanted to lock the golf clubs in the closet behind her desk, so when her client came tomorrow, she could hand them over. She didn't like the idea of something this valuable being in her car overnight.

Normally she didn't do back-door dealing for clients, but this guy was special. He was a golf fanatic, which she knew only too well, because she did all of the bookkeeping for his personal and business expenses. He was a moderately successful businessman who had built his company up from nothing, and liked to work in a golf game whenever he could. He'd had the dream of owning these ridiculously-priced clubs for a while, but she had threatened him with dire consequences if he even thought about increasing his dividend check for that expense; his business was cyclical and with the current economy, it couldn't take much more of a hit if he was going to stay in the black.

When she'd gotten the idea of helping him get the clubs he wanted, while also saving him some bucks, she'd started searching online. It was only by chance that she'd seen Aimee's ad when it popped up on her radar. She hated to see entrepreneurs not being able to enjoy the fruits of their labors, especially when they worked as hard as this client did, so she was happy to go the extra mile and help him out. Even if she didn't get the whole golf obsession thing, personally.

Elizabeth pulled into the valet area in front of the building. It was after-hours, but there were always a few guards on duty. She went to the front desk and sweet-talked one of the younger guys into helping her get the clubs out of her car and into the elevator. She assured him that she could handle the bag from there, so he left her in the lift by herself. She balanced the clubs in the corner so she could press the button. Her face was sweaty, so she blew some air up into it as she rode the elevator to the twelfth floor. Her hair was hanging down in spots, no longer perfectly contained in its prison of hair pins, but she disregarded it. She was alone and there was no one to see her not being perfect except herself.

The door opened to a dark and empty floor. It was after tax season, so nobody was working late tonight. They'd all earned a rest, now that May had finally rolled around.

Elizabeth dragged the clubs to her office, and before locking them up in her closet, pulled her binder out from the large side pocket of the golf bag where she'd stowed it. Once the bag was safely locked away, she sat down at her computer and logged on. She sent off a quick email to the client telling him of her find and letting him know he could come pick up the clubs tomorrow after nine when she knew her secretary would be in for a half-day of weekend catch-up work. Then she sent off an email to Betty, Aimee, and Kiki, thanking them for coming to the meeting and promising to stay in touch about the next one.

About to log off the computer, she spied a pile of papers on the corner of her desk. Sighing long and loud, she reached over and pulled the stack to her, removing her fingers from the log-off keys. *Might as well stay and work. I've got nothing better to do.*

Elizabeth remained until well after midnight, calculating profits and losses and constructing balance sheets and statements for client after client, wishing for the thousandth time that they were her own financials she was looking at.

7

aimee

AIMEE COULDN'T WIPE THE SMILE off her face. That book club meeting was the most fun she'd had in a long time. She was already planning to go to the library tomorrow to see if she could check out the club's next title. If that didn't work out, she would go to the used bookstore. They usually had a good selection. She'd decided against spending any of the golf club money on new books. She had to stretch it as far as she could and every dollar would count.

As she pulled into her driveway, her happiness faded rapidly into trepidation. There was a light on in the living room, and Jack's Aston Martin was in the driveway. Aimee instantly felt sick to her stomach. She parked off to the side so he would be able to leave whenever he was done yelling at her, threatening her, or stealing from her.

She turned off the ignition and sat in the car for a few seconds, looking over at her purse. *Should I take the money in with me? What if he's here for the clubs? What if he gets angry and takes my purse?* It sounded nuts, but she wouldn't put it past him at this point. She made a split-second decision, pulling out the envelope and shoving it under the front passenger seat. It was probably just crazy paranoia, but better to be safe than sorry. She didn't worry about Jack taking her Toyota. Neither he nor Tiffany would be caught dead in it, since it wasn't worth more than seven thousand dollars on a good day. It was five years old and not the luxury model. She'd picked it out herself, loving the smooth lines and great gas mileage. Jack had always refused to ride in it.

Aimee zipped her purse shut and got out of the car slowly, reluctant to face the angry confrontation she knew was waiting for her. Sighing as she walked up to the front door, she wished Jack didn't have a key anymore.

She wasn't two steps into the house before he accosted her, his face already red, showing how steaming mad he was.

"Where are my golf clubs, Aimee?"

Aimee smiled at him, using every bit of confidence she had left to not tremble in his presence. "I have no idea. Where did you leave them?"

His voice rose, and spittle began to fly. "You know very well I left them in the garage the other day. You saw me do it."

"Oh, really? I don't remember seeing you do that," she said calmly, putting her purse down on the front hall table, infinitely glad she had thought to leave the money in the car. Otherwise, she would have been clinging to her bag in fear, and Jack would surely have gotten suspicious.

"Don't play stupid with me. You were looking right at me when I took them out of my trunk."

Aimee shrugged. "Sorry. Like I said ... I don't remember."

Jack followed her into the kitchen, standing too close as she reached into the refrigerator to grab the orange juice and pour herself a glass. She was going to offer Jack one, but changed her mind. A picture of Kiki's and Elizabeth's faces flashed across her memory. It distracted her from Jack's tirade, as she wondered what *they* might do in a situation like this. *Kiki would probably tell him to go to hell. Elizabeth would probably ... I don't know ... list all the reasons he should leave, in very neat and professional handwriting.*

She poured the orange juice into the short, clear glass and turned to put the container back in the fridge, but Jack stopped her.

He grabbed her wrist, squeezing it hard. "If you did something with my clubs, you're going to be sorry."

"I'm already sorry, Jack. Sorry I ever met you." Aimee looked him straight in the eye, her nostrils flaring with the anger that was coming over her. *How dare he touch me and threaten me like that! In my kitchen, of all places.*

He squeezed her harder, so much that it made her drop the container of juice, spilling it all over the floor and onto her pants. He didn't apologize after he let go

"*Ow*, Jack! That hurt! What's your frigging problem?" Aimee looked down incredulously at the mess. Jack was an asshole, but he'd never been violent with her – except for that one time when he'd been drinking. "Are you drunk?" she asked, backing up, headed for the sink to get a sponge.

"No, I'm not drunk, you stupid bitch! I want my golf clubs!"

"Hey!" she said, pointing a finger at him. "That's *enough*, Jack! You can't call me that name in my house. Get out! I don't want you here anymore."

Jack advanced on her, a mean sneer twisting his handsome face into someone she didn't recognize. "That's the thing, Aimee," he said in a dangerous, low voice. "This isn't your house. It's *my* house. I paid for it and I own it. Just like I own you."

Aimee didn't like the look in his cold gray eyes. It was predatory and practically promised cruelty. She knew Jack well enough to recognize a threat when she saw it. She moved quickly to her right, putting the kitchen island between them. "Jack, you need to leave. If you don't, I'm calling the cops."

"Go ahead, call them. What are you going to tell them? That you stole my golf clubs?"

Aimee swallowed hard, trying to manage the sick feelings that were rising up from her stomach. "No. Because I didn't. Like you said to me when you took that vase you bought for me for my birthday last year and gave it to Tiffany – everything we bought when we were together is joint property. What's yours is mine."

She wasn't prepared for his sudden response, so he had a good head start on her. He raced around the island, nearly getting to her before she took off running. She tried to keep the large granite barrier between them, but the spilled orange juice foiled her plans. She went down with a solid thud, her head hitting the tiled floor with a loud crack. She only had a couple seconds to relish the intense pain ripping through her skull before Jack made it over to her.

He grabbed the front of her shirt and pulled her up, screaming in her face. *"Where are my fucking golf clubs, you bitch?!"*

Luckily darkness came and took her. The last thing she remembered was a fuzzy vision of an angry monster floating above her, bits of his spit hitting her face, before she passed out.

Aimee came-to later and found herself alone. She was still lying on her back on the floor, her hair stuck to something on the tile. She sat up gingerly, wincing at the hair being pulled out of her head, fighting off the waves of nausea. She looked back and saw that her head had been stuck to a disgusting combination of blood and gooey orange juice.

She reached up slowly to gingerly touch the back of her head. Her hair was matted in one spot – the place that had smacked the floor – and she could feel wetness there. She got onto her hands and knees and crawled over to the sink, using the edge of the counter to pull herself up while holding off the dizziness. She turned the water on to lukewarm and then leaned over, using the removable nozzle of the faucet to rinse out the worst of it from her hair. She winced at the pain caused by the flow hitting her open wound. Trying to feel the injury with her fingers, all she came up with was more blood and a terrible stinging pain.

Dammit. I think I need stitches.

She shut the water off, put a dishtowel over the back of her head, and shuffled over to the front hall table where she'd left her purse. She found it on the floor, its contents spilled out all over the place. She sent out a thank-you to the universe that she'd thought to leave the money in the car. Her fears sent her to the front door where she peeked out the window to see if it was still there. She breathed a sigh of relief when she saw that it was parked where she'd left it, and that it appeared to be unmolested. Unlike herself.

She went back to her purse, putting everything that wasn't

broken back inside, awkwardly with one hand. Jack had apparently decided her phone wasn't necessary and had destroyed it. The front was broken, and it wouldn't power up. She tried pushing the button several times, but nothing happened. She sighed, throwing it in her purse anyway. Tomorrow she was going to use Jack's golf club money to buy herself a new one ... in red, to commemorate the blood seeping out of her wound. She had some decisions to make, now that he'd acted out like this. Staying in this huge house was no longer an option. She couldn't afford the mortgage payment anyway, and Jack had a key. Unfortunately, she didn't know the law well enough to know whether he was right when he said it was his house and he could come and go as he pleased. And she couldn't afford a lawyer to tell her otherwise.

Aimee stood up and walked out to her car, not even bothering to lock the front door. What was the point? The thieves had keys anyway.

She arrived at the hospital at ten o'clock. The emergency room was packed. She sat in a corner with an icepack given to her by one of the nurses, wrapped in her kitchen towel and held to her head. She watched as men, women, and children came in, suffering from illness, accidents, and who knows what. She hated that she had to be here. She was a statistic now – a battered woman. When Jack had gotten violent with her once before, he hadn't even remembered it the next day. He said he didn't believe her when she told him what he'd done. The bruise on her arm from him grabbing it and squeezing it that time could have been from anything, he'd said. But he stayed away from her after that when drinking. And he drank rarely. She knew that deep down inside, he didn't believe in his innocence any more than she did.

Jack was a liar and a cheat. Aimee prayed that he would see the truth about himself when he woke up in the morning and looked in the mirror. She wanted to hate Tiffany for taking him away from her, but at moments like this, she had perfect clarity and knew the truth – Tiffany had done her a favor. The thought made her smile. And it almost made her feel sorry for Tiffany. Almost.

"What's the smile for?" said a familiar voice.

Aimee looked up into the eyes of none other than Kiki.

"Oh ... hey, Kiki! Um, nothing. Just thinking about my ex."

Kiki raised an eyebrow as she sat down next to Aimee. "That's different. Normally when people think about their exes, it's not a smile I see. Especially in the E.R."

Aimee smiled, not wanting to elaborate. Instead, she asked, "How's your friend?"

"Better. I just sat with her for a couple hours to keep her company. No one else is visiting her."

"That's sad. Is she a friend from work?"

"Yeah."

"Where do you work anyway?"

Kiki stared at her for a few seconds, making Aimee wonder what the big secret was.

"Are you in the FBI or something?"

Kiki smiled and then laughed for a second, before saying, "Aimee. Do I look like I work in the FBI?"

Aimee shrugged her shoulders. "Maybe you're undercover."

Kiki stopped laughing. "Undercover as what?" Her smile slowly left her face, making her look almost sad.

"A supermodel?"

Kiki grabbed Aimee across the shoulders in a spontaneous hug, her smile back full force.

"*Owowowow*," said Aimee, wincing and grinning at the same time. "What was that for?"

Kiki released her. "Sorry about your head. *That* was for not saying I'm undercover as a prostitute."

Aimee looked at Kiki, aghast that she would say or even think such a thing. "What? Why on earth would I say something like that?!"

Kiki raised an eyebrow but said nothing; she just looked down at herself and then back up at Aimee to stare at her silently.

The gears started turning in Aimee's head until the final connection clicked into place. She felt her face getting red and hot. She leaned in and whispered to Kiki, "Are you saying you're a ... lady of the night?"

"No. I'm not saying that. But I'm also not saying I'm a super-model, either."

Aimee frowned at her, sitting back and talking in a normal tone again. "Okay. So you're not a ... prostitute, and you're not a supermodel – even though I know you could be one if you want-ed to be – so what are you then? What is your job, I mean?"

"I'm an exotic dancer." Kiki watched Aimee steadily, her ex-pression giving nothing away.

"Whoa. That means stripper, right? That is *so* cool. I wish I could do that," said Aimee wistfully.

"You're nuts," said Kiki, shaking her head. "You obviously have no idea what you're talking about."

Aimee shrugged. "What's there to know? You dance around to cool music, you strip down to your undies, and guys pay you wads of money to shake your butt. Sounds easy and fun to me. I have natural rhythm you know."

Kiki looked at her wryly. "First of all, where I dance, it's full nudity. And second of all, you don't always have to dance just on stage. Sometimes it's in guys' laps. And there are drugs and pimps trying to get in on the action and recruit ... it's awful."

"Then why do you do it?" asked Aimee softly. She kept the rest of her thoughts to herself, not wanting to hurt Kiki's feelings by making her feel bad about her choices. *Why would a girl this beautiful and this smart do something she obviously hated, when she could probably do anything with her life?*

Kiki didn't answer for a second. Then she said, "I've been ask-ing myself the same question for a while now."

"I hear ya," said Aimee, taking the blood-stained kitchen towel off her head and resting it in her lap. "I need a job, bad. Maybe you could give me the number of one of those pimps. I can't seem to get a job doing anything else."

Kiki's face hardened. "I'd never let you do that. You're a nice person ... smart and cute. You don't want that kind of life. It's not like *Pretty Woman* out there. Girls are beaten and killed every day."

Aimee looked at her, searching her eyes. "I guess we both need to find a new job, huh?"

Kiki nodded, looking off into the distance. "Yeah. Big time." She focused her attention back on Aimee. "So, what happened to your head, anyway?"

"Well, I'm a bit of a klutz, actually."

Kiki frowned and then put her hand on Aimee's arm and squeezing it gently. "Listen, Aimee. Anytime a girlfriend tells me she's a klutz when I ask her about a bloody injury, it makes the hairs on my ass stand up."

Aimee laughed, feeling all warm inside because Kiki had called her a girlfriend. "No way do you have ass hair."

"Whatever. My point is, 'I'm a klutz', is code for 'My husband or boyfriend beat me.'" She pulled her hand off Aimee's arm. "So, tell me what really happened. I'm not going to judge."

Aimee felt tears coming up in her eyes. *Why does she care about what happened to me?*

"And no tears," Kiki said, pointing at Aimee's face. "Those come later, after you tell me and preferably when we have alcohol in front of us."

Aimee laughed in spite of herself. She liked Kiki's style of bossiness. It felt different than Jack's. "Well, when I got home from our book club meeting, Jack – my ex – was there."

"Did he break-in or something?"

"No. He has a key."

Kiki rolled her eyes. "Let me guess. You didn't change the locks."

"No, I didn't. I guess I should have?"

"Of course you should have; why are you even asking me that? That's the *first* thing you do when you kick your man out. That's Breakups 101, babe."

"Oh. Well, I've never done a breakup before, so I didn't know."

"Okay, so the asshole came in with his key. Then what?"

Aimee started to squirm. "Well, he wanted to know where ... some of his things were, and I told him I didn't know. So he got mad."

"What was he looking for?"

Aimee looked down at the speckles on the floor tiles. "Just some stuff."

"Some golf clubs, maybe?"

Aimee's eyes shot up to bug out at Kiki. "Did he call you? Talk to you?" She felt herself go into full-fledged panic mode, her blood pressure instantly maxing out. Visions of a life behind bars began haunting her brain.

Kiki put her hand on Aimee's arm again. "Hey, *relax*. I've never seen the guy. But I did see your sale of a particularly valuable set of man-toys in the parking lot tonight, remember? I may not be a rocket scientist, but I can put two and two together."

Aimee frowned. "Oh. Yeah. Well, Jack *is* ridiculously smart, and he knows I did something with them. So he got mad and kind of came after me. I slipped in some orange juice he made me spill and landed on my ass."

"Looks like you landed on your head."

Aimee half-smiled. "Yeah. My ass and my head. They both hurt."

Kiki reached over and rubbed Aimee's back a couple times. "They'll heal, don't worry. And for the record, Jack is not ridiculously smart. He let you go, right?"

Aimee thought about the logic for a second and wanted to agree. But something kept her quiet. She had a hard time getting into her own corner.

"Say it," demanded Kiki, suddenly serious.

"Say what?"

"Say 'Jack's an idiot'."

"Why?"

"Because it's true. And if you can't see the truth of it now, well, just say it because I'm bossy and I told you to. Either way works for me."

"Fine. Jack's an idiot," said Aimee, smiling tremulously.

"Feels good, doesn't it?" asked Kiki, a mischievous grin on her face.

"Yeah. It kinda does. Jack's an idiot."

"There you go."

"He's a flaming idiot."

"Oooh, I like that one."

"He's a flaming, asshole idiot!"

Kiki smiled, but then her eyes went up, her attention suddenly pulled away.

Aimee followed Kiki's gaze to see what she was looking at.

Standing in front of them was a cop in full uniform. He looked intimidating as hell, but Aimee couldn't decide if it was the gun on one hip and the club on the other, or the fact that he was totally gorgeous.

"Hello," he said, glancing back and forth between Kiki and Aimee.

"Hello, officer," said Kiki politely.

Aimee tried to answer, but the words got stuck in her throat. She couldn't take her eyes off his face and body. He had blondish brown hair – kind of curly-wavy – broad shoulders, a barrel chest, and thick, hairy arms. He looked like a giant green-eyed summer bear – docile at the moment but deadly when angry.

Kiki nudged Aimee's arm, jolting her out of her daze.

"Oh, uh, hi. Officer ... ," she squinted up at his chest, " ... Officer Cleary. Hi."

Kiki nudged her again and whispered, "Don't overdo it," under her breath.

"May I talk to you for a second?" he asked Aimee.

"Me?" She could feel the panic rising again. And she had just started to feel better, calling Jack names. Now she was back to seeing herself in prison garb – a bright orange jumpsuit – rooming with a woman who called herself Butch.

"Yes. Please. I just want to talk to you for a minute ... ask you a few questions. We can do it in private if you prefer."

Aimee asked the first thing that popped into her head. "Am I under arrest?"

The police officer looked at her with a confused frown on his face. Then he smiled a little. "Did you break the law?"

Aimee looked at Kiki, her eyes as big as saucers.

Kiki shook her head 'no'.

"No. I don't think so."

"Okay, good. After you." He gestured for her to walk in front of him, toward the front doors of the emergency room.

Aimee looked back at Kiki as she started to walk away. "Can you wait?"

Kiki checked her watch. "For another ten minutes. Then I have to get to work."

"Okay. I'll hurry," she said, glancing up at the police officer as she walked past him to go outside.

He pointed to a bench just outside the doors, usually taken up by smokers if the butts on the ground were any indication, but currently unoccupied.

Aimee sat down and stared at her hands gripping her towel in her lap, unsure what to do or what to expect. She prayed he wasn't going to ask her about the sale of a certain set of golf clubs.

"I see you've been injured," he began.

"Yes. I fell."

"May I ask how it happened?"

"Well, I'm a bit of a klu ... " She started to give him the same story she'd told Kiki, but then decided that if Kiki knew the code for 'my ex beat me' then the cop probably did too. So she opted for a slightly altered version of events. "Actually, what happened is, I was in my kitchen getting some orange juice, and I dropped the container. And then before I had a chance to clean it up, I slipped on it and landed on my ... butt ... and my head hit the floor." She looked up at him and noticed the intensity of his gaze immediately. She wanted to hold it – to stare back at him – but she couldn't. She felt like she was lying, and she didn't want to lie to him. He was a cop, yes ... but he seemed ... nice, too.

"You know, if you're involved in something that you want to tell me about, maybe I could help you."

Aimee looked up at him. "Involved in something? Like what?"

Officer Cleary looked back at the emergency room. "I noticed your friend in there. Do you work together?"

Aimee looked at him in confusion before comprehension finally dawned. She couldn't help it ... she burst out laughing. First a little and then a lot.

He got a frown on his face. "Did I say something funny?"

Aimee put her hand on his arm, noticing right away how warm and strong it felt. "No, sorry," she pulled her hand away and put it on her heart. "I'm just dying a little right now, realizing that you think I'm even remotely capable of working with Kiki."

"I don't think it's so remote at all. No offense, but it seems to me a perfectly reasonable assumption."

Aimee rolled her eyes. "Oh, please. Me? An exotic dancer? That'll be the day."

The officer took a deep breath and then let it out. "Well, okay. I may have very slightly misjudged your friend, but I stand by my original assessment. And if you're in trouble, I'm here to help."

Aimee stopped laughing and looked up into his eyes. They were kind, she could see that. She also noticed the concern there. "Do you always hang around the E.R. looking for damsels in distress?"

"No," he smiled, "I don't. I happened to be here bringing someone in for detox. I just got lucky seeing you on the way out."

Aimee smiled. "Well, that's nice to hear you say. But I'm okay, really."

"Yes, but I don't think you've told me what really happened." His smile was gone now, and it was replaced with something more dangerous-looking. "You're wearing a wedding ring, but your husband isn't here with you."

Aimee felt herself scooting away a little.

He watched her and then relaxed his posture, smiling. "Don't be afraid. I just ... I guess I get this feeling that you're in some kind of trouble, and I can't shake it. I usually go with my gut on stuff like this. I'm rarely wrong."

"I thought that gut-stuff was only on T.V."

"Nope. It's real. For some of us."

"Well, to clarify, I am technically still married, which is why I have the ring on. But my husband ... left ... several months ago. So I'm on my own now." Aimee looked through the glass leading into the waiting area. "My friend has to leave soon. I need to get back. I'm sorry." And she really was sorry too. Even though he was intimidating, he made her feel safe with his concern and his gun.

Officer Cleary pulled a business card and a pen out of his front shirt pocket, writing on the card as he talked. "I'm going to put my personal cell phone number on my card. I want you to keep this handy. If you ever need help, night or day, you call me. Don't hesitate, just do it. Okay?" He handed her the card.

Aimee reached out and took it from him, looking down and noticing his full name. "Joseph Cleary."

"That's me. But you can call me Joe."

She looked up and noticed he was smiling. "Do you always give out your personal cell phone to damsels in distress?"

"Only the really pretty ones."

Aimee blushed so hard, she was afraid her hair was going to catch on fire. She stood suddenly, anxious to get away from him. Not because she didn't find him attractive, but because she had no idea what to do in a situation like this. Jumping from an ex-husband's attack to the warm happiness of a cute cop giving her his number and practically promising to be her knight in shining armor was too much for her brain to handle right now. "Thanks, Joe. I have to go now."

Joe remained seated. "No problem. Good luck in there. Remember to call me ... if you need anything or want to talk about what happened."

Aimee waved the card at him. "Thanks." She walked away, sliding the card into her purse. She wanted to look back to see if he was still there, but she forced herself to keep her eyes forward. She concentrated on walking as carefully as possible so she wouldn't trip. She didn't trust herself not to do something colossally stupid right now, especially since she had an audience made up of the cutest guy she'd ever seen up close. Jack was handsome in a lawyerly kind of way, but Joe Cleary? He was something else entirely.

Aimee pushed open the door of the E.R. and practically ran over to sit with Kiki, who was smiling as if she had a really good secret.

"What are you so happy about?" asked Aimee, sitting down, feeling slightly flustered.

"Oh, I don't know ... maybe that hot cop making a move on you in the E.R. It's kind of sweet, actually."

"He wasn't making a move. He was just doing his job."

"You don't really believe that, do you?"

"Yes."

Kiki frowned at her.

"No. Maybe. I don't know."

The nurse opened the sliding glass window at the desk and said, "Aimee?"

Aimee stood. "That's me. I've gotta go. See you soon?"

"Sure. Two weeks."

"Have a good night ... at work."

"I'll try," said Kiki, unfolding her long frame from the waiting room chair.

"Stay away from the pimps," whispered Aimee, smiling.

Kiki grinned back. "No problem."

Aimee walked up to the front desk and followed the nurse's instructions to move through the double doors into the actual examination area. She looked back at the emergency room doors, watching as Kiki walked out, drawing every eye in the place toward her. Aimee tried to remember if she'd ever seen anyone that pretty close-up, and decided that she hadn't. It was kind of depressing to think that someone like that was stuck in a dead-end job, unhappy, and as far as Aimee could tell, without a man in her life. It made her own prospects seem nearly hopeless. She pushed through the doors and was greeted by a young doctor who looked rushed and unhappy. *Great. This guy's about to stick me with a needle in the back of my head. Thanks a lot, Jack, you jerk.*

8

kiki

"YA LATE," SAID ANTHONY, THE host – slash – bouncer at the front door of Lola's, the steakhouse and strip club where Kiki worked. "Duke's pissed. Ya'd better try to avoid him if ya can."

"Thanks, Auntie. I'll keep my eyes open."

"Don't call me dat. You know I don't like it. It's Anthony, not Auntie." His version of 'Anthony' sounded more like 'Ant-Knee'.

"It's your Jersey accent. It confuses me."

"My accent ain't dat bad."

Kiki rolled her eyes as she walked past him. "Whatever you say, Auntie." She worked for a bunch of guidos. It was so ridiculously cliché, it was funny. She had to catch herself to keep from imitating their accents outside of work; they were addictive.

Kiki walked past the front of the steakhouse part of the business and over through the double doors leading to the strip club section. She was heading to the dressing room and had almost made it there, before the general manager waylaid her.

"Kiki. Ya late. *Again.*"

"Yeah, I'm sorry about that. I was visiting with Cindi in the hospital. You know her, right? Cindi? Cute blond? Green eyes? She's worked here for five years?"

Duke rolled his eyes. "Don't play games. Ya know I care about ha. But I ain't gettin' involved. Ya know my policy."

"Yeah, yeah, I know. You're all about the business. So much for being family." Duke, Anthony, and their father, the patriarch of the Lola's Steakhouse and Dancing empire, were fond of saying that all the employees, especially the dancers, were part of the big DeLucca family.

"Ya know, Kiki, ya push me too far an' ... "

"And what, Duke? Are you going to fire me? Because if you are, please, do it now. Save me the drunken feel-ups and drooling idiots for tonight, would you please?"

Duke put his hands on his hips just below his ample love handles, "Ya'd betta rememba it's those drunken idiots who are butterin' ya bread, young lady. Y'outta be more appreciative. Maybe ya forgot who paid for dat nice little townhouse and dat boom-boom car ya got."

Kiki got up into his face. He was several inches shorter than her, and she liked looking down at him, knowing how much he hated it. "Oh yeah? Well, I butter *your* bread, little man, so I think *you'd* better be more appreciative of *me*."

He held up his hands and backed off. "What? What'd I say? Ya know I love ya, Kiki. You're my favorite girl. Always have been. Who sends the high rollers ya way?" He poked his chest with a fat thumb. "Duke does, dat's who. Nobody loves Kiki more'n Duke DeLucca."

Kiki tried not to smile, but it was hard. He tried to act so mafia tough all the time, but he was just a goofball trying like hell to please his dad and act all full of his second generation Italian-ness ... and failing miserably on both counts. Kiki nodded. "That's right. You're my biggest fan, Duke. I know. I appreciate you."

Duke smiled and stepped closer to her, reaching his hand out to touch her.

Kiki moved her shoulder out of the way and held up her finger in his face. "Hands off the merchandise, Dukey Doo. Or I'll lay you out right here on this floor."

"I hate when ya call me dat, Kiki. Cut it out. I was just gonna say it's okay if ya late. If it was one of the udda girls, it wouldn't be. But choo? ... " he tapped his right breast. "... Ya gotta special place in Duke's heart."

"Duke, that's your lung. Your heart's on the other side."

"Whateva," he growled at her, scowling, "just go get dressed. Ya're on in twenny minutes."

Kiki smiled, happy that she'd managed to get Duke cranky before starting her set. He was much more fun to be around when his feathers were ruffled, and it was so easy to get them that way. It was worth the little bit of effort.

Kiki went through the black door with the *Employees Only* sign on it and saw that the back of the house was packed. The girls were laughing and goofing around – all but one of them. Shawnda was in the middle of putting on her makeup, looking over at Cindi's empty spot in the line of lighted tables with mirrors attached to them.

Kiki went over and dropped into a nearby chair. "What's up, girl?"

The black beauty looked over at Kiki, her eyes big pools of sadness. "Nothin'. Not in the mood to be here. At all." She looked back at the mirror.

"Are you ever in the mood to be here?"

Shawnda sighed. "No. What about you? What's up?" Her eyes connected with Kiki's in the mirror.

"Nothing. I went to see Cindi."

Shawnda's eyes perked up. "Really? How's she doin'?"

"Good. Better. I think she's going to be fine. Her nurse said the head injury isn't going to leave any permanent damage."

Shawnda turned and grabbed Kiki's hands, relief washing over her face. "Oh my gawd, girl, I was so worried. I couldn't even bring myself to go see her." Tears appeared in her eyes and she instantly looked sad again. "What kind of shit friend am I?"

Kiki squeezed Shawnda's hands and then let them go. Grabbing a menu off the nearby table, she fanned Shawnda's face. "Dry 'em up, girl! No time for tears. You're on in five!"

Shawnda smiled, using a delicate fingertip with a very long acrylic, French-manicured fingernail on it to keep the tear from spilling over and ruining her makeup. "The show must go on, right?"

"Yeah," said Kiki sadly. Then she snapped out of her little melancholy moment and said in a serious tone, "You know, we need to get out of this shit job. Let's do it. Do it with me."

Shawnda picked up a bronzing brush and swiped it over strategic places around her face, pausing to turn her head from left to right to survey her results. "This is the best place in town, you know that. Where you wanna go from here? Downtown? *Huh-uh.* You're better than that. I'm better than that. We got a good deal going here."

"I don't mean get out of here, as in *Lola's* ... I mean get out of *dancing*. Like, permanently."

Shawnda put her brush down and turned to look at Kiki, a what-are-you-crazy?-look on her face, saying nothing.

"I'm serious," said Kiki.

"No, you're not. What? Are you going to go back to school? Become a doctor?" Shawnda laughed at her own joke before going back to her bronzing.

"No. But I could go back to school and do *something*. I have savings."

"You'll spend that savings in a month. You have expensive taste. You need a job that pays biiiig tips to afford your own self."

"I could cut back. I haven't spent that much." *Not by a long shot*, she thought, but she never shared that personal stuff with anyone.

"Well, I ain't leavin'. But I do have some plans. I'll be making some changes soon."

Kiki eyed her suspiciously. "What kind of changes?" In their business, if you said you were staying in but making some changes, it usually only meant one thing.

Shawnda didn't answer.

Kiki was instantly pissed. "No, Shawnda! You can't!"

Shawnda put her brush down and turned in her seat to face Kiki. "I talked to Bobby. It's all worked out. He promised he's going to get me some good clients – regulars – who have money and aren't into kinky shit. It's going to be fine. You should come with me."

Kiki dropped her face into her hands. She shouted a scream of frustration in them and then looked up at Shawnda, who was now sitting there with a definite chip on her shoulder. "Shawnda, please. Come on, you're better than this! You're beautiful, smart, capable ... you could do anything with your life. You don't need to sell yourself like that!"

"Shut up, Kiki. Not everyone has what you have."

"What? What are you talking about? What do I have that you don't have?"

"You're white for one."

"Oh, *fuck* that, Shawnda. That's just an excuse. You are amazing. Gorgeous. You don't need some drugged out pimp hooking you up with losers for pocket change."

"Who said anything about pocket change? I told you, Bobby is getting me *good* clients."

"There's no such thing as a good john, Shawnda. And I know you're smarter than that. They pay big money and then think they own you. They make you do things they can't make their wives do. Think about it!"

"Whatever." Shawnda turned back to her mirror, leaning in closer to get a better look at her false eyelashes. "I'm doing it. It's too late to back out now. I have my first client tonight."

Kiki stood up, disgusted with her friend. "Well, when you get your face beat in, don't come crying to me saying you didn't know it would happen. I warned you."

Shawnda pick up a hairbrush and threw it at Kiki's retreating form. "Get outta here. You're bringin' me down. I have to go dance now with a sad face, thanks to you. My tips are gonna be terrible."

Kiki leaned down and picked up the brush, walking over and putting it gently back on the makeup table. She bent over and kissed Shawnda on the cheek. "I'm only kidding. When you get your face beat in, I'll visit you in the hospital, just like I did Cindi."

Shawnda reached around Kiki's leg to pinch her on the butt, but Kiki was too quick, twisting out of the way.

"I told Duke, and I'm telling you now," said Kiki, as she walked away toward her own makeup table, "hands off the merchandise."

Shawnda smiled at her in the mirror and then went back to her primping, not saying anything in response.

Kiki grabbed a keychain out of her satchel and threw the bag down on the floor under her table. She used the smallest key on the ring to open up the locked drawer in front of her. It released a mechanism, unlocking the other drawers on either side. Inside was over a thousand dollars in makeup, eyelashes, brushes, and other beauty accoutrements.

As she began picking out the ones she was going to use for her set that evening, her eye fell on a few colors she knew would look good on Elizabeth. She'd noticed Elizabeth's pretty blue eyes, just begging for a little bit of smoky eyeliner to emphasize their size and sparkle.

And the warm golds and browns she kept in the second drawer would be perfect for Aimee. She had such a peachy complexion – it would be so easy to draw that healthy glow out with minimal fuss.

She shut the drawers, cutting off the thoughts of making over her book-nerd friends. She wasn't even sure if they qualified as friends yet. *No use getting ahead of myself.* In her experience, most women weren't comfortable with exotic dancers as friends. And her friends who were exotic dancers themselves, weren't the most dependable. They either left the game or joined a new one like Shawnda was planning to do. Then they got addicted to drugs or alcohol, or ended up dead.

She pulled some false eyelashes and the glue she use to put them on out of her drawer. "Not me," she said to the mirror before picking up a compact with cream foundation inside. She applied it with a special brush she had just for the purpose of smoothing out her skin tones before painting them back on, applying perfect shadows and sparkle in just the right places when she was finished. "I'm outta here. *Soon.*"

"Who you talkin' to, Kiki?" asked Duke, materializing out of a dark corner of the room.

"Duke, you know you're not supposed to be back here. Get out." Kiki ignored him, working her magic with her brushes, opting for a very dark, almost black look to outline her upper lids. She was feeling a little morose after seeing Cindi all beat up and now hearing Shawnda talking stupid. She was going to do her *Nine Inch Nails* set. That always got the money flowing into her coffers, and it let her drop into one of her darker moods at work. It was a win-win. She worked off her negativity and made more money while she did it. If she was for sure going to get out of the dancing game, and she'd pretty much made up her mind in that exact moment that she was, she needed to make some serious bank tonight.

"I just wanted to tell ya dat dat guy I told ya about is here. The high rollah. I told him all about ya, and he said he's looking forward to meetin' ya."

"How do you know this guy, anyway?"

"He's on da Board."

Kiki's hand froze in mid-blush-application. "The Board of what?"

"Da Board of Edjacation, whattya think? No, da Board of Lola's."

"You guys have a Board? Is he family?" Kiki couldn't remember hearing this news before. She thought she knew everything about the family, including all the DeLuccas here and still over in Italy. Their family tree had branches that went everywhere, and they were true Catholics – there wasn't a single DeLucca couple with less than five kids.

"No, he ain't family. He's one of da lawyers dat Pops hired this year. Tryin' to class up the place."

Kiki went back to her makeup. This was just Duke talking out of his butt again, trying to act like he was more in the know than he really was. "The place is as classy as it's going to get, Dukey Doo."

"Well, da Board don't think so. So Pops invited them to come and check it out. I don't think it's their usual thing, ya know?"

"No, I *don't* know. All men like stripteases. It's in their DNA."

"Don't I know it. Thank the Good Lord for dat." He did the Catholic cross on his chest. "Anyway, da guy's sittin' at table twenny. He's got a suit on. See what you can do about gettin' it off. At least the tie anyhow."

"Oh, I'll get it off, alright," said Kiki under her breath. An uptight lawyer in a suit? Easy pickings. He'd be putty in her hands before the end of the first song.

"Okay, well, get yaself extra sexy. Ya need to impress him."

Kiki gave Duke her scariest warning look. "Duke. Leave. Before I put lipstick on you."

He backed up a step, hands out. "Hey ... keep dat girl stuff away from me. Ya know I ain't like dat." A sweat had broken out across his forehead.

Kiki smiled. "I know you wear our underwear and heels when we leave them here. Don't worry, Dukey Doo. Your secret is safe with me."

Duke pointed a shaking finger at Kiki's face as he backed away some more. "Dat ain't true! Ya betta not be tellin' people dat! And stop callin' me dat doo doo name or whateva!" He turned and rushed out of the dressing room.

The girls sitting around listening in on the conversation started laughing. Kiki smiled, turning back to the mirror. She posed, pursing her lips and turning her face left and right, admiring her work and making an air kiss at her reflection. *Perfect.*

Reaching down into her satchel, she pulled out part of the costume she would be wearing for her one and only dance tonight. It weighed just a few ounces – a pair of barely there underwear and a bra in dark blue lace with rhinestones to set off the cut of the lines. A new pair of thigh-high silk stockings with a seam up the back completed the underthings part of the costume.

She stood and turned to the rack of clothing behind her. It contained her costumes, ones she'd had custom made to fit her measurements. Out came the dark navy, pinstriped business suit with all its accompanying pieces – a prim, white, button-down Brooks Brothers shirt, a pencil skirt that ended way too high above the knee, and a suit jacket, all in matching, light wool fabric. She unlocked the case behind the clothing rack and pulled out the dark blue designer platform stilettos with the five-inch heels.

She put the underwear on and the hose, making sure the seams were perfectly straight and centered on the backs of her legs. The clothing ensemble and shoes followed, effectively transforming Kiki into a six-foot-two-inch-tall, high-powered business woman – or at least, that was the illusion. She stood in front of one of the full-length mirrors nearby, turning to admire herself in profile. All she needed were the finishing touches.

From one of the drawers she took out a long string of white pearls with a knot in them, putting them on over her head and resting them between her breasts. Then she quickly twisted her hair up and stuck a few pins in the knot she'd made. A few loose curls hung down at the sides of her face, and the rest was caught up in a loose bun. Just a couple of pulls on the pins and all of it would drop down in a wavy mass.

She stood there, her image reflected in the mirror, every inch a man's sexual fantasy. Tonight she was a conservative businesswoman on the outside, like Elizabeth, ready to be revealed as the sexy stripper she was on the inside. It was a very well-received fantasy at Lola's, guaranteed to bring in the biggest tips.

The pearls would stay on for the entire dance. Kiki knew that guys liked pearls on naked women. It made them fantasize about being the ones to give her their own set of special pearls. It was so easy to manipulate their minds into reaching for their wallets.

Kiki walked over to the door that led to the stage and stepped through so she could watch Shawnda do her thing and possibly catch a peek of Mister Important Board Member. As soon as her eyes adjusted to the dim lights, she was able to pick him out. He sat in front, engaged in conversation with the man next to him. His tie was cinched up as tight as it would go, his jacket still on. *Man, how uptight can a guy possibly be?* He was gorgeous, if you like the perfectly groomed, aristocratic-looking type. Maybe he was English; he had that European air about him.

Kiki looked over at Shawnda and could tell that this guy's attitude was pissing her friend off. Shawnda was really working it, swinging her hips, leaning over to give him her best cleavage shots, and otherwise focusing a lot of her attention on the guy. But even Kiki could see from her vantage point that it was a lost cause. He was definitely not interested.

Kiki was fascinated. She'd never seen a guy sober who could ignore Shawnda like that. Maybe when they were totally blotto and so drunk they couldn't see straight, but not sober and if they had eyeballs that worked. The girl was stacked and she knew how to dance.

Kiki smiled, thinking about how pissed Shawnda was going to be when she came backstage. Maybe she'd be too angry to go through with Bobby's plans for her. *Wouldn't that be sweet?* Kiki wanted to be around for that conversation. Bobby didn't like being told no. He hung around the club all the time, recruiting for his bottom line. A total sleezeball. Kiki would like to witness him getting shut down by a pissed off Shawnda. Not even Bobby would mess with her when she was in one of her moods – at least not when there were witnesses around.

Shawnda's number came to an end, so she grabbed her boa and other parts of her costume that she didn't want to lose and strode off the stage. She tried to pass by, but Kiki grabbed her arm.

"What?" demanded Shawnda, not hiding the fact that she was mad.

"What happened out there?"

"Nothin'! I was totally working that stupid pole and that suit just sat there." She held up a five dollar bill. "Five fuckin' dollars from him. I'm going to have to screw *two* dicks tonight to make up for this." She jerked her arm out of Kiki's grasp. "Good luck, that's all I got to say. The guy's gotta be gay."

Kiki hadn't thought of that. They didn't get a lot of gay guys in the club, unless they were there hanging out with their girlfriends. Groups of girls did come into the club occasionally, out of curiosity more than anything else.

Kiki reached into the small pocket of her coat, pulling out the black librarian-style glasses she kept there. They weren't prescription – just clear plastic lenses. They added to the effect of the smart, conservative businesswoman, though. She looked over at the DJ who got on the microphone.

"Gentlemen ... ladies ... Lola's invites you to place your drink orders and get ready for the next number which starts in two minutes. Two minutes is all you have, and you'd better hurry. Because tonight, performing in one of her rare appearances as the executive pussycat, is Kiiiiiikiiiiiiii ... " He waited for the cheers to die down. "And please, don't forget to tip your waitresses aaaaand the dancers."

The regulars continued to cheer. Kiki tried not to smile, but it was hard. They were mostly drunks and pervs, but even so, it was nice to be appreciated. She rarely did this act because the heels were a pain in the ass and the routine was more complicated than her others with the restrictive material of the costume and the timing of different parts of it; but it was usually worth it. She made good tips with this one, and the patrons tended to remember it and request it pretty frequently. If this one didn't work on the uptight Board member, nothing would.

The DJ queued up the Nine Inch Nails song *"Closer"* and set the light system to a darker tone, with an occasional sparkling of white and deep blue from the spinning balls and lights above the stage.

The first few seconds of the six-minute song beat through the place. People who had been talking stopped, their attention pulled to the stage almost against their will, it seemed.

Kiki stepped out from the wings, taking long, measured strides to the front of the stage to the beat of the song, looking like she meant business, the lights flashing on and off to illuminate and then hide her face.

For those who had never seen her before, her beauty, presented mysteriously like this, was simply stunning. Even with her hair up and glasses on, she was like something off a magazine cover. The magic of the strange music, and the lights and the percussion coming out from the walls and floor, dragged men into her world, willingly or not. They sat, all of them without exception, staring at her coming onto the stage, getting closer and closer with every beat. They had no idea what they were in for.

She started with a simple movement – removing the glasses. She dragged them off slowly, and then put one of the stems onto her tongue, showing just enough of its pink, slipperiness outside her mouth to suggest she would like to lick something other than what she held in her hand at the moment. Every guy in the house imagined it was him she wanted to lick. Money started to burn holes in their pockets.

At first she just looked out into the crowd, but then she looked down, locking her gaze on the guy in the suit. She winked at him, causing hoots of excitement to break out from the guys in the surrounding area. Then she turned away and strutted from the group of them, pulling her jacket down, first off one shoulder and then the other. Six beats later and it was off all the way, thrown to the side to be collected by a guy wearing all black who nobody ever noticed grabbing parts of costumes as they were flung off. It helped to have them out of the way to avoid tripping and breaking the mood.

Kiki bent over a few times as she danced, making sure they caught a glimpse up her too-short skirt and what was underneath, just as the lyrics from the song suggested something very dirty and honest at the same time, the artist Trent Reznor singing about exactly what he wanted to do to her. The lyrics perfectly framed what was on the minds of every straight guy in the place. She wanted to be sure that not one word of business would be discussed when she was on stage tonight. It was her personal mission to blow this guy's mind, just because she could.

She came back to the front of the stage, doing some well-rehearsed and perfectly timed moves to the music, while also taking off her blouse, slowly, one button at a time. She pulled the edge of the shirt off her left shoulder, looking down to the left and bringing her hand up to run across her body, first down at her crotch and then up to her stomach and breasts. She turned slyly to look at the guy in the front row again. He wasn't talking to his friends yet. That was a good sign. His hand sat lax on his drink, still full and getting clearer in color with the rapidly melting ice.

Kiki's other shoulder came out of her shirt, and in one smooth movement, she pulled the entire thing off.

She changed tactics now, suddenly acting all innocent, as if she were just standing in her bedroom alone getting undressed and maybe these men were just peeping toms – eyes she didn't realize were watching. After she had the zipper on the skirt down though, she looked out at the men, running her eyes over all of them, and raised a finger, wagging it slowly back and forth to the beat of the music, as if chastising them for watching. Then she changed the finger to one that curved and gestured for them to follow her. She took two steps back and then dropped the skirt, stepping out of it and tossing it off to the side.

Now she stood in front of them, in just her stockings, bra, underwear and pearl necklace. It was time to drop the bomb then – the first bomb. She took catwalk steps forward as she reached back and pulled out the two pins that held up her hair.

Her mane of shiny, perfectly mussed hair dropped down below her shoulders, causing more than a few of the men watching to practically swoon. She shook her hair out a little, making sure some of it fell across her face, so a few strands would stick to her lips. It gave her that freshly-ravaged face that she knew they loved.

She spent a little bit of time dancing now, working the stage and the pole. She was athletic, and it showed in her muscle tone and control. She could take turns on the pole, hanging upside down from it, and holding several positions without support for long periods of time, giving the men ample opportunity to view her assets from all angles. She could move from the pole to the stage and back again, as if she did it all day, every day. If it was possible to be a natural at stripping, Kiki had that talent – that something special that made her sexiness seem effortless.

The song would be over soon, so Kiki knew it was time to give up the goods. She'd gone around to the edge of the stage on hands and knees collecting bills from the drooling men. Everyone but the Board member had contributed. He just sat there and watched, almost no expression on his face. He may have fooled everyone else in the place, but not her. His tie was loosened. Not a lot, but enough to know that she'd gotten him hot. She raised her eyebrow at him, almost daring him to do something – she didn't know what. He raised an eyebrow back, as if meeting her challenge. *Interesting,* was all she could think before she had to move on with her routine.

She turned from them so her back was facing the crowd. She slowly lowered one bra strap, looking over her shoulder to see if they were paying attention. She still had them. *Of course I do.*

She lowered the second strap and checked again, looking at them coyly, building their anticipation. Turning back toward them, she made sure to give them ample shots of her cleavage, helped by her upper arms pushing her breasts together as she acted shy about removing the last layer of clothing.

When the yells and shouts of enthusiasm from the men got sufficiently loud, she closed the deal and took the bra off, sending them into a frenzy of excitement. She turned around and bent over, giving them a shot of one of her best assets – her rear end. Then she turned back, working her magic with the panties, until she was finally standing there, in just stockings, heels, and pearls. She did a few more dance moves and then blew a kiss to the guy in front, making one more round to collect her tips and then strutting off stage at the end of the piece – perfectly timed so the last moment they saw her, the simple, single piano notes of the song finished chiming.

Shawnda greeted her at the stage door with three other girls, a silk robe held up in her hands. Kiki threw it on and quickly tied it closed.

"Damn, girl!" said Shawnda. "Have you been practicing at home or what?"

Kiki smiled. "Good, huh?"

"Good? Child, please. You just blew them guys' minds. They all a mess now. I hope my john ain't out there. I'll just be a big disappointment to him at this point."

Kiki play-slapped her. "Hey, you got five bucks off that guy. I got nothing. Zero. He zipped me."

"Whaaaat?" said the group of girls.

"Seriously. Shawnda wins the prize. She got blood from a stone tonight."

Shawnda smiled big. "Well, aallll right. I guess I haven't lost my touch after all."

Kiki drew her into a big hug. "Of course you didn't. You're brown sugar, baby. Pure sweetness."

"Oh, that's right. How could I forget?"

Kiki pulled away. "Don't ever forget it. Now watch out. I have to go get changed. I'm getting a headache from all this noise." Now that Kiki had made up her mind to leave Lola's she just wanted to get home and think – put together a plan or something.

She had already gotten back into her street clothes when Duke came rushing in. "Whattya doin'? Put your costume back on. He wants to meet ya. Plus ya got othah sets to do."

"Sorry, Duke. I've got a headache. I'm outta here. For good." Kiki grabbed her satchel and stuffed her lingerie in it, stepping back from the table.

"What am I s'posed to tell him? And Pops?"

"Tell him he should have tipped me if he wanted to talk to me. And tell Pops thanks for the ride. He can mail me my last paycheck." She brushed past Duke, ignoring his pleas to come back. She went to turn left and leave out the back door, but at the last minute she changed her mind and turned right, so she could leave by passing through the club. Let Mr. Important Guy see her blowing him off. She smiled at the idea.

She saw him long before she reached him. He was standing near the bar, talking to another guy in a suit and Pops DeLucca, the owner. He looked up at her quizzically.

She knew he was trying to figure out who she was, to place the face that seemed somehow familiar. Her transformation from naked dancer to girl in a short skirt was complete, changing her look enough to call it a disguise. She stared him down the entire way as she approached, breaking contact as she kept on walking by.

She didn't even stop to say goodbye or look back to see what he did as she left. *Let him drool.* Guys like him were all the same.

They thought they were a gift to women. She didn't have time for someone who thought he was too good to tip a hard working girl, sweating her tits off for the lost and lonely.

She heard Pops yelling behind her, but she ignored him too. She was done with this place. She'd made over five hundred bucks with that one dance. It was good enough to pay for groceries for the next few weeks, and she had no rent or car payments. She'd paid all her debts off two years ago. She was going to be fine. All she had to do was figure out what she wanted to do with the rest of her life.

9

elizabeth

$\mathcal{T}$HE TWO WEEKS SINCE THE last book club meeting had dragged. Elizabeth put the last file of the day on the corner of her desk, wishing she could throw it in her trashcan and light it on fire instead.

It never ended. Numbers in and numbers out, the same conversations over and over with clients who could never seem to understand that: one, they couldn't spend every nickel that came into their bank accounts, and two: that they did, in fact, have to pay *some* taxes. She just didn't get that sense of entitlement many of them had. That somehow they should be able to benefit from all the governmental presence in their lives without actually paying for it. One client told her today, the one associated with the file she wanted to burn, that the IRS didn't need to take his hard-earned money for taxes ... all they had to do was have the Treasury Department print some more hundred dollar bills. She'd had to use all of her willpower not to jab a pencil into her eye, listening to him whine over the phone. It wasn't the first time he'd used this argument with her.

Elizabeth grabbed her suit coat and purse, taking her keys out of her desk. She carefully locked her file drawers and left the office, checking her watch to be sure she wasn't going to be late. She had exactly twenty minutes to make the ten-minute drive. *Perfect.* She liked it when she had time to go slower and not worry about traffic lights.

She pulled into the parking lot at the same time as Aimee did, smiling at her enthusiastic grin and happily frantic wave. Elizabeth walked over to the driver's side of Aimee's car since it was taking her a while to get out. She could see her struggling with something on the front seat next to her.

"Can I help you with something?" Elizabeth offered.

"Oh, sure. Hi! How are you, Elizabeth?" Aimee said, handing out a plate with plastic wrap over it.

Elizabeth took the plate from her. "I'm well, thank you. Oh, what do we have here?"

Aimee got out, carrying another plate, also carefully wrapped. "A little surprise. I hope you aren't on a diet."

"No ... ," said Elizabeth, eyeing the plate from different angles trying to figure out what was under the plastic.

"Not that you need to be on a diet," said Aimee, "you look great. I didn't mean anything by that."

"No, don't worry about it. No offense taken. I never diet."

"I wish I could say the same," said Aimee, slamming her door shut. She walked to the trunk and opened it up, reaching inside to pull a platter out.

Elizabeth looked at the interior of the trunk, trying not to be nosy. But it was nearly impossible after she got a look at some of the things inside. "Is that a ... ? What *is* that?"

Aimee looked at what Elizabeth was pointing at and blushed a little. "Oh. That's a needlepoint-covered footstool I got at an antique store. And that's a child's chair I got at another place. Oh, and an old Victrola record player speaker thingy."

"Huh," said Elizabeth. "Do you collect antiques?" She had several clients who did, and she'd seen their appraisal reports. Sometimes they were good investments, but usually the clients never got rid of them, so they never took advantage of the appreciation.

"Not really. I just have a few pieces I like, so I ... uh ... put them in here."

Elizabeth gave her a penetrating look. "You put your favorite pieces in your trunk." She said it as a statement, not sure she understood, but noticing that Aimee looked uncomfortable.

"Yeah. It's a long story. Oh, check it out! There's Kiki."

Elizabeth looked up, actually hearing Kiki's arrival before she saw her. Kiki was driving the bright orange muscle car that had been parked by Aimee the last time they'd met in the parking lot.

The car eased into the empty space on the other side of Aimee's with a rumble and a loud growl before the engine shut off and Kiki stepped out on the driver's side.

"Hey, chicks. Looks like I'm right on time."

Elizabeth and Aimee greeted her warmly.

"You're early for the meeting, actually," said Elizabeth. "But just in time to carry something." She gestured with her chin at the platter in Aimee's trunk.

Kiki came over, throwing her big purse over her shoulder to free up her hands. "Give that to me," she said to Aimee, making as if to take her plate. "You have your hands full. Ooooh goodies. What's under here?" She went to pry the plastic up on the plate in Aimee's hands, but Aimee slapped her fingers away.

"Don't touch. You have to wait. Take the platter."

Aimee waited for Kiki to take it out before shutting the trunk; but Kiki stopped her before she could push it down more than a few inches.

"What's that thing? Is that an old record player in there?"

"Yes," said Aimee. "Well, part of one."

"Are we doing some more parking lot deals tonight?" asked Kiki, raising an eyebrow at Elizabeth.

Aimee smiled and shut the trunk. "Nope. No deals. Just food." She pressed the lock and alarm button on her keychain. "Ready?"

They looked at one another and nodded their heads, turning in unison to walk to the bookstore and chatting as they went.

"So, how was work for the past couple weeks, Elizabeth?" asked Aimee.

"And what exactly is your work?" added Kiki.

"Well, I'm an accountant, and work was ... work."

"That sounds ... good, I guess," said Aimee.

"Actually, it's dreadfully dull and it's making me crazy, but thanks for being polite about it."

"Phew, I'm glad you said that, because I was just about to say how boring it sounded."

"Kiki!" admonished Aimee, "That's her job. Don't tell her it's boring."

Kiki shrugged. "I'm just saying ... "

"No, don't worry about it," said Elizabeth, happy to know there was someone out there she could vent to. "It's awful. I hate it."

"Then why do you do it?" asked Kiki.

"Because she needs to make a living," said Aimee. "Like I need to but can't seem to be able to."

They'd reached the doors. Elizabeth grabbed the handle since her plate was the smallest. "After you," she said, nodding at their thank yous as they walked past her. She didn't argue with Aimee's assessment because it was true enough.

They arrived at the glassed-off area set aside for the meeting. They could see Betty already in there, well into another set of booties, this time in a bright orange color.

"Those are some hellaciously ugly baby booties," whispered Kiki.

"Sshh!" admonished Aimee, giggling.

Elizabeth agreed silently. *What kind of mother puts fluorescent orange booties on her baby's feet?*

They went through the door, going over to claim spots in the comfortable, overstuffed chairs and couches.

"Hello, Betty!" said Aimee cheerfully. "How have you been?"

"Well, I'm still alive, if that's what you mean," said Betty, not looking up from her knitting.

Elizabeth smiled at the expression on Aimee's face. She could tell Aimee didn't know whether to take what Betty said as a joke or to feel bad that she'd somehow insulted the old woman.

"Well, that's gotta be some kind of miracle," said Kiki, "what with all the smokin' and drinkin' I saw you doing at that bar up the street last Friday."

Betty cackled and looked up from her knitting, her needles going still. "Aren't you a pistol?" She turned her gaze to Aimee. "Don't listen to her, sweetie. I don't drink at the bars. I drink alone – one shot of whiskey each night before I go to bed. It's the secret to longevity. My mother taught me that, and she lived to be a hundred and five." She went back to her knitting.

"Is that true?" asked Aimee as she put her plate down on the coffee table in front of them, dropping her purse on the floor. "Maybe I should start doing that."

"Perhaps you should wait on that," said Elizabeth. She could just imagine Aimee getting tipsy every night on the basis of Dr. Betty's recommendations. Something told Elizabeth that Aimee was about as gullible as they came.

"I only do that if I'm sick," said Kiki. "My Irish uncle used to call it a hot toddy."

"You're Irish?" asked Aimee.

"No."

"But ... ?"

Kiki smiled mischievously at her. "Uncle is just an expression."

"Oh," said Aimee.

Elizabeth could tell by Aimee's expression that she had no idea what Kiki was talking about. Elizabeth wasn't even sure *she* knew what Kiki meant.

Kiki put the platter down on the table and started unwrapping it. "Aimee, don't tell me I can't unwrap this now. I hate secrets. I have to see what's under here."

Aimee waved at the table. "Go ahead. It's just a few things I whipped up for us to munch on while we talk about the book."

"Shall I go get us some coffees?" asked Elizabeth. "We can do decaf if that's an issue for anyone."

"Sign me up," said Kiki as she finally got to a part of the plastic that she could move off the platter.

"Me too ... decaf," said Aimee.

"Just some warm soy for me. I'm lactose intolerant," said Betty, now watching Kiki wrestle with the unwrapping of the mystery treats with interest.

"Okay, I'll be right back."

Elizabeth came back to the room five minutes later with four hot drinks and was stunned at what she saw. Sitting on the table were the most delicious-looking, beautiful confections she'd ever seen that were not on a Martha Stewart magazine cover.

"Oh my goodness, what *are* these?"

"These ... are works of art," said a respectfully sober Kiki. "There's no other way to describe them." Her eyes didn't move from the items on the plates, even while she spoke.

Elizabeth looked at Aimee whose face was a delightful pink. "Aimee, where did you buy these?" Elizabeth was thinking about all the high-end clients who would love to receive these as gifts from their grateful accounting firm.

"I didn't buy them. I made them."

Elizabeth eyes widened of their own accord. "Are you *joking?*"

"No. I made them ... today, actually. I had a lot of time on my hands, and I was excited about the meeting. Baking helps me keep my mind off stuff."

"I'm almost afraid to eat them," said Kiki, her voice almost reverent.

"I'm not," said Betty, putting her knitting to the side of her leg and bending over with a groan to grab one from the plate nearest her. "They sure are pretty. Let's see if they taste as good as they look." She took one of the small, delicate pink mini cakes with the sculpted flower and tiny silver pearl on top and bit it in half.

All three women watched her in fascination. She took a few chews and then closed her eyes.

Elizabeth glanced over at Aimee and could see she was on the edge of her seat, waiting for the verdict.

"Mmmmmmm," said Betty, her eyes opening back up and a smile lighting up her face. She finished chewing and said, "Utterly divine. Simply delicious. Young lady, you are a culinary angel." She popped the other half of the cake into her mouth, pausing only a second to remove the small silver ball from her mouth.

"Oh, you can eat that too. It's edible."

"Not good for the dentures, though, sweetie." She placed the ball on the edge of the plate, as far from the other cakes as possible.

"Oh. I didn't realize. I'm sorry."

Betty waved at her before taking another cake. "Don't apologize for giving me food fit for goddesses. These girls have all their teeth. They can eat your silver balls all night long."

Kiki snorted.

Elizabeth shot her a look, trying to remain serious, but losing the battle. She and Kiki both reached for one of the tiny tarts that were on the plates nearest them. They took a bite at the same time, exchanging looks of surprise and pleasure.

Kiki was the next to give a review. "Damn, girl. You can bake your ass off. Where'd you learn how to do all this?" She swept her hand over the display of six different confections.

"YouTube. Television. Magazines."

Elizabeth nearly choked on her tart. "You learned how to do this watching *YouTube?*"

"Sure. There are a lot of great videos on there, from some really talented people. Plus, I experiment a lot."

"Oh, my god," said Kiki, popping a tiny yellow cake into her mouth, not bothering to swallow before continuing, "she's like ... a culinary savant or something."

"Hey!" said Aimee, laughing. "Careful now!"

Kiki smiled as she finished chewing, unabashedly licking her fingers.

"I think she means that it shouldn't be possible for you to be this good without ever having taken a serious course in professional baking. You have one of those spooky talents." Elizabeth looked down at the little cake in her hand that she'd just taken off the plate. "How did you get the tart so perfectly sweet? And this cake thing so fluffy?"

"Oh, well, with the tart it's all about not overworking the pastry and watching the heat on the filling. It can be tricky. And with the cake, the way you manage the eggs ... that's key. It's mostly chemistry. I was always good in high school chemistry."

Betty cackled. "You're one smart cookie. Maybe you could bake some of these for my mahjongg club sometime. The girls would go bananas for it." Her eyes narrowed as if picturing something unpleasant. "I'd love to show Madge Wilson a thing or two. She brings her horrible lime jello molds with nuts floating in them every week. Can you imagine? If I never see another jello mold in my entire life, I could die a happy woman."

"I promise. I'll do some for your mahjongg club someday. Just tell me when."

"How much would you charge for twenty of them? Ten of the cakes and ten of those red tarts?"

"Oh, I wouldn't charge you, don't be silly."

"Of course I'm going to pay for them. These must take you all day to make."

Kiki nudged Aimee's arm. "Make her pay you. She looks like she's got dough."

"Ha! I'm not rich, but I've got enough to pay for some pretty cakes. Especially if they'll shame Madge into leaving her lime jello at home for the rest of my life. I've still got a few good years left in me." She held up her finger, shaking it at the girls. "And let me tell you ... life's too short to be tortured with jello molds. I think it's time I put my foot down. You've inspired me with your pretty little cakes." She smiled at Aimee, revealing her perfect dentures with their fake pink gums.

Aimee looked uncomfortable, shrugging her shoulders and not saying anything. Elizabeth was reminded of a turtle pulling itself into its shell.

"How much did you spend on the ingredients?" asked Elizabeth, looking at Aimee.

"I don't know. Maybe seven, eight dollars?"

"And how long did it take you to make them?"

"Ummm, maybe two hours? A little less? I can make a lot in two hours, but I only had you guys, so I just made this much. Once I get going, I can do a lot in a short period of time. It's like an assembly line kind of thing."

"Okay, well, if you were to figure in how many you could do maximum in those two hours, take twenty cakes as a percentage, add up the cost of materials and then determine what you want your hourly rate to be, multiplied by the hours worked, you could figure out what you should charge."

"Uh, sorry ... you lost me at hello," said Aimee, smiling awkwardly.

"She's saying you should charge about eighty cents to a buck for each one – assuming I've guessed how many you can make in two hours and a fair wage for standing on your feet in the kitchen by a hot oven properly," said Kiki.

Elizabeth looked at Kiki, impressed with her ability to put that together so fast. "You're good."

Kiki lifted an eyebrow and shrugged. "What can I say? I like money."

"Okay then," said Betty, clearly energized at the idea of bringing down the jello mold empire Madge had so carefully built over who knew how many decades. "Twenty cakes and tarts. How about I pay you twenty-five dollars, and I'll come get them from you before my mahjongg game next Monday. Say around eleven?" asked Betty.

"Shrewd," said Kiki.

Betty gave her a sly nod.

"Okay," said Aimee, looking a bit overwhelmed, "that sounds fair."

"You can give me your address later." Betty looked at the other two. "Are we going to talk about books now, or what?"

"No," said Kiki, matter-of-factly.

"No?" asked Elizabeth. "Why not? I have a list of talking points."

"Because I have something else I want to discuss first. I have an announcement to make."

Aimee sat up straighter. "Oh, goody. Announcements."

Elizabeth gestured with her hand for Kiki to continue, unoffended by being put off her agenda. She was feeling like throwing the agenda in the garbage anyway. She liked chatting with these girls. "By all means. Announce away."

"For the first time since I was sixteen years old, and that's more time than I care to admit, I am officially unemployed."

Aimee's mouth dropped open in surprise. "No more dancing?"

"Nope. No more dancing."

"You were a dancer?" asked Elizabeth.

"Yes. Why?"

"Probably because she thought you were a street walker," said Betty, knitting away.

"Betty!" said Elizabeth, shocked out of her gourd. "I didn't!" She looked at Kiki in horror, hoping she couldn't read her mind and find out that it was exactly what she had thought Kiki did for a living.

Kiki smiled. "It's okay. I know what people think. It doesn't bother me. But no, I wasn't a prostitute. I was an exotic dancer – a drug free, pimp free, exotic dancer, for the record. But I'm done with it, as of two weeks ago. I've officially retired."

"So what are you going to do now?" asked Aimee, fear in her voice.

"I don't know. Plant some window boxes with flowers. Suntan. Relax. Maybe start a business. I'm not sure yet."

Elizabeth leaned forward, suddenly very intrigued. "You're thinking of starting a business? What kind?"

"I don't know. I haven't thought too hard about it. But I have some money to invest. My expenses are low. I could live lean for a while if I had to." She paused for a moment looking at each of the girls before turning back to Elizabeth. "Why do you ask?"

Elizabeth sat back. "Just curious. I work with business owners all the time. In fact, I was thinking today about possibly doing the same thing – quitting and starting something on my own."

"An accounting firm?" asked Aimee.

"No. No way. I want out of that business."

"So, what then?" asked Betty. "Going to be an exotic dancer?"

Kiki smiled. "You could do it. You've got the bod. All you'd need is a few lessons. You could make a lot of money."

"Oh, I hardly think I could do something like that. I have no rhythm. And I'd be too afraid to let a stranger see me in my underwear."

"It's more than underwear," said Aimee, "it's the full monty. You have to show them your hoo-hah and everything." She looked at Kiki, nodding for confirmation.

"Hoo-hah?" asked Kiki.

"Yeah. Hoo-hah. Your ... you know ... lady parts."

Kiki started laughing.

Elizabeth joined in. She looked over and could see a smile on Betty's face too.

"What do you guys call it?" asked Aimee, slightly miffed.

"Vagina," said Elizabeth.

"Va-jay-jay," said Kiki.

"Hairy clam," said Betty.

The three girls were momentarily shocked into silence before they started laughing so loud, they received hard stares from patrons of the store outside the glass meeting room.

Elizabeth held up her finger, signaling them to stop laughing so loud, but all that did was make them start snorting instead, trying to keep the guffaws in.

Kiki was the first to recover. "Oh. Em. Gee. You did not just say what I think you just said."

"What? Hairy clam? I most certainly did too," said Betty, not laughing, just knitting away as if nothing was happening.

"Stop," gasped Aimee, "just stop. I'm gonna pee my pants if you keep it up."

"Yes, okay, no more ... colloquialisms. I drank too much coffee," agreed Elizabeth.

"Fine," said Kiki, back to business now. "So, Elizabeth, why don't you quit if you're so unhappy? Just do it. Start your own thing. If you're an accountant you must be good with numbers and know what it takes to make a business succeed."

Elizabeth felt the humor leave her body instantly as she thought about her job. "To be honest, I have no idea why I don't leave. I guess I just never seriously considered it an option. But after today, it's looking more and more attractive."

"Wow. You guys are amazing," said Aimee. "I wish I could do that ... just have a job and then decide to quit and do something on my own."

Kiki looked at her. "Why can't you?"

"Well, I don't have the job to quit in the first place."

"So, that just means you have one less obstacle," said Elizabeth. "It's easier when you don't have to make that decision."

"Well, you have to have money to start a business. And I have none."

"Find a partner with money. You have talent. You could open a bakery or a coffee shop. You already have one customer right here." Elizabeth pointed to Betty.

"I hope I get a lifetime discount, since I'll be your first," said Betty.

Aimee smiled, almost sadly. "That would be so amazing. But it's just not possible for me right now. I have to find an apartment, get a job, figure out how I'm going to support myself. Starting a business is a luxury I can't afford."

Elizabeth looked at the pitiful expression on Aimee's face and wished there was something she could do to help. "Something will turn up for you. I'm sure of it."

Aimee perked up visibly. "I know. I'm hopeful. Don't worry about me." She clasped her hands together. "So ... congratulations to Kiki, right? That's a big step. Retirement at ... 30?"

"Thirty-two. And it's only temporary. I'm just going to take another week off to marinate and then decide what to do."

"Well, here's to new beginnings," said Elizabeth, picking up one of the last few cakes on the plate in front of her.

The others each picked up a cake or tart and held them up, touching them together and smiling. "New beginnings!" they each said, before popping the confections into their mouths and smiling as the sugar, flavors and textures melted together onto their tongues.

10

aimee

$\mathcal{T}$HE LAST BOX WAS PACKED. Aimee looked over the stacks and sighed heavily. She'd made herself stick to ten of them. That's it. Everything she owned had to fit in one of those cardboard boxes, or it wasn't coming with her. Where she was going, she didn't yet know. But when she found a place, she'd be ready. There was one suitcase next to the boxes that held her favorite clothes, shoes, and toiletries. She could get all this moved in one carload, and it made her happy to be so organized.

She could have taken more time to do this and probably allowed herself more boxes, too. But Jack's behavior had escalated to the point that she just didn't trust him to be rational anymore. She needed to pack light and be able to move quickly, just in case.

Her phone rang and she looked at the caller ID. Jack again. It was to the point that it was almost harassment. He was calling her several times a day and always angry for no reason.

"Hello, Jack."

"What are you doing?"

She pulled the phone away from her head and looked down at it, annoyed. She put it back to her ear and replied, "None of your business, Jack. Why are you calling? Do you need something? Have you finally decided to pay my support?"

"Aimee, I'm tired of playing games with you. I want to know what you've been up to, and I want to know where my golf clubs are. I'm going golfing tomorrow, and I need them."

This was Jack's newest thing. For some reason, he'd decided that he had a right to know what she was doing at every moment of the day, just like he'd done when they were married.

"Jack, we're not married anymore. Well, technically we are, but we're separated and almost technically divorced. You have a new girlfriend or fiancée, or whatever she is, to harass and boss around. Just stay out of my business. And forget the clubs. They're gone."

She had to hold the phone away from her ear because of the screaming coming from Jack's end. She looked for the red button and pressed it, cutting off his call.

"I've had a lifetime of that crap, Jack, and I don't have to put up with it anymore," she said out loud, looking at her boxes. She smiled at her newfound confidence and stuck the phone in her back pocket, heading back to the kitchen. She had a batch of cookies in the oven, a new recipe she was trying. She'd been working on it off and on for days, trying to get just the right combination of flavorings and ingredients. She was pretty sure this one was going to be perfect.

The front doorbell rang. Aimee grabbed the cookies out of the oven and set the sheet on the cooling racks before rushing down the hall and looking through the peephole. She was always worried it was going to be Jack, there to cause trouble again. She felt reasonably safe during working hours, though. He rarely left his office between nine in the morning and six at night, especially with his soon-to-be wife Tiffany there. The girl wasn't that dumb. She knew he was a cheater, so she kept a close eye on him.

Betty was standing out on the front porch.

"Betty! Come in!" Aimee threw the door open wide.

"Hello, sweetie, how are you?"

Aimee smiled and leaned in, giving Betty a kiss on the cheek. Betty smelled of lotion and powder, just like an older lady should, in Aimee's opinion. "I have your cakes all ready. I even found a cute little platter for them at the dollar store. Come see."

Betty followed her into the kitchen where Aimee led her over to the granite-covered island. Among the baking pans, potholders, and other evidence of recent baking, was a pink platter with a two-inch high rim, filled with gorgeous cakes and tarts, just as Betty had ordered for her mahjongg club.

Betty clasped her hands together in glee, her shiny bone-colored purse swinging on her forearm. "Oh, those are just *lovely*. Absolutely *perfect*. Madge is going to be furious." She looked at Aimee with bright eyes and a devious grin.

Aimee smiled back. "I'm glad you're glad. But are you sure you want to get Madge so upset?"

"Oh, yes. Definitely."

"Okay, then. Let me get them wrapped up for you, and then I'll help you get them out to your car."

Aimee went about wrapping up the cakes and finished just as a voice came from the doorway.

"Who's she? The cleaning lady? Since when can you afford one of those?"

Aimee turned with a gasp, her joy disappearing like a puff of smoke. "Jack! What are you doing here? Aren't you supposed to be at work?"

"Cleaning lady? Did he say cleaning lady?" asked Betty, a frown spreading across her face.

Aimee put her hand on Betty's arm. "Ignore him. He's not a very nice person."

"I asked a question, and I expect an answer," he insisted. "Who is this person and why is she in my house?"

Aimee sighed, stepping in-between Jack and Betty. "This is a friend of mine, Jack. And she was just leaving." Aimee turned to Betty and said in a lowered voice. "Let me carry this out for you. Come on."

Before Aimee grabbed the platter, she quickly picked up her spatula and used it to put a few of the still warm cookies in with the pastries, carefully readjusting the plastic wrap once they were settled in nicely. She kept her eyes down and moved with the platter in her hand to leave the kitchen, praying Jack wouldn't cause any more trouble. She could feel her face burning in humiliation as it was. She was so embarrassed that Betty had seen him and heard how nasty he could be. And this was Jack being nice, actually. *Please, please don't let him get crazy in front of Betty.*

Aimee left the kitchen, Jack stepping to the side to let her pass. She had expected Betty to follow, but Betty had other ideas.

"Young man ... didn't your mother ever teach you any manners?"

"Excuse me?" was Jack's surprised response.

"You heard me. *Manners.* I'm pretty sure you're not as stupid as you look, so let me give you a little piece of advice."

"I don't need any advice from the cleaning lady, I can assure you," he said arrogantly.

"Ha! I wouldn't clean up after your messes if I were on welfare and eating cat food right out of the can. Your kind of dirt doesn't clean, if you catch my drift." She looked over at Aimee and gave her a nod. Then she turned back to Jack. "Now shut up and listen, because I'll bet you don't do that as often as you should. Remember the adage – as you sow, so shall you reap. One day you're going to look back on all of this, if you're a very lucky man, and regret the things you've said and done. Change your ways, before it's too late."

"Go to hell," said Jack in a low, menacing tone.

Betty sucked her teeth, staring Jack down, even though she was nearly a foot shorter than him, and then said in a sunny voice as she turned and left the kitchen, "Have a nice day, asshole!"

Aimee stood in the hallway, frozen in place and unable to move.

"Come on, sweet pea," said Betty, "let's get that platter out to the car. I have some friends waiting for me who are getting closer to death's doorstep every minute. Can't waste any time. I want to see the looks on their faces when they see these treats you made."

Aimee felt Betty gently push her shoulder to get her moving, which woke Aimee up from the living nightmare she had just watched unfold in front of her. She walked, Betty still behind her keeping up her prattle all the way back to the car.

Aimee had to force herself not to look back at the house. She half expected Jack to start throwing her boxes out the front door. *No, he'll probably want to go through them first before throwing them out, to see if there's anything in there he or his girlfriend might want.*

Betty opened the back door so Aimee could place the cakes on the seat. When Aimee finished settling them in and stood up, Betty put her hand on Aimee's arm.

Aimee looked down at the little old lady who was looking up at her with a very serious expression.

"Aimee, honey, do you have a gun?" Betty asked.

Aimee looked at her confused. "A gun? No. Why?"

"Because if I were you, I'd get one. *Soon.* That man is a keg of dynamite ready to blow. And I have a feeling he's wanting to blow on *you.*" She emphasized her point by poking her finger into Aimee's shoulder.

Aimee nearly crumbled. She felt so terrible that Betty had seen all that. "Jack's a jerk, I know. And I'm super sorry he was so rude to you. I don't know what's gotten into him lately. He was always bossy, but the last couple weeks ... I don't know ... "

"I can tell you what it is," said Betty, getting into her car and rolling down the window. It was one of the old hand-crank kind. "He's jealous of you."

"Of me?" laughed Aimee. "That's a good one."

"You're happy. He's not. That's obvious. Miserable people despise happy ones. It reminds them how worthless their lives are."

Aimee thought about that for a second. "Well, I'm not miserable, but I don't know that I'd call myself *happy*, happy."

"You seem happy to me. Always smiling, always positive-minded. That man in there doesn't like it. That's as plain as the nose on his snobby face."

"I have been happier since I started going to the book club meetings. Even though there've only been two, it's made a difference in my life. Doesn't that sound crazy? My life must be pretty pitiful." She looked down at the ground, embarrassed about how weak she felt.

"No, it's not crazy at all. Women need connections with other women. That's how we're wired. That's why I play mahjohngg, even though I have to suffer through Madge's jello molds the whole time. I'd bet my false teeth that man in there never liked you to have women friends. Am I right?"

Aimee searched her memory, digging up past moments of friendship. "I never really thought about it much before, but all the friends I had were wives of Jack's friends."

"And where are these so-called friends now?" asked Betty, starting her car.

Aimee answered in a soft voice. "They've all pretty much disappeared. It's as if we were never friends."

"They weren't. Glad you've figured that out. And I'll tell ya, I don't know that man in there from Adam, but I know for a fact, he's the reason you never had friends. There's nothing wrong with you, girly. You're as sweet as a gumdrop and as gentle as a lamb. There's a million women out there who'd love to call you friend, like me and Elizabeth and Kiki, if I'm not mistaken. Don't let that man take your fire from you. You can do much better."

Aimee smiled tremulously, finding herself very close to tears over Betty's kindness.

"Now I have to get going, or I'm going to be late. One more thing – I saw those boxes. Are you moving out?"

"Someday. I don't have a place yet."

"Well, take my advice. It's free. Go find yourself something today. You're not safe here, and I hate to see good girls like you get hurt. I'll see you at the next meeting, and I'll be expecting you to tell me that you have a new place to live then."

Aimee smiled through the haze of the tears floating in her eyes. "Okay, Betty. I'll see what I can do. I appreciate your advice."

"Oh, shoot! I almost forgot to give you the money for the cakes!" Betty reached over to the passenger seat and unsnapped her shiny, vinyl purse, pulling out a twenty and a five. "Here you go. Your first dollar made in your baking business!" She handed over the money and waved as she backed out of the driveway, smiling big and only going into the grass a little.

Aimee waved back, staying outside until the car was gone from sight. She wasn't looking forward to going back into the house. She walked up to the front porch and sat down on the swing. Betty's advice was weighing on her.

"Aimee, where are you?" came Jack's voice from inside.

"I'm on the porch."

Jack came out and stepped over to where she was sitting. "I need to talk to you."

Aimee shrugged, looking out at the street. "So, talk."

"Inside."

"No. I'm not going back inside with you, Jack. If you need to talk, do it here." *Where it's safe and I know you won't get violent in front of the neighbors.*

"I'd prefer to talk inside."

Aimee looked up at him, angrily. "I'm sure you would. But I wouldn't. So either talk here, or leave." She could tell by his reaction that he was surprised and not happy.

"What's gotten into you lately, Aimee? You've become suddenly very unreasonable. All I want to know is what happened to my clubs. And I need to talk to you about our life insurance."

"What's gotten into me is I'm sick of your attitude and the way you treat me. You sent me to the emergency room, Jack, in case you forgot. I had to have *stitches* put into my head. So forgive me if I'm not in the mood to just follow your orders, as usual."

"That was your fault, not mine."

"Whatever," said Aimee, disgusted with him. She was starting to wonder what she'd ever seen in him.

"I'm serious about my golf clubs."

Aimee said nothing in response. She decided she was better off playing dumb in that department.

"And about the insurance, I want to put Tiffany on as the beneficiary. With the baby coming, she needs it more than you do."

Aimee was angry that he was taking this from her too, since he was perfectly capable of getting a new policy for his new girlfriend. And Aimee knew she would need the money if he died and stopped paying support, at least until she got on her feet. She tried not to let his cut about the baby slice her open, but it did. And he knew it too; she could tell by the look on his face.

"Why don't you just change it yourself?" He'd managed to take whatever he wanted without consulting her before. She couldn't see why this should be any different.

"Well, I just need you to sign a paper for it. Just a technicality."

"Do you have the paper?"

"No, but I'll bring it over to you."

"Mail it. I don't want you to come here anymore."

Jack sighed loudly in irritation. "This is my house, not yours. I'll come here whenever I want to."

She could tell he was starting to get angry again. It was interesting to her that he had acted all nice when it came to the insurance paper, but now he couldn't pull it off anymore.

"Are you done?" she asked, looking out at the street. She couldn't even stand to look at his face anymore.

"You're pitiful, you know that?" he spat out. "You just sit here all day, feeling sorry for yourself, doing nothing but wasting time in the kitchen. You know you can't cook. That's why we always had to hire caterers when we had a party. That's why we had to eat out all the time."

Aimee said nothing in response. She battled with the inner demons that wanted to rise up and agree with him. She thought of her friends at the book club and how they had raved about her cakes. And she thought of Betty who'd just paid her twenty-five dollars to take her cakes and use them to bring down Madge's jello mold strangle hold. The demons and memories of Jack insulting her cooking for ten years disappeared in a puff of smoke, and Aimee turned her attention to Jack, looking him right in the eye. "Go to hell, Jack."

He took one step toward her, a furious expression on his face, but then stopped when a voice reached their ears.

"Hello, Aimee, how are you today?" asked the postman, approaching them from the front walkway. "Beautiful weather, isn't it?"

Aimee smiled brightly. "Sure is. How have you been, George?"

"Never better." He stepped up onto the front porch, nodding perfunctorily at Jack. They had never met. "Got some mail for ya," he said, handing it to Aimee.

"Thanks for the personal delivery," she said, smiling and standing up to take the stack of envelopes from him. "Have a good one. Say hello to Sally for me."

"My pleasure. Will do. You have a nice day too, now." He left, continuing on to the next-door neighbor's house.

"You and the mailman are on friendly terms."

"Yeah. We sleep together every Wednesday. In your bed."

Aimee was totally unprepared for his reaction.

He shoved her hard, sending her to the porch floor. She banged her knee on the chair that was in the way. A small scream of surprise left her lips.

"Whore," he growled, before storming off the porch, getting into his sports car and squealing his tires as he left.

Aimee sat up carefully, slowly picking up the envelopes that had scattered around her. She stood gingerly, keeping the weight off her injured knee as much as she could. She knew she should probably be upset right now ... crying too. But all she could do was smile through the pain. Today was the first time she could remember ever standing up to Jack, and it felt good. No, it felt *wonderful*.

She limped back into the house and glanced at the boxes that had been cut open and rifled through. Betty was right. She needed to get the hell out of there and fast. She could see the laptop computer screen on the kitchen counter from where she stood. It was open to an apartment listing service.

No better time than the present. She made herself a bag of ice for her knee and sat down at the computer, determined to find a new place to live before the day was out.

11

kiki

$\mathcal{K}$IKI CAME IN FROM HER back porch where she'd been trying to catch some of the afternoon's dying rays for the tan she liked to maintain. She'd sworn off tanning booths after reading a scary article about them online, but she couldn't make herself stay out of the sun.

"What to do, what to do?" she said out into the open space of her living room. She hadn't realized when she'd started this whole unemployment thing that she'd be so bored all the time. She'd already read an entire book that day and two the day before. But she was tired of being a hermit.

She walked over to her laptop set up at the dining room table and sat down, glancing at its clock. "Five o'clock ... let's see who's up for a drink." She tapped out an email, leaving the *To* field blank.

I'M BORED. WHO'S INTERESTED IN GRAB-BING A DRINK OVER AT O'MALLEYS?

She stared at the email, wondering who she should send it to. Not Cindi. She'd spend the entire time talking about her pimp, and that would just piss Kiki off. It was one thing to complain, but a totally different thing to do it and then go back to him. She had no patience for that tonight.

Shawnda wasn't going to be on the list either. She was too busy with her new job and her old job. Another one of those complainers who didn't have the guts to get out of the rat race.

She considered her other option for a second and couldn't think of a reason not to do it, so she quickly typed Aimee's and Elizabeth's email addresses into the empty space and clicked *Send*. They'd never met outside of the book club before, but what the hell. *The worst they could do is say no, right?*

Kiki didn't know why she felt so nervous about a stupid email. She got up and went to the kitchen to take a bottle of chardonnay out of the fridge and pour herself a glass. She loved the stemware she'd gotten on sale at Nordstrom. She'd splurged, but not as much as she could have using the sweet thirty percent off card she'd received in the mail - one of the perks of being a regular customer there. She didn't drink wine that often, but when she did, she liked to do it in style.

She took her glass back to the table, intending to surf the Internet, but she already had two new messages waiting in her inbox. She sat down, her heartbeat picking up a little.

"This is stupid," she said at her computer. "What am I getting so worked up about?" She didn't know why Aimee's and Elizabeth's answers were so important to her, but they were. She couldn't remember the last time she'd had a friendship with someone not in the business of selling sex or the idea of it.

She clicked on Elizabeth's first.

YOU ARE LIKE AN ANGEL OF MERCY. WHEN?

Kiki smiled, clicking open Aimee's next.

YOU TOTALLY READ MY MIND. WHAT TIME?

Kiki's heart warmed at the idea of drinks with her two buds. She thought about emailing Betty, but decided against it. It would probably end up being past her bedtime anyway, if things went well.

She sent a group email response.

SEVEN O'CLOCK. WEAR HEELS.

She smiled and clicked off the computer, snapping the top down and picking up her wine glass to take a sip. Her thoughts jumped to what she was going to wear, so she got up and walked to the stairs, taking them up to her bedroom.

She'd opted for the two-bedroom townhouse plan instead of the three bedroom, so she could have a bigger closet. And even though it was the size of a small room itself, it was still packed to the gills. She set her wineglass down on the dresser just outside the entrance and went in.

Her eyes scanned the selection available. *Sexy or conservative ... hmmm ...* She opted for something in-between, knowing that Elizabeth would no doubt be coming from work and Aimee from home. She reached over and pulled out one of her many black dresses. This one ended a few inches above the knee but fit pretty snugly – not too much, though – just enough to let the world know she had something to brag about underneath without actually showing off every detail. *Perfect* she thought to herself, as she reached over to the cubby that held a pair of black heels with a two-inch wide band across the instep. She loved the layered wood look of the heel and the casual elegance of the easy, summer slip-on style. The soft Italian leather made them one of the more comfortable pairs she owned.

She put the dress still on its hanger on a hook on the back of her closet door, dropping the heels on the floor nearby. She needed to take a shower and rinse off the suntan oil, and she needed to do her hair and makeup. She had at least ninety minutes of primping ahead of her and she needed to get going if she was going to make it to O'Malleys by seven.

12

elizabeth

*E*LIZABETH COULDN'T KEEP THE SMILE off her face. She'd just read Kiki's email confirming they were all meeting at seven. She wiggled her toes in her heels, glad she'd made the decision to wear these shoes today. Normally she went with conservative flats, but this morning, she'd been in a mood. Maybe she'd been picking up on Kiki's vibe.

But Elizabeth knew it was more than that. She'd been thinking a lot about the conversation she'd had at the book club meeting with the other girls. She was flat-out jealous of Kiki having quit her job like she had. Making that kind of decision took serious guts, and Elizabeth had been admonishing herself all week over being such a wimp. She wished she had that kind of bravery in her heart.

A knock at her office door interrupted her train of thought. The senior partner was standing there, holding up a file. "Got a minute?" he asked.

"Sure, Bill, come on in." She eyed the file in his hand warily, afraid she knew whose name was on it.

He walked over and stood next to her desk, choosing to tower over her rather than sit in the chair across from her like everyone else did. He had a habit of doing that, which really pissed Elizabeth off. She was pretty sure he knew it, too.

She made a split second decision and stood up. The heels she was wearing gave her a two-inch advantage over him, destroying whatever power play he'd been trying to use on her. For about two seconds.

"I need you to stay late tonight and work on this file." He threw it down on her desk.

She recognized it immediately as the client who didn't believe in paying taxes, preferring that the government just print some more hundred-dollar bills to cover his tab. "I have plans. I can't."

"Cancel them," he said as he turned to go. "Make him happy. He wants you and only you."

Elizabeth was angry and frustrated, too tired to keep the emotion out of her voice. "He's your client, Bill, not mine."

Bill stopped in his tracks and turned, raising an eyebrow at her. "Excuse me? I'm sorry ... " He put his finger up to his ear. "Did I just hear you tell me Mr. Bridgestone isn't your concern?"

Elizabeth squared her shoulders. "No. What you heard me say was that he's your client, not mine. If he needs to be taken care of, it should be you doing it, not me." She flipped open the file jacket and studied the first page for two seconds, before saying, "There's an entire weekend of work to be done on this."

She'd never stood up to Bill this way. Ever. She always just took whatever file he didn't want to deal with and completed the work without complaint or comment. She'd lost count of how many hours of Bill's work she'd done. She wasn't the only one in the firm who had and wouldn't be the last. Bill called himself the rainmaker, and he was very fond of saying that the rainmaker makes rain; he doesn't crunch numbers.

Bill dropped his hands to his sides, clenching his fists once before letting them go loose again. "Do the work, Elizabeth," he said in a very controlled and almost arrogant voice. "And next time, think harder before you respond to me. I'd hate for you to say something that you'd regret."

Elizabeth said nothing. She just clenched her teeth and steamed internally, watching Bill's back as he exited her office. No doubt he was heading out to go have a few cocktails at his very exclusive country club.

Maybe if I spent every afternoon drinking martinis with the good old boys, I could be the rainmaker and you could crunch numbers for a change. That's what she wished she could say, but she just thought it instead. *No need to get fired over Mr. Bridgestone.* The guy was an ass, but he did have a big account at the firm.

The front door of the office slammed shut behind Bill, and she could hear Sandy, the receptionist, gathering her things. The front waiting area lights went off, and then Sandy yelled, "Goodnight, Elizabeth! Have a good weekend!"

"Yeah, right," said Elizabeth softly. This file was going to take the full two days to get straightened out. "You too!" shouted Elizabeth, not wanting to be rude. It wasn't Sandy's fault that Elizabeth's job sucked and that Bill was a pompous, chauvinist prick.

She sat down at her desk, and began working on the file, all the while looking up from time to time to stare at the email from Kiki. Another one popped up around six o'clock, this one from Aimee. Elizabeth clicked on it sadly.

I'M SO EXCITED! AND I EVEN HAVE HEELS.
SEE YOU GIRLS SOOOON!!!

Elizabeth smiled at Aimee's obvious enthusiasm. Then she looked at the stupid folder sitting on her desk, knowing she'd be there until midnight with it, while Kiki and Aimee were having wine and hanging out. She was pissed.

Elizabeth took one more look at Aimee's email and felt a spark light up in her heart. She made a command decision, only a very small piece of her hoping she wouldn't live to regret it. She stood up, grabbed the file, and marched out of her office, heading to the one located three doors down – the one on the corner of the building with the gorgeous views of downtown Orlando. Bill's office.

She walked in and slapped the folder down on his desk, grabbing a post-it note and a pen from the carefully arranged and nearly bare surface. She wrote out a note and stuck it to the folder, placing the whole thing in the center of his desk blotter so he'd be sure to see it when he came in on Monday. Of course, that would be sometime around ten o'clock and long past the time Mr. Bridgestone would have expected this little problem he'd created to be resolved. Bill had the privilege in his position to hold old-school banker's hours. She, on the other hand, came in at seven every morning, seven days a week. She left after ten most weeknights and after four on weekends. But not tonight. And not ever again. She'd had it up to her eyeballs and was tired of drowning in Bill's work and covering for his ass.

She went back to her office and took her favorite Mont Blanc pen out of the drawer and the picture of her sister she had in a frame on her desk and stacked them neatly together. She looked around the room and saw nothing else urgently personal to worry about. She'd get the rest later, when she worked her last two or three weeks as part of her take-this-job-and-shove-it offer. She quickly sat down and typed out a letter of resignation before she could second-guess her crazy, impetuous decision. Her heart was racing, but she felt free. For the first time in years and years, she thought maybe she could be the captain of her own destiny, instead of following the path laid out for her by others.

She printed out the letter, signed it with a flourish using her favorite pen – a graduation gift from her mother who had passed away several years earlier – and delivered it to Bill's desk. She put it next to the file with the post-it that said "Not My Client" on it. Bill was going to have an absolute fit when he saw it, but she didn't care.

She went to her office and bent down, reaching into the bottom drawer of her file cabinet. She took out a small box of chocolates she had recently purchased for a client and put the box on Sandy's desk instead. She used one of Sandy's *While You Were Out* message notes and wrote, *"Sorry for all the trouble that's coming"*, placing it under the ribbon that was on the box and putting the whole package on Sandy's computer keyboard. Elizabeth knew exactly who was going to suffer when she left. First it would be Sandy, and then it would be any number of the other accountants on this floor. But she refused to feel sorry for them. If she could get out, so could they. Maybe if Bill had to deal with a mass exodus, he'd stop being such an ass all the time. But it wasn't her problem any more. *I'm finally free!*

She went back to her office and took the few things she couldn't live without, locked her drawer and cabinet, and headed out the door. She had the perfect amount of time left to drive the speed limit to the bar and not worry about catching red lights all the way. Her heels clicked along the marble floor as she headed to the elevator.

13

aimee

AIMEE WAS JUST PUTTING THE finishing touches on her makeup when she heard the front door open. Her heart leapt into her throat when she realized who it had to be. The panicked part of her looked at the bathroom window, wondering if it would be worth it to climb out, jump from the second floor balcony somehow, and run around the house to the car. But then she realized her purse was downstairs with the keys in it, so even if she were capable of said ninja moves, she wouldn't make it very far. She had to go down and face the devil who surely awaited her.

"Aimee?! Where are you?" came Jack's angry voice from the foot of the stairs.

"Coming down." She left the bathroom reluctantly, picking up the heels she'd left on the floor and carrying them down by the straps looped over her finger. As soon as she saw his eyes light on her, she knew there was going to be trouble.

"Why are you dressed like a whore?"

Aimee felt herself getting angry, even though she'd promised herself she wouldn't lose her temper. "Don't use that word in my presence. It's nasty and it doesn't apply to me."

Jack tried to grab her as she went past, but she slipped out of his grasp and moved down the hallway from him.

"Leave me alone, Jack. I'm leaving soon. Get what you came for and go."

"You're going out? What ... ? On a date? No. No, you're not going anywhere." He shook his head, his nostrils flaring and his lower jaw jutting out.

"No, it's not a date. I'm going out with some girlfriends, not that it's any of your business." She was proud to be able to say that she had friends now. Jack had taken nearly everything from her, but he wasn't going to take this.

"Bullshit. You're meeting some guy."

"So what if I am?!" she yelled. "You're engaged to your pregnant girlfriend, *Jack!* You've moved on! So have I!"

Jack grabbed her purse off the table by the stairs and started rifling through it, getting frustrated and finally dumping out its contents onto the floor.

"What are you doing?!" shrieked Aimee, afraid to go and rescue her stuff. "Get out of my purse!" She didn't want to get too close to him so she stayed where she was, wishing she hadn't left her purse there for him to get to.

"Ha!" yelled Jack, picking up her car keys. "See you later, Aimee. Have fun sitting on the couch all night." He turned and left the house, obviously very pleased with himself.

Aimee wanted to run after him and jump on his back, tearing his hair out and taking her keys back; but she knew that would only get her back in the E.R. and effectively give him that much more power over her, letting him know that he'd made her that upset.

She turned to go into the kitchen, tears welling up in her eyes as she heard his car zoom out of the driveway. The heels she'd been carrying dropped to the floor as she sat in front of her laptop on the kitchen counter. She slowly started typing out her email message to Kiki and Elizabeth as the tears flowed down her face, smearing her newly applied mascara.

HI GIRLS. SORRY. CAN'T COME. LOST THE KEYS TO MY CAR. HOPE YOU HAVE FUN. XOXO AIMEE.

She got off the chair and shuffled over to the pantry. *Might as well bake something.* It always calmed her to make something beautiful. She kicked her shoes to the side, because she hated wearing them when she cooked, and pulled out the flour and sugar. As she moved around the kitchen absently grabbing the necessary things, she tried to figure out who this batch of cookies would go to. She rarely ate more than a taste of what she made herself, but she had so few friends, there was a definite oversupply problem. Before she could decide whether to give them to the postman or her retired neighbors, a beep from her computer broke through her daze of unhappiness and alerted her to the fact that she had a new message in her inbox.

She shuffled over to read it, almost sure it would be an offer for another penis enlargement drug. She got at least ten of them a day. Or maybe this time it would be another multi-million dollar lottery that she'd won, or an inheritance from someone in Nigeria or the People's Republic of Congo.

Her eyes lit up when she saw that it was a message from Kiki.

WHAT'S YOUR ADDRESS? I'M COMING OVER TO GET YOU. NO EXCUSES.

Aimee smiled. It was like Kiki could read her mind and see past the stories she made up to keep from being too embarrassed. She half wanted to lie and say something about being sick, but instead, typed out her address. Worse than facing her friends and having them know what a horrible person her ex was, would be giving her ex the satisfaction of ruining her night.

She walked over and put away the flour and sugar, lining them up carefully in the pantry, and put her baking pans back in the cupboard. The rest of her life might be a complete mess, but this little part of it, the part that took place in the kitchen, was perfectly organized and ran like clockwork. She liked having that tiny bit of control, especially since the rest of her life seemed so chaotic.

Aimee walked slowly upstairs to the bathroom to try and repair the damage done by her tears. After taking one look in the mirror, she decided that starting all over was her best bet, and began washing her face. She needed the cool water to calm down her red eyes. After she'd dried herself off and was in the middle of putting on moisturizer, the doorbell rang.

She panicked, worried that Jack had come back. But then she realized he wouldn't have the courtesy to ring the bell, so she hurried downstairs as she rubbed in her face cream, throwing open the door as soon as she reached it.

Kiki stood on the doorstep, looking as gorgeous as ever, towering over Aimee in heels that made her six feet tall. Slung over her shoulder was a super cool black bag that Aimee remembered seeing in the window of a store in the mall she was afraid to go into because the things in it were so expensive.

"Nice place," said Kiki, stepping forward to come in. Her heels thunked soundly on the wood floor.

Aimee moved back, giving her room to enter, and then shut the door. She watched as Kiki's eyes roamed around the foyer, taking in the re-packed boxes that Jack had ripped open the day before and the contents of Aimee's purse thrown out on the floor. Kiki's gaze stopped at Aimee's face.

"Something tells me there's more than just lost keys going on here."

Aimee smiled at her tremulously and then lost it. She started crying and turned to grab some tissues off the nearby table. She was embarrassed that Kiki was seeing her like this. She hated crying in front of people.

"Tell me what happened, Aimee. Who do I need to go beat up? Is it the ex?"

Aimee smiled, imagining her Amazonian friend going after her short, uptight husband. That was a match she'd like to see.

"It was Jack. He came over when I was getting ready, and when he saw that I was going out, he took my keys. I don't have a spare set."

"Okay, I can do easy math ... Jack equals asshole. So. First order of business is fixing your face. Show me to your makeup area."

Aimee started walking up the stairs. "I can do it. I was just about to when you got here. You can make yourself at home, it will only take me a minute. There are some bar stools in the kitchen."

Kiki followed Aimee up and went right into the bathroom behind her. "I'm doing your makeup. Don't worry, I'm an expert. Show me your stuff so I can see what I have to work with."

Kiki had a very determined but gentle look on her face, so Aimee capitulated. She was too woozy and wienie-feeling to fight her off anyway. She'd only once had a person do her makeup before, in the mall, and they'd done a horrible job. At this point, though, Aimee couldn't care less. Some of the excitement of going out had dissipated in the wake of Jack's cruelty.

Aimee pulled open the top drawer of the bathroom vanity where she kept all of her supplies.

Kiki looked inside, taking in the two old and very used-looking compacts that had been purchased at the grocery store and a mascara that was way past its prime. "Is this it?"

"Yep. That's all she wrote."

"Where are your brushes?"

"What? Like hair brushes?"

"No, goof, makeup brushes."

"I don't have any. I just use what comes in the compact."

"Those crappy sponges on plastic sticks? Good lord, girl, you need a serious lesson in Makeup 101. I'm surprised you never watched the videos on YouTube."

Aimee smiled. "Actually, I have. I just never did anything after I watched them."

Kiki pulled her bag up off the floor and set it on the counter. "Well, lucky for you, I came prepared." She started pulling out pots and brushes and tubes and setting them down next to the sink, one by one.

"Wow," said Aimee, picking up an eye shadow pot, "these are pretty. Where did you get all of them?"

"Here and there. I don't have a favorite brand per se. I just buy what appeals to me. I do prefer Chanel liners though. I think they have the best formulation there."

"Oh, yeah. Me too," said Aimee, smirking.

"Watch it, wise ass. I have the power now." She held up a brush from her supply. "You might want to be nice to me for the next fifteen minutes."

Aimee frowned, thinking how much Kiki's demand sounded like one of her ex-husband's, minus the angry threat underneath.

"What? What'd I say?"

"You sound like Jack," she said softly.

Kiki grabbed Aimee's chin, forcing her to lift her face. "I'm not that asshole. I'm your friend. I was just giving you the kick in the pants I think you need. You tell me if I'm being too mean, and I'll stop." She dropped her hand and pulled her purse off the counter, letting it fall back to the floor. "I need a chair for you."

Aimee gestured toward the toilet.

Kiki shrugged. "If you insist."

Aimee dropped down and faced her friend.

Kiki frowned. "No. Too low. Come sit on the counter."

Aimee got up and did as she was told, balancing her butt on the small piece of counter that wasn't a sink and wasn't covered in makeup. Within minutes she felt the cool glide of foundation on her skin, being applied with a wide brush. It was so relaxing she closed her eyes. "This feels good," she said.

"It's called being pampered. Every woman should have it done at least once a week, in my book."

"Pampering costs money I don't have."

"Well, when times were tough or when I was saving money, I still did it – I just did it to myself. You can give yourself a manicure, take a bubble bath, massage your own feet. Whatever. The point is to be good to yourself. You don't always have to wait for someone else to do it for you."

"Wise words, I think," said Aimee. "I wish I had known you before I met Jack."

"*Pfff.* If you had known me before him, I don't think I would have let you marry him. I haven't met him yet, but I can see he's a dick."

Aimee smiled. "You're a very intuitive person, Kiki. He *is* a dick." She giggled, enjoying talking mean about him. "A big dick with a small dick."

Kiki snorted. "That's the spirit. But save it. Elizabeth is going to want to hear it, and you're going to mess up my work moving around like that."

"Oh. Okay," said Aimee, taking a serious tone. She felt something being put into her hands. "Take my phone and text Elizabeth. Tell her we'll be a little late."

"How late?"

"Ten minutes, max."

"Do you plan on teleporting us over there?" She opened her eyes, looking at Kiki's devilish expression.

"No. I plan on showing you what's under my baby's hood."

Aimee's eyes opened wide but she didn't say anything. "What's her number?"

"Just look it up under Elizabeth. Hit that down button and you'll find it."

Aimee scrolled while reading out loud, "Aimee, Anastasia, Apple, Babiecakes, Beautyqueen, Candygirl, Ditzy, ... you have some interesting sounding friends ... "

"Nicknames. Dancers. Keep going."

"Ah, here it is. Elizabeth."

"Hit that button on the right and select SMS and then start typing."

Aimee did as she was told. An answering beep came with a return message. "She says, *See you then.*"

"Good." Kiki held her hand out for her phone and Aimee put it in Kiki's palm. Back into the bag it went with a thud. Kiki grabbed a brush from the counter and said, "Close your eyes."

Aimee followed her instructions and soon felt a feather or something just as soft dusting across her eyelids. "What are you doing now?"

"Eyeshadow."

"What color?"

"Just wait and see."

Aimee could tell from the way Kiki said it that she was concentrating on something. "Do you always carry a full makeup kit around in your bag?"

"Not always. But often."

"Why did you tonight?" Aimee could feel a large soft brush moving across her cheeks now. *Must be the blush.*

"Because I was hoping I would catch someone at a weak moment who would let me do a makeover on them."

Aimee smiled. "Is that your hobby? Turning sad, sorry, sacks into cover girls?"

"You could say that," said Kiki with a smile in her voice. "Okay, now this is only going to hurt a little. I need you to sit still."

Aimee opened her eyes. "What's going to hurt?"

Kiki held up some tweezers. "You have some strays."

"Oh." She eyed the metal implement a couple more seconds and then noticed Kiki's determined look. She rolled her eyes and sighed in defeat. "Okay, fine. Just leave me *some.*"

"Don't worry. I'm not going to go full-out on you, even though in my opinion it wouldn't hurt. We just need to thin the jungle a little bit."

"Hey!" said Aimee in mock offense ... and then, *"Ouch!* Wow, that one hurt. Oh! *Ow,* that one too!"

Kiki laughed. "Stop faking. It doesn't hurt that much."

Aimee didn't say anything She just sat there, willing herself not to cry the now happy tears that threatened to appear. She'd never had a big sister, but this is how she pictured she would be – someone there to be in your corner, someone who did makeovers on you after you cried and made you feel like a silly kid pointing out the amateur way you'd done it before ... someone to show you the way.

"Can I say something to you without sounding weird?" asked Aimee. She was feeling so close to Kiki, even though they'd just met, she wanted to share what she was thinking. Something about

Kiki just made her drop her guard and feel totally comfortable with being herself. She'd never had a friend like that before, ever.

"Maybe, maybe not. Depends on what it is."

"Well, I'll take a chance. I just wanted to say that I'm really glad you came over. You're like ... the big sister I never had."

"I'm pretty sure you're older than me."

"You know what I mean. And I think you're older."

"Yes. I know. And if it makes you feel less insecure, I always wanted to have a little sister. If she had been like you, that would have been cool with me."

Aimee didn't hesitate – she spontaneously hugged Kiki and then broke away when Kiki protested.

"Hey! Watch it, lady! We're at a very critical stage here. Save the hugging for the end."

"Okay, sorry," said Aimee, not sounding apologetic at all. She could tell from Kiki's tone that she wasn't mad about the show of affection.

"Just one more minute and I'll be done. Look up."

Aimee looked up at the ceiling. "I heard sharing mascara is bad for your eyes. Like you can get a disease or something."

"That's why I swipe these from the Mac store in the mall," explained Kiki, holding up and waving a clear, disposable wand in front of Aimee's eye.

"Wow. That's dedication to your craft."

"Trust me ... I spend enough money in that store that they practically throw them at me. Last time I was there they gave me an entire bag from their supplies. It had like five hundred of 'em in it."

"Cool. No one's ever done that for me ... given me free makeup stuff."

"They don't give away disposable wands in the grocery store where I know you buy *your* makeup."

"Hey!"

Kiki shrugged. "I calls it likes I sees it." She stepped back and looked at Aimee, surveying her work. "Okay, last part. Lips." She searched the bathroom counter's offerings for the perfect shade.

"You're not going to use lip liner on me, are you?"

"No, absolutely not. That's not your style."

"Hmph," said Aimee thoughtfully, "I didn't even know I had a style."

"You do now," said Kiki, picking up a tube of gloss.

"Let me see," said Aimee anxiously, making as if she were going to turn around to look in the mirror.

"No!" shouted Kiki, putting her finger out to stop Aimee's cheek from going any farther to the right. "Not until I finish. Now open." She opened her own mouth, showing Aimee what she wanted her to do.

Aimee parted her lips and kept trying to talk. "Uts at?"

"Gloss. The non-tacky kind. Only place I've ever been able to find it is Sephora. But it's cheap, so even *you* could get some and not have a stroke over it."

Aimee rolled her eyes. "I ike oo end oney en I ah it."

"Well, we just need to figure out how you can *have* some money again so you can start pampering yourself a little more." She finished what she was doing. "Rub them together a little ... not too much!"

Aimee rubbed, just enough to spread the color evenly.

Kiki took the small brush she'd been using to apply the gloss, and smoothed it across Aimee's lips once more. When she was finished, Kiki backed up and gestured toward the mirror, saying, "Done! Behold my masterpiece."

Aimee hopped off the counter and turned to look, adjusting her dress as she stared at herself. She couldn't believe the difference a little bit of expertly applied makeup had made. "I can't even really see it." She leaned in closer to the mirror. "I notice a big difference in how I look, but I can't really see much makeup." Her voice held a note of wonder. "I'm ... pretty."

"That's the key. Do more with less. And yes, I am a genius. But I can only do so much. You have a naturally pretty face. I just highlighted your existing assets."

Aimee grabbed Kiki's arm without breaking her stare at the reflection. "You have to show me how to do this."

"No prob. Ready to go?" She started throwing her stuff into her purse with abandon.

Aimee hugged her fast around the waist and then went out ahead of her, going downstairs. "I just have to grab my shoes in the kitchen. Meet you at the front door!"

She was buckling the straps on the heels when Kiki came in and set her purse down on the counter. She looked around, taking in the high-end appliances and the perfect details on all the woodwork and granite.

Jack had insisted on the best when the house was built. He always did when it came to his own things or making an impression on people, and he liked to throw cocktail parties.

"So, this is where the magic happens, eh?" asked Kiki.

"What magic?"

"The baking? That magic spell you cast over all of us last week with those cakes? I still dream about them."

Aimee smiled, standing. "You're crazy."

"No, I'm not." Kiki came around to look at Aimee's computer. It was an old model, but Aimee didn't care. At least it worked. "Looking for apartments?" Kiki asked.

"Looking and failing to find apartments is more like it."

"Aren't there any vacancies?"

"Sure, there are plenty of those. But without a job, no one will rent one to me. I must have called fifty places today. I even offered to pay several months' rent up front. Still no deal. I'm going to have to go on welfare or something and get section-whatever-it-is housing."

"No. That is unacceptable."

"Tell me about it. If my parents could only see me now. They'd be so proud ... not."

"Where are they?"

"They died. A few years ago."

"Oh. I'm sorry to hear that. Mine did too."

"Bummer. Were you close?"

"Nope. Not at all. I've been on my own since I was fifteen."

Aimee frowned. "That's awful, Kiki. Did they die when you were really young?"

Kiki shrugged. "No. They died three years ago, one year apart. They were selfish. Weak. You know the sad story. But I turned out okay."

Aimee looked at Kiki, knowing that this girl had turned out more than okay. "You're a super person, Kiki. Smart and funny and generous. I'm sure if they could see you now, they'd be proud *and* feel bad that they didn't take better care of you when they were alive."

Kiki shrugged, saying nothing in response.

"Yep," said Aimee cheerily, now back in the mood to hang out with girlfriends. "Oh, wait a sec. I gotta get something." She went over to a cabinet and reached inside, pulling out a cookbook. It was thick and heavy. Aimee felt Kiki watching her, but she didn't care. She almost wanted her to see, so she could share the secret with someone else. She opened up the book to reveal the hollowed out interior. Inside was the manila envelope with the money in one large stack inside.

Kiki smiled. "I've seen that in movies but never in real life before. I hide my cash in a laundry detergent box."

"I'll bet that makes it smell good."

"It does," said Kiki grinning.

"Well, I had to think of the one place that neither Jack nor Tiffany would look and the last thing either one of them would take, and this was it."

"Who's Tiffany?"

"She's the practically prepubescent twit that works for my ex and who also now happens to be engaged to him and carrying his baby."

"What the hell?"

Aimee looked up at her, an embarrassed expression on her face. "Awful, right?"

"He's worse than a dick. He's a man whore."

Aimee laughed. "Yes. That and more."

"You mean to tell me that they come into your house and take your stuff?" Kiki sounded incredulous.

"Oh, this isn't my house," said Aimee bitterly. "Jack is fond of telling me every time he comes over that it's *his* house. He's only letting me stay here out of the kindness of his heart."

"And they take your stuff? Him and his girlfriend?"

"Yes, and they take my stuff. But neither of them cook, so they leave the kitchen alone."

"You realize what has to happen now, right?" asked Kiki, a serious expression on her face.

"Uh, no. Other than going out for drinks, you mean?"

"Yeah. I mean, what needs to happen in your life right now."

"Yes. I do, actually. I need to get a job. I need to get an apartment. And I need to get a life ... and not necessarily in that order."

"Okay, well I can help with two out of the three." Kiki leaned on the counter, giving Aimee a penetrating stare. "How would you feel about moving in with me? Temporarily, I mean."

Aimee was shocked into silence. And paralysis. She just stood there, her mouth partway open.

Kiki bent down a little, peering into her face. "Hello? Anyone home?"

Aimee shook her head a little to clear the fog. "What? Oh, sorry. I thought. Never mind."

"You heard me, Aimee, don't play games. Say yes. You need a place to stay, and I have an extra room. Plus, you planned on paying rent anyway – you can just pay it to me."

"Seriously?" Aimee didn't want to hope too hard that this could be true. She had zero misgivings about moving in with Kiki, regardless of the fact that it would make her ex completely insane. Maybe that was part of the attraction, actually.

"Seriously. Let's do this. We can put your stuff in the car right now."

Aimee bit her lip, not usually one for making spontaneous decisions.

"It's in a gated community and no one can get in without permission from a resident. And I have a fully alarmed place that's wired into the police department."

"Where do I sign?" asked Aimee, a grin dawning across her face. She'd had enough of the surprise visits from Jack to last a lifetime. The idea that she could be safe from his prying eyes and demands made her nearly giddy with pleasure.

"Okay, let's hurry. I don't want to be too late to O'Malleys," said Kiki.

Aimee walked with her friend to the front hall.

"This stuff?" Kiki asked, pointing to the boxes.

"Yes. That's it."

"What about your cookbook?"

"Oh, shit ... I mean shoot. Okay, be right back." Aimee took off in a rush to the kitchen. She heard Kiki yelling from the front door.

"Grab your cooking stuff! I don't have any!"

"Oh man, oh man, oh man," muttered Aimee, grabbing a box from the corner of the room where she had packing central set up. This was going to be box number eleven.

In went the money book. Then six other cookbooks that Aimee couldn't live without. Next went her favorite mixing bowls – three of them – and several wisks, spoons and her set of very expensive gourmet knives. She grabbed her pastry brushes and rolling pins out of one drawer and then looked around the kitchen in desperation. She had so many things in here that she used. *What to take and what to leave?* The cookie sheets and jelly roll pans weren't going to fit in the box.

Kiki came into the kitchen. "I have half the boxes in. I don't have room for all of it in one trip." She gestured to the box Aimee was in the middle of packing. "We'll take that one and come back later for the rest."

"I'm just worried that if Jack sees I'm in the process of leaving, he'll make it impossible for me to get back in."

"I'll handle him, don't you worry. Grab that box and let's go."

Aimee didn't argue. She completely trusted Kiki when she said she'd handle Jack. She pitied him, actually. She could tell that Kiki could be a very determined person when she wanted to be. Aimee was jealous of that particular trait.

Aimee dropped the box on the back seat of Kiki's car and went around to get in the passenger side. She looked over the dashboard as she buckled her seatbelt and Kiki climbed in. "I've never been in a car like this."

"What? A Camaro?"

"Is this a Camaro? Cool. No, I meant like, a guy's car."

Kiki rolled her eyes. "This is no guy's car. This is a badass bitch's car." She looked over at Aimee and lifted an eyebrow. "And don't you forget it."

Aimee laughed. "Yes, ma'am!"

"That's better," said Kiki. "Now hold onto your bobby socks. I'm about to show you how a badass bitch's car rolls." She looked up pointedly at the strap on the ceiling near Aimee's door. "You may want to grab that oh-shit handle up there."

"The *what* handle?" asked Aimee, following Kiki's gaze. "Oh. I get it." She put her hand through the loop and gripped it. "Ready to roll."

Kiki turned the engine over and gave the car a little gas.

Aimee could feel the rumbling make its way up through her legs and butt to reach her chest. "Whoa. How fast does this thing go?"

"You don't want to know," said Kiki, backing out of the driveway and shifting the car into drive. She pressed on the accelerator, laying rubber in the road outside of Aimee's house with a roar and a squeal.

Aimee twisted around to see the black trails on the asphalt and the smoke of burned rubber behind them. She looked over at Kiki with a huge grin on her face. "Jack is going to hate that."

Kiki smiled, keeping her eyes on the road. "That's what I figured."

They laughed most of the way to O'Malleys.

14

kiki

$\mathcal{K}$IKI PARKED THE CAMARO JUST outside the front entrance of the bar. She knew it would get plenty of admirers, making it impossible for someone to break into it with so many people around. She had a pretty good car alarm on it and a GPS tracking device too in case someone got stupid and tried to steal it. But she was more concerned right now with the cookbook bank that Aimee had in one of the boxes. If her guess was right, that was where the golf club money had gone. The pieces of Aimee's puzzle were slowly falling into place. Kiki felt really good about giving her a place to stay. She planned to set the rent very low so Aimee's money would last long enough, at least until she got a job and could stand on her own two feet. Kiki wasn't going to let her friend wallow in her sad circumstances for long. She hated negative vibes.

"I haven't been out for drinks in ages," said Aimee, getting out of the car and meeting Kiki on the sidewalk.

"I haven't been to this place in ages," said Kiki, ignoring the many admiring looks she was already getting.

"Everyone's staring at you," whispered Aimee.

"They're staring at you, too. Just ignore them."

"I can't," she giggled. "I'm not used to people looking at me like that. It's girls too, not just the guys."

"Yeah. Try not to take it personal when they look like they want to scratch your eyes out."

"Oh. Okay. Good advice."

Kiki noticed Aimee moved a little closer to her side, eyeing the women warily although trying valiantly to look like she didn't care.

"Look, there's Elizabeth at the bar," said Kiki.

"Elizabeth!" squealed Aimee, running over on her tiptoes to get to her.

Kiki watched as Elizabeth's face lit up and her arms opened for the inevitable hug. It was either that or get mauled. Aimee's intentions were clear, since she had her arms up and open wide before she was even halfway there. Kiki was jealous of Aimee's easy joy. Even her dick of an ex-husband hadn't gotten her down for long. Kiki hated to think what she'd do to a guy who tried to control her like that turd was obviously controlling Aimee. It was now her personal mission to break Jack's hold over her. Maybe she could get Elizabeth to help. She seemed to have a good head on her shoulders – smart and serious with good business sense.

"I figured it out," said Elizabeth, when Kiki walked up.

"Figured what out?"

"How I had miscounted."

Kiki looked at her in confusion for a minute. "Miscounted?"

"The money. That I paid Aimee? I had put my grocery money in the stack by accident. I meant to put it in my purse, but inadvertently included it with the other cash."

Kiki smiled. "That's been bothering you for two weeks, hasn't it?"

"Guilty." She shrugged. "What can I say? I'm anal about money. It's a curse."

"Don't worry about it. I am too."

Aimee nodded. "Me too."

Elizabeth and Kiki laughed.

"What?" she said in mock offense. "I could be anal with money, too. You guys don't know."

Kiki waved the bartender over. "What do you guys want? First round's on me."

"White wine," said Aimee and Elizabeth at the same time, grinning at each other when they realized they had the same taste.

"Three chardonnays, please," said Kiki, giving the cute guy behind the bar a half-smile. He stared at her in shock, momentarily frozen in place.

The other two girls looked first at him and then Kiki. Then back to the guy.

"Yoo hoo! Three chardonnays," said Aimee in a singsong voice.

The bartender snapped himself out of his reverie and quickly moved to get three glasses.

"Wow, you had that guy on cloud nine with just three words. I'm impressed," said Elizabeth.

"Don't be. It gets really old after a while."

"Well, if you don't like it, why do you make yourself so beautiful?" asked Aimee, taking a pretzel out of the bowl on the bar and crunching down on it. "If you went out without makeup and wore, like, ugly pants or something, maybe no one would look at you. Or maybe not so much."

"No makeup? Are you kidding me?" asked Kiki, acting shocked and appalled. "Wash your mouth out with soap, girl. I never go out without makeup on. And I never *ever* wear ugly clothes. Life's too short to wear polyester."

"Sounds like a curse," said Elizabeth, laughter twinkling in her eyes.

"It is, girls. It truly is," said Kiki, sighing dramatically.

Aimee turned to Elizabeth. "So, what's new with you? How was work?"

Kiki paid the bartender while she waited for Elizabeth's answer.

"Well, actually, I have really, really big news."

"Dish it, baby," said Kiki, handing out glasses of wine and taking a sip of hers. She closed her eyes for a moment while the liquid slid across her tongue, before swallowing and inhaling the tiniest bit of air so she could catch the flavors better. "Mmmm. Good."

"Well, I quit today. I *actually* quit my job."

Aimee grabbed Elizabeth's arm in a death grip, almost causing Elizabeth to spill her wine. "No! Oh my god, that's *huge* news! Huge!"

"Wow. That is big," said Kiki. "What happened?"

Elizabeth shrugged. "I don't know. I think I just snapped or something. The head partner came into my office and put this horrible file down on my desk and told me to cancel my plans for coming here and for the weekend, and then he walked out to go have cocktails with his friends."

"Penis!" said Aimee, loud enough that a few guys nearby looked over and laughed. Her face went a little red. "Oops. Too loud?"

Kiki nodded, saying nothing. She was looking forward to what Aimee would say after she'd had another glass of wine. A quick glance showed she had nearly finished her first one already. *Uh-oh.*

"Yes. He is ... that," said Elizabeth. "He always has been. But for some reason, today, it was just too much. So I took that file, put it on his desk, and wrote out my resignation letter."

"So do they even know you quit?" asked Aimee.

"Not yet. They'll find out on Monday. He never comes in on weekends."

"Because he's had you to do it," said Kiki.

"Exactly," said Elizabeth, nodding at her.

Kiki raised her glass. "I propose a toast. Here's to saying go eff yourself to dicks, pricks, and penises who try to keep us from enjoying our girls' night out."

Aimee and Elizabeth raised their drinks. "Cheers!"

They all clinked their glasses and took sips of the wine.

"Wow," said Aimee, finishing off her glass, "this is good stuff."

"No garbage wine for my friends," said Kiki, glad the bartender had done the smart thing and poured them something fresh and nice from an area of Napa she happened to like.

"So, what are you going to do now?" asked Aimee. "Start your own firm?"

"Nope. I'm out of that game. I'm going to open my own business, but not doing accounting for other clients. I'm going to do the accounting for my own place."

"What kind of place?" asked Kiki, a serious look on her face. She really wanted to know what this intelligent woman had planned for herself. Kiki was at a loss as to what she wanted to do, but she was thinking along the same lines as Elizabeth. She wanted to sink or swim based on her own efforts. Not those of a strip club owner or Board member or anyone else.

"I don't really know. Something fun. That's the only criteria I've come up with so far." She smiled. "I know this sounds crazy, but I feel free. For the first time in a long time."

Kiki nodded. "I do know what you mean, actually."

"Me too," said Aimee. "Especially now, thanks to Kiki."

Elizabeth looked at the two of them, glancing back and forth. "What'd I miss?"

Kiki frowned. "I had to stage a little intervention at Aimee's house. Her ex is a serious ... "

" ... penis. He's a serious penis, is what he is," finished Aimee, signaling to the bartender for another glass of wine.

"Hey, don't knock the penis," said Kiki, smiling. "They're not always bad. In fact, sometimes they're very, very good."

Elizabeth laughed. "Agreed. Okay, so he's a prick. Does that work?"

Kiki shrugged. "It works. It doesn't adequately express how much of a jerk he is, but it'll do." She took a sip of her wine before continuing, getting a nod of approval from Aimee first. "He tried to keep her from coming out by stealing her keys. He's also been bullying her. She probably didn't tell you this, but he sent her to the E.R. last week, after our meeting."

"No!" gasped Elizabeth. She reached over and rubbed Aimee's arm. "Sorry, hon, I didn't know about that. Are you okay?"

"Yes. I ended up seeing Kiki there when she was coming out from visiting her friend."

"Oh, yeah, I remember that," said Elizabeth. "How is she? Your friend?"

"She's good now. But back into the mess that started it all. She's part of the reason I quit. I had to get out of the game before it took me over. Too many girls get lost there in that garbage."

"I'm glad you did that," said Elizabeth. "It took a lot of guts."

"She's got guts in spades," said Aimee. "I need to borrow some of them."

"Don't worry. As my roommate, you qualify for ass-kicking lessons, on the house."

"You guys are roommates now?" asked Elizabeth. "Sounds like fun."

Kiki looked at Aimee. "It's going to be an adventure, I think."

"You know what, guys?" said Aimee. "We're all in the same boat now, kind of. We're all unemployed and looking for a new life! How cool is that?" She grinned at Kiki and Elizabeth.

"The big question is, what are we going to do with this opportunity?" Kiki raised her eyebrow, looking at both women and waiting for their responses ... wondering if they were thinking the same thing she was.

15

elizabeth

ELIZABETH LOOKED AT KIKI AND then Aimee. Her accountant's mind did a quick calculation. The three of them had talents and assets that could be leveraged for each other's mutual benefit. And their personalities seemed to mesh well. Maybe it wouldn't be such a crazy idea ...

"What do you guys think about combining forces?" she asked, purposefully being vague, wondering how they'd take it.

"I think it could work. We have some complimentary skills," said Kiki, taking another sip from her wineglass. "But it wouldn't work unless we were all in."

"That's what I was thinking," said Elizabeth.

Aimee looked from Elizabeth to Kiki. "What exactly are you guys saying? Are you talking about us doing something? Like the three of us? Together?"

Elizabeth nodded.

Kiki nodded too.

Aimee smiled, her lip resting on the edge of her empty glass. "Count me in. Sounds like fun. What is it we're going to do?" She went to take a sip of her drink, apparently forgetting it was empty. "Hey ... who drank my wine?"

Kiki took the glass from her. "You did, you lush."

Aimee stuck her lower lip out. "Party pooper."

Elizabeth took Aimee's glass from Kiki and put it on the bar, shaking her head at the bartender who asked if she wanted another one.

"Am I cut off already?" asked Aimee, clearly disappointed.

"No," said Elizabeth, "but before we get too tipsy, I'd like to talk about this some more. And we need your head in the game."

Aimee saluted. "Okay, coach. Go for it. I'm all ears. What's the play going to be?"

"Let's go find a place to sit," said Kiki, looking around.

Elizabeth spied an empty booth, just recently vacated by a group of guys. "There!" She pointed and got up off the bar stool she'd been sitting on.

The three girls quickly went over to claim the table before someone else could. The place was starting to fill up, making the few booths around the edges of the room prime real estate.

"This is perfect. We can stare at people standing at the bar this way," said Aimee. "I love people-watching."

"Scooch over, my butt's hanging off the side," said Elizabeth, nudging Aimee.

"Hey! Now I can't see the guys at the bar!" she complained as she was moved to the inside of the booth.

"Come over on this side, whiner" said Kiki. "The view's much better. I'll trade you."

The all stood up and played musical chairs so that Aimee was sitting on one side by herself with a full view of the bar and the other two were facing her.

Once they were settled in, Elizabeth began. "Okay, so here's what I propose, as the jumping off point for our discussion." She snapped her fingers at Aimee. "Hey ... focus."

Aimee held up her hand, still staring at the bar. "I know, but ... who is that guy? The one over there, the big one in jeans ... "

Elizabeth and Kiki looked over.

"Which guy in jeans?" asked Kiki. "They're all wearing jeans."

"The hot one. With the wavy hair. Holding the beer."

Elizabeth shared a smile with Kiki and said, "You just de-scribed at least half of the guys here."

Aimee waved them away in frustration. "No, silly. *That* one. Oh my god!" Aimee looked at Elizabeth and Kiki in a panic. "He just caught me looking at him."

"Oh, I see which one you mean now," said Kiki smiling.

"Is she talking about the one walking over here?" asked Elizabeth.

"Yep."

"He's coming over here?" squeaked Aimee, her eyes as big as saucers.

"Be cool, Aimee. He's looking right at you," whispered Kiki under her breath.

Elizabeth looked at Aimee in amusement. She'd never seen someone so freaked out over a close encounter with the male kind. Clearly, Aimee had been out of the dating game for a while.

"Hi," said the deep male voice coming from the cute guy Ai-mee had pointed out. He really was cute, too. *Holy hunk,* thought Elizabeth. *She sure can pick 'em.*

Aimee looked up. "Hi," she said. Her face was bright red.

He looked at Kiki and Elizabeth and nodded, saying, "Hello," before turning his attention back to Aimee.

"Hi," said Elizabeth, happy to see he was here for Aimee and not Kiki as she had originally suspected he might be. She want-ed Aimee to get some attention from the guys here. She had a feeling that women standing near Kiki didn't get that experience very often, and Aimee was definitely in need of validation of her cuteness.

"So ... I don't think I've seen you here before," he said to Aimee.

"No. I never come here. But you look familiar to me ... "

Elizabeth had never seen him before, but she didn't come here very often.

"We've met once before. I gave you my card. Outside the hos-pital ... "

Aimee's face colored and her hand flew to her mouth. "That was you? Oh, wow. You look different out of your police uniform."

Kiki snorted, looking at Elizabeth and lifting her eyebrows.

Elizabeth said nothing, deciding to watch it all play out in silence.

"Is that a good thing?" he asked.

"Yes. I mean no! I mean yes! Oh, shoot. I don't know."

"She said you were hot," said Kiki.

Aimee looked like she wanted to be swallowed into a hole in the floor. Her face turned even redder as she whipped around to look at Kiki, her mouth opening up but no sound coming out.

Kiki shrugged. "She did. I'm not lying."

Elizabeth decided to do something totally out of character and joined in, keeping a straight face. "She did. I witnessed it."

Aimee rolled her eyes and bit her lower lip, before bursting out, "Fine! Okay, I said it. I admit it, okay? Geez." She put her head down on her arm on the table. "Somebody shoot me," she mumbled. Then she lifted her head, looking up at her admirer with a hopeful expression on her face. "Did you bring your gun?"

He smiled, bending down to sit in the booth next to her. "Nope. No gun tonight. But how about I buy you a drink?" He looked up at Elizabeth and Kiki. "You girls drinking tonight?"

"Chardonnay," said Kiki. "Napa Valley. The bartender knows."

The cop looked at Aimee – actually at the top of her head, since she was back to hiding her face – and said, "Do you mind if I buy you and your friends a glass of wine?"

Aimee picked her head up and looked at her friends. "Do I mind?"

Elizabeth and Kiki just shrugged their shoulders.

Aimee looked at him, suddenly all shy. She cleared her throat and said, "That would be nice, Joe. Thank you."

He winked at her. "You remembered my name. I'll take that as a good sign. Be right back." He got up and went to the bar, leaving Aimee to her well-deserved teasing.

"Good pick, Aimee. A hot cop. I like it," said Elizabeth, smiling at her, honestly impressed. She got a good feeling about him. He

wasn't flashy or roostery. That's how she pictured a lot of cops –
walking around like roosters in the hen house. This guy was more
calm and collected, as if he were totally confident in his maleness
and didn't need to advertise it so obviously.

"He's that guy," said Kiki, "the cop who was all worried about
you in the emergency room, right?"

Elizabeth cleared her throat loudly. "Hello ... need to be filled
in over here."

"Okay, quick breakdown before he comes back," said Kiki.
"Aimee was at the E.R. with a cut-open head, thanks to Jack the
jackass."

"Don't tell Joe that! He doesn't know what happened!" said
Aimee.

"Whatever," said Kiki. "And this cop, Joe I guess, was coming
through on his way out, sees Aimee looking all sad and damsel-
in-distress-like, and he takes her outside and ... I don't know ... ,"
she turned to Aimee, " ... what happened then?"

"He asked me what happened, thinking it was a domestic violence thing, and then gave me his card with his cell on it. And he
said I could call him anytime."

"Well?" asked Elizabeth. "Did you call him?"

"What? *No!* Of course not!" said Aimee.

"Why not?" she asked.

"Because ... well ... I guess I didn't need his services," she finished lamely.

Kiki wiggled her eyebrows at Aimee. "You sure about that?"

"Shhhh!" Aimee said, trying not to smile, but failing miserably.

"Did you see his hands?" Kiki asked. "Big. Thick."

"Veiny," added Elizabeth.

Kiki looked at Elizabeth, her head cocked to the side, saying
nothing.

"What?" said Elizabeth defensively. "I notice that stuff. I like
veiny hands."

"What else do you like veiny?" asked Kiki.

"Well, funny you should ask ... ," said Elizabeth, looking over
at Aimee and seeing she was about to have a heart attack.

"He's coming back," said Aimee. "Stop talking about big, thick, veiny things."

Two seconds later, Joe sat back down in the booth, somehow managing to carry three glasses of wine and one beer in his hands.

All the eyes around the table were focused on those hands. Elizabeth noticed that they were exceptionally veiny ... and thick.

"Oh my god," whispered Aimee, before she could stop herself, staring at his hands.

Joe looked at her, confused. "What's wrong?"

"Your ... hands ... " She gulped.

He held his hands out in front of him, first palm up and then turned palm down. "What's wrong with my hands?" He rubbed them a few times and clenched and unclenched his fists.

Elizabeth looked over at Aimee and thought for a second the poor girl was going to swoon, but instead, she grabbed her glass of wine and took a big gulp.

Joe picked up his beer. "Cheers."

The girls picked up their glasses and clinked them together.

"What's the toast?" asked Kiki.

"Here's to weekends not spent in the emergency room," he said, smiling at Aimee.

"I'll drink to that," she said, taking another big gulp. She used her fingertips to wipe off her mouth.

"Well, I don't mean to break up your party, here." He moved as if to go, but turned to Aimee before he did. "Maybe I could get your number ... so I could call you sometime ... if that's okay ... "

Aimee got a scared look on her face. "I don't know ... ," she said, tentatively.

"Give me your phone," said Kiki, gesturing for Joe to hand it over. She was pulling her own phone out of her bag.

He handed it to her wordlessly and everyone at the table watched as she typed two sets of numbers into his keypad. When she was done, she handed the cell back to him.

"The first one is her cell number. The second one is her house number. We're roomies."

Joe smiled and held his phone out to Aimee. "Is this okay with you? I don't want to call you if ... you're not into it or whatever."

"I have baggage," she burst out. A split second later she got a panicked look on her face and whispered loudly, *"Did I just say that out loud?"*

Kiki nodded, laughing but trying to hide it.

"Don't we all," said Joe, standing up. "I'll call you. If you want to talk to me, pick up the phone. If you don't, that's okay, just don't answer. I'll probably try three or four times before I give up." He smiled before casually walking away, going back to the bar and his group of friends who weren't trying to hide their curiosity.

"I wish Betty were here," said Aimee, her head back on her arm.

"Why?" asked Elizabeth, wondering how a ninety-something-year-old woman could possibly make this better for her.

"Because she has a gun," said Aimee's muffled voice.

Elizabeth looked at Kiki. "She's a serious lightweight. Did she drink before she came here?"

"Not that I know of. But she's under a lot of stress. Her ex is seriously bad news. Lawyer. Cheated on her."

"I can hear you!" came Aimee's cranky voice.

"Well, sit up and join the conversation then, you big baby," said Elizabeth in a friendly, encouraging voice. "You made it through your first potential hook-up scenario unscathed. You're in good shape. You got the hottest and probably nicest guy in the place to ask you for your phone number."

Aimee sat up, a smile dawning on her face. "I did, didn't I?"

"Yes," nodded Elizabeth, "you did. Now, can we talk about our plans? Because if I don't get to these talking points before we leave, I'm going to be so stressed by the time I get home, I'll probably clean my whole house before I go to sleep."

"That sounds like a condition," joked Kiki.

"It is. It's called OCD. I'm pretty sure I have a mild form of it."

"I think all accountants do," said Kiki.

"Okay, so as I was saying, before Officer Hottie came to drool over Aimee, is that I suggest we come up with a basic plan. An outline. And then we meet over the next few days to hammer out the details. Since none of us are currently employed, I figured we might as well put this free time to good use."

"I agree with your proposal," said Kiki, without hesitation.

"I agree too, even though I'm not really sure what I'm agreeing to," said Aimee, her head up now and her happy look back on her face.

Elizabeth could see it was taking a lot of Aimee's concentration not to look over at Joe, so she sighed and said, "Go ahead. Look over there once. I know you want to."

"What's he doing?" Aimee whispered.

Kiki looked over. "He's pretending like he's watching the soccer game on T.V., but he keeps checking you out. Hook, line, and sinker, baby. You've got him. He'll call you tomorrow. I'll bet he doesn't even wait the standard three-day period."

Elizabeth looked over. "You're right. I agree with that."

"Standard three-day period? What's that?" asked Aimee.

"Guys like to play this game and pretend that they're not as interested in you as they really are. So they wait at least three days to call. Makes you wait by the phone and shit. Very annoying," explained Kiki.

"Some guys aren't playing. They really don't care enough to call sooner," said Elizabeth.

"True. Either way, it sucks."

"And you guys don't think he'll do that?"

"No. He looks serious," said Elizabeth.

"And not desperate," said Kiki.

"Does that make a difference?" asked Aimee.

"Of course," said Kiki.

"Yes," said Elizabeth. "Because some guys who might call you the very next day are desperate. Like they can't get a date with anyone because they're so freaky or whatever. You don't want one of the desperate ones. They can go all stalker on you later if you're not careful."

"So ... how do I know if he's one of those ... if he calls me the first day?"

"Oh, we can already tell you. He's not," said Kiki.

Elizabeth noticed Aimee looking to her for confirmation of Kiki's statement, so she said, "Kiki's right. He's not. It's obvious. I'm ninety-nine percent sure."

"How do you guys know all this?" asked Aimee, bewildered.

"Internet dating," said Elizabeth.

"Any kind of dating," said Kiki.

"How am I going to learn all this stuff?" asked Aimee, back to being distressed.

"Don't worry," assured Kiki, "we'll give you a crash course."

"I don't know about Kiki, but I'm an expert. I've been on at least twenty online dates, and I know all the games and B.S. that goes on. I will be your Obi-Wan Kenobi."

"I'm going to be a jedi internet dater?"

"If you choose to accept your destinyyyyy ..."

Kiki groaned. "Oh, god, that was bad."

"I know, right?" said Elizabeth, smiling and taking a sip of her wine. It felt good to joke around with girlfriends like this. At that moment she couldn't have been happier that she'd started that book club.

16

aimee

$\mathcal{A}$IMEE WOKE UP WITH A headache. She looked up at the ceiling and experienced a quick moment of panic as she tried to place exactly where she was. She turned her head on her pillow, first to the left and then to the right, taking in the tasteful yet feminine decorations on the walls and the cute knick-knacks on top of the furniture against the walls. Her hand brushed across sheets that were so soft, she was sure they had to be over a thousand thread-count.

Then she remembered. This was *her* room. In her new townhouse. The one she was sharing with Kiki. A huge smile bloomed across her face ... until the pounding headache came back and reminded her what she'd done last night.

She groaned as she rolled out of bed, her toes sinking into ultra thick, super plush carpeting. She smelled coffee coming from somewhere, and even though she wasn't much of a coffee drinker, it beckoned her with its heady, fresh-roasted aroma. She looked down and saw that she was wearing her pajamas, deciding quickly that she could risk going out without getting dressed first. She left the bedroom and descended the stairs silently, not sure exactly what to expect.

Aimee got to the bottom of the staircase and saw croissants on a plate at the dining room table. As she moved toward the kitchen, Kiki emerged.

"Good morning, sleepy head," Kiki said cheerfully. "Coffee?"

"No, thanks. It smells great but I'm more of a tea person, actually."

"Earl Grey? Green? Mint?"

"Earl Grey sounds amazing. And a pain reliever if you have one of those, too."

"Coming right up. Have a seat at the table there and drink that juice first. Your body needs the vitamins."

Aimee sat down and did as she was told, gulping the juice down in four swallows. She had no idea she was so thirsty. As soon as the flavor registered on her tongue, she knew it was fresh squeezed; it tasted like liquid heaven. "Mmmm ...," she said with a satisfying smack of her lips as she set the glass down.

"Honeybells," said Kiki, setting a cup of hot water with a tea bag floating in it on the table in front of Aimee. She sat down next to her. "They have the best juice. I get them in season and freeze gallons of the stuff."

Aimee reached over and took a croissant. She bit into it but wasn't impressed by its tasteless, dry and cardboard-like consistency. She tried unsuccessfully to keep the frown off her face.

"I know. They suck. But they're the best I can find around here. We need to go to Paris to get the good ones."

"I can make better ones than this in my home kitchen," said Aimee, chewing the pastry and swallowing it down anyway because she needed to get something into her stomach to ease the queasiness there.

"I'm happy to support any cooking challenges you wish to undertake in this house. I'll even provide chopping services and clean up after you. You can call me Alice."

"Why Alice?"

"She was the maid on *Brady Bunch*."

"Oh. Well, I have to get more of my stuff first."

"Yes," said Kiki, standing up, going back into the kitchen and coming out with a pad of paper and a pencil. "Our to-do list for the day."

Aimee held out her hand and Kiki passed it to her. She took a sip of her tea while she read the items off. "Get ready to go out. Get Aimee's stuff. Move Aimee's stuff in. Eat lunch. Meet with Elizabeth. Make business plans. Eat dinner. Party." Aimee looked up. "I like everything but the last one. My headache is pounding too hard to even consider another glass of wine."

"It'll go away. You just need to hydrate. And maybe stick to something other than white wine. You were knocked on your ass last night."

"I know, I'm like a total lightweight or something. But in my own defense, I really hadn't eaten all day before I met you guys."

"Well, that'll do it. Why didn't you eat?"

"I don't know. First I was too depressed; then I got the email about going out and I was too excited."

"Well, as you can see, I've scheduled meals in there, so you'll be better tonight, hopefully. Not that I don't enjoy seeing you have a good time. It's pretty decent entertainment."

"Ha, ha."

"What are you going to say to him when he calls?"

"Who? Jack?" asked Aimee, confused about the change in topic.

"No, Joe."

"Oh. Shoot. I forgot about him," said Aimee putting her hand to her forehead. "What did I say to him last night? The memories are kind of faint ... is the reality as bad as I'm remembering it?"

Kiki laughed. "No. It wasn't bad. It was cute. I think he fell in love with you a little last night."

"You're kidding," said Aimee, totally not believing a word Kiki was saying, sure that she was just being nice to spare her feelings. She was pretty certain she'd made a fool of herself – probably slurred her words and everything.

"Serious. I promise." Kiki held up her hand, pledging her honesty.

"Well, if he calls, I have no idea what I'll say. I'm just going to have to wing it. And pray that Jack doesn't find out about him."

"Jack has nothing to do with this," said Kiki. "You don't need his permission to have a life of your own."

"I know, I know. I'm not saying that. I just ... I want to avoid making him mad, because lately, he's seemed a little unhinged. He never used to get physical with me, but the last few times he's been over, especially when he sees me being more confident or happy, he gets crazy."

"He realizes he's losing control of you."

"I don't know. Maybe that's it."

"Guys like him ... control freaks ... they can't handle it when someone they've mind-fucked for years goes off the range like that. It makes them question everything they thought they knew about themselves and you ... "

"You sound like you speak from experience," said Aimee, softly.

"When you work at places where I've worked, you start to see patterns. Your ex is like the pimps I've known – guys who have hurt friends of mine. Some girls even end up dead when guys like that lose it."

"That's awful," said Aimee, truly horrified that this kind of thing happened and that Kiki had actually seen it. "You mean, it could have happened to you?"

"Well, I never hooked, but it's why I'm out of that business and currently seeking other opportunities. After a dancer gets older, there's not a lot in the same field other than selling your body. And this body ain't for sale at any price." She stood up. "Now hurry and finish your breakfast. We have a schedule to follow."

"Bossy much?" Aimee asked, smiling.

"More like enthusiastic and excited. And I want to get you moved in so you can get away from Jack for good. He worries me."

"Me too," said Aimee, gulping down the rest of her hot tea and wincing at the sharp scalding, taking another quick bite of her crois- sant to ease the pain. Now she was as motivated as she needed to be to follow Kiki's list. Getting away from Jack for good was the best idea she'd heard in months. Maybe even years. She couldn't wait to say goodbye to that house for the last time. All it held for her now was bad memories. She was ready to move on and never look back.

Aimee raced to her room where Kiki had stacked all of her boxes and her suitcase. She threw the suitcase on the bed and pulled out an outfit of jeans and a t-shirt. Her sneakers were in there too, so she grabbed them and dropped them on the floor. Investigating the room a bit showed her that she had her own shower and bathroom attached, fully stocked with towels and hair and body products. She smiled, realizing that she expected no less from Kiki – the woman who was focused not only on pampering and beauty, but on taking care of her friends.

How did I get so lucky?

Within seconds, she was stepping into a steaming hot shower and sighing in contentment. *This is exactly what I needed.*

17

kiki

KIKI WASTED NO TIME, PUTTING the breakfast dishes into the dishwasher and wiping away the few crumbs that had found their way to the counter and table. She had showered earlier before Aimee had gotten up, so she quickly dressed in jeans and a casual blouse. Her wedge sandals and gold bangle bracelets finished the look.

She texted Elizabeth, asking her if she'd like to meet them at the Coconut Grill around noon for lunch, figuring they could start working on their business ideas over a meal. Seconds later a response came, firming up their plan. Now all Kiki had to do was get Aimee's stuff over to the townhouse and they'd be ready to roll.

Kiki walked over to her bedside table and took out the small pistol she kept there. It was loaded. Since no kids ever came to her house, she didn't worry about keeping it locked up or the bullets out of reach. She had a permit to carry it, but she had never actually taken it out of the house except to go to the shooting range to learn how to use it. *Should I bring it?* She didn't know this Jack guy, but he sounded like a class-A jerk from what Aimee had said.

She shrugged, deciding she might as well have it along, shoving it into the satchel she planned to keep carrying. Normally she would have switched to a smaller purse on a warm day like today, but she needed to carry the gun, the to do list, and she'd also decided to throw in her latest bank and stock account statements – in case the subject of money or investment came up during lunch. It felt a little strange to her to be sharing such private information with two virtual strangers, but she decided that it was no different, really, than sharing them with some anonymous bank employee when asking for a loan. Besides, they needed to get all their cards out on the table today to see if this crazy idea of working together was worth even thinking about.

She walked out of her room and across the hall to Aimee's, knocking on the door. "Come on! Bus leaves in five minutes!"

Aimee's wet head poked out of the door a couple seconds later. "We're taking a bus?"

Kiki walked down the stairs. "Yes. It's called a Camaro. Hurry up."

"Five minutes. Be right down."

Kiki heard the door shut behind her. She didn't believe for a second Aimee could be ready that fast, so she sat down on her couch and started reading a magazine. She especially loved *Elle Decor*. She'd used color schemes and decorating ideas from several issues to inspire the look in her townhouse. Her home was the calmest, chicest place she knew, and made it completely possible for her to unwind after a night at the club. She folded over a page that featured a room done in salmons and gray browns, intrigued by how it was both feminine and masculine at the same time, inspiring and relaxing too. She heard Aimee emerging and shoved the magazine in her bag, standing and grabbing her keys off the nearby coffee table.

"Ready?"

"Ready!" said Aimee cheerfully. "Back to my old house?"

"Yes. How long do you think it'll take to get it all?"

Aimee frowned as she thought. "Mmmm, maybe thirty minutes."

"Will Jack be there?"

"I doubt it. He likes to golf on Saturdays."

Kiki raised an eyebrow at her. "Isn't that hard to do without clubs?"

Aimee cleared her throat, not meeting Kiki's eyes. "Apparently not."

"Good," said Kiki, not wanting Aimee to feel bad about the stupid clubs. "We're golden. Come over here so I can show you how to set the alarm when you leave." Kiki gave her a quick run-through, showing her how to turn it off and on, and how to enter in a code that looked like it was turning off the alarm but was actually alerting the police department to a home invasion.

"So, if someone forces me to open the door for them, I press in this code, and it will shut off the beeping but will call the police and tell them a bad guy is in here with me?" asked Aimee.

"Yes. Exactly."

"Huh. That's convenient. But what if the bad guy knows about this feature?"

"He won't know if you did the good code or the distress code, regardless. Unless you tell him of course, which we would never do."

"Of course. Let's just pray we never have to use that one."

"Yes. Let's," agreed Kiki, shutting and locking the door behind them.

Fifteen minutes later they were pulling up to Aimee's old house, very happy to see the driveway empty.

"Good. Jack's not here."

They walked up to the front door and Aimee dug in her bag for her key.

Kiki tried the handle and the door opened on its own. "Not locked," she said, searching Aimee's face for her reaction. She saw fear.

They walked cautiously into the foyer, Kiki looking left and right to try and figure out if they were alone. There were no obvious signs of someone else being there. There was no broken glass, and no sounds other than their own footsteps reached their ears.

ELLE CASEY

"I think maybe I forgot to lock it last time," said Aimee, sheepishly.

"Okay, good. I was a little worried for a second there. So what's first? Kitchen?"

"Yes. That's the only place I need to pack anything, actually. Everything else is already at your townhouse."

"You didn't have a lot of stuff."

"No. Jack took almost everything and I was never much of a clothes maven. Jack gave me an allowance, but it didn't go far."

Kiki looked at her, disgusted with the whole idea. "An allowance? Are you friggin' kidding me?"

Aimee frowned and shook her head. "Nope. Pitiful, isn't it?"

"Ridiculous is more like it. Come on," she nudged Aimee's shoulder, "let's get you the hell out of this shit hole."

They went to the kitchen and Aimee took over. She directed the packing of her precious culinary tools like a drill sergeant. Kiki was happy to follow her orders, glad to see that Jack hadn't managed to completely eat all of her soul. That's what he was, as far as she was concerned – a soul eater.

Kiki's back was to the front hall, so she didn't see anyone coming in. But when she looked up to ask Aimee which thermometers she wanted Kiki to include in the box she was packing, Aimee's expression told her everything she needed to know.

Kiki swung around and found herself face to face with a guy - a short, angry guy, who couldn't be anyone other than Jack.

"Who the hell are you and what are you doing in my kitchen?" he said, gritting his teeth together, his face glowing red.

Oh, shit. This isn't good. She'd been around mean drunks before at work, but at least she had a bit of an advantage there with their slowed reflexes and sloppy coordination. This guy was sober and fueled only by rage. Kiki risked a glance toward her purse and saw that it was near the front door, and of totally no use to her right now. Jack was between her and her gun.

"Jack!" squeaked Aimee. "What are you doing here?"

"I think a better question would be what the hell is *she* doing here?" He looked over at Kiki and said, "Get the hell out of my house before I call the police."

That got Kiki's back up immediately, but she knew she had to be smart, or this guy was going to go ballistic. "Yeah, sure. No problem." She glanced over at Aimee and said, "I guess I'm gonna go. I'll talk to you later."

Aimee looked stricken. Her mouth opened and shut, but she said nothing.

Kiki turned her back and made her way down the hall, praying Jack wouldn't follow her. She needn't have worried, as he was too intent on meting out punishment to Aimee.

Kiki reached down when she got near the front door and grabbed her purse, shoving her hand inside and closing her fingers around the cold, wood and steel handle of the gun. She yanked it out, dropping the bag on the ground and striding back toward the kitchen. She got there just before Jack had made it around the kitchen island, obviously in pursuit of a very sad and scared-looking Aimee.

"Stop right there, before I decide to be a hero," said Kiki, lifting the gun and aiming for Jack's chest. She kept her finger off the trigger because she could feel her heart racing a mile a minute and she didn't trust her finger not to accidentally pull back in a spasm of gut-wrenching fear.

Jack stopped in his tracks, staring at Kiki in disbelief. "What the ... is that a *gun?*"

"Oh my god, Kiki, is that a gun?!" cried Aimee, clearly in total freak-out mode. "Don't shoot him!"

"Thank you, Aimee," said Jack, satisfaction coloring his voice.

"I don't want you to go to jail, is what I meant, Kiki" said Aimee, looking only at her friend.

"Hey!" said Jack. "What's that supposed to mean?"

Aimee turned to him, a cold look coming over her face. "It means, Jack, that I'd be perfectly okay with her shooting you if I thought she wouldn't go to jail over it."

Kiki smiled. She liked this Aimee better than the sad or cowed one.

"Get out," Kiki said. "And stay out. You don't live here anymore."

"You can't kick me out of my own house!"

Kiki moved her finger to the trigger and took two steps closer. "You sure about that?"

Jack held his hands up in surrender. "Fine, fine ... you crazy bitch. I'm leaving. But I'll be back." He pointed at Aimee. "You know you can't keep me from coming into my own house."

Aimee got an inspired look on her face. "Give me my car keys back, you jerk."

Jack stole a look at Kiki and then reached into his pants pocket, taking out the keyring and throwing it on the counter. "Here. Thing's a piece of shit anyway."

Aimee said nothing, her eyes glued on Kiki's hands.

Kiki moved farther into the kitchen and stepped to the side, giving Jack room to walk by. "Mess with Aimee and you mess with me. *And* my gun."

Jack didn't say anything until he got to the foyer. Then he turned and said menacingly, "You're going to be very sorry you did this." He slammed the door behind him on the way out.

Kiki rushed to the entrance of the house, stepping out and shouting, "Touch my car and you die!" She waved the gun at him making sure he could see it. She watched as he clicked something in his hand and the garage door went up. He disappeared inside, and shortly thereafter an engine started. An Aston Martin backed slowly down the driveway. *Sweet ride*, she thought, wondering what the hell Aimee was doing driving that old granny car while this jackass drove this design marvel.

Aimee come up behind her, stopping in the doorway. "Well, that was exciting."

Once Jack's car was clear of her Camaro, Kiki turned to look at her. "Yeah. Let's get the rest of your stuff and get the hell out of here. He's going to be back, either with something dangerous or the police."

Aimee turned and ran to the kitchen, throwing open drawers and tossing things into boxes and even a few trash bags. "Put it all in! Just go! I'll sort it out later!"

Kiki wasted no time following her and emptying the few remaining cabinets and drawers. She grabbed two fully loaded trash bags and ran them out to her car, throwing them into the backseat before turning to go into the house for more.

Aimee followed with two boxes stacked on one another, leaving them by the curb to fit in once the trunk was open.

Within fifteen minutes they had the rest of Aimee's possessions loaded and had gotten into the car. Kiki turned to look at Aimee before she started the engine. "Are you ready?"

"Ready for what? To go? Heck yes."

"No, I mean ready to start your new life."

Aimee smiled. "Double heck yes."

Kiki held up her hand. "Give me some skin on that."

Aimee gave her a high-five, laughing when their hands nearly missed. "Oof, we suck at that."

The distant wail of a police siren hit their ears at the same time. Kiki took one look at Aimee's face and turned the key, slamming down on the gear shift and pushing down hard on the accelerator. They peeled out of the neighborhood, going well over the speed limit.

"Was that for us?" asked Aimee, her hand gripping the oh-shit handle.

"I don't know. I figured we'd better not risk it."

Aimee started giggling and Kiki glanced at her sideways. "You losing it?"

"Maybe. A little."

"Good," said Kiki, smiling. "I think you're entitled. Your ex acts like a mean pimp."

"That's sad. I was married to a mean pimp," said Aimee. "Is there such thing as a nice pimp?"

"No. Not in my experience."

Aimee sighed. "I hate that I stayed with him for so long. I'm a serious wimp."

"Don't do that to yourself. That's in the past. It's onward and upward from here. No more pimps."

Aimee rolled down her window and shouted, "No more pimps!" at the passing houses.

Kiki laid on the horn. "Whooo *hooo!* No more piiiiimps!" She looked in her rearview mirror and blanched. "Oh, shit. No more yelling. Cops." Kiki grabbed Aimee's arm. "Don't turn around. Just be cool."

"Ohshitohshitohshit," whispered Aimee over and over, her hands folded tightly in her lap. "Just act casual. Caaasscchjjuuuul. I'm casual. I'm cool."

Kiki tried not to laugh. "Shut up. Seriously. They're ..." She didn't get the words out before they heard a *whoop!* – the police car's signal that they needed to pull over. The red and blue flashers were going now, too.

"Oh, fuck me sideways. I'm screwed."

"Is your gun ... illegal?"

"No. I have a permit. But that doesn't make it okay to point it at your ex."

"Even if he deserved it?"

"Well, maybe. But I don't think we want to get into that with them. Just don't say anything, okay?"

Kiki pulled over to the side of the road and waited for the officer to get to her window before she did anything. The last thing she wanted was for him to think that she was reaching for something dangerous, so she put her hands on the steering wheel, up high where he could see them. Better to figure out what he was after them for anyway, first. She was trying to remember if she'd noticed a tail light out, when he arrived at the passenger-side window.

Kiki's smile lit up her face as soon as she saw who it was. "Well, hello, Joe."

Aimee's eyes almost bugged out of her head. She stayed completely silent.

"Hello. Um ... Kiki is it?"

"Yes, very good. You remembered. I'm impressed."

Joe looked at Aimee. "Hi, Aimee. Nice seeing you again."

"Yeah, um ... you too." She had a frog in her throat and tried desperately to clear it out. She sounded like she was going to hawk up a loogie any second.

Kiki tried to save her. "So, what's up with the lights?"

Joe broke his gaze away from Aimee and smiled. "Well, we got a report of a crazy woman waving a gun around inside someone's private home. Drove away in an orange and black Camaro. Would you happen to know anything about that?"

Kiki weighed her options, unsure about how to answer. She could lie and risk pissing him off and maybe blowing Aimee's chances for a future date. Or she could tell the truth and get booked for assault. *Hmmmm. What to do, what to do?*

"It's mine!" shouted Aimee. "I did it! Take me to jail!"

Joe looked at her in shock at first. Then he looked at Kiki. "Does she own a gun?"

"No," said Kiki, disgusted with Aimee's complete lack of self-control. "She doesn't own a damn gun. I do, though. The permit's in the glove box if you want me to get it."

"Sure. Do that for me. I'll be right back."

He returned to his car, talking into a speaker on his shoulder.

"Shit, Aimee, what are you trying to do?"

"Keep you out of prison," she said, pouting.

"Well, at this rate, you're going to get us two tickets to pokeytown instead of just one."

"I'm sorry. I panicked."

"No shit," Kiki said, but laughing anyway. "Kind of dramatic, aren't you?"

Aimee pressed her lips into a thin line and then said, "Sometimes. I might get a little out of hand ... but only *sometimes*. When the stakes are high."

"Or you've had a glass of wine."

"Maybe then, too." Aimee looked at Kiki, worry in her eyes. "So what's your plan? Full confession? Surrender?"

"Not exactly. Just follow my lead. And don't *lie.*"

"Fine," huffed Aimee, staring straight ahead.

Joe came back to the window, this time on Kiki's side. "I'm ready for that permit."

Kiki handed it over, explaining, "I have the gun with me, in my purse. But what I did was ..."

Joe held up his hand and said, "Ah! Wait. Don't say anything else. I don't want to hear it."

"How come?" asked Aimee, before she quickly put her hand up to her mouth. "Oopsy. Sorry. Ignore me."

Kiki rolled her eyes. "So what's the deal? Am I in trouble?"

"For owning a properly permitted gun? No. Nothing unlawful about that." Joe smiled and handed her the permit back.

"You didn't call for backup?" asked Aimee meekly.

"No. Do you want me to?" He was addressing Aimee directly. Her face colored under the attention.

"No, Officer Joe, we do not want you to call for backup," answered Kiki wryly, noticing that Aimee was clearly too flustered to speak with her brain connected in any way to her mouth. Officer Joe was flirting with the poor girl, and she had no idea.

"Just do me a favor ... steer clear of Jack Parsons, would you please?" he said.

Kiki gave him a winning smile. "There's nothing I'd like more than to never see that jackass again as long as I live."

"Me too," mumbled Aimee, looking down into her lap.

Joe looked like he was going to walk away, but then he stopped and bent down to look in the window again. "Call you later?" he said to Aimee.

Her head whipped sideways to look at him, her eyes wide open. "Me? Oh ... yeah. That'd be ... good ... no great! No, good ... oh, crap." She looked the other way, out her window, trying to hide her beet red face.

"I'll take that as a yes," said Joe, before he stood up and tapped his fist on the open window ledge of Kiki's door two times.

Kiki shifted the car back into drive as Joe walked back to his car. "Thanks, Officer Joe!" she yelled out the window.

He waved a pen over his shoulder in response.

Kiki looked over at Aimee before pressing on the gas. "I guess you have friends in high places."

Aimee smiled tentatively at first and then more broadly. "I guess I do."

18

elizabeth

*E*LIZABETH CHECKED HER WATCH AGAIN. *Twelve minutes after. Should I call them?* No sooner had the thought flitted through her head than the door swung open and a jubilant Aimee and slightly more subdued Kiki entered.

"Elizabeth!" exclaimed Aimee. "I'm *so* sorry we're late. It's totally my fault. Well ... actually, the gun slinging part was Kiki's fault, but it only slowed us down a little bit. The rest was me. I went a little crazy with putting stuff away at our place. And I had to bake a batch of cookies. I had the dough already made, though."

Elizabeth looked at her, not knowing exactly what to say to that. She wasn't even sure how much she had understood.

"Allow me to clarify," said Kiki calmly. "We went to pack the rest of Aimee's stuff, her ex showed up, I flashed him my gun, we got pulled over, Aimee pulled some strings with her hot cop boyfriend, we were let go, went back to the townhouse, emptied all her stuff out, threw some cookies in the oven, and then spent about ... ," she checked her watch, " ... fifteen minutes too long putting things away."

Understanding dawned on Elizabeth's face. "Good lord, you guys know how to have a busy morning."

"No moss, baby, no moss," said Aimee.

Elizabeth raised an eyebrow in question, happy to see Aimee so energized.

"I think she's a rolling stone now," explained Kiki. "Let's get a table. I need an iced tea or a shot of tequila or something."

The hostess arrived and led them to a spot near a window. Once they were settled in with three sweet teas between them, Elizabeth starting asking questions.

"Okay, so I'm not even sure what I should ask about first. Ex-husband? Gun? Cop boyfriend?" She looked at Aimee. "Are we talking about the guy from the other night? Joe?"

"Yes," said Aimee, "but he's not my boyfriend."

"Yet," said Kiki, perusing the menu.

"Yet. Maybe. I don't know. Anyway, we were packing, as Kiki said, and my ex showed up. He started to get ugly, like he always does these days, and Kiki had a gun in her purse."

"Whoa. So, did you threaten him with it?" Elizabeth was fascinated. She'd never known a woman who owned a gun. Some of her male clients had them, but they never carried them around as far as she knew.

"Kind of," said Kiki, looking up. "You would have done the same thing. The guy's an ass."

Elizabeth held up a hand. "I'm not judging. I'm all for standing up for yourself against violence." She looked over at Aimee. "I'm glad Kiki was there with you."

"Me too. I'm so glad I don't live there anymore. And I got fresh-squeezed juice this morning, too. Jack's never done that for me."

"Yes. I'd make a great wife. But don't get used to it. I only do that on weekends."

"You could do it once a year and I'd still be grateful. It's just so nice to wake up and not feel desperate for a change."

"How long have you and Jack been ... having problems?" asked Elizabeth.

"Oh, I don't know. I guess it's been about nine months. Not quite a year, I think. He started cheating on me around my birthday. At least, that's my theory."

Elizabeth was disgusted. "What's wrong with men? Why can't they just keep their you-know-whats in their pants?" She grabbed her drink and took a long sip of her tea, frowning at no one in particular.

"It's just as much women's faults as it is theirs," said Kiki.

"What?!" said Aimee in a clipped tone. "Are you saying it's my fault he cheated?"

"Hell no. I'm saying that if women in general stopped sleeping with married men, men would only have other *men* to turn to."

"Oh," said Aimee. "I'd never thought of it that way."

"They'd still have prostitutes," said Elizabeth, although still impressed at Kiki's thought process. She'd never considered throwing the blame on the cheating women before. It made sense in a way.

"They could have a singles-only policy," said Aimee, smiling again. "The men would have to come in with a certificate of singlehood. That could be our business - a singles registry."

"While I appreciate the entrepreneurship and the way your mind works, I have a better idea that might not take so much time to get up and running with actual customers," said Kiki.

"What's that?" asked Elizabeth, now totally focused on what Kiki was going to say. She liked cheater-bashing as much as the next girl, but she was anxious to get down to business.

"After lugging about fifty pounds of kitchen gadgets into the house and tasting Aimee's confections, I had a flash of brilliance. I vote we open a cafe bakery kind of thing. A place where people would hang out and have coffee, some cake or pie or tarts, maybe with wifi so they could bring their laptops. A gathering place."

Elizabeth nodded her head absently as her mind sped through some calculations. "Where are you thinking?"

"Well, that depends. Do we want our weekends free? If so, downtown. It would be slow on weekends and we could hand over the reins to trusted employees. But if we want maximum exposure, then maybe someplace not so business-oriented. Like somewhere near a hip shopping district. There are a few near downtown that might give us the best of both worlds."

"I like where you're going with this. I mean, restaurants in general are difficult to get profitable. But I have had some very successful clients in the business so I know it can be done. You just need to have the right ingredients."

"Ingredients. That's a good one," said Aimee. She lost her smile. "The only problem is, I'm afraid you guys are putting way too much faith in me. I'm really not an expert at anything. I can make a few things in the kitchen, but a whole menu?" She looked at the other two, a slightly panicked expression on her face. "I don't think I could do it. And I'd hate to let you down. I've never had any training at all."

"That's the beauty of it, I think," said Kiki. "You're a natural genius. Talent like yours isn't learned. Sure, you could fine-tune it. But you have enough skill to do what I'm thinking about. If you need to go take some courses as part of the business planning, I'll support that." Kiki faced Elizabeth. "What do you think?"

"I agree. There will be several things we need to do before the business opens anyway. Aimee could go over to the culinary institute and take some weekend courses. They have all-day sessions, taught by professionals on specific things."

Aimee was looking back and forth between the other two, her eyes beginning to shine. "You guys, you have no idea how incredibly excited this makes me. To be able to think about taking actual courses like that? I mean, it's a dream come true." She started playing nervously with her straw. "But the problem is that I don't really have anything other than that to contribute. I've never even waited tables. And I'm a tea drinker not a coffee person, so I don't know how to work one of those fancy machines. I can enter receipts into a bookkeeping program, but I can't analyze the information. I'm afraid I'd feel like dead weight. And you know I have zero money to invest." She cast her eyes down to the table, suddenly very concerned with a smudge on its surface and getting it off with her napkin.

"All of us will bring a strength or two to the table. I'm bringing investment cash and accounting skills. I'll be the number cruncher. I've also put together plenty of business entities, and I have some contracts we can use and a family member who's an attorney who will help us. He's my cousin, and I do his taxes free every year, so he owes me. I also love coffee, so I could learn how to run the fancy machine." She smiled encouragingly at Aimee who'd picked up her head again, not looking quite as bummed as she had a couple seconds ago.

"I'm bringing investment cash too, and style. I'm going to find the spot and design its interior. I know exactly what we need. Like the bar in *Friends* but not a bar. A coffee slash tea house with cakes and other sweet things, sandwiches and soups. We'll keep that other stuff simple so we can really emphasize the confections. We'll have comfy chairs and tables too. Inside and outside seating. Flowers. But chic. Oh, and I can wait a mean table, but I'm picturing this as a 'get your food at the counter' kind of place. We'll hire a hot guy to bus the tables for us."

"And take out the trash," said Elizabeth, getting even more excited after hearing Kiki's ideas. This felt really right.

"I could do some special things. I've been experimenting ... ," said Aimee, now taking on a distracted expression as she gazed off into the distance.

"Okay, so are we all in agreement then?" asked Elizabeth. "We're all in, at least in theory, on opening a cafe together?"

"I'm in," said Kiki without hesitation.

"I'm in. If you guys don't mind dead wood," said Aimee, smiling shyly.

"We won't let you be dead wood. You might feel like the walking dead by the time we have this business up and running, but you will never have to worry about not pulling your weight. Right, Kiki?"

"Damn straight."

They exchanged conspiratorial smiles across the table. Emotions were riding high. Elizabeth couldn't remember the last time she'd been this excited about something.

The waitress came over to take their orders. Once she was finished and had walked away, Elizabeth said, "We need to put together a business plan. I want to draft it all up in the next couple of days and throw together the pro formas - estimated financials - so I can get an idea of the level of investment required." She looked at Kiki, not entirely sure that Kiki knew how much it could cost to start and run a business. For all Elizabeth knew, Kiki could have only ten grand to share. That wasn't going to be near enough. "I'm guessing, just off the top of my head and depending on where it is, we're looking at an initial investment of between one hundred to two hundred and fifty thousand. That doesn't include operating capital. We could do it with less, but we'd have to really work hard at finding deals and cutting corners. It would mean more work."

Aimee choked on her drink.

Kiki reached over and patted her on the back a few times.

"One hundred and *fifty thousand dollars?* Are you *nuts?*" said Aimee. "I can't do this. No way. You guys could buy a house with that money. What if it fails? What if I'm terrible? What if Jack's right?" She slammed her mouth shut and just looked at the others, tears swimming in her eyes.

"Take a breath, Aimee. It's not a lot of money to start a business. A club costs nearly a mil. Sometimes more. We're getting off easy." She reached over and put her hand on Aimee's, stopping her from completely shredding her straw wrapper. "And for the record, whatever Jack said about you, it was wrong. You kick ass in the kitchen. No one can say any different. We've tasted the proof."

Elizabeth nodded her head. She was glad to hear Kiki wasn't as naive about the investment as she had feared, and she was in full agreement about Aimee's abilities.

Kiki let go of Aimee's hand after patting it a couple times and sat back in her seat. "Do you want to each put up half, or what? We can do it in thirds and I could front Aimee's part to begin with. She could pay it off with her share of the profits over a period of several years."

"I'm not sure. I'll ask my cousin and see what he thinks is best. From a tax perspective, it really doesn't make much difference. I suspect we'll have a loss at least the first year. Aimee probably doesn't need one. I could use one. What about you?"

"Well, I'm going to take some gains if I cash out some stock to pay part of my share; so next year, yes, I'll probably need some losses to offset."

Elizabeth was now definitely impressed. She'd had no idea that exotic dancers even thought about investing in the stock market, let alone tracked their short- and long-term capital gains. She silently admonished herself for judging Kiki like that. She'd been called stiff and unfriendly for years, as a result of the professional constraints of her job. Some of it may have been earned, but not all; so she knew what it was like to be judged unfairly. She smiled to herself as she imagined what it would be like to be part owner of a chicly bohemian coffee house. She had a feeling people would look at her differently, and she liked it. A lot. She was already feeling like a changed woman - more free and creative.

"Okay, we'll figure it out. I just want to be fair to both of you and myself. I'd like to think of this as a lifetime partnership. Someday, if this takes off, it will fund our retirement."

"Yeah, and we can all cash out to go live on a tropical island somewhere. Where the men wear coconut suntan oil and deliver us drinks in a pineapple," offered Kiki.

"I am likin' the idea of the cafe, ladies," said Aimee, lifting up her drink. "And the guys in suntan oil for sure. I'm poor, but I'm motivated. So if you guys will loan me the money to participate, I promise to bake my buns off for you. Here's to our new business!"

The other two raised up their glasses to join Aimee's. They clinked them together and said, "Here's to ..." They all stopped and looked at each other.

Elizabeth said, "We need a name for our new place."

"Well, for now, we'll call it 'Desperation Depot' since it's what lead us here. Desperation, I mean," said Kiki.

"Here's to Desperation Depot, until we find a better name," said Elizabeth.

"Hear, hear!" said Aimee, enthusiastically.

Kiki took a drink of her tea and asked, "What's our timeframe, do you think? Three months? Six?"

"That depends on the location. Three months is very ambitious. But it could happen."

"I know a realtor who does commercial stuff. He helped the DeLucca's find the club I worked in. I'll contact him and get him on finding a spot. I assume since we're all currently unemployed, we can take time to go visit possible candidates?"

"I still have to work until my month of notice is up, but I'm not worried about leaving to do our business. Feel free to call me anytime."

"Aren't you worried about a reference from your old boss?" asked Aimee.

"No. I have enough clients who will give me references. I have a feeling several will ask to go with me. They've already told me if I ever leave, they're jumping ship, too."

"Will you tell them no?" asked Kiki. "I would keep a few, if it were me."

"I might. It could be a good idea to have some money coming in, just in case."

"Take the nice ones," suggested Aimee. "That way you won't be cranky at work."

"Good idea," said Elizabeth. She liked Aimee's simplified outlook; it was deceptively brilliant.

Their salads arrived, so they spent the next few minutes eating and critiquing the food. Now that they had all decided to be restaurant owners, the quality of the food and presentation took on a whole new meaning.

"My lettuce is kinda wilty," said Aimee.

"I don't like the greens they're using," said Kiki. "Too much iceberg and not enough spring mix."

"This dressing is from a jar," added Elizabeth. "Homemade is so much better."

They all looked at each other. Elizabeth was the first to speak. "We're really doing this?"

"Yes," said Kiki firmly. "We are."

"Absolutely," agreed Aimee. "I mean, what do we have to lose? ... Besides all your money and my new home, of course?"

Aimee cracked them up with her devil-may-care expression. It was nice to see her not being shy or doubting her skills.

"So, what are we going to call it? I'm afraid Desperation Depot might make people afraid to come in," said Elizabeth.

"I have an idea," said Aimee, excitedly. "Let's put words on pieces of paper that kind of describe us, and then put them in a pile. We'll pull out two papers at a time and see if that prompts any ideas."

"Brilliant," said Kiki. "I'm game."

Elizabeth pulled a sheet of paper out of the portfolio she'd brought along. She carefully folded it over several times in various places and then went about ripping it up into small squares. She divided the pile into three and gave each girl her own.

Kiki reached into her purse and came out with three pens, all of them with the steakhouse strip club logo on them.

"Wow, can I keep this?" asked Aimee, looking it over. "I've always wanted to go here."

"I'll take you sometime. And yes, keep it. I have hundreds."

Elizabeth decided she was going to use her pen at work for her last few weeks there, to remind her of the fun she was getting ready to have with her two friends. She hoped her coworkers would see it too. Let them wonder what she was doing with a pen from an infamous strip club.

"Okay, so write one word on each piece of paper and then fold it in half. Put them in a pile in the middle of the table." Aimee moved some of the dishes and glasses a bit to make room as she continued her directions. "Put nouns and adjectives only. Use words that describe us or our lives or our dreams for the business."

After ten minutes of pens tapping on foreheads and chins, interrupted occasionally by spurts of scribbled creativity, there was a small mountain of papers folded up in the middle of the table.

The waitress came to take their dishes away and three sets of hands shot out to cover the pile in the middle.

Elizabeth looked up apologetically. "Sorry. We want to keep these."

The waitress rolled her eyes and cleaned up the table, avoiding their mess in the middle.

As soon as she was gone, Aimee said, "Okay. So, we pick out two papers and see if it gives us a good name. Elizabeth, you go first."

Elizabeth took out two slips of paper and opened them up, smiling as she read their contents.

"Don't leave us in suspense. What are they?" asked Kiki.

Elizabeth laid them out on the table.

HOT CAKES.

"*Hot cakes*. Hmmm. Uh, no. I don't think so," said Aimee, confirming with the others that it was a negative.

"Try again," said Kiki. "Your turn, Aimee."

Aimee picked out two papers and put them on the table.

TALENTED TARTS.

Kiki spoke first. "I'm seriously tempted."

"My turn," said Elizabeth, putting the slips back into the pile. "I'm afraid we'd have a hard time getting signage for that name. People would think it was a whorehouse."

Aimee burst out laughing and quickly covered her mouth. "Sorry. Go, Elizabeth. Your turn."

She put her two choices down in front of her.

COOKIE ASSKICKERS.

"Now *I'm* tempted," said Aimee, trying to look serious but clearly failing. She hid her smile behind her glass, clearing her throat a couple times.

Kiki grabbed several papers and just started opening them. She shuffled them around on the table, face-up, putting several in a row.

HOT COOKIE ASSKICKERS.

Elizabeth reached over and moved some.

TALENTED HOT MUFFIN BADASSES.

"Who put all the superhero words in here?" asked Kiki.

Aimee raised her hand halfway. "Guilty. I was inspired by your gunslinging. I couldn't seem to help myself."

Elizabeth tried again.

DESPERATE TALENTED HOT MUFFIN SEXY ASSKICKERS.

"This is not working," said Kiki, staring at the words.

"Maybe we should use a computer program," suggested Aimee. "They have these things on the Internet that will pick random words for you."

"But it shouldn't be random," said Elizabeth. "I don't think we need to go to desperate measures to just pick a good name for our business. This should be the easy part."

"I like that one," said Kiki.

"What one?" asked Elizabeth, looking down at the papers. "HOT SEXY TARTS?"

"No. Desperate Measures."

"I don't see that here," said Aimee, searching the pile.

"It's not in the papers. Elizabeth just said it. *Desperate Measures*. It kind of describes us. We all reached a moment of desperation in our lives, and we took desperate measures to move forward. And now we're about to do something really amazing as a result."

Elizabeth pursed her lips, mulling the idea over in her mind. "Not bad. I like it." She looked at Aimee. "What do you think?"

"Well. I like that it has 'measures' in it. I'm going to be doing a lot of that with the cooking. And I do feel pretty desperate right now."

"You guys don't think using the word 'desperate' is going to cause people not to come in?" asked Elizabeth.

Kiki shrugged. "I don't see why it would. Who hasn't been desperate at least once in their lives? Everyone should be able to identify. In this economy, everyone's feeling a little desperate. Maybe it'll strike a chord with people."

Aimee slapped her hand down on the table. "I like it! I vote, *yes!*"

"Fine," said Elizabeth, putting her hand down on the table, palm down. "I vote, *yes*, too."

"Make it three," said Kiki, sweeping up all the papers into her hand and crushing them into a ball. "Desperate Measures it is. I assume you'll do the formalities with the State?" She looked at Elizabeth for confirmation.

Elizabeth nodded. "I'm on it today. As soon as I leave here."

"Awesome," said Aimee. "So what's next?"

"You and I have to go finish putting all that stuff away," answered Kiki.

"Yes, and we have lots of other things to do. I can put together a task list right now if you'd like." Elizabeth looked to the others, and as soon as she saw their acquiescence, she took out her portfolio again. She got busy writing down three lists - one for each of them - doing her best to make sure the work was divided as evenly as possible. She tore off the sheets and handed one to each of the girls, explaining as she did. "Okay, so Aimee, your job is to let us know exactly what you'll need in the way of equipment and supplies. That means you need to get your recipes together and work on that menu. You make a proposed menu, and we'll all vote on it. Once you have our approval, you tell me what ingredients you need and in what proportions. I'll do some estimating of customer order volume and with the costs of those raw materials, we'll be able to calculate our costs of goods sold."

"Um, you lost me about part way through that explanation," said Aimee, looking worried.

"Don't fret. I've written it down, step by step. First thing is menu development. Then, equipment and ingredients. Once you have that together, I'll give you new things to do. Essentially, you'll be in charge of getting the kitchen set up so it operates efficiently for you and the menus you envision."

Aimee nodded her head, looking less worried. "Okay. Menus I can handle. And equipment."

Kiki was reading over her list. "I can get started on this today. I'll call that realtor. I already have a couple locations I noticed that went empty this past year in mind. One was already some sort of restaurant, so maybe we can save some money there with build-out." She pointed to something on the list. "What's this? I think it says 'project board'?"

"You're in charge of decor. I was thinking you could put together one of those boards that has fabrics, paint chips, pictures of furniture and that kind of thing. Show us the vision you have for the space. You probably can't do all of it until we actually have the space picked out, but you could do some."

"Oh, I'm all over this, baby. I'm already in the paint store in my mind right now." Kiki's eyes were gleaming.

"What else is on your list?" Aimee asked Kiki.

"I'm supposed to work on the business plan too. Let's see ... I need to give a synopsis of the business goals, the market for our products and location, and ... I saw it somewhere here ... oh, yeah - I have to do a SWOT analysis. Whatever that is."

Elizabeth explained. "It's strengths, weaknesses, opportunities, and threats. It's a marketing exercise that helps you go through the motions of evaluating your position in relation to your competition. We need to know all these things so we can develop our brand in the most effective way."

"We're going to have a brand?" asked Aimee, sounding impressed. "That's so cool."

"Yes. We are going to develop a brand. Then people will recognize us, and if we decide to open more locations, it will make it easier to ramp up sales in a meaningful and efficient way."

"I'm getting the feeling efficiency is important to you," said Aimee, not unkindly.

"It's the accountant in me. Sorry. I just know that it's lack of efficiency that sinks businesses."

"I'm perfectly okay with anyone's obsessive tendencies entering the picture so long as they enhance our bottom line," said Kiki. "We all have our issues."

"What's yours?" asked Aimee, playfully.

"I hate frumpiness. I will have to insist that we and our employees look nice while we work."

"I'm okay with that," said Elizabeth.

"I'm okay with it in theory. But I will admit to being frumpy probably way too often. It's more comfy to cook frumpy than fancy."

"I'll make sure your uniform is comfy, don't worry. But I cannot tolerate frump. Besides ... you're a beautiful girl. You need to show it off more."

"You're silly. I'm at least fifteen pounds overweight and too lazy to do anything about it."

"You and me are joining the gym later. I'm not dancing any-more, so if I don't go, I'm gonna get wide."

"I need to get into the gym, too," lamented Elizabeth. "I've always worked too many hours to fit it in."

"Well, we're going to end up working more hours than we ever have in our lives, but I'm not going to let that stop any of us from doing what we need to do to take care of our bodies. Why don't you join us, Elizabeth? Come to the same gym."

"Yeah!" agreed Aimee. "We can sweat and oogle cute guys together."

"Which one are you thinking?" asked Elizabeth.

"Club 30. They're all over. They even have them downtown and in the shopping district I was thinking about, so we can trans-fer our memberships to be near work, if you want."

"Excellent idea. I'll do it with you. Just tell me where to sign."

"Let's go now!" suggested Aimee. "After lunch. We'll do it all together."

"We've got time," agreed Kiki.

"Good. Let's do it. I'll follow you over." Elizabeth grabbed her purse and took some cash out of her wallet, leaving it on the table with the check. "Thirds everyone?" she asked.

"Thirds," confirmed Kiki, putting her part down.

Aimee added to the pile and handed it to Elizabeth to count.

Once she was sure it was all there, Elizabeth put it back on the table and stood, the others joining her.

They left the restaurant and hugged out in the parking lot. "I'm so excited that we decided to do this," said Elizabeth. She felt like singing and dancing right there in public, but she restrained her-self. Just barely.

"Me too," said Aimee. "This is going to be the funnest, most exciting thing I've ever done."

"Ditto," said Kiki, kissing Elizabeth breezily on the cheek. "Follow us to Orange Ave. I know a shortcut."

"Good. See you soon," said Elizabeth, getting into her Buick. She smiled at herself in the rearview mirror. Desperate times called for Desperate Measures. No truer adage was ever penned.

19

aimee

$\mathscr{A}$IMEE WAS PSYCHED. SHE COULDN'T stop humming all the way to the gym. She paused in her wordless rendition of *Walking on Sunshine* to mention, "I haven't belonged to a gym in ages."

"Me neither. I'm terrible about exercising. I need a partner to keep me going. That's going to be your job."

"Ha! That's going to be *your* job for *me*. I hate exercising. But I'll do it, I promise. I know I need to."

"Consider it a gift to yourself. You deserve to feel and look good. Not that you don't look good now, because you do."

"I could stand to lose a few. I know that. But you're right. I'm tired a lot and I know it's because I'm out of shape."

"And you've been stressed, too. That doesn't help. But don't worry. We're going to get both our butts in shape and never look back."

Aimee looked askance at her. "You don't have an ounce of fat on you anywhere. You're already in shape. Promise you won't laugh at me in aerobics class or whatever. I'm not very coordinated."

"I'm not going to laugh. Dancing kept me in shape, but that's obviously no longer an option. So if I don't start exercising now,

I'm gonna start spreading, and that is unacceptable. Asses run big in my family. Like axe-handle-wide big."

Aimee laughed. "Asses run big on *me*, forget my family."

Kiki smiled, negotiating the traffic, glancing in her mirror as she did.

Aimee turned around, making sure they hadn't lost Elizabeth. "She's still there. Do you think she's excited?"

"Elizabeth? Yeah. I think she is. She had a shit job, too, like me. You had a shit husband. We were all in the shits."

"You're telling me. I'm so glad she's doing this with us. She's so organized, and it seems like she really knows about businesses."

"Yes, I agree. She's smart as hell." Kiki turned into a parking lot and negotiated the Camaro into a tight spot. The place was packed.

"You seem to know a lot about money, too," said Aimee, worried about being nosy, but not quite able to keep herself from wanting to know details.

"I grew up with very little. I always swore I was going to have nice things when I got older, and I knew I had to be smart about money to make that happen. So I educated myself. And my brokerage is good about giving me all kinds of free info on the market."

"The market?"

"Stock market. I've been investing for years. Since high school."

"I don't really know about that stuff. I hear things on the news, but it's all Greek to me."

"I could teach you. It's not that difficult. I don't do anything crazy. I'm mostly a buy and hold kind of girl, but I've done well. I stick with stocks of companies I like personally, and so far, that strategy has never let me down."

"That's so cool. So you're like that guy ... Jimmy Buffet."

"Huh?"

"You know. That *guy*. The financial guru who's like a gajillionaire."

Kiki seemed to think about it for a second before the light of understanding dawned across her face. "You mean *Warren* Buffet." She chuckled.

"Jimmy Buffet, Warren Buffet, same diff."

"Yeah. Just a cheeseburger in paradise apart, I think," said Kiki.

Aimee laughed, unbuckling her seatbelt, now that they were parked. "That's why I like you, Kiki. You don't judge."

Kiki shrugged. "Who am I to be doing that? I made my fortune shaking tits and ass in front of drunk pervs."

"Yeah, but I'll bet you did it with style," said Aimee.

"You bet your cherry tarts, I did." She turned off the engine and unclicked her seatbelt. "We're here. Let's go get physical."

"Oh no, you did *not* just Olivia Newton John me."

"Oh, yes I did, and I'd proudly do it again. Don't make me bust *Grease* out on your ass."

Aimee held up her hands in surrender. "I give. Please. Have mercy on my soul. I'm hopelessly devoted to keeping you happy so you won't feel the need to do that."

Kiki stuck out her tongue before she got out of the car and said, "Don't tempt me. I had a crush on Danny for years. I'm still not completely over it."

Elizabeth joined them at Aimee's side. "Danny? Danny who? Is that your boyfriend?"

"No. She's talking about Danny in the movie *Grease*. John Travolta."

"He was cute," agreed Elizabeth. "Still is."

"Elizabeth, I have some cookies for you in the car. Don't let me forget to give them to you."

"Mmmm, I love cookies. I won't forget."

They all walked into the gym together discussing the merits of musicals involving male dancers. Within seconds of stepping up to the front desk, they were accosted by a salesman who nearly started salivating when they told him they were interested in three new memberships.

As they took a tour around the gym, Aimee noticed Kiki getting agitated. She tried to figure out what was bothering her, but couldn't put her finger on it. She touched Kiki on the arm to get her attention. "What's up? Don't you like the gym?"

"Yeah. Sure. It's nice." She seemed distracted.

"Something's wrong."

"No. I'm fine."

Aimee frowned. Kiki wasn't telling the truth and Aimee knew it, but she couldn't force her to talk. *Time for detective mode.* Aimee narrowed her eyes. She was going to watch every move Kiki made, analyze her facial expressions, and ask enough questions until she figured it out. This was how she had eventually caught Jack with his cheating. Everyone has a tell. Everyone gives away secrets without realizing it. She just had to pay attention to details.

Kiki kept looking over at a part of the gym that had freeweights. They hadn't gone over there yet because they'd all decided they weren't the free-weight type. Aimee decided to up the ante with Kiki.

"Excuse me," she said to the salesman who was in the process of negotiating rates with Elizabeth. She was giving him a run for his money if the frustrated look on his face was any clue. "I'd like to go see the free-weights area. I changed my mind about not using them." She looked at Kiki's face. Instant frown. *Bingo! Something or someone is a problem for Kiki over in the free-weights.*

"I'll meet you guys at the front," said Kiki casually, making a big effort to look nonplussed.

Aimee could see her stress as clear as day, and she wasn't going to let Kiki get away with running from it. Not when Aimee was this close to figuring it out. She grabbed Kiki's arm. "No, come with us. We're workout partners, remember? We need to stick together. We can do this, right?" She raised her eyebrows in challenge at Kiki.

Kiki narrowed her eyes at Aimee. "You're a sneaky little devil, you know that?"

Aimee winked at her. "I have been accused of worse."

"Fine. I'll go look at the free-weights, *partner.*"

"What am I missing?" whispered Elizabeth, bending over so she could reach Aimee's ear.

Aimee whispered back, leaning close so Kiki wouldn't hear. "She's afraid of someone over there. I'm making her face her fears."

"Who?"

"I have no idea."

"Are you sure this is a good plan?"

"No. But it's fun."

Elizabeth smiled. "Well, then. Let's go see the free-weights." She straightened up and said in a regular tone of voice. "Bill, could you show us that area over there? We've changed our minds."

Bill sighed heavily, indicating he was already worn out from Elizabeth's questioning about schedules, peak usage hours, age of equipment, and about twenty other things Aimee would never have thought to ask. "Follow me," he said, not nearly as enthusiastic as he'd been twenty minutes earlier.

The closer they got, the more nervous Kiki acted. Aimee kept a close eye on her. When they were halfway there, she noticed a guy that Kiki was deliberately avoiding looking at. A scrumptious one.

"Holy hotness. Do my eyes deceive me or is there a god in our midst?" Aimee said, looking directly at Kiki.

"Who? That guy over there?" asked Kiki pointing to someone only half as cute as the one she was pretending not to see.

"Please, Kiki. You're not fooling anyone. Who is that amazing hunka burnin' love over there? Fess up or I'll go ask him myself."

Kiki whipped around and grabbed her arm. "Don't!"

"Sheesh, okay. I won't. But you have to tell me who he is *now*. We're workout partners and roommates. I'm pretty sure there's a rule that says we have to talk about guys together."

"I want in on this," said Elizabeth, "especially if you're talking about tall, dark, and mouthwatering over there in the gray shirt and black shorts that I wish were just a tad tighter." She licked her lips for emphasis.

Kiki sighed loudly. "Yes, that's him. I'll tell you later. Until then, be cool. And stop staring at him ... *Aimee!*"

"Oh. Sorry. I'm trying, but he's really, really cute. I can't help myself." And now he was only about ten paces away. Aimee had to force herself to look at Bill instead. The poor guy was ready to bail; he kept looking at his watch and the door. Aimee figured it was probably a slow month or something that kept him hanging on at all.

"So, this is the free-weights area," he said in a bored tone. "Any questions?"

Aimee giggled. Bill wasn't even going to bother telling them about it. She raised her hand. "I have a question," she said, a mischievous tone in her voice.

"No, she doesn't," said Kiki, pushing her arm down and trying to steer her away from the area.

"No, I really do!" said Aimee, twisting away from Kiki so she could stay in front of Bill. "I'm wondering if ... um ... " She wanted to stay there longer but couldn't think of any legit questions to ask. She was saved by Elizabeth's OCD-driven ingenuity.

"I'd like to know how many hand barbells you have of each weight level. I want to be sure during peak hours there will be enough to go around."

Bill rolled his eyes, but began reciting his equipment list to her as she stood there nodding, while looking over several times at the hot guy.

Aimee had plenty of time to pretend she was looking at the floor and ceiling while she checked him out from every possible angle. Luckily, he was standing in front of some mirrors while he did bicep curls.

Kiki started tapping her foot. "I'm ready to sign, Bill. But if you don't put a contract in front of me in about two minutes, I'm outta here."

Bill perked up and said, "Be right back!" before disappearing like a jackrabbit into one of the offices ringing the outside of the workout area.

"Nice move, Kiki," said Aimee.

"Somebody had to stop the madness."

"I was just giving Aimee enough time to do her inspection. I've seen enough to join," said Elizabeth.

Just then the hot guy put down his weights and grabbed a towel to wipe his face. Aimee knew the exact moment he caught Kiki's reflection in the mirror. The towel stilled in his hand and slowly dropped down to his side, as his eyes locked on hers. His head tilted to the side as if he were trying to place her. Then recognition seemed to dawn as his eyes widened. He threw down his towel and made a move to walk toward her.

Aimee nudged Elizabeth so they could both watch the sparks start to fly across the room. No one said anything. Kiki's face got a light pink color near her cheeks, giving her a beautiful glow.

"Time to go," she said, spinning on her heal.

The guy stopped in his tracks when he saw her walking away in a hurry. He blinked a couple times, shrugged, and then returned to the bench where his cell phone was sitting. He picked it up and started pressing buttons, no longer looking in Kiki's direction.

"Dammit. We almost had a connection there," said Aimee.

"You're playing matchmaker?" said Elizabeth.

"Yes. I think. Isn't he cute?"

"More like drop-dead gorgeous."

"And so is Kiki." Aimee sighed. "They'd make beautiful babies," she said dreamily.

Elizabeth snorted. "Could you see Kiki with a bunch of rug rats running around her feet?"

"Yes, actually, I could see that."

Elizabeth didn't respond right away. Then she said, "Yeah, me too, I guess. She has that whole momma bear thing going on."

"Totally," agreed Aimee.

"Come on. She's going to run out of here if we don't go sign those contracts right now."

"Okay. But at least we know he goes to this gym. It shouldn't be too hard to find him again."

"I'm putting that on your to-do list."

"What?"

"Finding out who that guy is and why Kiki's so afraid of him."

"Hmmm," said Aimee, her most devious voice coloring her words, "a mission impossible ... I accept."

20

kiki

$\mathcal{K}$IKI WANTED TO GET THE heck out of there. This sales guy was-getting the perfect setup for a slam-dunk of a deal. She needed to be gone before Lola's board member lawyer decided to get brave and come talk to her.

She'd recognized him from the club. The guy who'd had a front row seat for her final performance. Normally, she wouldn't care who saw her after work; but for some reason, she did now - especially with this guy.

"Okay, I'm all set. Here's your application and my credit card info, Bill. Ready to go, Aimee?"

"In a minute. I have to give him a check." Aimee took her time filling out the slip, making sure her handwriting was perfect.

Kiki sighed heavily. "You know the bank's not going to care if your curly-cues aren't on every letter."

Aimee ignored her, finishing her signature with a flourish. "There. All done. Now we can go, Miss Pushy Pants." Aimee smiled at Bill, but he didn't bother returning the nicety. The sale was over and now he just had work to do.

Elizabeth had already finished and put away her copies of the paperwork. "Where are you girls off to now?"

"We're going back home to put stuff away and get going on the planning. What about you?"

"Same. Going home to get started on the pro formas."

They walked out the front door together. "How about we make a plan to meet here tomorrow for our first workout, and then we can sit at the juice bar after and discuss our progress?" suggested Aimee.

Kiki couldn't very well insist that she didn't want to come here, now that she'd just signed the forms and promised Aimee she'd be her workout partner - even though that's exactly what she wanted to do. "Okay. That's fine with me. Except they're closed on Sunday so it'll have to be Monday."

"Excellent," said Elizabeth. "Monday it is. What time?"

"Ten in the morning?" Aimee looked at the others, obviously excited about the prospect of her first day.

"Ten it is. See you girls Monday, then." Elizabeth leaned in for hugs, which were happily given.

"Bye! Call us if you have questions!" said Kiki from across the parking lot.

"Will do!"

"Oh wait!" exclaimed Aimee. "I forgot to give Elizabeth her cookies!" She waited for Kiki to unlock her door and grabbed the plate off the seat, running over to Elizabeth's car to deliver them.

Kiki started the engine and put on her seatbelt, trying to act very busy with adjusting the mirror and radio to keep Aimee from asking her questions. She should have known it would be useless.

The first thing Aimee said when she got back to the car and climbed in was, "So who's the guy?"

"What guy?" *It's worth a shot.*

"Don't play games with me. I am the master of no fun. There will be no games today. I'm talking about the level-ten hot guy in the free-weights section. The one who was coming over to talk to you before you ran away."

"I didn't run."

"You ran. And frankly, I'm pretty disappointed. I thought you were fearless."

"I am. Except with that guy for some reason."

Aimee got a concerned look on her face. "Oh, no! Is he like ... one of those pimps you told me about? Oh, shoot, I was thinking about setting you *up* with that jerk. Now I feel like a total idiot. I'm so sorry ... "

"No, no, Aimee, you're getting the wrong idea. He's not a pimp. Not at all." She sighed. She was in too deep now to *not* say anything about him. "He's a member of the board for Lola's ... the place I used to work. I think he's a lawyer."

Aimee frowned. "Might as well just call him a pimp, then."

Kiki laughed. "Not all lawyers are assholes."

"Yes, they are."

Kiki couldn't keep the smile off her face. She couldn't remember now why she was so reticent about telling Aimee the secret. It really wasn't that big of a deal. "Well, maybe a lot of them are. But I don't even really know this guy. He was there on the night of my last performance, sitting in the front row."

"Oh, wow. That's kind of sexy, actually. Did he ask you out after?"

"No. He didn't tip me, so I refused to speak to him."

"He *stiffed* you? What a bum! See? I told you. They're all pimps at heart ... think the world owes 'em."

"He wasn't the type to go to that kind of club. I could see it all over his face."

"Well, why was he there, then? Trying to get a free look?"

"The manager told me this board, which is made up of mostly attorneys, had gotten involved to class up the place. Try to get it more profitable. I don't know ... maybe the DeLuccas are going to sell it to someone or something. Franchise it. I have no idea."

"Huh. So this guy was at the club, a place he doesn't normally go, watching you shake your tooshie, and then you blew him off?"

"Yeah. That's about right."

"So now he's going to want you bad."

"Not necessarily. Life is not like *Pretty Woman*, Aimee. Most guys don't want an exotic dancer for a girlfriend."

"You're not an exotic dancer anymore, first of all, and second, any guy who doesn't bother to get to know you first before he rejects you is a butthead anyway and not worth your time."

Kiki smiled. "I like the way your mind works, Aimee."

"It's just common sense. You have a lot to offer the right guy, so you have to be selective."

"You could be talking about yourself, you know. Seems like that Joe guy might be a good candidate."

"*Pffft.* Right. I'm damaged goods, Kiki. I can't afford to be picky like you. But that doesn't mean I'll go with just *any* guy. I've already been tied to one prick for long enough."

"What are you talking about? You're not damaged goods, that's ridiculous." Kiki was angry that Aimee felt this way about herself. That guy Jack had really done a number on her self-confidence.

Aimee's voice lost its cheer and energy. "I didn't really tell you this before; I thought you might have guessed it ..." She sighed sadly before continuing, "I can't have kids. I'm barren."

Kiki barked out a laugh. "Barren? Have you been reading too many historical romances, or what? Who says that anymore?"

"I thought it sounded more dramatic." A small smile began to show at the corner of her lips.

"Oh, it does." Kiki was still chuckling. "How do you know it's you that's the problem? Maybe it's him."

"Well, he got Tiffany pregnant. And we tried for several years without success, so you do the math."

"Did you ever see a specialist?"

"Not exactly."

"What's that mean?"

"Well, I asked my gynecologist to check me - which he did - and he didn't see any reason why I couldn't have kids. But Jack would never agree to pay for a fertilization specialist, so I guess the only proof I have is years of trying with nothing but failure ... and now a pregnant paramour, of course."

"Again with the eighteen hundred's language."

"It's more ..."

"Yes. I know. It's more dramatic. Anyway, it could still be him. Maybe he has slow swimmers or something. Why didn't he allow you to go to a specialist?"

"He didn't want to spend the money."

Kiki rolled her eyes. "Please. That guy drives an Aston Martin, and your house is like five thousand square feet. Do you know how much those things cost?"

"Yes. I took care of all of our accounting. He has his spending priorities, and I wasn't at the top of that list. Ever."

"What a toad. How could you have ever married that guy? I mean, no offense, but I don't see any redeeming qualities in him. He must have been awesome in bed. But even so, you could do so much better."

Aimee laughed. "Ha! That's funny. Thank you for saying that. I wish I believed it. I have this little devil on my shoulder telling me I can't do better. Isn't that sad? And for the record, Jack stunk in bed. I think. He's the only guy I've ever slept with. I don't think I've ever had ... well ... you know."

"Had what?"

Aimee sighed. "*You* know. One of those things ... that everyone talks about."

"Are you talking about an orgasm?"

"Yes."

"Trust me, Aimee ... if you'd had one, you'd know it. You wouldn't wonder. It's too obvious to not know." She looked over at her friend. "You poor thing. You're what? Thirty-three? Thirty-four? And you've never had an orgasm?"

"Thirty-three. And, well, maybe I have had one. But not with him." Her face was turning pink.

"That's just plain sad and disturbing ... that you've been with that man for over ten years, and he's never given you an orgasm. *And* he's somehow convinced you that it's your fault. A-mazing." She shook her head, feeling really bad for her friend. She reached over and patted Aimee on the arm. "I'm so glad you're not with him anymore. He doesn't deserve you. We need to get you some man-created orgasms *stat*. The self-initiated ones are okay, but they really don't compare in my book."

Aimee laughed. "I'll take your word on that." She got sober again and said, "Jack wasn't always bad. Or maybe he was in the beginning and he just hid it better than he does now. When we first met, I had just graduated high school and was going into community college. I did two years - almost finished my associates - and then Jack and I got married. I wanted to keep going for my four-year degree, but he convinced me to stop."

"Why would he do that?"

"Well, at the time, he said he needed me to be home for him, to run our household and help him with his new law practice. But looking back, I think it was more to just control my every move. He never liked it when I spent time out of the house doing my own thing."

"God, that's so sad. You're such a smart girl. How come you put up with that for so long?"

Aimee shrugged. "I'm not sure. In the beginning, I was flattered that he was so possessive. It made me feel desired and special."

Kiki started shaking her head. This was a story she'd seen played out over and over in the lives of women she knew.

"I know. You don't approve. Neither do I. It's kind of embarrassing, actually. I can't believe I acted so weak for so many years. I let him brainwash me. *Ugh.* I hate thinking about it now." She turned and looked out the side window.

"Don't beat yourself up. Lots of smart women fall for that shit."

Aimee turned back toward Kiki, and Kiki noticed her friend's smile had returned.

"The side benefit to being a shut-in is that I kind of threw myself into cooking. If I'd had friends and interests outside of the home, I wouldn't be of any use to you in starting Desperate Measures."

"I think the name of this business is taking on more and more meaning for all of us," said Kiki, nearly lost in thought. *How do beautiful, loving, smart women get into these situations that she and her two new friends found themselves in?*

They arrived at the apartment after passing through the security gate with the clicker Kiki kept in her car, and immediately began unpacking the rest of Aimee's things. In two hours, the kitchen was completely reorganized to Aimee's liking and a fresh batch of cookies was in the oven.

"Okay, so what's next?" asked Aimee, a smudge of flour on her cheek.

Kiki reached over and gently brushed it off. "Now we sit down and brainstorm ... and make some phone calls. I want to get this business planning done A-S-A-P. I know we talked about six months to opening day, but I'm thinking more like three."

Aimee's eyes went wide. "You think we can get it done that fast?"

"We ... can do anything we put our minds to."

Aimee nodded her head. "Yes. You are absolutely right. Let's do this."

They sat at the table for the next three hours, pausing in their business planning only to take care of cookies. By the time they were finished, they had a draft of a menu and a list of equipment items that Aimee would need.

"There. The list is done. Now we just have to figure out how much this equipment is going to cost," said Kiki. She took her first bite of a cookie, her eyes going wide as the taste made its way to her palate. "Holy crap, Aimee! These things are amazing! I can't believe you did this in my kitchen." She examined the cookie more carefully. "I didn't think my oven was capable of putting out something of this quality."

"I could do better with a professional oven," said Aimee, obviously pleased with the compliment.

Kiki shook her head. "We need to get this planning done and fast. These cookies are going to be a hit." She popped the rest of it in her mouth. "So ... back to business. Equipment costs?"

"Why don't you let me work on that while you work on the location and maybe sketch out some design ideas?"

A big grin split Kiki's face. The idea of designing Desperate Measures from the ground up was incredibly energizing. "You don't have to tell me twice." She whipped out her cell phone and scrolled through some names until she found the one she wanted. She pressed the green button and waited for an answer.

"Yo, you got Rich," came the voice on the other end. Rich was one of the DeLuccas' friends, also suffering under the delusion that he should aspire to be and sound like one of the characters in *The Sopranos*.

"Hey, Rich. I need you to do me a favor."

"Don't tell me, let me guess. Ya feelin' sick and ya need Doctor Rich's hot beef injection to make ya feel bettah."

Kiki rolled her eyes. "Do you *get* many girls with that line, Rich?"

"No. Nevah."

"There may be a reason for that. You might want to think about coming up with something a little less obvious."

"Yeah, sure. So, no Doctor Rich then?"

"I just vomited a little in my mouth. Would you stop, please?"

"Oh, dat hurts. Kiki, ya break my heart into very small pieces when ya do dat. All da time ya do it, too. Nevah evah do ya say yes to me. How many times have I tried to take ya out? T'ree? Four?"

"Try thirty five. Listen, Rich. Focus. I need your help, seriously. I want you to find me a piece of real estate."

"Oh. Well why didn't ya say so? Whaddya need? I'm ya guy. You'll nevah get stuck ..."

"Yeah, yeah, I know. *'You'll never get stuck in a ditch, with Rich.'* Classy tagline, Rich. I have it memorized ... it's so hard to forget. Anyway, it's for me and a couple friends. We're starting a new business. A cafe bakery kind of place. We need something commercial, and it's better if it's already got a hood thingy," she paused to look at Aimee who nodded her head in agreement, "and near downtown and a higher end shopping area. Not too big, but large enough for about ten tables or so."

"Oh, so ya ain't openin' another Lola's." He sounded disappointed.

"No. I'm out of that business, Rich. For good."

"Dat's what they all say. But honestly, Kiki, you bein' gone makes Lola's no fun anymore. I only went because-a you."

"So you're not going anymore?" she asked slyly, knowing full well that Rich was a lifer at Lola's. As long as there was one girl there - and all she needed to have for qualifications was a pulse - he was going to be throwing his dollars on the stage.

"Well, I wouldn't go dat far. But I will say in all honesty, may God be my witness, dat I don't like it as *much*. The other girls just don't have da same pizzaz dat you got. Maybe ya could just come back for special appearances and shit like dat."

Kiki was getting annoyed. She'd only ever been able to take Rich in small doses at the best of times. He was a regular at Lola's and tipped well, but he had to. Otherwise, the girls would have completely ignored him. His two good qualities were that he was tenacious and he knew everybody who owned property in the city. He had found real estate for the DeLuccas for years, and Kiki had always heard how he was able to help negotiate better terms from landlords than any other realtor they'd ever worked with. Knowing Rich, he probably grossed the person out so much, they agreed to his terms just to get rid of him.

"Oh, Rich, sorry - I've gotta go. Duty calls. Talk to you soon?"

"Yeah, yeah, I'm on dis. I already have something in mind for ya ... I just have to call and find out da status on it. I'll call ya back in a few hours. Dat good enough for ya? Fast enough?"

"Yes, that's perfect."

"Listen, Kiki ..."

"Yeah?"

"Now dat you're, uh, outta da business and all ... maybe you'd like to go to dinner or somethin' ..."

"Oh, shoot, Rich, I have to go. I'll think about it. Talk to you later!" She hung up the call before waiting for his response. She shivered, grossing out over the visual of Rich on a date. With her.

Aimee raised an eyebrow. "What was that all about? You look like you're going to be sick."

"Ugh. Rich. He's so cheesy, I can hardly stand talking to him sometimes. He's almost as bad as a caricature of a used car salesman. Polyester suit and everything. I just pictured him semi-naked."

"Oh, God, why would you do that? And why are we using him if he's so awful?"

"Because he can find the perfect place. He goes in the category of 'necessary evil'. The DeLuccas used him for Lola's and about five other places they own. He's like an idiot savant when it comes to commercial real estate. He's a social misfit, but apparently the ability to act like a normal person isn't in the job description around here."

Aimee shrugged. "If you trust him, I trust him." She went back to working on the menu. "I'm almost done with the ingredients list." She was typing away on her laptop. "I'm going to send it over to Elizabeth with the menu and equipment stuff. Anything you want me to add from you?"

"No. Just tell her I said hi. I'm going to go online and research design ideas."

Kiki spent the next hour researching color palettes, furniture, and artwork. Ideas sparked other ideas and plans took shape in her mind. She could already picture it - warm, cozy, and vibrant all at the same time. Three independent women, dedicated to creating new lives for themselves, and willing to take desperate measures to make it happen.

elizabeth

$\mathcal{E}$LIZABETH INCORPORATED THE INFORMATION SENT over from Aimee into the pro forma financials she'd been working on for the past few hours. Things were looking really good. Now all she needed to know was the rental amount of the location and she'd be done with this first draft. She was distracted from formatting the reports she was going to print by a text on her phone.

GOT TIME FOR A COFFEE?

It was her cousin, Marcus. "Awesome," she said out into the empty apartment.

YES. COME ON OVER.

She pushed 'send' on her phone, and before she could put it back down on the table, her doorbell rang.

She opened the door to find Marcus standing on her front step with his phone in his hand and a big smile on his face.

"Hello, gorgeous!" he said brightly, walking up to give her a little hug. It was more the type of hug you'd get from a girlfriend than a male cousin, but she was used to it.

"Hello, Marcus. Don't you look dapper today." He was wearing a tweed jacket with a burgundy bow tie, his hair slicked down neatly, instead of flying all over for a change. "You look good in tweed."

"I do, don't I? This is my new style. I'm going for the academic look. What do you think?"

"Well ... you're a lawyer ... so I'm not sure why you'd want to go for the academic look but ... "

"Because, sweet pea, I've accepted a position at UCF as an adjunct professor, and I need to fit the part."

"Marcus, that's great! When did you decide to do that?" Marcus had been a divorce lawyer for many years and did some business law work for a few select clients as well. He'd been good enough to answer her questions over the course of her accounting career about things concerning her clients, and she'd returned the favor by doing his taxes.

"I've always wanted to do this." He didn't meet her eyes when he answered, instead taking a little too much interest in a nearby potted plant.

Elizabeth eyed him suspiciously, closing the door behind him. "That's funny. I don't recall hearing you mention it before." She and Marcus were pretty close. And he had a tendency to go off on different life tangents for the express purpose of chasing tail. Male tail, that is.

"Fine. You've sussed me out. There was this totally gorgeous hunk of a professor who made a visit over to the office, and it just got me thinking ..."

"Thinking what?" she laughed. "That you'd put on a jacket with elbow patches, get a job over there, and land yourself a hot date for Friday night?"

"No. But is there anything wrong with that? I mean, seriously. What do you expect me to do? Internet date? Go on Rent-a-nob dot com? I don't think so." He brushed some imaginary lint off of his lapel.

Elizabeth rubbed his upper arm, soothing his ruffled feathers and trying really hard not to laugh. "No. No one expects that of you. Dating sucks. Rent-a-... what did you call it ... ?"

"Nob. Rent-a-nob dot com."

"Yeah, that. Don't go there. Internet dating sucks. I hear ya."

"Try doing it as a gay divorce lawyer."

"And you think your prospects as a gay professor will be better?"

"Sweetie, they couldn't get any worse."

Elizabeth shrugged. *To each his own.* "Come into the kitchen and sit with me. I have your favorite coffee, and I need your help."

"I live to serve," he sighed as he followed her in. "So what's new in your incredibly exciting life as an accountant?" He obviously was expecting to hear the same old answer, which was usually 'not much'.

Elizabeth smiled as she put down a cup of coffee in front of him, waiting until he took a sip to respond with, "I told my boss to take his job and shove it, and partnered up with an exotic dancer and a divorcée to open up a cafe bakery called Desperate Measures ... but other than that, not much."

Marcus choked on his coffee, leaning forward as he desperately tried to keep from staining his Brooks Brothers jacket and fine cotton shirt.

Elizabeth handed him a napkin.

Once he had gotten himself together, Marcus glared at her. "You did that on purpose. You knew I was going to cough up a lung, and yet you said it anyway. You don't like the jacket, do you? Or is it the tie?" He craned his neck trying to see it for himself.

Elizabeth smiled. "No, I actually *do* like your jacket *and* your tie. I think the whole professor thing suits you. If I were a gay man, I'd be all over you right now."

Marcus dropped his glare, partially mollified. "Thank you. You have excellent taste, as usual. So, tell me. Are you having a mid-life crisis? What exactly is motivating you to drop a nuclear bomb on your oh-so-carefully-crafted life?"

"I'm not old enough to have a mid-life crisis."

"Lack of sex can age a woman. It's a proven fact."

She slapped the back of his hand. "I have sex. Sometimes."

"Having carnal relations with your vibrator doesn't count, love bug."

Elizabeth gave him the stink eye. But deep down she was wondering if there wasn't a grain of truth to what he was saying. She felt older than she should, and budding romance always made her feel young again. Maybe after this business was up and running she could try Internet dating again. *Ugh.* Even the thought of it made her want to go do another spreadsheet. She was better off with numbers than another failed attempt at connecting with someone who valued nothing other than tits and ass.

"Whatever, Casanova. Just drink your coffee." She got up and grabbed a plate off the counter, bringing it over and setting it down in front of him on the table. "Try one of these."

Marcus reached over and took one of Aimee's cookies, biting into it just before lifting his cup of coffee to take another sip. His hand froze when the cup was nearly to his lips. He cocked his head to the right, chewing now more slowly, a frown creasing his forehead. "Hmmm ..."

"What?" Elizabeth asked innocently. Marcus looked like he'd just thought of something, but couldn't put his finger on exactly what it was.

"This ... mmmmm ... my *goodness*. What is this heavenly confection you've tempted me with, young lady?" He slowly reached his arm out, the half-cookie still in his hand, wrapping it around the edge of the plate to drag it closer to him. "Mine."

Elizabeth smiled. "My new business partner baked those."

"I want in. Where do I sign? How much do you want?"

Elizabeth couldn't help but laugh, feeling instantly validated in her decision to go into business with Aimee and Kiki. "We're not taking on any partners."

Marcus pouted, pulling the cookies in tighter.

"But, you can have all the cookies you want, in exchange for legal advice."

"Done. Just so you're aware, I can eat my weight in cookies in a very short period of time before starting the process all over again."

"That's not a problem. I'm working the financials. I'll put an extra line-item in for your cookie budget."

"That's my girl. Now what kind of legal advice do you need?"

"Two kinds, actually. One, to help us set up the business and issues with the partnership."

Marcus waggled a finger at her as he chewed another cookie and took a quick sip of coffee. "No. Not partners. Members. You will have an LLC. It will be better for you to manage; and for tax purposes, as you know, it will be cleaner."

"Fine. So we need that. And one of the partners, Aimee, she's in the middle of a hairy divorce. She needs help. Badly."

"Who's her attorney?"

"She doesn't have one as far as I know. Her ex is a lawyer, and I'm pretty sure he's taking advantage of her."

"Who is it? Do I know him?"

"Jack. Jack ... Parsons."

Marcus choked for a second time that visit. "Jack?! *Gah* ... Jack Parsons? Excuse me ... sorry ... did you say, 'Jack Parsons'?"

Elizabeth nodded.

"Whatever your friend needs, I'm here. I'd like nothing better than to see Jack Parsons' ex wife take him down, down, down. Like all the way down."

"Why the hatred, Marcus?" Elizabeth was smiling, realizing that this was somehow personal to her cousin. And he might be flighty when it came to finding boyfriends and trying new fashions, but he was one hell of a divorce lawyer. All the high-profile cases came his way because he always ended up getting his clients what they wanted. He was like a dog with a bone. Eventually he just wore the competition down; and he was very good at finding dirt.

"Homophobe. Big time. Looks down his nose. Poop doesn't stink. Zero ethics. I've heard things ..."

Elizabeth leaned in and dropped her voice. "Like what kind of things?"

Marcus leaned in and whispered, "Very bad things." And then he winked at her and sat up. "I'm not a gossip. Leave this to me. I'll take care of it. Have her call the office and set up an appointment to come see me Monday morning, first thing. Tell her to tell Lana I said to fit her in immediately."

"I'll make the appointment for her."

"Oh, she's one of those?" he frowned.

"No. She's capable. But she's a nice person, and this Jack guy has really intimidated her. He sent her to the emergency room not that long ago."

Marcus sneered. "Dirtbag. It will be my pleasure to take half of his paycheck. Or more if I can manage it." He stood. "And now, my dear, I must depart. I have things to do, people to see. All manner of important goings on in my life right now."

"You're going to watch *Glee* on your DVR aren't you?"

"Like I said ... important things." He leaned in to kiss her cheeks. "Kiss, kiss. Loves ya."

Elizabeth followed him to the front door.

"Will you be joining the little missus Monday?" he asked.

"Maybe. Should I?"

"Are you her financial advisor?"

"Yes," Elizabeth said without hesitation.

"Then I will see you there. Toodles!" He stepped down to the sidewalk and sauntered over to his convertible M.G. He never walked fast anywhere.

"Bye, Marky Mark!" she yelled.

He waved his hand out of the convertible top, driving away with a muffled putt-putt-putting.

Elizabeth went back into the apartment to send Aimee and Kiki an email informing them of their Monday morning meeting at their new attorney's office. She decided to spring the news about the divorce part of his services later.

22

aimee

$\mathcal{A}$IMEE WRUNG HER HANDS NERVOUSLY in her lap. She hated attorneys. All attorneys ... Elizabeth's assurances that her gay cousin wasn't like the rest of them notwithstanding.

Kiki reached over and squeezed her hands. "Just relax. You're going to be fine."

"I'm so glad you're both here with me. How much of a wimp could I possibly be, right?" Aimee looked at first one and then the other of her friends, feeling ashamed of her weakness.

"You're not a wimp just because you need support during a tough time. Besides, we're not just here for that. We're here about Desperate Measures too, don't forget."

"That's the only reason I agreed to come," mumbled Aimee. She was so nervous about Jack's reaction to her getting a lawyer, it made her stomach hurt. She kept telling herself it was a necessary evil, but all she could think about was how much easier it would be to just let him have his way. She didn't mind starting over with nothing so she could leave all of the Jack part of her life in the past.

The door to the inner office flew open.

ELLE CASEY

"Ladies!" said a bright and cheery voice from the doorway. "Step into my inner sanctum!"

Aimee looked up into the bluest of blue eyes she'd ever seen. Elizabeth's cousin had wavy blond hair, the kind that reminded her of that guy on *The Mentalist*. *Thick, sun-streaked, and playboyish,* was the only way she could think to describe it. She stood in place, staring. His good looks, matched with his prim and proper clothing, complete with small polkadot bow tie, made him a sight to behold.

"Wow," she said, before she thought to stop herself.

He smiled hugely. "I'm going to take that as a good wow." He held out his hand. "You must be Aimee ... "

She smiled back, automatically responding to his good nature. She took his outstretched hand gently and shook it. "Yes. I'm Aimee. I guess that makes you Marcus."

"Indeed it does. So happy to make your acquaintance." He turned his attention to Kiki. "And the statuesque tigress to my right must be Kiki?"

"Right again," she said, shaking his hand and smiling politely. "Nice to meet you."

He kept staring at her. "You could totally pull off a Cher lookalike gig, you know that? You have some of the bone structure ... "

"So I've been told."

"Well," he said as he turned to go into his office, "if you ever do, I'll be buying a ticket. Come in, ladies. We have much to do before your hour is up. Come in, come in."

They followed him inside and took their seats as he shut the door. After making his way around the desk to his high-backed leather chair, he began speaking again. "So. You have a new business, is that what I hear?"

The heads around the table nodded in tandem.

"And a misbehaving almost ex-husband who needs to be reminded of the laws of the State of Florida, is that right?"

Elizabeth and Kiki nodded firmly, but Aimee just shrank a little down into her seat.

Marcus addressed himself only to Aimee. "Sweetie, I know what you're thinking right now. Do you want to know *how* I know?"

"Because you're psychic?"

He smiled. "Aren't you a peach?" Then he got serious again. "No. I know because many of the ladies who come to my office and sit in that chair where you're sitting, feel exactly the same way. And later they tell me what they were thinking as they sat there, during their first appointment. Usually it's something like ... oh ... how they don't want to fight ... or how they just want to move on without causing a fuss. Am I close?"

Aimee couldn't help but smile. "Yes. Very."

"Good. Well, let me tell you something. In all my years of practicing law, I've never *once* had a client come to me later and say, 'I should have gone with my first instinct.' You know what they *do* say, Aimee?"

"No."

"They say, 'I'm so glad you made me see this through to the end. I feel strong again. I feel like I'm in control of my life again. And I know I'm never going to let a jerk like that take my life over and make me lose myself again.'" He fixed her with a stare, as if she and he were the only ones in the room. "Do you want to take your life back, Aimee? Because I can help you do that."

Tears sprung to her eyes as she whispered, "Yes. I'd like that very much."

"Well then!" he nearly shouted, clapping his hands together once very sharply and making them all jump, "let's get this party started! Ladies, Kiki and Elizabeth, you may remain here for part of this conversation, however at some point I will ask you to step out so that my client and I can discuss some things in confidence. But first, let's talk about the nuts and bolts." He paused to take an expensive-looking pen out of his drawer along with a pad of paper.

Aimee snuck glances at her friends and noticed that the expressions on their faces mirrored her inner thoughts. They were inspired and moved. Marcus was freaking awesome. Aimee felt like Rocky Balboa on the stairs, getting ready to train and then kick some serious butt. She reached on either side of her and squeezed her friends' hands.

Marcus went on to gather the basics about the marriage and how it had come to an end. His laughing and joking manner took a back seat to his probing and frowning concentration, his head nodding or shaking from side to side in all the right parts. When Aimee told him about the insurance he held up his pen and pointed it first at her and then the two other girls. "No. You will not be signing over that insurance policy. Over my dead body, and I promise you, I'm hard to kill. Two people have already tried. True story. But, as I said ... No. Capital N, capital O." He looked at Elizabeth. "You know where I'm going with this, right, Lizzie?"

"Yes." She turned to look at Aimee. "Your insurance policy is an asset. It's worth possibly quite a bit of money. If he wants you to sign it over, it must mean you're the owner of that policy, which means he can't do anything to it without your written authorization."

"Right," said Marcus. "And speaking of, we'll want to get together a detailed list of all marital assets. Do you have something like that?"

"Um, well, I used to."

"Used to?"

"Well, Jack made me keep binders of all of our expenses. They're back at the old house. He's probably figured out I've left though, so I don't know if I'll be able to get back in."

Kiki patted her hand. "We'll get back in. Consider it done, Marcus."

"What are these binders like, Aimee? And what did you do with them?" asked Elizabeth.

"They have receipts taped into them for anything we bought. I put the amounts into software on the computer, too. They're sitting on shelves in the home office."

"Get me a copy of that data, both what's on the computer and in the binders. Every bit of it," said Marcus, making notes on his pad.

Aimee started to get really uncomfortable.

"I can see you squirming, Aimee. What's wrong?" asked Kiki.

Aimee looked at all of their faces and wasn't sure how to say what she was feeling. "Well, I'm not sure. I guess I feel like I'm being sneaky."

Marcus put his pen down and folded his hands. "Okay, time to get real, sweet pea. Did Jack, or did he not, have repeated sex with another woman during your marriage and get said other twenty-something-year-old woman pregnant?"

"Yes." Just hearing it out loud made her feel awful all over again. Just like the day she found out.

"And did he, or did he not purchase ...," he looked down at his notes and then back up again, "...a townhouse for said girlfriend using your marital savings?"

"Yes. He did." She was feeling more and more humiliated by the second.

"Aimee, the guy used you to wipe his feet on. Did he or did he not make you drop out of school? Cut you off from the world? Tell you that you sucked at the one thing you love - baking? And cause you to fall and crack your head open?" finished Kiki, obviously losing patience.

Aimee looked down, feeling terrible and knowing she wasn't going to be able to stop the tears. "Yes. That's all true. I'm an idiot."

Elizabeth handed her a tissue and took her hand. "Aimee, no one is saying you're an idiot. And you're not. We know this is hard for you. You're a lover, not a fighter. But if you need to, you can lean on Kiki and me for the fight part. You have to stand up for yourself, that's why we're reminding you of the reasons you have to be strong. You might not realize this now, but you *need* to do this. For yourself ... your soul. Don't let him take *everything* from you."

"He already has."

"No. He hasn't," said Kiki grabbing her other hand and squeezing it. "You still have the sweet, funny, loving person that's inside of you, hiding behind the wimp that's going to have to take a rest for a little while; because the time for running away is over. It's time to stand up for yourself, like Lizzie said."

Aimee looked up and saw Kiki smiling at Elizabeth. Aimee looked at Elizabeth in time to see her stick out her tongue at Kiki.

Elizabeth caught Aimee looking and said, "I hate that nickname. Marcus has been teasing me with it since I was a little kid."

Aimee felt emboldened by her friends' support. And she loved that they teased each other in the middle of the chaotic pain. It totally made her feel like she'd always imagined the girls in the story *Little Women* felt like - sisters who had a tight bond that really came into play when the chips were down. And the chips were definitely down right now. At least in her life. "I hear what you're saying. And I'm going to try. I really am." She hoped that was good enough for them because it was all she was capable of promising right now. She hadn't realized until this moment just how much Jack had taken from her. It wasn't just the house and the money and the fidelity of their marriage. He had taken some essential part of her and snuffed it out, or caused her to bury it so deeply, she didn't know if she'd ever get it back. She sighed in resignation.

"She's on board," assured Kiki. "Let's move on."

"Okay," said Marcus. "I just need a few moments alone with my client, and then you ladies will be free to go. And I hope your first order of business will be to get those binders for me."

Elizabeth and Kiki stood. "You bet," said Elizabeth. Thanks, Marky Mark, for all your help."

"I'm not finished with you. You'll come back in for a few minutes to discuss the new business when we're done here. It'll only take five minutes."

Aimee waited for the other two to leave and shut the door behind them before she began speaking. "Marcus, I just want to apologize. I'm so sorry I'm such a wimp. I really appreciate your help. I'm sorry if I'm not the most ideal client." She felt so bad that Elizabeth was calling in favors for her so that she could have a lawyer. Jack was such a jerk. He was going to make this Marcus person wish he'd never agreed to this.

"You're worried about what Jack's going to say."

"Yes."

"And do."

"Yes."

"To you and to me, if I'm not mistaken."

Aimee looked up. "How did you know? You *are* psychic, aren't you?"

"No. I've just been doing this for too long. I'm not sure about the psychology behind it, but so often I see the women being cheated on tending to be very sweet, nice people, who have a bad habit of blaming themselves for everything terrible that happens to them."

"Well, that's true, that I do that - but I'm not sure that makes me a nice person. The divorce is mostly my fault."

"How do you figure?"

"Well, for years, Jack wanted to have children. And I can't. So it was a big disappointment. Plus, he liked to entertain his clients and colleagues, and I wasn't very good at that. I think ... I think I embarrassed him with my ... goofiness or whatever. I don't know." She couldn't finish. It was too humiliating. She felt like she was sitting with a therapist, and she wasn't even able to pay him.

Marcus got up and came around the desk to sit at her side, taking the seat that Elizabeth had been in. He reached over and grasped her hands, pulling them out of her lap so they rested in between the two of them. His hands were warm and dry, soft to the touch. They were the hands of a lawyer who shuffled paper all day and left the manual labor to someone else.

"Look at me, love bug. Right here in my eyes. I know it's difficult and you might feel like crying, but that's okay."

Aimee really didn't want to, but she did it anyway because she knew he was just trying to be nice. As her eyes made contact with his, she was immediately struck by the kindness she saw there. And it was in such stark contrast to his lawyerness, it caused her to pause her normal inner diatribe against herself.

"I'm going to share a secret with you. This will be just between you and me. Those two wonderful ladies outside that door don't need to know this part, okay?"

Aimee nodded her head wordlessly. She was on the edge of her seat wondering what he was going to say. It felt like it was going to be monumental.

"Years ago, when I was young and foolish and fancied myself in love, I found myself in an emotionally abusive relationship. Over a period of three years, I suffered the slow and insidious breakdown of my sense of self. Little by little - with what seemed like innocuous, harmless comments - my lover tore the foundation of *me* down, brick by brick, until almost nothing of me remained ..."

Aimee's heart squeezed painfully for him. He was so beautiful with those earnest blue eyes. *Who could have done such a thing?*

"You know what the worst part is?" Marcus asked.

Aimee shook her head, unable to speak.

"I *let* him do it. I left me ... Marcus ... in the dust. I became this other person - the one I thought he wanted me to be. I would have done anything to please him, to make him happy. I left my friends and family behind ... " He paused, rubbing the back of her hands with his thumbs and looking down for a moment. When he looked back up, his eyes were shining with unshed tears. "When I'd finally been brought down to my lowest point ... when I had finally let him convince me that I was worthless and would never measure up to anyone's standards of beauty, intelligence, or worth, someone stepped in and saved me. She grabbed me by the shoulders and gave me a good, hard shake and told me to snap my sorry butt out of that horrible dark place and get away from him. She made me see the web of hatred and self-loathing that my lover had spun around me. I'd been trapped willingly, but she wouldn't let me feel the shame of it. She said something to me that I'll never forget, and it helped me, so I'm going to say it to you too. Maybe it will give you that little ray of hope it gave me, and the inspiration to keep on going and trying to get out of the darkness."

"What did she say?" whispered Aimee.

"She told me that the only person's expectations I ever needed to measure up to were my own. No one decides for me who I am, who I need to be, or what I should be doing with myself, but me. And she told me I was perfect, exactly the way I was, faults and all. Because faults are what make us human, and ultimately unique and wonderful."

Marcus reached up and took Aimee by the shoulders, gently shaking them for effect. "This is me, giving you a good shake. Now, snap your sorry butt out of that well of pity that you're drowning in and take responsibility for your happiness." He grabbed a tissue and used it to wipe the tears that were streaming down her face. "Jack does not get to decide who you are, what you can do, or what you *should* do. Jack does not decide what your world is going to be like. You are gorgeous, fierce, loving and lovable ... today is the day you take your life back. One thing at a time. Yes, it's going to be hard sometimes. You've buried the real Aimee down in there somewhere, and she's afraid to come out. Be patient with her. It will be worth it, I promise." He sat back and just stared at her, practically insisting she respond.

Aimee didn't feel forced though, she was compelled by her own curiosity and newfound sense of hope to speak up. "What ever happened to that guy? The jerk who tried to destroy you?"

"He destroyed a few more lost souls before drinking himself to death."

"That's horrible," she said, feeling sick for Marcus and wondering how he could possibly have ended up so fabulous with such a terrible experience in his past.

"He was a gay man who was never okay with who he was. He battled it and hated himself for it nearly his entire life. He couldn't deny who he was, always drawn to relationships with other men; but he hated them for being attractive to him, so he launched this psychological warfare on those around him in an effort to cleanse his conscience. At least, that's what my dime store psychological handbook said." He smiled, making light of the analysis of his painful past.

"Well, Jack isn't gay, so he wasn't torturing me over something like that."

"No, but he's got issues. I don't know what they are - but they did cause him to systematically tear you down, to the point that you want to run and hide whenever his name is mentioned."

"I don't want to feel that way anymore."

"I know. That's why I shared my secret with you." He stood and went to the door. "I'm going to let the girls in now, if you're ready."

"In a second. I just want to thank you first." She stood up and went over to him, giving him a quick hug. "Sorry. I'm a hugger." His hand reached around and patted her on the back.

"Don't apologize. It was my pleasure. I hate to see a beautiful soul being hidden away."

Aimee released him. "Okay. You can let in the troops. And thank you. Again. For sharing that part of your life with me." She returned to her seat, blowing her nose and doing her best to wipe her face clean.

The girls joined her, looking at her worriedly. Aimee smiled, trying to reassure them that she was okay.

Marcus went back to his chair. "Okay, so last on the list of things to do is business start-up."

"Yes," said Kiki. All three women nodded their heads.

"You want an LLC. Are we doing an even split?"

They all looked at each other and nodded affirmatively.

"Good. I need you to send me what each of you are contributing for your share - just a simple email will do. Are you planning on franchising?"

"Not at this time," answered Elizabeth.

"Adding additional investors?"

"No," said Kiki.

"Are any of you married, other than Aimee here?"

"No. But is that going to be a problem for her?" asked Elizabeth.

"Maybe. Maybe not. I just ask that you not share with Jack or anyone he knows any information about this business. If you start it during the marriage, it could get mixed up in the process. I'd prefer if you officially start it after the divorce judgment is final."

"Can you fast-track it?" asked Elizabeth.

Marcus smiled a little deviously. "I have some ideas on that. It's possible. Let me get back to you."

"We were hoping for a three-month start-up," said Kiki, looking anxious.

"It could be possible ... if my theory proves out. I'll let you know."

"Feel like sharing that theory?" asked Elizabeth.

"Not yet. Give me a few days. In the meantime, I don't want any of you signing any documents or officially declaring the existence of this business."

"We won't," said Elizabeth. "Right, girls?"

Kiki and Aimee agreed they wouldn't.

"Okay, that's all I need for now. Elizabeth, keep in contact with me about the business." He looked at Aimee. "Aimee, go home and open up a new email account. Use a brand-new password you've never used before. Send me the address. This will be just for you and me to use. Don't share the username or password with anyone except these two girls, if you want. Do not write the password down on anything. Do not use one that Jack could guess - meaning, don't use your birthday, anniversary, pet names, etcetera in the password, okay? Pick something random. Got it?"

"Yes." Aimee nodded her head, feeling good about having some sort of action plan to follow when she left his office. When she'd walked in it was just a place of business for Elizabeth's cousin. Now it almost felt like a safe haven - one guarded by a strong, kind, and compassionate warrior.

Marcus waved a finger at all three girls. "You ladies have a mission. Get me copies of the binders and computer data." He stabbed his index finger into the top of the desk for emphasis. "I want it on my desk by tomorrow."

"Yes, sir," saluted Elizabeth as she stood. "Come on, girls. We need to go do what the boss says."

Marcus smiled winningly. "I like that. The boss. Feel free to call me that all the time," he said as he came around to open the door for them.

"Not gonna happen, cousin," said Elizabeth, giving him a kiss on the cheek and a quick hug. "See you soon."

Kiki went next, giving him a hug and kiss on the cheek too. "Thanks, Marcus. You're a gem."

Marcus smiled. "My pleasure. I always love to spend time in the company of beautiful women."

Aimee came next. Just looking at him made her want to start crying again. Who knew her personal savior would come in the form of a gorgeous gay lawyer wearing a polka dot tie?

Marcus took her into a strong hug, not at all what she would have expected from a serious lawyer. She let herself enjoy it though, melting into the strength he shared with her.

"You take care of yourself, you hear?" he demanded.

"Yes. I hear you. And thank you again. This means ... more to me than I can say right now."

Marcus let her go and stepped back. "All you have to do in return are two things..."

"What two things?" she asked curiously, hoping it wouldn't be expensive.

"First, find Aimee again." He winked at her. "And second, you need to keep me in those cookies. I'm addicted. They're like crack to me."

Aimee looked at him confused. "Excuse me?"

"I gave him some of your cookies," explained Elizabeth. "Actually, he stole all of them from me. I only had one before he took off with the plate."

Marcus looked hurt. "You promised I could have lifetime cookie access in exchange for being your attorney. I just assumed that started at the first taste." He worked really hard to look affronted.

Aimee smiled. "I'll bake you as many as you want." She felt good being able to pay him back in some way for all his help. If she knew Jack, he was going to make Marcus suffer.

"Be careful what you promise. I am an absolute fiend for cookies." He patted his only slightly rounded belly. The girls stepped out of his office and out into the hall leading to the foyer. "I'm going to let you show yourselves out. I need to jump on a few things before I head to court for a hearing." He wiggled his fingers at them. "Tah-tah!" he said before closing the door.

They walked silently out of the office, only speaking to thank Lana, the secretary, before going down to their cars.

"Well, that was a trip," said Kiki in the parking lot. "You didn't warn us that we were going to be in the presence of a god, first of all."

Elizabeth smiled. "He hates it when people say he's handsome."

"I hate when people say I'm pretty, so I can relate," said Kiki. She looked at Aimee and then Elizabeth. "Was that conceited? I'm sorry. It's not like I think I'm all that."

"You are all that," said Aimee, looping her arm through Kiki's elbow. "And so is Marcus. He's like an angel or something."

"Angel? Maybe. Just don't piss him off in the courtroom. He's like an angel of death, then. Jack's going to be very sorry if he tries to pull any funny business on my cousin."

"So we're going over to get those binders now, right?" asked Kiki.

"Yes," said Elizabeth, looking at Aimee.

"Are you guys sure you want to do that? I could go by myself. Seriously." Aimee felt so guilty about bringing them into the mess she had created.

"If it were my ex-husband and me needing to go back into that house, would you let me go alone?" asked Kiki.

"Well, no. But that's different."

"In what way? Because you're tougher than me?"

"Heck no. I'm a marshmallow compared to you."

"Okay then. In what way?"

Aimee felt so uncomfortable. She couldn't explain herself.

Elizabeth rescued her with her common sense. "Fact is, it doesn't matter. We're like the three musketeers here. We can't get this business off the ground until we have this divorce final. So it's in all our interests to get this stuff done now. Consider this part of our business start-up planning."

Aimee smiled, feeling a million times better. "I can do that." The guilt was already weighing less heavily on her shoulders.

"Done," agreed Kiki. "Now let's go. We can get the binders and fit in that workout we talked about after, if you girls are interested."

"I need to do it," said Aimee. "I have energy to work off. Anger I think, too."

"Okay, I can run home and get my things after we get the stuff for Marcus," said Elizabeth. "So I'll follow you guys over to Aimee's old place?"

"Yep. I'll go slow so you won't lose us," said Kiki, smirking only a little.

"What are you trying to say?" asked Elizabeth. "Are you knocking my car? I'll have you know that it gets excellent gas mileage for a sedan."

"Gas mileage isn't sexy," said Kiki. "Camaros? Now *they* are sexy."

Elizabeth smiled. "See you at Aimee's."

Aimee decided it probably was wise of Elizabeth not to get into an argument with Kiki about cars. The Camaro obviously meant a lot to her and Elizabeth did drive a Buick. Even Aimee knew there was no comparison between the two when it came to sheer power.

Aimee and Kiki got into the car and left the parking lot, headed in the direction of Aimee's old place.

"Do you think Jack will be there?" asked Kiki.

"I hope not. He golfs on Mondays sometimes. Other times he's doing I don't know what with his girlfriend or working."

"The slut."

"Yes, the slut."

"I think we should just call her that from now on."

Aimee giggled. "Okay. He's probably with the slut."

"Okay, well, just in case, do you have the phone number for your boyfriend handy?"

Aimee looked at her confused. "Marcus?"

Kiki shook her head. "No goof. *Joe.* Marcus is my new boyfriend, so stay away."

Aimee smiled. "Marcus is neither of our boyfriends, and yes, I have Joe's number in my purse."

"Good. I hope we won't need it, but just in case, be ready to dial. Put it in your phone."

Aimee did as she was told, worrying the entire time that Kiki might be as psychic as Marcus seemed to be. She hoped she was wrong about that.

23

kiki

$\mathcal{K}$IKI PULLED HER CAR INTO the driveway of Aimee's house.

"It looks empty," said Aimee, hope in her voice.

"Let's hope it stays that way while we're here."

They got out and went to the front door. Aimee tried her key, but it wouldn't work. "He changed the locks. I knew he'd do that."

"Asshole. You still have stuff in there. He has no right to do that."

"Well, he did it."

Elizabeth joined them on the front porch. "What's going on?"

"He changed the locks."

"Oh. Well. I guess we tried." She shrugged.

"Bullshit. We're getting inside," said Kiki. *There is no way this douche bag is going to keep Aimee out of here. He's done enough intimidating for one marriage.* "What other entrances are there?" she asked Aimee.

"There's one around the back and a side door going into the garage."

"Come on. Show me."

All three women went around first to the side of the house and then to the back. All of the locks had been changed.

"So what now?" asked Aimee. "Gym?"

"Don't give up so easily, Aimee," said Kiki, her eyes roaming across the back of the house. "That window up there. Could it be unlocked?" She was pointing to the master bedroom window.

"Possibly. I used to open it sometimes in the evening, when it was nice outside. I don't remember locking it ever."

"What are you thinking, Kiki? You can't climb up there," said Elizabeth, her tone making it clear she thought her friend was crazy.

"Not without a ladder, I can't. Aimee, do you have any nice neighbors here? Someone who might loan us one?"

"Um, maybe. There's a retired couple two doors down who are usually home."

"Let's go."

They got lucky. The lady of the house was home, and she was more than happy to loan them a ladder to get a cat out of a tree. They carried it together, down the sidewalk.

"I feel really foolish," said Elizabeth.

"I just hope Jack doesn't come back while we're doing this," said Aimee.

"He probably feels all secure in the fact that you won't be able to get in, so he won't bother coming around much," said Kiki.

"What if he's moved the binders?" grunted out Elizabeth, now struggling to keep her end of the ladder up.

"He won't," said Aimee, also a little breathless. "He doesn't want Tiffany getting her ... hands on them."

"Why do you say that?" asked Kiki, not yet feeling the strain, but switching her hand position to get a better grip.

"I get the feeling he's hiding as much from her as he ... hid from me." Aimee's breath was starting to come out in huffs.

"I wouldn't be surprised. How did you figure that out? Did he say something?" asked Kiki.

"Well, I suggested he take the binders ... and have her start taking care of his expenses ... and he just got ... all nervous and said he didn't want her ... involved in his business. *Phew!* This ladder is *heavy!*"

"What an ass. That Tiffany girl deserves what she's getting. I cannot figure out why a woman who has slept with a married man expects him to be honest with her. It just blows my mind," said Kiki.

"Yeah. And she's having a ... child with him. Aimee, I hope you don't ... hate me for saying this ... but you're lucky you didn't get pregnant ... when you were married to him. Dammit, this ladder *is* heavy!" Elizabeth hiked it up higher, readjusting her hold. "Could you imagine the heartache you'd be going through right now with custody issues ... added to all this?"

"I know. Don't even make me ... think of it. It makes me glad I'm barren." She grunted out a breath of air as she tried to lift the ladder higher.

Kiki could tell she was almost ready to drop it. "Not much farther, girls, just keep going ... "

"Barren? Who says that anymore?" asked Elizabeth.

"Seriously," agreed Kiki. "That's exactly what I said."

"It's more dramatic," said Aimee.

"As if you need more drama in your life right now," said Kiki, dryly.

"You have a point there," agreed Aimee, gamely.

They finally arrived at the house and worked the ladder around to the back, leaning it up against the house under the window.

"Phew! Okay. So who's going up?" asked Elizabeth, breathing heavily and looking at the other two as she wiped her hands together, trying to dust off the dirt.

"Aimee, do you want the honors? Ready to take back control of your life?" Kiki lifted her eyebrow in challenge.

Aimee smiled. "Yes. As a matter of fact, I am." She huffed out a big breath of air before mounting the ladder and going all the way to the top without stopping. "Okay, guys!" she shouted down, nervous energy evident in her voice. "This is really high! I'm trying not to freak out!"

"Just try the window. Don't let go of the ladder!" yelled Elizabeth. She rolled her eyes at Kiki. "Are you having a small heart attack like I am right now?"

"Yes. But she has to do this."

Elizabeth looked up to watch their small friend trying to remove the screen from the window. Three seconds later it came falling down to the ground. "I know. You're right. I just keep thinking about how I want to protect her."

"Me too. Something about her just brings that out in people. Marcus was good with her today."

Elizabeth smiled warmly. "Yeah. He's pretty amazing. He's had his own hard times. I wouldn't be surprised if he shared a little of it with her today."

They both heard Aimee's shouts of glee at the same time and looked up.

"Yay! It's open!" Her bottom half disappeared inside.

They let go of the ladder and went over to the back door, waiting to be let in. Aimee's face eventually showed up in the window and she waved, a huge smile on her face. The door lock slid back, making a faint clicking sound. Aimee pulled the door open and started to say something she was obviously excited about, when the faint sound of a *beep-beep-beep* came from the front of the house.

"What's that?" asked Elizabeth looking at Kiki and Aimee.

"Do you have an alarm?" asked Kiki.

"Not that I know of?" Aimee said questioningly, doubt shading her voice.

Kiki pushed the door open wider, yelling, "I think you just set off an alarm!" as she ran inside to locate it. The other two followed on her heels.

Kiki stopped at a small white box near the front door. She flipped up the lid to reveal a keypad, looking over at Aimee's stunned face. "Any idea what the code would be?"

Aimee shook her head slowly. "It could be anything. Birthday, anniversary, a word ... I don't know."

"Okay, where are the binders? We have about three minutes to get them and get the hell out of here before the cops show up."

Aimee stood as if frozen in place. The pace of the beeping increased.

"*Go,* Aimee!" yelled Elizabeth, not unkindly, but trying to get her moving.

"Oh, *shoot!* Come this way!" she ran across the foyer and into a room, passing through it quickly to access another next to it. Kiki and Elizabeth entered after her.

"There!" she shouted, pointing to a big built-in shelf. Lined up, five feet high and four feet wide, were four full rows of binders.

"Holy shit, Aimee. Those have all your receipts in them?" asked Kiki incredulously.

"I've never seen anything like this," said Elizabeth, sounding stunned.

"That's all of them. For the past five years. Everything we ever bought."

"Grab 'em!" said Kiki, snapping out of her daze. "Where's the computer?"

"There. On the desktop."

Elizabeth ran over and clicked the mouse. "What's the password?"

"Jack."

Kiki rolled her eyes. *Of course it is.* She kept her thoughts to herself, not wanting to rub anymore salt into Aimee's wounds today. She'd had plenty of that done already.

"It's not working."

"We don't have time for this. Just unplug the tower and bring it."

"I don't think you need to," said Aimee, not sounding exactly sure of herself.

"Why are you saying that?"

"I'll explain later. Let's just get the binders." She moved over to the shelves and started pulling them down, beginning on the top row. "These are the most recent. I'd start here, in case we run out of time."

The telephone rang in the kitchen.

They all froze in place, staring at each other.

"That's the alarm company," said Kiki. "Go talk to them."

ELLE CASEY

"What am I supposed to say?!" said Aimee, in full-on panic mode.

"Try to guess what password Jack used," said Kiki, her anxiety increasing. "If you can't figure it out, stall them! Tell them your husband did it and forgot to give you the code or something, I don't know! Wing it!"

Aimee raced off to answer the phone. As soon as Kiki heard Aimee pick up the line, she jumped back to the task of running binders out to the car. On her second trip, Aimee came dashing out of the kitchen.

"They said they aren't sending the police, but they're calling Jack's cell phone. He's going to come!" she screeched.

"Get some binders and move your ass!" said Kiki, feeling a little panicked herself.

Elizabeth came running by, her arms full of binders. *"Go! Go!"* she yelled.

They were on the last row, when Elizabeth yelled from the front door. "Does Jack drive a sports car? A red one?"

"Yes!" yelled Aimee. She and Kiki froze, carrying the last of the binders in their arms.

"He's here! He just parked behind Kiki!"

"Ohmygod, ohmygod, ohmygod," chanted Aimee, "we are *so* screwed. He's going to kill me! These binders are his life!"

Kiki made a split second decision. "Aimee, go out the back! Now! Hurry!" Then she yelled toward the front. "Elizabeth, lock that front door!!"

They all met in the front hallway. "Let's go! Out the back. Go! Hurry up!"

They hauled butt to the kitchen and out of the house, going through the back door. Elizabeth grabbed half of Aimee's books from her while they ran across the back part of the house and snuck around the side of the garage, slowly making their way toward the driveway where Kiki's car was parked. Elizabeth's car was at the curb. She wasn't blocked in, but Kiki was. They stood at the corner of the garage, both Kiki's and Elizabeth's cars in sight. Jack was somewhere in the house, since he wasn't in his car anymore and they couldn't see him in the front yard.

"Aimee!" yelled a very angry male voice from near the back door.

"Run!" said Kiki.

They took off to their cars, throwing open the doors of the Camaro as fast as they could with their arms full and tossing the binders in without worrying about keeping them organized or even closed. The books fell into a heap on the floor of the back seat, joining the few that were already piled there. The rest of them were in her trunk. Kiki briefly thanked the designers of the Camaro who had come up with a trunk big enough to haul dead bodies around in - or several binders full of incriminating evidence against cheating ex-husbands.

"What the ... Aimee!" shouted Jack, from the side of the house. They'd been spotted.

"Elizabeth, get to your car and haul ass outta here! When you're far enough away, call us!" yelled Kiki.

Elizabeth wasted no time, sprinting over to her car and jumping in. Kiki heard the engine start as she and Aimee scrambled to get into the Camaro.

"What are you going to do?" screeched a panicked Aimee. "His car is in the way!!" She turned to look out the windshield and screamed bloody murder.

Kiki looked up in time to see Jack coming at them at a jog from the side of the house, bad intentions written all over his face.

"What the *fuck* are you doing breaking into my house, you whore?!" he yelled, spittle flying out of his mouth and his face beet red.

Kiki started the engine and threw the car into drive.

"Jack! Stay away!" screamed Aimee. *"Stay away from me!"*

He got near the front of the car, and stood there for a couple seconds, fuming, his clenched teeth making his jaw stand out, his eyes narrowed in a vicious look that made shivers go up Kiki's spine. *He's mad enough to kill.*

Kiki took a deep calming breath and stared him down, challenging him with her eyes. "Go ahead, ass wipe. Make my day," she said in a conversational tone, squeezing the wheel over and over, waiting for him to make his move.

He slammed his fists down on the hood.

"Don't fucking hit my car, asshole," said Kiki loudly. The fear flew out of her heart to be replaced by indignation. No one touched her car like that. *No one.*

"Oh yeah, bitch? What are you going to do about it?" He hit her car again. Only harder.

"Well *this*, for one," she said in a low, menacing tone.

"Kiiiikiiiiii," whined Aimee. "What are you doooinnnggg?"

Kiki put one foot on the brake and one on the gas. She pushed the brake down with her left and pushed on the accelerator a bit with her right, revving the engine and causing the car to surge up in the back and bounce a little, making it look as if it were going to leap forward and run him over.

Jack jumped back. "You crazy bitch! What are you going to do? Run me over? I'm calling the cops. That's *assault*." He pointed his finger at her sharply.

"Kiki, don't run him over! I don't want you to go to jail!" begged Aimee.

Kiki didn't take her eyes from Jack for a second. "Shush, would ya? I have a plan." Then she started talking softly again, as if to herself. "That's right, little bastard. Come on over here to the side of the car. Here ... I'll roll my window down and give you a nice target. You look like the type to hit a woman."

She kept her right hand on the wheel and slowly cranked her window down, making sure he'd see that her face was now exposed. She yelled out to Jack, "Get out of the way or I'm going to run your small dick over!"

He took the bait, running over to the side of the car as he roared, intending to attack Kiki. But she was waiting for him. Aimee screamed like a wild woman, coming completely unglued at the idea of Jack getting to her friend, but Kiki didn't have time to explain what she was going to do. She whipped the wheel to the left at the same time she slammed her foot down on the accelerator, a split second later letting up off the brake.

The Camaro's rear wheels spun out, sending small rocks and debris up behind them to pelt Jack's car, making a sound like a miniature machine gun. The back end of the rear-wheel drive vehicle spun out to the right, swinging the car around until its front end was pointing toward Aimee's lawn. As soon as Kiki let up off the accelerator just a bit, the tires grabbed and propelled the car forward, narrowly missing Jack, but at the same time making it impossible for him to reach Kiki's open window before she and Aimee were shooting out across the front lawn.

"Hold on!" Kiki yelled, spinning the car to the left again, leaving a big skid mark in the grass as she got the car pointed out toward the road.

Aimee screamed and grabbed onto the dashboard with one hand and the oh-shit handle with the other. The car continued, careening forward and running over landscaping rocks and the curb before bouncing back onto the street and zooming over to the other side. Kiki jerked the wheel one more time to the left, getting the car under control, and headed out of the neighborhood.

Once the car stopped rocking and Kiki was able to convince her brain to let her foot off the gas, they found themselves three blocks away, the engine humming along quietly as if they hadn't just totally pulled a page out of the *Dukes of Hazzard* playbook to escape the clutches of Aimee's crazy almost-ex-husband.

Aimee slowly peeled her hand off the dashboard and released the vinyl loop by the window. She dropped her face into her hands, her shoulders quaking. Kiki looked over at her nervously, feeling terrible.

"Aimee, hon, I'm sorry. I know I scared the shit out of you back there. I'm sorry about the grass, too. I'll pay for it. I didn't mean to get you in any trouble."

Kiki was shocked to hear laughter as a response.

Aimee pulled her hands away from her face, and Kiki was able to see for the first time that Aimee wasn't upset. She was laughing her butt off.

Kiki felt her own smile starting to come, unbidden, reveling in the joy she saw on her friend's face.

"*That!* Was *the most. Amazing* thing. I have *ever* seen a woman do. In my *entire life!*"

Kiki felt her heart fill with pride. "Yeah. It was pretty friggin' awesome, wasn't it?"

"Holy cannolis. Let's do it again!" She bounced up and down on the seat, clapping her hands. "Do it again! Make Jack pee his pants again!"

Her enthusiasm was infectious. Kiki would never go looking for trouble like that, but she glanced up in her rearview mirror, just playfully acting as if she were going to turn around and go back for more. Unfortunately, the hilarity of the moment ended in a flash, the moment she noticed the tiny red dot behind them getting closer and bigger.

"Oh, hell," said Kiki, pressing on the accelerator.

"What?" asked Aimee, a big grin still on her face. "Are we out of gas or something?" She looked at Kiki's gauges curiously.

"No. We have company. Behind us."

Aimee turned around, and her smile disappeared instantly. "Oh, shoot. What are we going to do?" she asked, the panic creeping back into her voice.

"You are going to call Joe. Right now!"

"Okay, okay!" said Aimee, scrambling for her purse and phone. A few seconds later, Kiki heard Aimee's voice. "Um ... hello? Joe? ... Yeah, hi. This is Aimee. I'm not sure if you remember me but ... oh you do? Oh ... that's so sweet!"

"Aimee! Kind of urgent here!"

"Oh, shoot, yeah, Joe, I hate to do this on our first call, but I really, really need your help. Well, actually, my ex-husband is following my friend Kiki and me in his car, and well, he's super angry right now. I'm afraid he's going to try and hurt her or me or both of us. I don't know ... yeah, we're um ... hold on a second." She looked at the passing street signs and then at Kiki. "Where are we?"

"Tell him we're about a mile north of that donut place near Maggie's. He'll know what I'm talking about." Kiki was in the neighborhood near Lola's now. She knew this area well and felt confident that she could stay one step ahead of Jack here, at least for a little while.

Aimee repeated the location to Joe and then said, "Hold on, I'll ask." She turned to Kiki. "Are we going north or south?"

"South."

"We're going south." Aimee nodded her head a few times and then said, "He said to keep going south slowly and he'll catch up. He's not far."

"Tell him he's got five minutes, max."

Aimee relayed the information and stayed on the phone with Joe while Kiki concentrated on not getting stuck in front of Jack at any stoplights. She had to run two yellows to make sure that didn't happen, and for the first time in her life was very upset that there were no cops around to pull her over for doing it. It was the longest five minutes of her life before she saw those red and blue lights in her rearview mirror.

"Oh, thank God," said Kiki, breathing out a sigh of relief. "Joe's back there." Kiki watched as Jack slowed down and pulled to the side of the road, the police car directly behind him. Kiki kept driving, listening in on Aimee's conversation.

"Yes. The red Aston Martin. That's Jack, my ex-husband. He tried to attack Kiki at my house when we were getting some of my things out, and then he chased us." She was silent for a few seconds.

Kiki glanced over in time to see a sweet smile creep onto her friend's face.

"Okay. I can do that. Alright. I'll talk to you later, then." She pulled the phone away from her face and put it in her lap, pressing the red button with her thumb and sighing as she stared out the windshield.

"What? What'd he say?" asked Kiki. It sounded like something good, and she knew Aimee could use some good news for a change.

"He wants to meet me after his shift. He's going to give Jack a ticket for speeding. He said that will give us enough time to get out of the area."

"Wow. Talk about a prince charming. I think you found yourself a good one, there, Aims."

"I don't know. I'm not sure if I'm ready to date."

"Why not?"

Aimee shrugged her shoulders and said nothing. Her phone rang in her lap. "It's Elizabeth." She pushed the green button. "Hello, Lizzie." She rolled her eyes. "Okay, Elizabeth. Do you want to meet us at Kiki's?" She paused and then gave her the directions, finishing with, "See you there in ten."

"When was the last time you had sex?" asked Kiki when Aimee hung up the phone.

"What?!" said Aimee, half laughing and half sputtering.

"I'm serious. You said you weren't ready to date, so I guess that means you and Jack were close and you're not ready to let him go."

"*Pfft.* Right. I think it's been ... six months? Maybe longer?"

"Oooh, ouch. That sucks."

"Not really. He wasn't very good at it."

Kiki smiled. "Oh, that's right. Okay, so if you're not pining for Jack, why not? You're single. Joe's single, I assume. He's hot. He's at your beck and call when lunatics are after you." She looked over to make sure Aimee was paying attention and to see her reaction before she continued. "Plus he has those big, veiny hands you like so much."

Aimee reached over and smacked her lightly. "Stop. You're embarrassing me."

"Please. You have nothing to be embarrassed about. You're talking to a stripper here."

Aimee smiled. "You weren't a stripper, first of all. You were an exotic dancer. And you're not one anymore. And how exactly is that supposed to keep me from being embarrassed?"

Kiki shrugged. "I'm not sure. It just sounded good at the time."

Aimee laughed. "Oh, Kiki. You're a real hoot, you know that?"

"Yeah. I'm a hoot," she agreed, thinking the exact same thing about Aimee. *Wait until Elizabeth hears about what she missed.*

24

elizabeth

*C*CAN'T BELIEVE I MISSED all that. You guys have all the fun," said Elizabeth.

"I wouldn't call it fun," said Aimee. "More like heart-attack -inducing."

"We're just lucky Officer Hotstuff was working nearby."

Elizabeth smiled. "Sounds romantic to me. Like your knight in shining armor came galloping up to save the day."

"Shush. You guys are goofy," said Aimee, trying not to smile but failing, her face going pink.

"Alright, girls, let's get these binders into the house," said Kiki. "I don't want to leave them in my car, even though Marcus wants them tomorrow."

"Then we can go to the gym, right? I have to work off this nervous energy. I feel like I've had four cups of coffee," said Aimee.

"Adrenaline rush," said Elizabeth, grabbing an armload of binders. "Gotta love the ex-husband hot pursuit."

"Or not," said Kiki, opening the door leading into the town-house from the garage.

"Wow, this is nice," remarked Elizabeth, as she got to the top of the stairs. "I'm glad we have you in charge of styling the cafe. You have a knack for it."

"Thank you," said Kiki, smiling under the praise. "I do love doing it. I'm addicted to *Elle Decor* as you can probably tell." She motioned to the pile of magazines on the nearby coffee table.

"Well, your future subscriptions should be part of our expenses for the company. I think it's important that the look of the place stays fresh."

Kiki set her stack of binders down on the couch. "I agree. Now ... what are we going to do with all these binders?" She looked around the room. "Oh! I know. Follow me." She led the other two up the stairs and into her room.

"Oooh, I haven't been in here yet. Wow, that bed looks comfy," said Aimee.

"It is. I splurged. After working my ass off until three in the morning, I liked having a super nice place to finally crash."

Elizabeth looked around, appraising the space. "I'm seriously impressed with you, Kiki. You have a beautiful home, an amazing eye for detail, and even your vehicle purchase was made with keen investment sense."

"Wow, thanks. That means a lot coming from an accountant. I am pretty proud of myself, actually. It wasn't easy, but I did it."

Aimee put her binders on the bed and sat down on the edge of it, bouncing up and down as if testing its firmness. "When we hit the big time, I'm buying a bed like this." She quit the bouncing and stood up. "Of course, that would be after I have a place of my own. I guess I should do that first."

"Don't worry," said Elizabeth. "As soon as we have your divorce out of the way, we can get started on making that happen. I figure by month eighteen you'll be able to move out on your own."

"Wow, that soon?" asked Kiki.

Aimee frowned. "I thought it would be sooner." She looked at Kiki. "I don't mean that I don't love living here. I just figured ... I don't know ... that I'd be independent before then, I guess."

"Well, most businesses don't make money their first year. Some don't until their second or third. But I was able to gather a significant amount of information online from the local chamber of commerce that's invested quit a bit into market research. Plus, I have ... or *had* ... several clients in that business over the years, so I'm familiar with the fixed and variable costs. I think my numbers are as good as they can be. There's always the fickle customer that can throw those calculations off, one way or the other."

"Well, it will be my job and Aimee's job to manage those expectations as best we can and keep them from ruining your forecasts, right Aimee?" asked Kiki as she entered her closet. "Lizzie, help me move these shoe boxes, would you?"

"Only if you agree to stop calling me that name," she said, going to join her in the closet. "Holy crap, Kiki, how many pairs of shoes do you have?"

"Lots. Here." She started handing her boxes.

"Where should I put them?"

"On the bed for now."

Elizabeth took the first few boxes and handed them to Aimee who had come over to join them.

"They're empty," Aimee said. "Where are the shoes?"

"They're in here. In their slots. I just keep the boxes for ... emergencies."

"What kind of emergency requires a shoe box?" asked Elizabeth, handing more of them out to Aimee.

"I'm not sure. I've never actually had to use one. That's why I'm going to put the binders here and the boxes somewhere else."

"Like the recycle bin?" asked Aimee.

"Maybe. I'm not sure."

Elizabeth leaned closer to Aimee and whispered, "I'm not sure she's ready to let them go yet."

"I heard that," said Kiki, sticking her head out of the closet. "I'm not a hoarder."

"Except when it comes to shoe boxes," said Aimee, giggling as she put another four boxes on top of the ten or so that were already on the bed. "Is that it?"

ELLE CASEY

"Not even close," said Elizabeth, unable to keep the laughter out of her voice.

Aimee walked over, and her eyes bugged out when she saw the inside of the closet. "Holy poo on a stick, Kiki. What in the world ... ?"

"Told you," said Elizabeth.

"I'm not a hoarder!" said Kiki, acting like she was mad, but unable to stop smiling.

"You are *too* a shoe box hoarder. I think you need to join a support group or something," said Aimee as she looked over the stacks and stacks of boxes on the shelves above her head. "It looks like a shoe store in here ... only for people with big feet. What are you? A size nine?"

Kiki slid another stack off and said, "I don't need a support group. I have you guys. And yes, I'm a nine. I'm tall, okay? Just throw the damn boxes away if you want. I don't care. I don't need them. I don't think." She stopped, biting her lip.

Elizabeth rubbed her arm reassuringly. "Don't worry. We'll keep a few of them. Not *all* of them," she warned. "Just a few. You can pick ten you can't live without."

"Ten?" asked Kiki, still looking worried.

"Okay, a dozen. No more." Elizabeth gave Kiki her best stern look, thinking how funny it was that the normally totally in control and self-reliant, reasonable Kiki had some kind of issue with shoes and their boxes.

"I see you judging me," said Kiki, play frowning.

Elizabeth put up her hands. "No judgment here, babe. I have my issues and I'm sure Aimee has hers. It's what makes you ... interesting."

Aimee nodded as if in agreement. "Right. Interesting. Shoe box hoarding."

Kiki smacked her on the butt. "Watch it, roomie. You have to go to sleep sometime."

"Oooh, I'm scared," laughed Aimee, dumping another load of boxes on the bed. "I'm going to go downstairs and get the rest of the binders up here."

She left Elizabeth and Kiki to the job of moving the rest of the boxes, which they did in companionable silence for the next several minutes. Aimee came up with several loads of binders, each time a little more out of breath than the last.

"Holy crow, that's a lot of stairs," she said, putting a pile of binders on the bed to join the many others there. "That's all of them. From the car and everything."

Elizabeth and Kiki had arranged the shoeboxes under the bed, Kiki promising to pick out her twelve favorites soon so they could recycle the rest. For the next few minutes they moved the binders on the bed to the closet.

"Okay. That was a workout in itself," said Aimee, wiping her sweaty brow as Kiki slid the last binder into place. "To the gym now?" Aimee's phone rang before any of them could answer her question. Her face looked stricken when she saw the number.

"Who is it?" asked Elizabeth.

"Jack."

"Don't answer it," said Kiki.

"Oh, don't worry, I'm not," said Aimee, throwing the phone down on the bed and staring at it.

Elizabeth walked over and glared at it. "It's like a snake or something. I don't even want to touch it."

The phone quit ringing and a minute later a beep rang out.

"What does that beep mean?" asked Elizabeth.

"It means there's a message," whispered Aimee.

"Oh, for shit's sake. Give me that," said Kiki, grabbing the phone. "How do I listen to the message?"

Aimee reached over and pointed to a button. "Press that one."

"Where's the speaker phone?"

"There," said Aimee, pressing it.

Jack's voice came out loudly into the room. *"You're going to pay for that, Aimee. You think I don't know you're fucking that cop? I'm going to report him, and then I'm coming for you and those two whores with you. You took what's mine and no one does that. No one! Do you hear me?! Fuck you, Aimee! You're nothing but a worthless, stupid piece of shit! You always were. You know why I left you for Tiffany? Because she knows how to please a guy. She ..."*

The rest of it was cut off by Kiki, staring at the phone with a look of extreme distaste on her face, her finger on the red disconnect button.

Aimee was in shock - standing stock still and as white as a sheet, except for two splotches of color high on her cheekbones. Her hand fluttered to her neck. "Oh ... my god ... how ... humiliating ... " Tears sprang to her eyes before she dropped her face into her hands and started bawling.

Elizabeth went over quickly and put her arms around her friend. "Oh, Aimee, ignore that asshole. He is so, so ugly inside. None of that garbage was true ... none of it!"

"How do you know?" spat Aimee angrily, dropping her hands awkwardly. "He knows me better than anyone!"

"He doesn't know you at all, Aimee," argued Kiki. "I might not have slept with you, but I know for a fact you're a passionate person. Anyone can see that about you. If you weren't any good in bed it's because your partner sucked, not because of you. It takes two, you know." Kiki started pacing around her room. "I hate guys like that ... taking their inadequacies out on the women they're supposed to love. What the hell is wrong with that guy?" She stopped her pacing and came over to join Elizabeth and Aimee. Elizabeth released Aimee from her hug halfway to give Kiki access.

Kiki put her hands on either side of Aimee's face, forcing her to look into her eyes. "You listen to me. I'm not kidding. You are a gorgeous, lovable, *amazing* woman, who can bake her ass off. *You* are not the problem here. *You* are not the one with zero morals. *You* are not the one who destroyed your marriage." She dropped Aimee's face to take her shoulders and continued. "Your only problem is you're too nice. You put up with his shit for too long, and he took advantage of that. But never again." She shook her friend once gently. "Say it now, so I know you're listening."

"Say what," she said sniffling.

"Say, 'Never again'. Loudly."

Elizabeth nudged her.

"Never again," Aimee whispered.

"No. Not good enough. Do it again, louder."

"Never again," Aimee said in a conversational tone.

"Sorry. Lame. Do over."

Aimee smiled a little. "Never again." She sounded firmer this time.

"You can do better. He cheated on you with a slut half your age. He bought himself an Aston Martin and made you drive a Toyota, for chrissakes."

"Hey, I like my Toyota," said Aimee in mock offense.

"Aimee!"

"Okay, fine. Never again! There, are you happy?"

"One more time. With gusto."

"Never again!" she shouted.

"I like that," said Elizabeth, encouraging her. "It has a nice ring to it."

"Never again am I going to be your doormat!" Aimee yelled.

Kiki hugged her hard and fast before stepping back. "You're going to be just fine, Aims. You'll see. You just need to get back up on that horse and give it a ride."

"With a certain cop, I think," added Elizabeth.

"I'm not sure ...," said Aimee.

"I am. Call him," said Kiki, holding up Aimee's phone.

"Right now? What should I say?"

"Tell him you want to meet him. Tonight."

"He already said he wanted to meet after his shift."

"Good," said Elizabeth. "Now just find out where and when. And make sure it's a date and not just a thank you for saving me kind of thing."

Aimee sighed and took the phone. "I can't believe I'm doing this. I'm still not sure if I'm ready."

"If you're not ready now, you will be when he starts taking your clothes off," said Kiki.

"Kiki! As if I'd go all the way on the first date."

"You'd better!" said Elizabeth. She saw Aimee's reproachful look and shrugged her shoulders. "I would. He's hot. And he's rescued you twice and not played games either. That deserves some heavy petting at least."

Kiki nodded. "It's unanimous. You need to jump his bones. Tonight if possible."

Aimee shook her head as she dialed. "You guys are nuts."

25

aimee

$\mathcal{A}$IMEE FOUND JOE'S NUMBER IN her phone and dialed it nervously, almost hoping he wouldn't answer. But she had no such luck.

"This is Joe."

"Joe, hi. It's Aimee again." She cringed, imagining him thinking she was a semi-stalker, calling him twice in one day.

"Hey, Aimee." His voice softened. "How're you doing? Still freaked out?"

She smiled, going warm over his obvious concern. "A little. Jack just called and left a pretty mean message on my voicemail. But that's not why I called. I was wondering if you'd ... um ... like to meet. Or whatever."

"Yeah. I thought we already agreed to that. After my shift, right?"

"Yes. Well, I guess I need to know what time and where, then." She felt like a desperate loser. This was almost painful. She wondered if awkward dating scenes were part of the reason she'd stayed married for so long - so she could avoid them entirely.

"How about if I come pick you up around eight? That'll give me time to get cleaned up after work."

"That would be good. What do you think we'll do? I mean ... I'm just wondering what to wear." She thought she was going to die of embarrassment. She'd practically just asked him if they were going to have sex. Or at least, that's what it sounded like to her. Kiki and Elizabeth were both giving her the thumbs up, smiling like crazy and high fiving.

"I was thinking a late dinner and maybe a movie? Or we could just hang out after dinner. It's up to you."

"Okay," she said, relieved. Dinner and movies sounded safe enough. "Eight o'clock. I'll text you directions to the house."

"Good enough. See you soon."

"Yeah. See you later."

"And Aimee?"

"Yes?"

"I'm really glad you decided to call me."

"Me too," she said softly, her heart in her throat. She took the phone away from her ear and disconnected the call.

"What'd he say?!" asked Elizabeth excitedly. "I can't believe you did it. I'm so proud of you!"

"Yeah, what'd he say? Give us the details. Word for word. Don't leave anything out."

Aimee giggled. "You guys act like we're still in high school."

"As far as I'm concerned, the only thing that's changed is the styles. Now spill it, sister," demanded Kiki.

Aimee gave them all the details and then waited to hear their analysis. She'd forgotten how much fun it was to pick apart every word a guy said and try to read all the meanings possible into it.

"He's into you. Big time," said Kiki. "You'll get lucky tonight if you want to."

"Do I want to?" asked Aimee, kind of thinking she did, but afraid about the consequences. Not only was she worried about how it would make her feel emotionally, she also worried about what would happen if Jack found out.

"Why not?" asked Elizabeth. "What are you worried about?"

Aimee cringed, imagining what their reaction would be if she told them.

Kiki pointed a finger at her. "Don't you dare be worried about what Jack would think!"

"I'm more worried about what he'll *do*, than what he thinks," she confessed.

"Joe's a big boy. He can take care of himself," said Kiki, dismissing her fears.

"Seriously, Aimee. He has a gun. And he's twice Jack's size," agreed Elizabeth.

"Yeah, but Jack is crazy."

"He's also a lawyer. Hopefully that means he knows the law and will be smart about not breaking it with a cop around."

Kiki rolled her eyes. "Don't give him too much credit, Elizabeth. The guy's an idiot, obviously. But I'm not worried about him, and neither should you be, Aimee. Joe can handle him. Just enjoy yourself. Jack doesn't know where you live, and he has no way of finding you. So go have some fun. Get laid."

Aimee smiled. "Maybe." She started walking out of the room. "But first I have to work out. I have a puffer belly and there's nothing sexy about that."

Kiki and Aimee changed their clothes, and the three girls went to the gym for their first workout.

26

kiki

*T*WO THIRDS INTO HER WORKOUT, Kiki spied Lola's board member across the room. She'd been thinking about trying some free-weights to do some bicep curls, but immediately changed her mind, turning to go back to a leg lift machine she had already used three times.

"I thought we were going to do those curl things you mentioned," said Aimee. "We already did that machine enough times, didn't we?"

Kiki had been showing Aimee a nice circuit routine she'd used in the past to get into shape, which included using several machines in a row for various body parts, taking a quick break after doing three sets of twelve repetitions on each one before starting over and doing it one more time.

"Yeah, well I'm going to do one more."

Aimee looked at her, confused, and then glanced over in the direction Kiki had been walking.

Kiki knew her fib had been discovered when she saw the look of understanding dawn across Aimee's face. "Uh-huuuhhh, I see what's going on here. Mr. Hot Board Member is here now, so suddenly you're not interested in curling anymore."

"It's not curling, dummy. It's 'doing bicep curls'."

"Whatever. You're a chicken." She winked at Kiki deviously. "But I'm not."

"Aimee, no!" she said. But it was too late. Aimee had already left, headed over to the free-weights section.

"Damn little pest," mumbled Kiki, adjusting the pin into the weights so the load on her muscles wouldn't be quite as heavy as before. Her legs were already tired from the other sets she'd done, but she didn't want to get up now and admit that she was avoiding the guy, especially not after she'd given Aimee that big pep talk earlier, telling her to be all brave and fearless. She kept her eyes closed as she slowly went through another set of reps.

"Hi," said a male voice a minute later.

Kiki opened her eyes, looking toward the ground, noticing first that this voice was attached to a guy with a sprinkling of hair on tan legs. She really didn't want to look up the rest of the way because she was afraid she knew who the legs belonged to.

"Hello," she said, pretending to adjust the pin again, and then her seat.

"Need some help?"

"Nope. I'm fine," she said.

"Your friend said you did."

Kiki looked up in frustration. The guy obviously couldn't take a hint. "Well, I don't." She tried to stay annoyed, but *damn*, she thought. *He's even better looking up close than he is from a distance.* She turned away from him, trying to get a grip on her brain. *Focus. Lift. Don't arch your back.* She executed another slow, controlled leg lift.

"You shouldn't arch your lower back like that. You could hurt yourself."

She dropped her legs, the weights making a loud clanking sound as they came back together in a hurry. "Thanks for the tip. Now do you mind? I'm trying to focus here." Now she was just annoyed. Annoyed with herself. *Why should I care what this jerk thinks of me?*

He smiled.

"Why are you smiling at me?" She was used to this bitchy act being useful for getting rid of guys, not making them happy.

"You already knew that. About the back arching thing."

"Yes. I did. I've worked out before."

"I can tell. My name's Brent." He held out his hand.

Kiki sighed. "Kiki." She wiped her sweaty hands off on the towel that was hanging on a hook on the machine and shook his hand. Both of them had firm business-like grips.

"That wasn't too painful, was it?" he asked, referencing their introduction, refusing to be put off by her rudeness.

"Only a little," she said grudgingly.

"I could show you something better for your quads if you want. Less stressful on your back than those leg lifts on the machine."

"That's okay. I'm good here."

"You've already done three sets."

Kiki sighed again in frustration. "Have you been spying on me or what?"

"Yes."

She looked at him like he was nuts.

"I saw you here a few days ago and was going to come over and talk to you, but you walked away. I could have sworn you saw me, but I wasn't sure. So I saw you today and watched your routine for a little while. I like seeing what girls like you do for workouts."

Kiki was instantly offended. "What the hell is that supposed to mean?"

Brent backed up a step, involuntarily putting his hands up. "Whoa, it wasn't supposed to mean anything. Just that I admire you."

"You're a prick, you know that? Just leave me alone."

She got up off the machine and grabbed her towel, brushing past him to go find Elizabeth and Aimee. She was done here. The jerk had ruined it.

Before she got more than three paces away he was next to her, taking her gently by the arm. "Hey, Kiki, I'm sorry."

"Back off, asshole, before I take you down with a knee to the jewels."

He kept his hand on her arm but moved his other hand to cover his vulnerable parts. "Wow. You mean business. But seriously ... I obviously said something to offend you, but I have no idea what. I wish you'd tell me so I can apologize."

She stared at his face, which was way too close for comfort. His ice blue eyes and dark hair made for a heady combination. She couldn't help but think of Damon on *Vampire Diaries*. Guys this beautiful just weren't for real.

"You said 'girls like you'. I find that offensive. And I'm pretty sure any woman in my situation would."

Brent looked at her with a confused expression. "I would have thought you'd take it as a compliment."

Kiki jerked her arm out of his grip. "In what kind of twisted world have you been living where women like being treated like second-class citizens and objects?" She used her towel to wipe off the spot where he'd had his hand. She felt dirty, knowing he'd touched her skin there. "Just stay the hell away from me, or I'm going to call security."

He half smiled. "Do they even have security here?"

"I don't know. I'll call the cops if they don't."

Brent was looking at her with a bemused expression. "Honest to God, Kiki. I think you're beautiful and toned like an athlete. I just wondered what a female athlete did in her gym workouts. I'm sorry if you find that offensive. I really am. I had no idea that women didn't like their skills pointed out in the gym. My bad," he said, as he started to walk away, shaking his head.

Athlete? Is he messing with me? She wasn't sure. She spoke up to get his attention. "When you say athlete, what exactly do you mean by that?" She'd never heard an exotic dancer referenced in that way, so it seemed strange for an obviously well-educated guy to do it. And if it was some kind of pickup line it would probably go down in history as the world's worst effort, so he deserved to know that.

"I knew I'd seen you before, but I couldn't place where. Beach volleyball, right? You're a pro, aren't you? I swear I've seen you. On T.V., I thought."

"Are you telling me ... you think I'm a pro volleyball player?"

He shrugged. "You're not?"

"Uh. No. Definitely not."

He cocked his head to the side. "Well, how do I know you, then? I swear I've seen you somewhere before."

Kiki smiled mirthlessly. "I don't know," she lied. "But it was nice meeting you. Sorry about the misunderstanding."

"So my jewels are safe?"

"For now," she said, turning to go back to her machine.

"I was serious about showing you that exercise. I think you'd really like it."

She kept walking, intending to blow him off, but his next comment got to her.

"It'll help lengthen your muscles more, develop all of your quad instead of the more dominant parts."

She hated when someone got into her head like that and figured out how to push her buttons. He'd just pushed a good one. She was a sucker for a complete workout that challenged all her muscle groups together and each muscle individually. And she knew that the leg lift machine sucked for that.

She turned around with a sigh. "Fine. Show me your exercise." She walked with him back to the free-weights, catching Aimee's and Elizabeth's gazes from across the room. Both of them were smiling like loons and giving her a thumbs up behind their towels. She rolled her eyes and ignored them. *Idiots. I feel like I'm in high school again.* Aimee's earlier similar comments echoed in her head. *I guess it's my turn to go back in time.*

Ten minutes later her legs were burning with effort and Brent was urging her on. "That's it, babe, you can do it. One more, one mooorrre ... excellent!" He smiled at her, nodding his head. "I'm impressed. You're strong. Even stronger than you look."

ELLE CASEY

"You're no wimp yourself," she said, wiping her face off with her towel, breathing heavily. "Well, thanks for sharing, Brent. I need to get back to my friends. See you around."

She started to walk away, praying her legs weren't visibly shaking. She was wiped out.

"Hey, Kiki? Are you busy later? Say around seven?"

"Yes." She turned to look at him, even though she didn't want to.

"You're lying."

Kiki looked at him in mock outrage. "Says who?"

"Says me. You're no good at it. Listen, it's not a big deal. It's just that I have a client who has an opening tonight at a gallery, and I could use a plus one. I hate going to these things alone. They're dreadfully dull sometimes."

"So, you're asking me to go out on a dreadfully dull date with you?"

"Uh, yeah. I guess I am." He smiled, flashing the straightest, whitest teeth she'd ever seen not in a *Crest* commercial.

"No thanks. As tempting as it sounds." She couldn't help but smile back at him. His face was glowing from not only the sweat but merriment.

"Why not? Are you seeing someone?"

"No."

"Afraid then," he deadpanned.

"No, I'm not afraid," she said, trying not to let her hackles rise up at that, since it was exactly what he wanted.

"Yes, you are. Afraid you're going to have a good time. Which you probably would, since I'm a fun date. Or so I've been told."

"I'm not afraid. I'm just not interested."

"What if I said I have more workouts I could share with you? Free of charge."

"Tempting. But not enough. I'm busy tonight."

She turned to leave again but was stopped by his sincere voice.

"How about begging? Would begging make any difference? Because I'm willing to go there, if I have to. Although I'd appreciate it if you wouldn't make me."

"I think you already are," she laughed.

"Yeah, I guess I am. Come on, Kiki. Say yes. I promise not to offend you again. And if the thing is too boring, I'll take you out dancing instead."

Her eyes narrowed at him, but she could detect no underlying joke. He really didn't seem to remember where he'd seen her. It was dawning on her that she could, for the first time in so many years she couldn't remember, go out on a date with a guy who didn't look at her like a stripper. At least, until he put two and two together and remembered who she was. She decided not to over-think it and just go with her gut.

"Fine. What time and where?"

"I can pick you up."

"No. I'll meet you there."

"You're feisty. I like that." He seemed confused by his confession.

"You don't seem the type."

"I know. I'm usually not." He reached into a small bag next to a nearby weight bench and pulled out a card and a pen, writing something on the back before handing it to her. "Here's my card with the address and gallery name on the back. See you around seven?"

"Or so," she said, turning to go join her friends. "See ya."

She didn't wait for his reply, instead focusing on her friends' faces and chanting in her head as she walked away. *Legs, don't fail me now ... Legs don't fail me now...*

elizabeth

*E*LIZABETH STARTED FANNING HER FACE before Kiki walked up, trying really hard not to smile. As Kiki got within earshot, she started talking to Aimee in an overly casual tone. Aimee picked up on it right away.

"Wow, Aimee, is it *hot* in here or what?"

"Oh, *yeah*. Hot? Is it *ever*. Phew!" She started fanning her face too.

"I swear, I feel like I'm just going to *combust!*" said Elizabeth. "What about you, Kiki? Are you all *hot* now too?"

"Hot and *bothered?*" asked Aimee, her voice and expression pure innocence.

Kiki shook her head as the other two collapsed into giggles. "Geez, you two ... do you have any idea how dorky you are?" She tried to act annoyed but couldn't keep a straight face. "Come on, I've had enough. Let's go."

"What? Too hot for ya in here?" asked Aimee, going off into snorts, she was so pleased with herself.

Kiki just rolled her eyes. "Are you finished yet? The grown-ups have things to do today."

Elizabeth took Kiki's hand, forcing herself to stop laughing. "Okay. I'm going to control myself. For now. I want to hear all about your ... *hot* ... workout date over a fresh juice." She coughed a little to stop her laugh from getting out of hand again. "Come on. My treat. Let's go have a smoothie or something."

"I guess I can have a wheatgrass," said Kiki.

Aimee screwed up her face, looking like she'd smelled something bad. "Wheatgrass? I didn't know people actually drank that stuff."

They walked over to the juice bar. "We all are. It's a requirement after a workout. Helps get the toxins out," said Kiki.

"Maybe I like my toxins right where they are," suggested Aimee.

"Nope. Your toxins are going bye-bye," insisted Kiki. "Toxins can make your butt get lumpy if you're not careful."

Aimee got a scared look on her face and twisted around, trying to get a view of her rear end. "Seriously?"

"I've always been curious about what it tastes like," said Elizabeth. "I'm willing to try anything once."

"I'm so glad to hear you say that, Lizzie," said Kiki, sounding a little evil.

Elizabeth looked at her suspiciously. "You're making me nervous right now, Kiki. And don't call me that."

They ordered their shots of wheatgrass juice and then looked at Kiki for an explanation.

"Elizabeth and I have been invited to a gallery opening tonight. It starts at seven. I'll pick you up at seven-thirty so we can be fashionably late. It's downtown. Wear a short cocktail dress, preferably black, and heels."

Elizabeth frowned at her. "That guy asked you *and* me out on a date?"

"Yeah," said Kiki innocently.

"Waaait a minute," said Aimee, suspicion written all over her face. "He did not. You're just dragging Elizabeth along so you don't have to be alone with him, aren't you?"

"No."

"Kiki!" admonished Aimee. "After all that rah, rah baloney you gave me today? You have a lot of nerve being such a wimp. Shame on you." She put her hands on her hips for emphasis.

Elizabeth tried not to laugh at the comical scene it made. Aimee couldn't look mean if she tried. "I'm with Aimee on this one," she said. "You need to face up to your fears and deal with them head-on. You can do it. You're Wonder Woman." She reached over and shook Kiki's shoulder a little.

"First of all, I'm not Wonder Woman. And second of all, it's a public place with art. You like art, right? Maybe we can find a starving young artist to help us decorate our cafe. I only agreed to go there for that reason. It's business."

"Yeah, right," said Aimee.

"I do like art. But I'm not interested in being a third wheel on your date."

Kiki closed her eyes as if searching for strength. Then she opened them and her expression changed to one of desperation. "Pleeease? I really don't want to be alone with this guy."

"Then don't go, silly," said Elizabeth, not really understanding what Kiki was getting at. That she was nervous about something was clear. But what it was?... Elizabeth had no clue.

"Why don't you want to be alone with him?" asked Aimee. "Worried he'll make a move on ya?"

"No. I'm worried he'll ..." She looked at the wheatgrass shots that had just been put on the counter and grabbed one, slamming it down in one quick gulp. She wiped off her mouth with the back of her hand and said, "Never mind. Forget I mentioned it."

Elizabeth put her hand on Kiki's arm. "Tell me. Something's bothering you, and I want to hear what it is."

"It's no big deal, really."

Kiki was acting overly casual about it, which made Elizabeth's suspicio-meter needle go up to level nine. "Tell me or bad things will happen."

"Bad things?" she laughed. "Is that a threat?"

"Yes. A big one."

"Okay, miss threatening person, what bad things? What are you going to do to me if I don't tell you my deep, dark secrets?"

"It's not me who's going to do it. It's Aimee."

Aimee stood with her glass in her hand, staring down into the dark green liquid. She looked up suddenly, hearing Elizabeth's claim. "Me? ... Oh, yeah. Me." She narrowed her eyes and frowned. "Bad things, Kiki. Bad, bad things will happen. I'll make sure of it."

"Oh yeah, Mighty Mouse? Like what?"

"Like ... I'll take your shoe boxes and *recycle* them!"

"*No!*" gasped Kiki.

"Yes! And! I'll ... not bake you any more *cookies!*"

"Blasphemy!" said Kiki, trying to look seriously distraught.

"It's true. I'd go that far. I already know which boxes I'm going to crush and put into the blue bin first. I'll start with that pink Jimmy Shoe one."

"It's Jimmy Choo, dork."

"Whatever. It's going. In the bin. Today."

"Fine. You want to know what's bothering me so bad that you'd take it out on my innocent shoe boxes? I'll tell you ... it's that he doesn't remember where he saw me before. He's asking me out because I'm an athletic-looking woman. Not because I'm a stripper."

"And that's a problem because...," said Elizabeth.

"Because everyone I've dated since I was twenty-two or so has been fully aware of my career, if that's what you want to call it. He isn't. And he's a corporate lawyer who doesn't go into strip bars."

"Well, sure he does. That's where he met you the first time," said Aimee.

"He only did that for work. It's not his normal hangout."

"And it's not yours either. Not then and not now. Don't let thoughts of what his impressions *might* be allow you to judge yourself harshly, sweetie. That's not who you are," said Elizabeth, finally figuring out what Kiki's problem was. As tough and brave as Kiki was, she was not as sure about her life choices as she appeared to be. Even though they'd made her financially stable and allowed her to have a really comfortable life, she wasn't proud of herself. That made Elizabeth sad. Kiki had everything to be proud of and nothing to be ashamed about.

Aimee must have picked up on it too. "Kiki. Honey child. You are the most with-it, intelligent, gorgeous girl I know, present company excluded of course - you and Elizabeth are tied in awesomeness - and there is no man alive who is good enough for you. But maybe this guy could come close. Why don't you give him a chance? Nothing ventured, nothing gained, right?" She turned her attention to Elizabeth. "Why don't you go too? You stay home and at work too much. You need to get out. I say tonight, we all go out and then meet up tomorrow to do some business planning and boy gossiping. What do you say? Are you in?"

Elizabeth and Kiki exchanged glances.

"If you're sure I won't be a third wheel, I'll go to the gallery opening. But that's it! I'm not going anywhere else with you guys," she warned. "I'm serious."

"That's it, I promise. And you don't have to stay the entire time if the art sucks. You can come in, do a quick look around, and go if that's what you want. Or you could stay. Whatever ...."

Kiki looked so unsure of herself but hopeful, now that she knew Elizabeth was coming, that Elizabeth just had to hug her. "It'll be fun," she said as she squeezed Kiki once before letting her go. "I need to shop though. I don't have a little black dress."

"Whaaaat? Girl, what have you been doing with yourself that you didn't need a little black dress at some point?"

"Seriously. Even I have one of those," said Aimee.

Elizabeth shrugged. "I don't get out much. I had a bad break up a couple years back, and it kind of made me shy away from the whole dating thing."

"Yeah, but what about for work? Wouldn't you need one for cocktail parties with clients?"

"If I went to them. I avoided those, too." Saying it now made her feel like a shut-in or something. *Why have I chosen to close myself off from the world so much? When did that happen?*

"Well, I'm up for shopping if anyone else is," suggested Aimee. "I could use a new pair of shoes."

"Drink your wheatgrass and we'll make a plan," said Kiki, eyeing Aimee especially.

Aimee held her glass, the funny look still on her face as she stared down at the green juice inside. "Doan wanna," she said, like a petulant child.

"Drink it. Or no shopping."

Aimee stuck out her tongue before taking a sip of the drink. The expression on her face was classic. "Ewww! It tastes like ... *grass!*"

Kiki and Elizabeth laughed.

"Well, duh," Kiki said. "What did you expect? Bananas?"

"Something other than just grass," she mumbled. "Do I have to?" Her eyes were pleading for mercy.

"I guess you don't," said Kiki, gathering up her gym bag from the floor, "if you don't care about lumpy ass syndrome."

Elizabeth turned away, but not before seeing Aimee swig the last of her wheatgrass down in one gulp.

28

aimee

𝒜IMEE WAS MORE NERVOUS FOR this date than she ever remembered being in her entire life. Her fingers were shaking as she tried to rub her moisturizer in.

"Aimee, can I come in? I need you to zipper me."

"Yes, come in. I'm in the bathroom, trying not to throw up."

Kiki entered, turning so Aimee could fix her dress for her.

"Nervous?"

"Oh my god, like you wouldn't believe."

"Did you douche?"

"Kiki!" Aimee yelled, half laughing and half choking as she pulled Kiki's zipper up. "God, where do you come up with this stuff?" Then she thought about it for a second, immediately worried. "Should I have?"

Kiki smiled. "Not if you don't want to."

Aimee shook her worry off. "I don't need to do that. It's not like anything's going to happen." She kept telling herself that over and over, trying to convince herself that it's what she wanted.

"You never know. Best to be prepared in my book."

"But douching? I mean, is that *normal?* To do that before a date? God, it's been so long since I've gone out with anyone but Jack ..."

Kiki shrugged. "I guess it depends. Some people do it a lot. Some not at all. I was just messing with you. But seriously. Let's talk about make-up."

"Do mine!" said Aimee without hesitating. "You do it better than me, and I want to make a good impression."

"Step into my salon," said Kiki, motioning for Aimee to join her in her own bathroom.

Twenty minutes later Aimee gazed at a beautiful woman staring back at her from the mirror. "Wow. You are an artist. There's no other way to describe what you do. I really need to learn this skill." She leaned in to get a better look.

"It's easy. Remind me next time, and I'll give you a blow-by-blow lesson. But it's fun for me to do, so as long as you're my roomie, I'll keep doing it for you."

"Now I just need my shoes and I'll be ready." Aimee went to her room and put on the new heels she'd just bought on sale at the mall, returning to Kiki's room to get her feedback. "How do I look?"

"Gorjamuss. Totally gorjamuss. You're going to blow his mind. And maybe some other parts of him if he's really lucky."

"Kiki!" Aimee squeaked. "Holy crap. Now I'm going to be thinking about that all night, thanks to you."

"That'll make two of you, then," said Kiki, smiling devilishly.

"Do you really think so? Do guys really think about that a lot?"

"Pretty much every time they look at your mouth."

"No *sir!* Oh, shit. I think I need less lipstick. Or more lipstick. What should I do? I'm so confused!"

Kiki laughed. "Just relax. There's nothing you can do but be yourself. If he likes who you are when you're being Aimee, you're golden. If you have to pretend to be someone else to make him like you, he isn't worth it. Faking it gets exhausting."

"Wise words," said Aimee, nodding her head. "You should listen to them too."

"I will. And I have my crutch Elizabeth there to watch over me and smack me if I get out of line."

"I'm going to text her right now and remind her of that duty," mumbled Aimee as she tapped away at her keypad.

The doorbell rang as she typed the last letter of her message. "Oh no! He's here!" she stage-whispered.

Kiki looked at her like she was crazy. "Oh no! Run! Hide in the closet!"

Aimee instantly relaxed. Kiki did have a point. "Okay, fine. I'm a big girl, I can do this. It's not like it's my first date or anything."

"No. Of course not."

"Just my first one in twelve years."

"It's like riding a bike," Kiki said as they went down the stairs together.

Aimee froze before she got to the bottom, grabbing Kiki's arm in a panic. "What if it's Jack?!"

"It can't be. We have security, remember?"

"Well, how did Joe get in, then?"

Kiki peeled Aimee's hand off her arm. "I called the guard and told him to *let* Joe in. Now *relax.*"

"Oh. Okay," said Aimee, patting her chest a few times to calm its crazy rhythm. "Of course you did. That makes complete sense."

They stood at the bottom of the stairs for a moment. Aimee looked at Kiki, who just stared back at her. "Well?" Kiki asked.

"Should I answer it?"

Kiki rolled her eyes. "Only if you want to go out with him tonight." She left Aimee standing there and went into the kitchen.

A very small piece of Aimee wanted to run up the stairs and lock herself in her bedroom. But instead, she took a deep breath and went to the door, unlocking it and opening it up before she could chicken out.

Joe was standing on the front step, looking handsomer than she thought it was possible for a guy to be. She felt herself go weak in the knees. Now she knew exactly what her romance novels were talking about when they said that. She'd always thought it was silly before.

He was wearing khaki pants and an expensive-looking dress shirt, open at the neck. She could see his hairy chest beneath and tried very hard not to picture what the rest of it might look like. And that chest ... it was so broad it made her feel absolutely tiny. She loved that about him instantly. His waist was trim but not small. No one could ever describe Joe as small. His legs were thick too, and muscled - she could tell from the way his pants fit. *Good lord almighty, what have I gotten myself into?* She broke out in a sweat, wishing she had worked out an extra hour. Or three. *I should have douched.*

"Hi, Aimee. Ready to go?"

"Hi, Joe." She smiled shyly. "Yes." She stepped out and began to close the door behind her.

"Wait a second," he said, pulling a pink rose out from behind his back. "You may want to go put this in water first."

A smile bloomed across her face. "Oh, it's so pretty! And thoughtful! No one's bought me a flower in ... years," she said, losing a little of the happy glow that had appeared, remembering why no one had bought her flowers in ages. *Jack. Talk about a wet blanket.* "Come in, while I get a vase."

She opened the door back up, putting her clutch purse on the front table and leaving him in the foyer, before going into the kitchen. She caught Kiki standing in front of the sink, her mouth full of cookie.

"Caught ya!" she said, pointing at Kiki's mouth. "I need a vase. Where are they?"

"Oh vats fo fweet. Eee boough oo a fwowah." Kiki pointed to a cabinet above Aimee's head.

"Yes. He did." She grabbed Kiki's arm and leaned in, squealing as quietly as she could, "And he looks *ah-may-zing!*"

The sound of a man clearing his throat in the kitchen doorway made Aimee's blood run cold.

Kiki was looking over Aimee's shoulder, her eyes showing her surprise and then mirth.

"He's right behind me, isn't he?" Aimee whispered.

"Mmmm hmmm," said Kiki, struggling to swallow her food. "Hey, Joe. Want a cookie?" she asked, grabbing the nearby plate and leaving Aimee to walk over to him with it held out in front of her.

"Oh, no thanks. Nice seeing you again. Kiki, right?"

"Yes. And I can't take no for an answer. Our lovely and talented Aimee made these. You *must* try them."

Aimee was glad for the distraction so she could look into the cabinet Kiki had pointed out and get down a vase. She kept herself busy with unwrapping the rose and getting it in water, hoping to avoid facing the guy she had just called gorgeous within hearing range, for as long as possible. *So much for playing it cool.* She sighed as she turned on the water and filled the small blue bud vase. *Like Kiki said - I might as well just be myself. If he doesn't like the fact that I'm a flaming dork, he can just move on.* She turned and watched him roll his eyes in pleasure at the taste of her cookies, and sent a quick prayer out to the universe that he would like dorks.

"Ready to go?" she asked, trying to act like she wasn't so nervous she wanted to barf.

"Well," he said, chewing slowly, "I thought I was a minute ago. But now I'm not so sure." He reached over and picked up another cookie, taking a bite out of it and smiling. "I'm kinda busy with these cookies."

Aimee smiled. "Those are Kiki's favorite."

"I can see why," he said. "I've eaten a lot of cookies in my day. In fact," he said, leaning a hip on the counter, "I consider myself somewhat of a connoisseur. And these could very possibly be the best I've ever had. Even better than my mom's." He nodded his head as he continued to savor the flavors, raising an eyebrow at Kiki in a silent exchange of mutual cookie adoration.

Kiki's eyes widened. "Wow. I don't think I've ever heard a man admit that about someone else's cooking."

"Yeah, well, if you ever tell my mom I said it, I'll deny it." He winked at Kiki, and the vision of it made Aimee go all funny inside. *Oh my god, he is the cutest, hottest guy I have ever, ever seen. What is he doing with me? He's going to figure out I'm a goofy housewife and leave me in the dust.* She tried to smile, but felt her happiness sliding away.

Joe looked over and stood up, reaching out to take her hand as he popped the last bit of cookie in his mouth. "Come on. We have reservations." He grabbed another cookie off the plate, explaining, "One for the road. Thanks for sharing, Kiki."

"Oh, any time," she said, taking another for herself. "You two have fun!"

Aimee followed Joe out of the townhouse blindly, battling with herself the entire time. *Should I just try to have fun anyway, knowing this is doomed? Should I try to make conversation, or wait for him to do it? What does a cop like to talk about?*

She heard him clear his throat and realized she was standing like a statue outside the car door he'd been holding open for her. "Oh. Sorry," she said, snapping to attention and getting in, trying to keep her dress from riding up too high. It was loose at the bottom and fitted at the waist with a low neckline. When she'd put it on earlier it had seemed perfect. Now she was worried it wasn't right for the occasion. She fretted that her makeup was too much. Or not enough. She wondered if she should have just worn the lip gloss instead of the tinted stuff. *Is he thinking about blow jobs right now? Or just wondering when he can gracefully get out of the date?*

Joe got in on his side and put his key in the ignition, but he didn't turn the car on. Instead he turned a little in his seat to look at her. "Are you okay, Aimee?"

Aimee could feel her game-face disintegrating. *He doesn't want to go out with me. I'm a freak.* She turned her head quickly, looking out the side window so he wouldn't see her tearing up. *I'm going to be single forever. No wonder Jack was embarrassed by me.*

She felt him take her hand. "Listen. I know you've had a hard time recently. And if this is too stressful for you, this date thing, we can go do something else. No pressure." He rubbed the back of her hand gently with his thumb. "We can do anything at all. We can take a walk downtown, we could just drive around for a while, we could ... I don't know ... go to the batting cages."

She smiled through her tears. He was trying so hard - that had to mean something. She turned to look at him. "Batting cages?"

He gave her a guilty grin. "Yeah, well, that's me just trying to impress you. I figured maybe if I could hit a few home runs and look really manly, you'd give me a chance." He reached up to touch her face, wiping away a small tear that slipped from the outside corner of her eye. "Don't be sad. I promise I won't hurt you. At least not intentionally, and not carelessly. I'm a nice guy. You can call my mom right now and ask her if you don't believe me."

Aimee laughed. "That will *never* happen."

"Well, I'm just sayin'. If it would make you feel better, you could do it."

"I appreciate the thought. It's not that I don't trust you to be a gentleman ... " She looked down at her lap, not even really sure what she was thinking other than the fact that she was at an all-time low in the self-confidence department.

"Okay, so what is it? I can tell you're upset or nervous or something. I just want to put your mind at ease so we can enjoy ourselves tonight."

Aimee sighed heavily. *Might as well get it out of the way.* "Well, the truth is, I *am* nervous. Like *really* nervous. I haven't been out on a date in twelve years. Maybe longer. My divorce isn't final yet, and the last few years that I was married, I didn't get out much. I haven't kissed anyone but Jack in more than a decade." She cringed at how pitiful that sounded.

Joe took her hand and squeezed it. "Well, then. It's time you *did* go out, don't you think? A girl as pretty as you shouldn't be shut up in a house all day and night." He bounced her hand up and down a few times to get her attention.

She looked into his eyes and saw only sincerity.

"Let me take you out and show you a good time. I promise, you won't regret it."

"You sure about that?" she said, smiling tremulously, trying not to hate herself for it.

"Absolutely," he said, squeezing her hand one more time before letting it go and starting the car. "First stop, a surprise. And then out to dinner. After, you can choose what we do - a movie or whatever you want."

"Okay. I can handle that." *I think.* She was hoping it was the truth; it felt like it was. Now she just needed her badly bruised and battered ego to go along with the plan.

"What's the surprise?" she asked.

"Now if I told you, it wouldn't be a surprise anymore, would it?" He smiled, as he looked out the windshield, negotiating the small streets that led out of the neighborhood and into the city.

Aimee stared at him in profile, taking in the view of his strong jaw and full lips. She wondered how a guy this gorgeous and who seemed this nice could possibly be single at their age. He probably had a checkered past. *Maybe he has an ex-wife. Or two. Or three!*

"What is your little mind concocting over there?" he asked, good naturedly.

"Nothing. Much."

"I'm serious, you can call my mother. Here ... I'll dial it for you." He picked up his phone and started pressing buttons.

Aimee grabbed it away from him. "Joe! No! Don't call your mother! Are you crazy?" She looked down at it, trying to figure out how to shut it off. Then she heard a voice coming from it ... an older lady's voice.

"Hello? Joe? Is that you?"

A huge grin split his face. "Hi, Ma!" he said loudly.

Aimee was frantically pressing buttons, whispering, "Oh my god, I can't believe you actually called your mother. How do I shut this thing off?"

The voice came out over the speakerphone next. "Why are you pressing all those ...," *BEEP! BEEP!* "... buttons? Stop that, you're giving me a headache."

Aimee's fingers froze, the phone hanging in her hand, held out at arm's length in between her and Joe.

"Yeah, sorry about that. Listen, Mom ... I need you to do me a favor and vouch for me."

"For what? Are you in trouble again? I told Mrs. Malkovitch twenty-five years ago, and every year since then - it wasn't you who colored her poodle's hair pink with *Kool-aid*. She's not going to let it go, Joe, no matter how many times I vouch for you. I'm sorry, I don't know what else to do."

"Yeah, I know. It was Lolo Pancetti. That's not what I'm talking about. I have a girl here with me, and she's a little nervous about going out on a date with me, so I thought maybe you could tell her I'm a good guy."

"Lolo? I should've known. That kid was always doing stuff like that and blaming you. Wait a minute ... you've got a girl with you right now?" Her voice perked up. "Who is she? Put her on."

Aimee's eyes felt like they were going to fall out of her head, they were bugging so bad. She shook her head as fast as she could, whispering, *"No, no, no, no ...,"* but Joe wasn't listening.

"She's on right now. You're on speaker. Her name's Aimee."

"Aimee? Hello, hon. This is Estelle. I'm Joseph's mother. I can vouch for him. He's a nice boy. I raised him to be a gentleman. If he doesn't hold your doors open for you, you call me back, okay, sweetie? ... Can she hear me? Can you hear me, Aimee? Hello?!"

Aimee couldn't help but smile. "Yes, Mrs. ... Joe's mom." Joe's last name had escaped her, making her feel like a complete nincompoop in front of his mother, of all people. "Joe opened my doors for me already. He seems ... nice." She mouthed the words, *'I'm going to kill you'* at Joe who just shrugged, as if it wasn't his fault. Aimee could see a devilish grin just below the surface of his calm demeanor. She was willing to bet it wasn't Lolo whatever-his-name-is who had turned that poodle pink.

"One thing about my Joey, though, you gotta watch for this, is that he is very *picky* about his work. Everything is just so, with Joseph ... always has been. He won't cut corners, and he doesn't let anyone get away with any shenanigans. Don't get me wrong, it's a good thing, but don't ask him to fix any speeding tickets for you, because he just won't do it. Not even for his own mother."

"Mom, I told you before. I can't fix tickets for the ladies in your bridge club. For you, maybe. But not all of them."

"I didn't ask for you to fix all of them. Just a couple. For my partners."

"Mom, can we talk about this later?" He grabbed the phone, his thumb hovering over the *Off* button.

Aimee grabbed his arm, saying, "Wait," in a low voice. Then she spoke up. "Thanks for vouching for Joe. I feel better now."

"It was my pleasure, sweetie. Do me a favor, if you can. Talk some sense into him about the speeding tickets, would you please?"

"I'll try," said Aimee, trying not to laugh.

"Bye, Mom," said Joe, not waiting for her answer, pressing the button to end the call.

"There," he said, looking smug. "Are you happy? I'll have you know that my mom does not lie. She considers it a sin."

"But she believes in fixing tickets for her bridge partners."

"Of course. That's different. Those tickets are what she calls a travesty of justice."

"I'm sure," said Aimee, feeling much better about her choice to go out with him tonight. Crazy as it sounded, his mother vouching for him gave her a sense of security that at least she wasn't going out with a serial killer. Or another Jack. Jack hardly talked to his mother, and even if he did, Aimee doubted the woman would vouch for him. She was a pretty harsh person.

Aimee let her thoughts wander as Joe drove on, which did wonders for her nervous stomach. By the time they pulled up to a gravel parking lot, Aimee was almost feeling like herself again.

Joe shut off the car and got out, coming around to open her door and help her with a strong, steady hand. She tried to drop it once she was standing, but he held onto it gently. She smiled at him tentatively before looking around. "Where are we?"

"Just a place I like to hang out sometimes."

"It looks like an art studio."

"It is. They give lessons here in all kinds of media - clay, paint, photography. You name it, they probably have classes for it."

"Are we going to take an art lesson tonight?" she asked, confused.

He laughed. "Maybe another time. No, tonight I'm going to show you something that always helps me relax. I thought you'd be interested in seeing it."

He led her in between some buildings and into an attached garden. They walked along the gravel path that had flowering bushes on either side at varying heights, and stone benches spaced every so often, inviting people to stop and rest. Aimee noticed sculptures and statutes made of plastic, metal, clay, and stone, interspersed between plantings. One looked like a giant ostrich, made with recycled soda and water bottles of all shapes, colors and sizes.

"What is this place?" she asked in wonder. It was beautiful. Not only was the art and the landscaping nice, there were two huge trees with limbs that spread out forever, Spanish moss tangled amongst the branches and hanging down to trail almost to the ground. It gave the place a very mystical feel.

"I call it a contemplative garden. I'm not sure what it's officially called. I come here to think."

"I can see why. It's very peaceful."

"Yeah. Even when there are people around, it's quiet. I can escape the rat race here whenever I need to. It's never closed."

They sat down on a bench that was on the edge of a pond. Some artist had put a giant Loch Ness Monster sculpture in the center of it. "That is so cool," said Aimee, happily. It was fun looking at art that had a sense of humor and adventure mixed with a little bit of legend to it.

"That's my favorite piece out here."

"Is any of your work in the garden?"

"Nah. My stuff isn't this good. I just do it for fun. I started in second grade, and it hasn't improved much in quality since then."

Aimee laughed. "You're joking."

"No, unfortunately, I'm not. Even my own mother told me to give it up and find another hobby."

"No, she didn't!" said Aimee in mock outrage.

"She might have had the ulterior motive of wanting to recruit me for her bridge club, which I will join no earlier than at the age of eighty-five, but still. I've had enough people look at my work with pity in their eyes to know it will never leave the safety of my house to be on display anywhere. But I'm okay with that."

Aimee felt bad for him. *Poor guy.* He had an artist's soul but a policeman's hands. She looked down at their interlaced fingers, noticing that her hand was tiny compared to his. She tried not to stare at his thick wrist and bulging veins, but it was almost impossible after the conversations she'd had with Elizabeth and Kiki. She looked away, back out toward the lake, trying to shake thoughts of his probably amazing body parts out of her mind.

"What are you thinking about right now? I saw you get a panicked look again."

"I can't tell you. It's too embarrassing."

"I promise I won't laugh."

"Oh, God, no way am I confessing *that* one." She stood up. "Come on. Let's walk some more."

He stood up next to her, and she started to go, but her heel got caught on a piece of gravel, throwing her off balance. He caught and steadied her, his body rubbing up against hers as she gained her footing.

Aimee's breath hitched as she felt his hard form through the flimsy material of her dress. He still had his hands on her, and they were very warm, the heat radiating into her skin. The scent of his cologne drifted past her nose; it wasn't overwhelming, just a light woodiness that hinted of maleness. She looked up to see him staring down at her with his baby blues.

Neither of them said a word.

Aimee stared at his eyes and then his lips. She wanted to kiss him so badly, but then again, she was scared as hell to do it. *What if I've forgotten how? What if I'm terrible at it?*

She didn't have much time to worry about it, though, because his head dipped toward hers while his hands slid up her arms to hold her shoulders gently.

Their lips touched.

Her first sensation was that of surprise. Here he was ... this giant, muscled man ... but he had the softest lips. Her heart immediately started hammering away, as the kiss deepened and his arms went around her back. She soon realized she needn't have worried about knowing how to kiss this man; their mouths moved in perfect harmony, both of them seeming to know exactly when and how to entangle their tongues together. Her hands moved of their own accord, going around his neck, her fingers touching the hair there lightly.

It was a heady sensation, this sexy heat and rush of emotion that threatened to overwhelm her. She could tell he was enjoying this as much as she was. His head tilted to the side to bring the kiss to another level. The place between her legs started to tingle, and had to stop herself from grinding into him. When his hand moved down to press against her backside, she realized how excited he'd become right along with her. His hard length felt like it was practically laying against her nakedly, the thin material of her dress no barrier to the sensation.

The sound of nearby voices and gravel crunching under walking feet was like an instant cold shower. Aimee stepped back, breaking their connection and putting an end to the heavy petting that was starting to make her think crazy things - like the fact that having sex outdoors in a public park might be fun.

Joe grabbed her hands and pulled her back slowly. "I'm sorry," he whispered in her ear, before kissing her neck gently one time and standing up straight again. "Wow, Aimee. I'm ..." He dropped one of her hands to run his fingers through his hair, a confused expression on his face. "I'm not exactly sure what happened there. I didn't intend to maul you like that."

Aimee smiled shyly. "I'm not sure who was doing the mauling - you or me. But don't apologize. I liked it."

Joe smiled back. "Be careful. I don't need much encouragement. You're really beautiful, you know that?"

He was gazing into her eyes so seriously, she didn't know what to do other than blush. And blush she did. She could feel her ears burning brightly.

"Okay. I'm embarrassing you now. And I don't want you running away from me because I'm being too intense, so what do you say we get out of here and go to dinner, before I lose my mind again?"

"Good idea," Aimee said, glad he was making the smart decision to leave this tempting place, since she obviously lacked the strength to do it herself.

They got back into the car and Joe took her to a cute little Italian restaurant, where they were immediately seated in a nice little alcove with a view of a quaint garden complete with trickling fountain. The owner had greeted Joe like an old friend, giving him a robust hug and a kiss on the cheek, before escorting them to this private spot.

"Wow, this is really nice," said Aimee, looking around. "I've never been here before."

"The owner is an old friend," said Joe.

"I could tell. He looked like a big fan of yours."

Joe shrugged. "He's a good guy. He's got a huge family. He's brought lots of his Italian relatives over here. He's an immigrant himself but loves being an American. He got his citizenship ten years ago." Joe opened up the menus that had been delivered by a waitress. "All of their pastas are homemade, and the pasta fagioli soup is out of this world. It's made fresh every day with a family recipe that's hundreds of years old."

Aimee perused the selection. "There are too many things here. I can't choose."

"Well, I've had everything at least once. Some many times over. I recommend the ravioli and the lasagna. You can't go wrong with the classics."

Aimee shut her menu. "I'll take the ravioli."

"Good choice," he said, setting his menu down.

A waitress arrived and took their orders. As soon as she was gone, Joe folded his hands loosely and rested his forearms on the table. "So, Aimee. Tell me about yourself."

She felt immediately uncomfortable, not knowing what to say, but pretty sure he didn't want to hear about the sad sorry state of affairs that was her life right now. "What do you want to know?"

"Tell me where you grew up."

"That's easy. Here. Outside of Orlando, in Maitland."

"And have you always lived here?"

"Yep. Jack ... my soon-to-be-ex-husband ... started his law practice when I was still in college, so we kind of had to stay."

"Well, you don't have to stay now, since you're almost divorced. Will you? Stay, I mean?"

She looked into his eyes and it didn't seem like he was just asking her a casual question. The answer seemed to mean something to him. Or maybe she was just reading too much into the look on his face and the tone of his voice. "I'm going to stay. I'm starting a business with my two friends, so this is my home for good."

Joe smiled, seeming satisfied with her answer. "Me too."

"What about you?" Aimee asked. "Have you always lived here? What do you do when you're not working? Do you play any sports?" *Are you seeing someone? Divorced? Married? Please, please don't say you're married.*

"Well, let's see ... no, I haven't always lived here. I moved down here from Syracuse in high school and stayed. When I'm not working, I coach little league baseball and work with a couple committees putting together benefits to raise money for breast cancer research. I also like to watch football sometimes, soccer too during World Cup time. I like movies and reading a lot."

"And long walks on the beach?"

"As a matter of fact, yes. But I wasn't going to admit that."

"Your secret is safe with me. That's nice that you do the coaching thing. Do you have a son who plays?" Aimee tried to act casual with the question, picking up a crunchy breadstick and taking a bite. But the effect was totally ruined when the thing exploded and threw bread shrapnel everywhere, including over onto his placemat. "Oops. Sorry," she said, trying to collect the crumbs into a pile.

"Don't worry about it. It happens to me all the time. To answer your question, no, I don't have a son. Or a daughter for that matter. No kids. And no ex-wives if you're wondering."

"Oh, no. Me? No." She looked at him and saw a small smile playing at the corner of his mouth. "Okay, yes. I confess. I'm wondering what a guy like you is doing single and unattached. You are single, right? And not gay?" she asked weakly. *Oh please don't let him be dating someone else.*

Joe laughed. "Wow. It's been a long time since someone's accused me of that. No, I'm not gay. And I'm single, I guess because I'm picky. I date now and again, but if I don't feel something pretty much right away, I don't bother going out a second time.

I don't like to waste my time or anyone else's, going after something that isn't going to be able to turn into something more."

"Oh, crap," she said, slight disappointment coloring her words.

"What? What's 'oh, crap'?"

"Well, I was just thinking that if you don't call me tomorrow, I'll know why. I'm not sure if I like it that way or if I just prefer to wonder and guess about the mysteries of what a guy might be thinking."

He reached over and took her hand. "I'm going to call tomorrow. And the next day. And the next. You don't need to worry about that."

"But how can you say that now? You hardly know me." She wanted to believe it. She really, *really* wanted to believe it, but it seemed so far-fetched. *Love at first sight doesn't really happen ... does it? And certainly not to me. I'm pressuring him. Guys hate that. Why can't I keep my mouth shut?*

"I know you better than you realize. How about this: you are a beautiful woman who has been married to a guy who didn't appreciate her for over ten years. You've kept to yourself, at home, because that's how he wanted it. You've always put his needs first, and it's made you unhappy - but now you're making changes to have a better life for yourself. You're funny and like to laugh. You care a lot about your friends and worry about their happiness. You love deeply and you can cook your butt off." He squeezed her hand. "How am I doing so far?"

"Wow. Pretty good, actually. You're either really intuitive, or you've been stalking me. Tell me more."

"Okay," he said, warming up to the idea and leaning in a little closer while he dropped his voice. "You like me, but you're afraid of your feelings. You're wondering if I'm going to try and sleep with you tonight, and if it would be any good if you said yes."

Aimee whispered back before she could think to stop herself, "Are you? Going to ask me?"

"That's what I'm doing right now," he whispered, lifting an eyebrow and making her nearly swoon with the sexiness of it.

Aimee pulled her hand away and sat back, fanning her face with her napkin. She cleared her throat. "Um ... I have to use the ladies' room." She stood up suddenly and grabbed her purse, escaping to the safety of the bathroom without looking back.

She pulled her phone out of her bag as soon as she got inside and called Kiki. Kiki picked up after the third ring and Aimee wasted no time with pleasantries. "Kiki! Oh my god! I need some advice. He just asked me if I would sleep with him tonight, and I am *freaking out*. Freaking. *Out!* What should I say? What should I do?"

Kiki laughed. "Whoa, slow down there. What did you just say? He asked you to sleep with him? Where are you? At his place?"

"No, I'm in the bathroom at the restaurant."

"He asked you in the ladies bathroom?"

"No, dummy, he asked me back at the table."

"And you ran away to the bathroom to call me, didn't you?"

"Yes. I admit it, I panicked."

"Okay, this is easy. Do you want to sleep with him?"

"I'm not sure!"

"Do you stare at his hands and wonder what his dick looks like?"

"Maybe. Okay, yes."

"Do you look at his eyes and lips and imagine them worshipping your body?"

"Oh, shit. *Yes.*"

"Do you look at him and wonder what he'd look like naked ... and then get all hot and bothered about it?"

"Yes!"

"Then put the damn phone away and go back there and tell him you want to jump his bones. *Goodbye.*"

Aimee stared at the disconnected phone in her hand. "I guess I have my answer," she said to the empty toilet stalls.

She took a few minutes to collect herself and check her makeup and hair. Everything seemed to be in order - no lipstick on the teeth, no stray hairs messing up her 'do. She had no more reasons to stay in the bathroom, and if she continued to postpone the inevitable, she knew she risked destroying the mood that had come over them. *And that would be a damn shame,* she thought to herself. She couldn't remember the last time she'd been this excited about the idea of sex. Being with Jack was about as exciting as Monday night football for her, which was about as arousing as watching paint dry.

Aimee sat down at the table and immediately noticed Joe's smile. He wasn't mad. *Thank goodness for that.*

"Feel better?" he asked.

"Much."

"Sorry I scared you. I'll try to control myself from now on."

"No! I mean ... no, please. I'm fine. I liked what you said. It's just ... I'm not used to playing those games."

"It's not a game, Aimee. I was serious." His smile left his face.

"No, I know that. I don't mean games like you don't mean it. I meant like ... you know. Lover games."

"Oh. I see." He visibly relaxed and started to say something else, but their conversation was interrupted by the delivery of their meals.

They ate in companionable silence for a few minutes, waiting while the waitress refilled their water glasses and offered them freshly-grated parmesan cheese. Aimee sat there the whole time hoping they could move beyond this awkward moment. It felt like some of her fears were coming true. She had dorked out and possibly scared him off. She tried not to be sad about it. It wasn't like he was her boyfriend or anything, or that he had broken up with her. She'd been out of the dating game for a really long time, but she was still pretty sure you couldn't break up with someone after only one date.

"What do you think?" Joe asked. He motioned toward her food.

"Oh! About the food! It's good." She chewed a little more and paid attention to what she was eating, instead of focusing on her worries about her love life. "I mean, it's *really* good," she amended. "Wow."

"Yeah. This place is great. I come here once a week."

"So you're a regular. That's nice. For them."

"Yeah. The food is always consistent. Always good. That's important. I hate going somewhere and not knowing what I'm going to get. If it's the kind of place that's great one day and terrible the next, I'd rather not take my chances."

"Consistency is the key, is what you're saying."

"Yeah."

"I'll keep that in mind. Kiki and Elizabeth and I are opening a cafe bakery shop. I agree with you - I think being consistent is important in the food business."

"You gonna sell those cookies I tasted today?"

"Yes, I think so."

"Well, if the rest of your stuff is as good as those were, I have no doubt that you'll be successful."

"Thank you," she said, feeling all warm inside again.

"You have such a pretty smile, Aimee. Has anyone ever told you that?"

She blushed. "Not that I can remember."

"What a shame. A girl like you should hear that every day of her life."

"A girl like me?"

"Sweet, pretty, nice to people, caring. Pick your adjective."

"You flatter me," she said, looking down at her plate. She didn't know what else to say. She didn't want to compliment him back, since it felt like she would just be doing it in response to his kind words.

"Truth," he said, before putting a big bite of spaghetti in his mouth.

The rest of the meal of pasta and bread passed by quickly. Conversation turned to work, and Aimee learned that Joe was up for a promotion soon. If he got it, he'd no longer be driving around in a patrol car. He was thinking about becoming a detective.

"The only downside is, I won't be out there in a position to come rescue you," he said, sounding halfway serious.

"Oh, don't worry about it. I don't plan on getting into anymore situations with you-know-who. I have a lawyer now, and we're hoping to push the divorce through quickly."

"Well, that's good news."

The waitress came and took their plates away. Aimee looked down at her placemat and then at Joe's, immediately going red in the face again. His was perfectly clean - not a spot on it. Hers was covered in oil stains, sauce blobs, and bread crumbs, plus a few other things she couldn't identify. *Oh my god, I'm such a slob! How embarrassing.*

Joe followed her gaze and said nothing. He just picked up his placemat with one hand and grabbed the edge of hers with his other, sliding it over until it rested in front of him, and gently deposited his clean one in front of her.

Aimee sat there, stunned. He had read her mind and done the simplest, yet sweetest, most gentlemanly gesture he possibly could have. All without being asked. It made her nearly cry. She looked up at Joe, with misty eyes. "Thank you. That was very sweet."

"What? I have no idea what you're talking about." His tone said it all. This was the kind of consideration a guy like Joe gave to women as a matter of course. It's just who he was.

Aimee had never met a man like him before. And now she was worried she'd lose him before she'd get a chance to really experience what it felt like to be cared for and protected. The idea made her sad.

Joe tilted his head. "What's wrong, babe? You look bummed all of a sudden. Is it because I'm so messy?"

She smiled at that. "You really are messy. Look at all the stains on your placemat. How embarrassing."

"I'm hoping you won't hold it against me. Maybe you can just look at it as part of my quirky charm."

"Is that what it is? Quirky charm?"

"Absolutely."

"I'm not so sure quirky charm is such a good thing."

"Oh, trust me. It is. Can't be faked, and it's rare. I've been look-ing for someone with it for a long time. I always had a soft spot for it myself."

"Seeing as how you have it, right? The quirky charm thing?" she said, gesturing toward his placemat.

"Yeah. I'm looking for a good personality match. I figure the chemistry will come right along with it."

"Do you really think so?"

"I'm positive."

Aimee felt herself going warm.

"Do you want dessert or do you want to get out of here?" he asked.

"I'm ready to go," she said, wondering if he was thinking the same thing she was. She wanted to try another one of those kisses and see if it knocked her socks off like the first one had. She caught him staring at her lips and hoped it was a good sign.

Aimee opened up her purse and took her wallet out.

"What are you doing?" he asked.

"Paying for my meal."

"Oh, no ma'am you are not. Put that away."

"Why? I can pay my way."

"First of all, I asked you out, and in my world, women do not pay their way. I'm sorry if you think that's antiquated, but it's how I was raised and anything else just seems wrong. My mother would kill me if I let you pay for anything. Do you want that guilt on your shoulders?"

Aimee giggled, for some reason tickled pink that he was insisting on this. "No."

"Good. Besides, your money's no good here. Vincente won't take it."

She put her wallet back in her purse and waited for him to pay the bill. She tried not to feel guilty about making him pay for everything, and found it surprisingly easy to do. He wasn't just blowing smoke. She could tell - he really meant what he said. Jack had always made her pay half when they went out on dates. Even when they were married, she had her allowance and had to budget with it.

Once done with settling the check, they walked out of the restaurant and over to Joe's car. She liked that he drove something nice but not too flashy. The Honda Accord said to her that he liked style and comfort, but didn't feel the need to advertise his manhood - he was secure in who he was.

They sat in the car, Joe once again not immediately starting the engine. He turned to her and leaned in. "I've been wanting to do this for the past two hours."

He put his lips to hers before she really had time to think, and her heart nearly exploded with the emotions. *He still likes me! Even though I'm a dork! And messy!*

The kiss got hot and heavy in no time flat, and Aimee found herself madly wishing the front seats were more accommodating to heavy petting.

Joe pulled back, breathing a little hard himself. "Okay, Aimee. It's up to you what we do from here. Because if you leave this up to me, I'm going to want to get your clothes off right here in this parking lot, and that's no way to treat a lady. So please ... tell me what to do." He put his hands on the steering wheel and gripped it hard. "We can go to the movies, where I promise to keep my hands to myself. We can go to ..."

"The batting cages?" she asked.

"Yes. We could do that. Or we could ..." He didn't finish. He just kept staring out of his windshield.

"We could ...?" she asked, wondering if he was tempted like she was and thinking about getting more comfortable than they could in the front seat of his car. She didn't want to assume that he was as into her as she was with him. And even if he was, she wasn't sure if she should do what she wanted, which was to jump his bones and let the chips fall where they may.

"We could go back to my place." He turned and looked at her, without a smile and without judgment.

Her heart nearly stopped. "Let's go there," she said, trying to sound all cool about it but her voice squeaking anyway.

The whole ride there Aimee warred with herself, trying to decide if she'd made the right choice. *Will he call me after? Will I be unable to perform and be a big disappointment? Jack always said I was terrible in bed. Maybe he was right.* And on and on it went. By the time they reached his house, which was an adorable cottage in the old part of Winter Park, she had worked herself into a tizzy.

Joe came around and opened her door, taking her by the hand and bringing her into the foyer.

Aimee stood there awkwardly at first, not knowing what to do. Joe started to talk, but she didn't register any of the words. She lost her mind a little as she saw him standing there in the front hall, looking so incredibly hot in the white shirt that only gave her a hint of what was underneath. Some part of her brain that had lain dormant for more then ten years came alive and took over her thoughts, emotions, and control.

She took two big steps and pressed herself against him, reaching up to grab the back of his head and bring him down to meet her lips. In less than a second, they were locked into a passionate kiss. She pushed greedily into his body and felt him respond instantly.

He kept kissing her while pulling her backwards with him. He bumped into the wall and leaned into it for moment. Aimee took advantage of the support it gave and pushed more forcefully against him, wanting to feel his hardness on her most sensitive spot. She hiked up one leg to get better contact, and he responded by taking it and pulling her in closer. His other hand grabbed her backside, pushing it into him while he matched her slow, pulsating rhythm.

Aimee had never let herself go with abandon like this. It was exciting and maddening at the same time. He had too many clothes on and *she* had too many clothes on. She reached up to tangle her fingers in his hair for a moment before sliding her hands down and finding the buttons on his shirt, getting them undone as fast as possible. Their deep tongue-tangled kissing continued, their heavy breathing punctuated by the occasional moan as their bodies connected in just the right way. Aimee pulled his shirt off his arms and the tails of it out of his pants, flinging it carelessly to the floor once it was free.

Joe pushed himself off the wall and walked to the side and backward with her, stopping finally in the middle of his living room. A soft leather couch was at their knees and the nearby coffee table was quickly nudged out of the way without a second thought.

Joe grabbed her hands to still them, pulling away from her a few inches. "I want to see you." He turned her around to face away from him, unzipping her dress slowly from behind. It fell from her shoulders and down to her ankles, the material pooling up in a shiny pile, covering her black heels. She stepped outside of it and kicked it to the side. She was afraid to turn around and face him in her underwear and bra, but thanked the stars that she had worn her brand-new set of matching Victoria Secret lingerie.

He kissed her shoulder, ever so softly. His lips left a burning trail from there to her neck, sending shivers all over her body and making her nipples go rock hard. She started to turn, but he stopped her, slipping one bra strap off her shoulder and then the other, taking both of her breasts in his hands and gently squeezing them. She moaned in pleasure. His movements were so simple and yet so mind-blowing. No one had ever made her feel this way before.

She turned and grabbed his belt, working quickly to rid him of his pants. Soon he was standing there in his underwear too. She was happy to see he wore boxer briefs and was amused to see they were electric blue. All she could think was how he should be an underwear model with a body like his. She'd never fully appreciated the male form until she saw this specimen standing in front of her; especially since it had a big hard-on she could see outlined in blue, straining to get free. She rubbed it up and down with her hand, reveling at his sharp intake of breath. It made her feel powerful and just a little bit wild.

"I want to see you naked," he said, grabbing her and pulling her closer, kissing her hard and without mercy. She felt like she was being swallowed up in the sex, but even still, wanted more.

"You first," she said against his mouth.

He didn't need to be told twice. He pulled his underwear down, stopping at the bottom to drop to his knees, his face level with her belly. He took the edge of her panties and pulled them down, exposing her to his face. He leaned in and kissed her on her most private place, sliding his tongue into the slit for a second and sending shocks through her body.

"Oh!" came out of her mouth before she could stop it.

He looked up at her for a moment to verify she was okay before going back to what he was doing. Within seconds her legs started to quake. She was in danger of crumbling to the floor in a hotflash-induced collapse, his tongue sending her to a place she'd never dared hope to be. Something was building inside her, and she didn't know what it was or what to do.

"I'm ... I'm going to fall," she gasped, holding onto his hair, trying not to pull it too hard. But it was so difficult to remain gentle, the sensations taking over her mind and making her movements nearly involuntary.

He stood and lifted her up easily, as if she weighed no more than a feather, and carried her to the couch. "I'd take you to my room, but it's too far. I want you now."

The heady scent of her own sex on his mouth made her crazy. They began kissing again, as his heavy body come down on hers, his hardness pushing against her belly and forcing her body to sink farther into the soft cushions of the couch.

"Put it in," she begged. She was beyond caring what he thought about what she said or did at this point.

"I need protection," he said, visibly restraining himself.

"I'm infertile and have no STDs," she said in a rush.

"Me too. No STDs. Just got checked for work."

"Please. Don't wait. Do it now," she begged again.

The next thing she felt was pressure - delicious pressure she wanted more of. "Oh, God," she whispered, her anticipation making her feel like she was going to have a stroke. His tip was at her opening. He pushed it in, a little at a time, her slippery excitement making it as easy as it could be, considering how big around he was. Aimee had only a moment to consider how well-endowed he was before she was crying out in pleasure.

He moved it so slow, she was practically panting, wanting and needing to feel it go deeper. When he was fully buried, she expected him to start pulling out. But instead, he just pushed in more, and then moved his hips ever so slightly, pressing his body against her sensitive spots while keeping her stretched to the max.

She couldn't take it. She screamed in ecstasy.

He started to slowly pull out, going just as slowly as he did on the way in. Her body rose up to meet him, saying, "Please, please, please!" as she waited for him to come back in again.

He waited until he was almost completely out before coming back to her, a slow snail's pace making the sexy torture almost too much to bear. As their bodies touched again and his hips moved in that languid rhythm, she felt something begin to happen inside. She lifted her legs up to try and get him deeper, moving her own hips in rhythm with his.

"Oh my ... what's happening?!" she cried, not understanding what her body was telling her.

"Oh, God, Aimee, the way you're moving ... I'm going to come!"

She heard his words and felt the pulsing begin to announce itself. But it was coming from her, not him. She screamed out as wave after wave of orgasmic delight seized her body and turned it into jelly. She moved with its natural pulsing rhythm, unable to stop herself or the shocks of pleasure that kept coming and coming. Over and over it throbbed through her, as Joe then quickly started pumping, crying out himself in pleasure. She could feel his hard thickness send its seed into her, as Joe's back stiffened and he grunted once loudly, before finally relaxing again.

He moved a little and it caused another shock to her system. "Oh. My. God," she said. "Do *not* move."

He wiggled his hips.

"Noooo," she moaned. "It's happening again!"

He slowly massaged her with his pelvis, still filling her, only going partway soft.

Aimee couldn't take it. She started crying out in pleasure and confusion, her cries quickly turning to tears, as she made noises she had no idea would ever come from her mouth. When the sensations became too much, and began to turn more into tickles than orgasms, she grabbed his back, squeezing him to her. "Stop now. Stop. I can't."

He went still and leaned down, kissing her tears. "You are so beautiful right now. You have no idea."

"Why am I crying?" she asked, silent sobs wracking her body. She was overwhelmed and lost at sea, drifting on the emotions and sensations still haunting her mind and body.

"You're caught up in the feelings. Shhhhh, it's okay. Just relax. I'm here." He pulled out of her and laid at her side, stroking her hair and leaning down occasionally to kiss her cheek or lips gently. "Just relax, you're fine. You're okay."

Beneath his gentle ministrations, she found herself finally relaxing. Her heartbeat slowed to a normal rhythm and the heat that had been burning her up dissipated, leaving her feeling like she was floating. She almost couldn't feel the couch beneath her.

"So," he asked a minute or so later, a smile in his voice, "is it safe to say you enjoyed yourself tonight?"

Aimee smiled, reaching up to wipe the sticky tears from her face. "You could say that. I just hope you don't mind the fact that I'm a premature ejaculator."

He barked out a laugh. "You made me lose it pretty damn fast. I'm going to have to work on that." He stroked her breast softly. "Want to go out tomorrow?"

"Aren't you supposed to wait three days before you ask me again?"

"Screw that. I don't want to wait that long; I want to see you tomorrow. I'm not going to play those games."

"Good," she said, lifting her head to give him a quick kiss. "Me neither." She strained to sit the rest of the way up, Joe moving to the side as best he could to give her room.

"Where are you going?" he asked.

"The couch is kind of ... sticky," Aimee said, smiling so he wouldn't think she was complaining. "I'm just going to get my clothes back on."

"Oh, no you're not," he said, grabbing her and turning her around so she was lying on top of him. "I'm not ready to let you go yet."

Aimee thought her heart was going to burst with happiness. She'd just had her first guy-created orgasm of her entire life, and this gorgeous hunk who'd given it to her didn't want to let her go.

"Okay, but only for a few minutes. Then you have to take me home. I have a big day tomorrow."

"Doing what?" he asked. "You could stay here, you know."

"Nope. I have business planning to do and a workout at the gym."

"I can think of other ways you could work out," he said slyly, sitting up to kiss her neck.

She could feel him waking up beneath her. "You're kidding me, right? You're ready to go again already?"

"When I have a girl like you lying on top of me? Hell yes!"

She giggled and leaned down toward him, starting the kissing and fun all over again.

29

kiki

*K*IKI COULD NOT FIGURE OUT what her problem was. "I haven't been this nervous since my first show at Lola's," she said to her steering wheel.

Her phone rang and she picked it up. "Hello?"

"Kiki, hi. It's Elizabeth. Are you here yet?"

"I'm thirty seconds out. Where are you?"

"Standing out front."

"I see you. I'm just going to park." She hung up and waved to Elizabeth as she drove by, admiring her friend's choice in outfits. Elizabeth had that classic upper-crust type of beauty - understated but striking. Her chignon matched the Chanel-style black cocktail dress perfectly. Kiki was almost jealous of the look. Hers was always a lot less understated and a lot more wow-would-you-get-a-load-of-*that*.

She found a spot and got out, hurrying to join Elizabeth while silently bemoaning the humidity that was surely going to make her hair fluffier than she wanted it to be. "Hey, girl," she said as she arrived, giving Elizabeth a quick kiss on the cheek. "You look gorgeous, as always."

"I was just going to say the same to you. Those heels are outrageous. I don't know how you even walk in them."

Kiki turned her toe a little, lifting up her heel to reveal the red underside. "Christian Louboutin. Love 'em. Even though they're not known for their comfort. At least, not this style."

"Oh my goodness, you spend a lot on shoes. I've never done something like that."

Kiki shrugged as they walked toward the gallery entrance in the barely there evening light. "I used to, but not anymore. Now I have to pinch my pennies if we're going to make a go of this cafe."

"You got that right. I kept my checkbook at home tonight. Even if I see something I like, it's not going back with me. No matter what."

"Word up, sister. Desperate Measures ... hoo rah."

"So what's our game plan?" Elizabeth asked, stopping just outside the front door.

"Well, I'm going to go in, say hi and see what happens. I have my car, so I can take off if things get weird. Just ... stick by me until I give you the signal."

"What's the signal?"

"Shit, I don't know. Ummm, maybe I'll use a certain word. Yeah, that'll work. If I use the secret word, you know that means you can go and that I'm cool about being alone with him."

"Fine. What's the word?"

"I don't know. It has to be something I wouldn't normally say, but that could be worked into a sentence easily."

"How about 'popcorn'?"

"Popcorn?"

"Yeah."

"I guess so. It's not very sexy." She grabbed the door handle and pulled, letting the cool and crisp climatized air hit their faces and exposed arms.

"I'm sure you could find a way to make it sexy."

Before Kiki could respond, she saw Brent making his way over to them, first a smile and then a flash of confusion on his face.

"Hello, Kiki," he said, reaching her and giving her a chaste kiss on the cheek. "Thank you for coming. And you brought a friend."

"Brent, this is my friend and business partner, Elizabeth."

"Pleased to meet you," said Elizabeth, offering her hand. "I'm so glad Kiki suggested I come. I love gallery shows. Who's the artist?"

A girl in a serving uniform walked by and Brent waved her down, taking two flutes of champagne off her tray to give to the girls before taking one for himself.

"His name is Sebastian Buisson. Come. I'll introduce you."

Brent took Kiki by the elbow and steered her across the room. She looked over her shoulder, making sure Elizabeth was still behind her. Her friend was looking at some of the pieces hung on the white walls and lit by overhead lights, nodding in appreciation.

"I don't think I've heard his name before. Is he new?"

"He's been in France for the past ten years. This is his first showing here."

"Is he French?" asked Kiki.

"No, he's American. But I think he's spent a lot of time there. I seem to recall someone mentioning that he has a French parent."

Brent was leading them over to a small cluster of people who were surrounding a guy with dark, wavy, brown hair, long in a careless fashion, wearing pointed shoes, black pants and a black top. If Kiki believed there were vampires in the world, she'd suspect him immediately. He was good-looking, in a foreign guy kind of way. This guy had to have some European blood in him, maybe even the aristocratic kind. His cheekbones and chin were fabulous.

"Excuse me, Sebastian?" said Brent, nodding his head in apology to the three people he was obviously interrupting by coming over to make his introductions.

"Yes, Brent, hello." The strangers faded away leaving the four of them alone. Kiki could sense just a hint of an accent in Sebastian's speech.

"I want you to meet two ladies I invited here tonight. This is Kiki." He waited for them to shake hands. "And this is ... Elizabeth, right?"

"Yes," she said, shaking Sebastian's hand.

Kiki could tell Elizabeth had just gone from cool as a cucumber to as nervous as Aimee had been on her first date-after-divorce, in a split second. *Interesting. Time to make my exit.*

"So ... where's the popcorn?" Kiki asked.

Elizabeth's eyebrows shot up. She stuttered out, "Surely you don't need popcorn already? It's so ... early in the evening."

"Oh, no. It's fine. Feels like a good time for popcorn to me. I just *loooove* me some popcorn."

The two men were looking back and forth between Kiki and Elizabeth, obviously wondering what the hell was wrong with them, if the expressions on their faces were any indication.

"I just think maybe you should wait. Your craving for popcorn might not last, and then you'll wish you hadn't asked for popcorn so early on."

"Nope. I'm sure. Come on, Brent." She grabbed him by the arm and steered him away. "Let's go get some popcorn." She looked over her shoulder at Elizabeth, saying, "Enjoy the show. I'll talk to you later." She nearly laughed out loud at the expression on her friend's face. Elizabeth looked like she wanted to run, but didn't want to be rude. Her head was swiveling back and forth between Kiki and the artist. And he was just looking at Elizabeth, obvious interest in his eyes.

Kiki could have waited to bust out the secret word, but as soon as she saw the look on Sebastian's face when he looked at Elizabeth, she knew; she had to give them some time to sort out the sparks that had instantly started to fly. She just prayed Elizabeth wouldn't chicken out, or that she hadn't imagined the chemistry.

Kiki let her hand drop from Brent's arm, putting a few inches of distance between them.

"I'm pretty sure there's no popcorn here," he said, looking at her askance. She could tell from his voice he knew something was up.

"That's okay. My craving's gone."

Brent stopped and turned to look at her. "Are you going to tell me what's going on?"

Kiki smiled. "No. Are you going to show me some art?"

Brent smiled back, and Kiki was struck again by how handsome he was. He looked ... powerful. Confident, but not arrogantly so.

"Yes. I guess I am." He steered her over to a corner of the room. "Let's start here. You can let me know what you think."

Kiki looked up to see a large canvas, at least six feet tall and nearly as wide, covered in bright splashes of color that at first looked like random markings, but after a few seconds seemed to arrange themselves into a vision of a woman, leaning over a child. "Wow. That's pretty amazing, actually. Are you seeing what I'm seeing?"

Brent leaned over and read the tag that was next to the canvas on the wall. "Mother Loves Child? That's the title of this one. Is that what you see?"

"Yes, exactly. I'm impressed."

"Yeah, he's pretty talented. I commissioned a piece, and he just finished it." He looked at her. "I think you'd like that one, too."

Kiki had moved on to the next canvas. "I probably would. I definitely like his style. He's a bit of a tortured soul, isn't he?" she asked, when she saw the third one. It was darker, moodier.

Brent spoke softly at her shoulder, "I hear that he had a muse - a woman - but that she and he had a falling out. Apparently, he's struggling now with awakening the same feelings for the work that he had back when she was in his life. I think you'll be able to tell which are part of the post-muse period."

"That's so sad," said Kiki, almost to herself, as she looked at the next canvas. It was covered in bold strokes of midnight blues and deep greens, with dashes of burgundy and bright red in various freeform shapes. There were no figures here - just raw emotion.

"This one really gets to me, too. After seeing some of the others and then this one, it's kind of ... jarring," he said.

Kiki was trying to ignore the feel of his breath on her neck as he spoke from behind her, but it was difficult. He wasn't saying anything provocative or sexy at all, but it was making her want to lean against him anyway. He looked so proper in his expensive, tailor-made suit. She wondered what he'd look like with his hair all mussed and his shirt untucked. Even at the gym he'd looked perfectly put together. A glance down at his feet told her that he even took the time to shine his expensive Italian leather shoes. There wasn't a single scuff on them.

"So did you commission the piece recently?"

"Yes. Very recently. He finished it quickly. That's one thing I like about him; he's not just an artist, he's a businessman. When he has paid work to do, he prioritizes it."

"But aren't you worried about having such a sad piece in your place?"

"Oh, his commissioned work isn't like this. I gave him a picture, not a very high-quality one either, and just asked him for his interpretation of it. It came out stunning, really. I plan to give him more work."

"What was it of?"

Brent shrugged, his mind going to some far off place. "Just someone."

"Oh." *Probably an ex-girlfriend. I wonder if she knows her ex is a stalker.*

Kiki continued on in awkward silence with Brent at her side. They reached the end of the series of paintings at the same time Kiki finished her champagne.

"Can I get you another glass?" he asked, taking her empty flute and putting it on a nearby table.

"No, thank you."

"Popcorn?" he asked, a glint of humor in his eye.

"Sure, if you have some," she retorted, meeting his sass with a little of her own.

"Well, there isn't any here, but I know where we can get some."

"Is that so?"

"If you're not afraid. To be alone with me."

Kiki laughed, surprised at the turn the banter had taken. "Afraid? Please. I eat guys like you for breakfast."

He raised an eyebrow.

"Scared?" she asked.

"Me? Maybe a little. But I like living on the edge."

"Fine. Take me to your supplier," she said. "I'm just going to go say goodbye to my friend, first." She left him to walk over to Elizabeth, freaking out a little inside at the flirting she'd started. *What am I getting myself into? Do I really want to know how this turns out? Maybe leaving it a mystery would be better.*

As she walked up to her friend, she noticed a pretty blush spreading across her cheeks. Sebastian looked just as tickled as Elizabeth did.

"Sorry to interrupt. Brent and I are going to take off. I need some popcorn."

Elizabeth's eyes widened. "You're leaving? Oh." She turned to the artist. "It's been very nice speaking with you, Sebastian. Thank you for keeping me so entertained."

"You're leaving? Oh, no, please stay. You haven't even seen my work yet."

"No, I can't."

"Yes, you can," said Kiki. "Please. Stay. I'll be fine. You have your own car." She turned her attention to Sebastian. "As long as I can count on you to make sure she gets to it safely..."

He put his hand on his heart. "It would be my pleasure."

Elizabeth looked conflicted, so Kiki made the decision for her. "Good. Bye, Lizzie. See you tomorrow at the gym. Eleven o'clock?"

"Fine," she said softly. "As long as Sebastian doesn't mind."

"Not at all. I mean it. Stay and talk to me some more. These shows can be very dull sometimes. You are making it more than bearable."

Kiki turned to go, without waiting for Elizabeth's next volley of misgivings. Elizabeth wanted to stay, she could tell. She and Sebastian had made some sort of connection and Kiki wasn't going to be the one to bring it to an end.

Brent met her at the door and opened it for her, following her out into the humid night.

"So, where to?" asked Kiki.

"Did you park nearby?"

"Yep. Just over there."

"How about if I take you in my car and then I can bring you back later?"

"No, I'd prefer to have my own car."

"So you have an escape plan?"

"Yes," she admitted. There was no sense in trying to deny it.

"I don't bite, you know." He was smiling, not offended at her paranoia.

"How smart would it be for me to take the word of a possible biter that he's not a biter?"

"Probably not very. Okay, you win. Let me walk you to your car, and I'll drive over so you can follow me."

They walked until they were near her car.

"Don't tell me you drive the Camaro ...," he said.

Her hackles went up. "So what if I do?"

"Then I'm going to have to beg you to let me drive it."

Kiki smiled, surprised at his response. "Maybe someday. I don't let just *anyone* drive it."

They arrived at the back of the vehicle and Brent took his time walking around it slowly, his eyes appraising its smooth lines and flawless paint job. "Wow. This thing is unbelievable. Did you buy it in this condition?"

"Heck no. I restored it from junk."

His head whipped up. "No way."

"Yes way. Bought it from a little old lady out in the boondocks. Paid my guy to put her together piece by piece."

"Numbers matching?" he asked with hope in his eyes.

"Of course."

He grabbed his chest. "Oh god. I think I'm in love."

Kiki's heart skipped a beat. *He's talking about the car. Just relax.* "I made a couple of mods. There's A.C. and an alarm, decent stereo."

"So you drive this every day?"

"Yep. I know I shouldn't, but I can't help it."

"I don't blame you. I'd do it too." He looked at the interior. "Can I sit in it?"

Kiki shrugged. "Sure." She unlocked the door and got in, leaning over to unlock the passenger side.

Brent got in and sat in the passenger seat, his eyes roaming over the dashboard. He looked at Kiki when he was done with his appraisal. "I'm seriously impressed. You surprise me."

"Why? Because I'm a chick with a muscle car?"

"Well, maybe that's part of it. But the way you put this back together. I mean, except for your mods, it looks all original. Not a lot of people bother."

"I know. It just seemed like the right thing to do."

"You do that a lot, don't you?" he asked. "Do the right thing, I mean."

"I try."

He stared at her for a few seconds more. "Where do I know you from? Other than from the gym, I mean. It's making me crazy."

Kiki looked away, wondering if she should tell him the truth. "I don't know," she lied. "I don't remember ever seeing you before in my life." The lie felt wrong, wrong, wrong, but she couldn't help herself. She was starting to like this guy, and she wasn't ready yet for reality to destroy the good buzz she had going. He was gorgeous, smart, and loved muscle cars as much as she did - and he didn't hang around strip clubs. *What's not to love?*

"Okay," he said, slapping his palms on his legs and making Kiki jump. "I'll go get my car and meet you over here. Then we'll go to the popcorn place."

"I'll be waiting," Kiki said. She watched him get out of the car, admiring the cut of his suit and how it showed the muscles in his legs when it was stretched across them. She was going to have to get a better look at him in the gym next time. Before she'd been so busy trying to blow him off, she hadn't taken advantage of the close proximity and better view of his physique.

Kiki busied herself with fixing her lipstick and hair in her rear-view mirror for a few seconds before looking up at the sound of an engine purring behind her. A quick glance told her what she already suspected. The guy liked fast cars.

He was parked behind her in one of her dreams on wheels.

She shut off her engine and got out, stalking over to his window. She stood there while he rolled it down, smiling the whole time.

"Oh no, you are *not* driving an Audi R8. Get out." She motioned with her thumb for him to leave the car. "Come on, come on. I don't have all night."

He opened the door and exited the vehicle, gesturing at the seat. "Would you like to sit in her?"

"You're damn straight I would," she said, feeling like she was going into mild shock. She'd drooled over this car for years, dreaming that someday, maybe, she'd get to ride in one. She never kidded herself about actually owning one. They were about a hundred grand out of her price range. She was a savvy enough investor to know that when she had a hundred grand, it needed to go into real estate or stocks - not hot cars. But, oh, how she would have loved to have one of these.

She sat on the smooth leather seat and inhaled deeply. "Oh, God, it still smells new!"

"Gorgeous, right?" he said, leaning in and smiling over her shoulder. "Press that."

She did as she was told and watched the GPS come out of the dash. "Damn. I need one of those."

"Want to give it a test drive?"

Her eyes took on a mad gleam. She whispered, "Are you serious?"

"I'll trade you. One Audi R8 test drive for one sixty nine, numbers-matching restored Camaro test drive. One ... from here to Dean's."

"Dean's?" she asked.

"The popcorn store. Over by the mall."

She laughed. "You're on. Keys are in the ignition." She shooed him away so she could shut the door, pressing on the accelerator a bit and reveling in the roar of the engine. She paid no attention to the answering growl from her Camaro, now coming from behind her. She was too absorbed in the awesomeness of Brent's ride.

She tried not to giggle with mad glee as she pulled out of the parking lot and into the empty streets of downtown Orlando at nine-thirty at night. The engine purred, and she marveled at the smooth yet solid shifting mechanism she controlled with ease. The seat and pedals were in perfect position. This car was made for her.

Ten minutes later, she pulled up to the darkened windows of the popcorn store. Brent drove up and stopped beside her, awkwardly rolling down the passenger side window. "I guess they're closed. I know another place, if you're not tired of driving the Audi."

"Lead on!" she said recklessly. Anything to give her more time in the car. At this point she trusted him. No guy, no matter how rich or cool he was, would let just anyone drive his R8. He obviously considered her special. She just prayed he wouldn't change his mind when he finally figured out who she really was.

The second place offering popcorn in town turned out to be his apartment, located in a high-rise on the edge of downtown. She followed him into the underground garage and waited for him to lift the gate for her, since it closed after each car. She parked next to him in a designated guest spot. She noticed he took one with the number 2001.

She got out of the car and waited for him to come over. They exchanged keys, and she smiled. "That was amazing. Thank you so much."

"I thought you'd like that," he said, taking her by the elbow. "I got it a few months ago. I'm still not off cloud nine when I drive it around."

"Aren't you worried about what people will think when they see you in it?"

He pushed the code buttons giving them access to the lobby. "What do you mean?"

"You know," Kiki said, trying not to be too impressed with all the marble and glass around her. "That you're overcompensating."

"I never worry about that kind of thing," he said, in a dangerously low voice - dangerous because it was laced with a seductive tone that seemed to pull out emotions from her that she wasn't yet willing to share. He led her to an elevator and pushed the button for the twentieth floor, inserting a key at the same time and turning it to the right.

"Good," she said, suddenly at a loss for words and feeling not nearly as supremely confident as she had ten minutes earlier.

The door opened up into his condo. He had the entire floor. She had to force her mouth not to drop open at the view and the fact that she was standing in the middle of luxury like she'd never seen before except in her magazines. "Are you a drug dealer or what?" she asked, moving into the penthouse apartment to go stand at the floor to ceiling windows that looked out over the city.

"You could say that."

She whipped around to look at him and could see from his expression that he was messing with her. "Ha, ha, very funny."

"Actually, I do mergers and acquisitions for pharmaceutical companies. So in a way, it wasn't a joke."

"Well, what the heck are you doing at ..." She almost said, 'Lola's' but stopped herself in time.

"What was that?" he asked, coming up to hand her a glass of wine he'd just poured.

"Nothing. Wow, what a view." She was trying to distract him from her goof-up.

"Would you like a tour?"

"Sure. So long as it doesn't end in your bedroom."

"I promise, I have only innocent intentions."

"Fine then. Show me what you've got." She wanted to smack herself in the forehead for that one. First she tells him no funny business and then practically tells him to show her the goods. *I really need to watch my words better than that. He's going to think I'm making a move on him for his car.*

He took her around the apartment and stopped at the entrance to his bedroom. "Through this door is the bedroom and master bath. I'll let you take a look by yourself. I don't want you to think I have ulterior motives."

He stepped away and walked back toward the center of the condo, disappearing around a corner.

Kiki's curiosity got the better of her. She walked in and was instantly surrounded by the feeling that she was entering someone's very private space. Where the rest of the condo looked as if it had been decorated by a professional designer trying to please just about any taste, making it classy but bland, this room was more steeped in emotion. The woods were dark and exotic looking. The covers on the bed were a deep blue, setting off the cream-colored walls to perfection. There were pictures in frames on the side table next to the bed showing an older couple and a younger man, not Brent, joined by an alarm clock and an expensive-looking watch left carelessly near the edge. The lamp looked artistic - a one-of-a-kind creation made by someone with a real talent for glass-blowing.

She wandered into the bathroom and smiled at the man-things she saw next to the sink. He used one of those mugs with shaving soap in it and a brush for applying it, a silver razor lying nearby. His closet was twice the size of hers, with row after row of suits and racks of shoes. One side was dedicated to work things, the other to recreation. He obviously played a lot of sports.

She walked out to go back and join Brent in the living room, but stopped when she saw the painting that had to have been done by Sebastian Buisson. It was huge, taking up almost half of the empty part of the wall that faced the bed. It commanded the space. It had blues and reds and yellows and all manner of other shades, all fighting for space on the canvas. As her eyes adjusted to the rhythm of the strokes, she found herself intrigued. There was a figure there. A woman. She was standing in profile, looking off into the distance. She had long hair, dark. The strokes of paint that made up her face hinted at beauty. She walked over to get a closer look, losing the image as she did. But there was a small placard and photo on the wall next to it, and she wanted to get a closer look.

When she reached it she stopped. Staring at the photograph affixed to the wall and the caption underneath it made her blood run cold and then hot ... and then cold again. It was a grainy photo of a woman standing in a gym, exercise machines in the background. The caption read: *Mystery Woman*. It was then that she realized who the subject of the painting was. She was looking at a picture of herself.

elizabeth

𝓔LIZABETH WAS FASCINATED BY SEBASTIAN. She'd never met anyone like him. He talked about his work as if it were a living thing. It was so completely different than accounting, she couldn't wrap her brain around it. She found herself feeling sad that she'd never tried to paint before. *I wonder if I'm too old for art lessons.*

"Would you like to see my work?" he asked. "I could give you a personal tour."

"Oh, yes, definitely."

"Come this way. We can start with my older pieces and then finish with the more recent ones."

Elizabeth followed him to the first canvas.

"You must stand back to get the entire image to appear in your mind."

"What happens if I stand closer?"

"Well, you will find out. Look for the image here, think about it for a minute, and then get closer. Tell me what you see. Don't worry, you won't hurt my feelings if you don't like it." He smiled at her graciously, but his eyes said that her opinion did matter to him. A lot.

ELLE CASEY

She looked away from his face, trying to get the look in his eyes out of her mind. He was adorable, and she saw pain there. It made her want to give him a big hug. The rest of him made her want to do other things. He was seriously gorgeous, in a wild, less-conventional way.

She stared at the image on the canvas. Within a few seconds she saw a woman looking down, holding something in her arms. "It's a woman with a baby. Right?" She looked to confirm whether she was correct.

"Good. Now move closer."

Elizabeth followed his instructions and realized that as she got closer, she started seeing the brush strokes and the colors, but not the image that together they created. "Wow, that is just fascinating. I've never realized that about paintings before."

"They are not all like this. It is a hallmark of my work, however. I don't do it on purpose, it just kind of happens this way."

"You loved this person. Is she your mother?" Elizabeth asked.

"Why do you say that? That I loved her? How could you know that about me from the piece?"

"It's the body language of the woman. There aren't enough details to see a facial expression, but the way she almost shelters the child while touching its face ... I don't know. It says to me that you saw the love there and needed to express it. You treated the subject with love." Elizabeth felt her face go pink and then felt bad when she saw the sadness move from his eyes to his shoulders. They sagged ever so slightly. "I'm sorry," she said. "I got a little carried away there. It's silly."

"No, no, not at all," he said, suddenly enthused and upbeat again, looking as if he were purposefully shaking off the melancholy that had threatened. "It's correct, you are reading exactly the truth of this painting." His accent was getting stronger as he spoke faster and had so much emotion wrapped up in his thoughts. "I did love her - I still do, in a way. She is not my mother, but she is a mother to this child. She was a ... friend of mine for several years."

"A girlfriend?" asked Elizabeth, a little shocked that she'd actually said aloud what she'd been thinking. But she really, really wanted to know the answer.

"She was my muse, and yes, my lover. But not anymore." His voice lost its excitement.

Elizabeth put her hand on his sleeve. "Is it your child, too?"

"No. He was not my child. I met her when he was a baby. She is with the boy's father now."

Elizabeth took her hand back and looked away, trying to avoid the awkward silence her questions had brought upon them. She felt his hand take her elbow and his soft voice in her ear.

"Don't worry yourself over this. It means nothing to me now. Let's move on to the next piece. I am truly interested in your opinion."

She looked at him to see if he was being honest or just trying to make her feel better. From what she could tell, he was being sincere.

"Especially now that I know you are so perceptive. Or maybe I should be worried. I'm afraid I won't be able to hide anything from you."

Elizabeth smiled, trying to reassure him. "I'm really not that perceptive. I think you just do a good job putting your emotion into your work. You have a lot of ... passion." She felt herself start to sweat. *Great. I'm embarrassing myself now. He's going to think I'm totally corny.*

"What do you think of this one?" he asked, gesturing to the next painting.

They made their way around the gallery, Sebastian presenting each painting in turn, and Elizabeth sharing her interpretation of what she saw and felt when she looked at them. Sebastian became more and more enthusiastic as they progressed, now holding her hand and occasionally reaching over to stroke it with the other.

Elizabeth did her best to concentrate on his work, but his attentions and soft way of touching her and expressing his emotion without even realizing it was distracting and energizing. She was trying to remain neutral, but it became impossible. The more she started to like him, the more she loved his work. When she had first arrived, she had appreciated the artistic talent; now she appreciated the man behind the art.

The prices on these pieces were high, but not so high that she considered them out of her league. She wished she had spending money, but was glad she had left her checkbook at home. She wasn't sure that she had the self-control to keep from buying one of his paintings. The moody ones really got to her. A protective feeling came over her whenever she saw them, making her want to heal him of his obvious pain. She normally shied away from tortured souls, but this felt different. He wasn't tortured permanently; he had a temporary pain that didn't need to last forever.

His apology pulled her head out of the clouds. "Elizabeth, please forgive me. I've been talking for over an hour about myself and my work, and I've just realized that I have learned nothing about you. Please. Tell me ... what do you do for a living? Are you married?" He smiled and added, "I hope not."

Elizabeth smiled back. "No, I'm single. And for a living I used to be an accountant, but right now, I'm getting ready to start a new business with some friends. One of them is Kiki, who you met earlier."

"What kind of business?"

"A bakery cafe. Kiki's in charge of styling it, and I sure wish we could afford to put your work in there. But we're on a budget."

"For you, I would do whatever you want. Seriously."

"No, I couldn't ask that of you, but thank you so much for saying that."

Sebastian took her by the hands and stepped sideways so he was in front of her. "Please. Let me do this. I don't mean to put pressure on you, but I am feeling something in my heart that hasn't been there in a long time. To be honest, I want to leave here now and paint something." He squeezed her hand. "I want to paint you."

Elizabeth looked at him like he was nuts. "Whatever for?"

He tilted his head in confusion. "What do you mean?"

"I mean, why me? Why now?" Here she was at a gallery showing for the purpose of rescuing her friend, and now she'd somehow hooked up with the artist who was saying he wanted to paint her. Impressions flitted across her mind. *He's crazy. He likes me. He's an artist with one of those wild temperaments and needs to paint when he feels the fever. Why me? Why not someone like Kiki, voluptuous and gorgeous, not ... conservative and boring?*

"I don't question the feelings when they come over me. Please tell me you'll come. My studio is not far from here."

"If this is some elaborate ruse to get me to take my clothes off ... I'm not interested." *Not really. Okay, maybe a little.*

"No, please, not at all. I just need to paint something. I will be right back." She watched him walk over to the gallery owner whose face went from happy to irritated in two seconds. The woman shook her head several times 'no' but Sebastian's gestures and facial expressions clearly said he didn't give a hoot what she wanted. He turned and made his way back to Elizabeth.

"Come. Let's go. We can take my car."

"How about if I just follow you? I'm parked over there," motioned Elizabeth, now standing with him just outside the gallery.

"Okay, I will pull up here, to the front of the building, and you come behind me. We will drive about ten blocks. It's in a commercial warehouse space, near several other artists' studios."

They parted ways, Sebastian jogging off in the opposite direction. Elizabeth smiled at his distracted air. As she made her way to her car, she wondered what it would be like to be so carried away by your passion for your work that you ceased to care about other things, like what gallery owners would say or what women might think. She figured plenty of women would have said, 'No thanks,' and walked away from this craziness. But she couldn't help but think, *What would Kiki or Aimee do?* She decided that their lives being the way they were now, both of them would go for it - Kiki because she was a big risk-taker anyway, and Aimee because she needed some excitement and something different in her life right now. And that went for Elizabeth, too. *I'll just text them and let them know where I am, just in case he turns out to be a sociopath.*

She drove her car over to the entrance and within seconds a sports car pulled up on her passenger side. The window rolled down to reveal Sebastian's excited face. He was beaming at her.

"Follow me!"

He zoomed off and she followed nervously, not exactly comfortable with the speed he was going but not wanting to lose him. They arrived at a small warehouse building five minutes later. He pulled into the dark parking lot and slid into a space, jumping out of his car to come meet her at her door. He held out his hand to help her, and led her to a gray, metal door. He jingled a bunch of keys around until he found the right one, opening the door and gesturing for her to precede him inside.

The smell of paints and turpentine hit her first. It wasn't unpleasant at all. It made her feel like she was really in the lair of a true artist. He turned on the light, and she was immediately taken aback by what she saw. There were canvases everywhere - leaning against the walls, up on easels, stacked on tables. There were several palettes with dried blobs of paint left carelessly on surfaces - some even balanced on paintings themselves. She continued to look around while he busied himself with setting up an easel and some paints and brushes.

Elizabeth wandered over to the nearest group of paintings, moving them aside one by one so she could look at them. They were covered in dark splashes of emotion, moody and turbulent. Over in the far corner were some with lighter colors, but they seemed to lack inspiration. She didn't know why she felt this way; she was no art expert. It was just the sense she got.

"Okay, I am ready. Please come and sit. Just make yourself comfortable."

He gestured to a raised sort of stage. It was small, just big enough for a person to sit or lie down on. There was a cushion on it, covered in a black drape.

"How do you want me to sit?" she asked walking over to it.

"However you want. Just be sure to face me, so I can see you. You may even lie down if you like. Maybe that would be better."

She looked at him through narrowed eyes, trying to figure out if he was making some kind of move, but he was too busy mixing paint colors feverishly to even look at her. She shrugged, deciding that he was so wrapped up in what he was doing that he probably wouldn't even notice her much. She felt as though she'd gone from being a living, breathing person, to an art object. She didn't mind at all. It actually made her feel free and beautiful, in a weird way. She was flattered that a man so talented saw something in her that made him want to express himself.

She went over to the stage and sat down, testing the cushion a few times with her butt, bouncing up and down on it lightly. It was very soft, one of those memory-foam things that molded to the body. She suddenly felt very tired, remembering her workout and lack of sleep from doing the financials into the wee hours of the morning. "Were you serious? Can I lie down?"

He waved a paintbrush at her, looking only at the blank canvas in front of him. "As you like," he said distractedly, turning it so it was no longer in portrait position, but landscape instead.

She sighed. *So much for stimulating conversation.* She laid down on the stage and reclined on her side, kicking her heels off and letting them drop to the floor. The warmth of the room and the tiny buzz from the champagne, mixed with the sounds of brush strokes and his occasional humming, quickly send her into la-la land. Her head dropped from her hand to rest on her outstretched arm, and the last thing she remembered thinking before falling asleep was how amazingly beautiful he looked standing there - consumed by his passion, in front of his canvas. Dressed in all black with his hair in disarray and framing his angular and strong-featured face, he looked like a sexy character out of a fantasy novel.

31

aimee

AIMEE WALKED INTO THE TOWNHOUSE and called out, "Hello! Kiki? Are you home?"

"In the kitchen!"

Aimee found her eating another cookie. "Your butt's gonna get big if you keep eating those cookies like that."

"I'm stressing, okay? Cookies are good for stress."

"They're good for celebrating, too," said Aimee, grabbing one herself and winking at Kiki. She couldn't keep the smile off her face for even two seconds to worry about whatever was stressing her roommate out.

"Tell me your good news," said Kiki. "That goofy smile can only mean good things."

"Oh, it does. But it can wait until tomorrow, if you're too tired."

"Oh, hell no. You're not going anywhere. It's only one-thirty. Tell me about your date."

Aimee related the story of her first date with Joe, leaving out the details of what occurred at his house, but giving Kiki the basic idea.

Kiki hugged her spontaneously. "Oh, I'm so happy for you! Didn't I tell you? He's a keeper. And you just got right back up on that horse and everything was fine."

"Better than fine, actually."

"We were right about the veiny hands, weren't we?"

Aimee blushed. "I'll never tell."

"You don't have to. Your freshly-fucked afterglow is giving you away."

Aimee slapped Kiki on the arm. "Watch your mouth, girl."

"Oh, I'm sorry. Did I offend your puritanical sensibilities? How about this: your post-coital glow is giving you away ... is that better?"

Aimee screwed up her face. "Not really. I think I prefer the other."

"So, are you going on a second date?"

"Yep. He already asked me."

"Wow, not even waiting the three-day period. This must be serious."

"It is. I think it is. No, I know it is. Or I hope it is." She started to feel stressed. "God, I hope it is. I'd just die if it wasn't."

"No, you wouldn't die. You'd move on. That's life. The key is to enjoy what you have while it's good, and either fix it or get the hell out if it's not."

Aimee nodded in appreciation. "Wise words from a very smart girl. Now tell me about your night."

"Well, my night was ... interesting, I'll put it that way."

"How so?"

"Come sit at the table with me. I'll bring the juice."

Aimee sat down and waited for Kiki. She came out a minute later with two small glasses of orange juice.

"Okay, so I met Brent at the gallery, hung out, looked at some great art - I think Elizabeth and the artist kind of hit it off, actually. Did she send you a text?"

"Yes, she did. She sent me the address of some warehouse where he paints, I think?"

"Yeah. So anyway, we left and went to his apartment."

Aimee rubbed her hands together. "Oooh, this is getting good, fast."

"Hold your horses. Don't get too excited yet. So anyway, I got to drive his car, which was the highlight of the evening. An Audi R8, Aimee." She looked at her friend expectantly.

"That means absolutely nothing to me, but I get that it's a big deal from that crazy look in your eye."

"Trust me. It is. So I drove his car to his penthouse apartment in the city. Amazing. Marble, leather, silk ... the works. But then I got a tour, and in his bedroom, is a huge painting of me. Of *me*, Aimee."

"Of you? But how could he have a painting of you?"

"He commissioned it from the artist at the gallery. Sebastian Buisson."

"No sir."

"Yes sir."

"But how could he have done that? He didn't even remember you or where he met you."

"He took a picture of me on his cell phone at the gym."

"Oh, my god. That's kind of ..."

"Creepy, right?"

"Well, I was going to say flattering. But yeah, okay, I could see how you might find it creepy. What did he say when he showed it to you?"

"Nothing. What happened is, I went on a tour of the condo, and he stopped the tour before his bedroom and let me do that part myself. He said he didn't want me to think it was some sort of sad plan to get me in bed. So he wasn't there when I saw it."

"What did he say when you called him out on it?"

"Nothing. Because I didn't."

"What?! You didn't say anything at all? I'm shocked. That is *so* not like you."

"I know. I freaked. I tried to act like it was no biggie or that I hadn't even seen it, and then got the hell out of there."

Aimee laughed, picturing Kiki busting butt to leave. "How did you do that?"

"I don't know ... I told him you needed me. I pretended to get a text. Luckily, Elizabeth's text had just come in, so I had the beep to cover my lie."

Aimee slumped down in her seat, finishing off the last of her juice. "That is just hilarious."

"Hilarious?" asked Kiki in a miffed tone. "How is that hilarious? He could be a stalker or a psycho!"

"He didn't strike me as the type," said Aimee, still smiling.

"Well, maybe that type can hide itself."

"Or maybe he just thinks you're amazingly beautiful and wants to have an artistic image of you to keep him company, since you're this mystery woman who won't tell him who she really is."

"Well, he did actually title the thing 'Mystery Woman' or something like that. I'm going to tell him the next time I see him, if I ever do see him again. Maybe then he'll leave me alone." The tone of her voice should have been all self-assured, but it wasn't.

"I don't think that's what you want," said Aimee.

"What? You think I want a stalker after me?"

"No, don't be silly. I think you liked him before you saw that painting, and you're hoping it doesn't mean that he's a nut case."

Kiki shrugged, refusing to commit.

"If you knew for a fact that he wasn't crazy, would you like him and want to go out with him again?"

"If I knew that there was some valid reason for that painting that didn't include insanity at any level? Then, yes. I admit. I found him ... attractive."

"*Pfft.* Please. The guy is a god."

"Fine. He's hot. And he's incredibly smart, and he likes fast cars."

"Wow. It sounds like you found the perfect guy for you."

"Except for the insane part."

"Yeah. But the jury's still out on that aspect of his personality. And, don't forget to factor in how adorable your babies would be, if you two ever procreated."

Kiki looked at her like she was crazy. "Babies? Are you nuts? I'm not having kids, ever."

"Baloney. You'd make an awesome mommy. You should have at least three. Maybe four."

Kiki shuddered. "No way. Kids are noisy and messy."

"They give lots of good cuddles though and they give noodle necklaces, too."

"Noodle necklaces?"

"Yeah, you know ... how they paint dry rigatoni pasta and then put it on a string for you for Mother's Day? Noodle necklace."

"Well, there is the noodle necklace. You do have a point there." Kiki rolled her eyes.

"I wonder how Elizabeth's night is going," said Aimee.

"We'll find out soon enough." She looked at her watch. "It's after two in the morning. I'm going to bed. We're meeting Lizzie at eleven tomorrow for workouts and then lunch."

"Good. I need to lose about ten pounds, stat."

"Getting naked with a hot cop turning out to be good motivation?" teased Kiki.

"You bet your buns, girl," said Aimee, smiling as she made her way to her bedroom. She was beyond thrilled to feel so inspired about making herself look and feel as good as possible. And she thanked heaven for Jack's terrible temper. If she'd never slipped on that juice and banged her head, she never would have met Joe. It was so cool how every cloud in her life was turning out to have a silver lining.

32

kiki

$\mathcal{K}$IKI GOT UP EARLY AND spent the first three hours of the day fretting about the possibility of seeing Brent at the gym. She really didn't want to face him after running out like she had. *What would I say to him if I saw him there, anyway? 'Hey Brent, listen ... I have a question to ask you. Are you a psycho?'* She was pretty sure that particular question would tick him off, plus there was no hope of getting an honest answer, anyway. No one ever admitted to being crazy.

Aimee's voice came from upstairs. "Are you ready? It's time to go."

"Ready as I'm going to be."

Aimee came into the kitchen to join Kiki, and patted her on the back on her way to the sink to fill up her water bottle. "Don't worry about Brent. He probably won't even be there."

"What if he is?"

"Well, you'll talk to him. Apologize for running out, and then ask him what the hell that picture is all about."

"Just like that?"

"Why beat around the bush? That's not your style, babe. Go with what you know." She moved to the front door. "Come on! You're driving."

Kiki shook her head at this newfound bossiness of Aimee's. It suited her to be taking care of people and their feelings like this. Kiki was glad to see her friend feeling so good and happy about her situation. She didn't want to be one of those misery-loves-company-kind of people who gets grumpy when others are happy. She did her best to shake off her misgivings and started walking toward the door. Before she got halfway there, her phone beeped. She looked down at a message from Elizabeth flashing on her screen.

CHANGE OF PLANS. MEET ME AT MARCUS'S OFFICE. HE HAS NEWS FOR AIMEE.

"Hey, Aimee!" shouted Kiki at the open front door. "Change of plans!"

Aimee came wandering back in, looking down at her phone, all of her good mood having evaporated away. "I got the text. What do you think it means?" She looked and sounded panicked.

"Good news, probably. Come on. We'll do the workout after."

They got into the car and drove to the lawyer's office in silence. Kiki wanted to make Aimee feel better, but wasn't sure what she could say to make her worry go away. They'd see soon enough whether it was good news or bad; there was no point in speculating now. She turned on the radio and sang along to top forty nonsense, determined to at least provide some comic relief.

The receptionist ushered them in, and seated them in front of Marcus's desk to join Elizabeth, who was already there. She stood up and gave each of them a hug.

"How are you doing, Aimee? You look stressed."

"I am," she said, taking her seat. "Anything that has to do with Jack and this divorce makes me freak out."

"Well, don't freak yet. Maybe it's good news."

"It is good news. Maybe," said Marcus's voice from the doorway. "No, don't get up ... sit, sit. I don't have a lot of time. I have to be in court in forty-five minutes." He closed the door and walked quickly over to his desk, sitting down and putting his folded hands on its surface.

"Aimee. Darling. How are you?"

"Well, I was good until about twenty minutes ago. I'm very nervous right now."

"Lizzie tells me you got the binders, is that right?"

"Yes. We can bring them over later ... "

"No, don't worry about that now. And what about the computer?"

"No, we ran out of time," said Kiki.

"Well, I might be able to get that for you anyway," said Aimee, looking at her friends nervously.

"How?" asked Elizabeth. "I don't think you should break into the house again. It was really risky last time, and now he'll be waiting for it."

"Don't call it breaking in, love. It's still her home," admonished Marcus.

"Yes, I know that technically it's still her place. But entering through an upstairs window using a ladder, and racing to beat an alarm, feels like breaking in."

"Understandable," he said nodding, before turning back to Aimee. "Tell us what you're thinking."

"Well, a few months ago, I read an article online about the importance of backing up data. I told Jack and he said no, that we had everything in the binders and that if our system failed, we could just recreate the books."

"Meaning you could just do all that work," said Kiki, disgust in her voice. Every time she heard another little factoid about Jack, she hated him more.

"Yes. But I didn't listen to him. I didn't want to have to re-do the work. So I got an account at one of those cloud computer thingies. I'm not sure what it's called. Anyway, all the books are there. At least, I think they are. I backed up the whole hard drive to it."

Kiki reached over and hugged Aimee, letting go so Elizabeth could do the same. "You little rebel, you. Good for you!" she said.

"Thank you," said Aimee, smiling shyly. "I felt guilty about it at the time. But, I guess, not so much now."

"That's excellent, excellent news. Okay, so the reason I called you here was to share some information with you. It's all good news as far as I'm concerned. I spoke with Jack, who's apparently one of those attorneys who is so arrogant he doesn't think he needs a lawyer for himself. I won't bore you with all the details, but essentially, he's ready to make a deal to get this over with."

"Wow," said Aimee, shock in her voice. "I'm really surprised about that. I thought he'd fight more."

"Well, don't give up on that thought just yet. He is going to fight ... over the settlement. He thinks he's going to be able to block the use of those binders against him. But your backup drive of the computer, the entire hard drive, in fact, will be all we need. I assume that's the computer he used for personal things too? Did he have a password on it that you didn't know?"

"No. He had to give it to me to get into the books."

"Good. So he can't claim that it was not part of the marital property. In any case, I'm going to hire a really great accountant I know," with that he raised his eyebrows a few times at Elizabeth, "to go through those books of yours and do some forensics. If there are assets hidden anywhere that he's somehow referenced in the system, she'll find them. Once we know the value of the estate, we'll have some figures we can throw out at him."

"He's not going to give me anything. He already told me that about a hundred times."

Marcus held out his hands across the desk, signaling that Aimee should take them. She put her hands in his, and he grasped them firmly. "*Jack* is not in control of the law of the State of Florida, sweetie pie. Jack may *think* he's not going to give you anything, but he would be *wrong* about that. Very wrong."

"But what if he refuses to pay?" asked Aimee, getting a small measure of comfort not only from his words, but also his warm hands.

"He will go to jail for contempt of court."

Aimee's eyes bugged out. "But he put all of our money into a townhouse for Tiffany. And a car. There is no money left to get from him as far as I know."

Marcus shrugged, releasing her hands. "Cash, real estate ... it doesn't matter. They're all marital assets. He may think he bought that townhouse for Tiffany, but he really probably technically bought it for you. It wasn't his money to spend. Not all of it anyway."

"But I never worked while we were married."

"And why is that?" asked Marcus.

"Because he said he needed me at home to help with other things, so he could focus on building his practice."

"Exactly. His contribution to the marriage pot was building the business. Yours was managing the household so he could do that. It's considered an equal contribution under the law, and that makes you entitled to half."

"Holy crap," said Aimee. "That's a lot of money, kinda. Well, more than I have now." She looked at her friends, her heart feeling significantly lighter. "That means I could maybe have some money to invest in the business!"

Kiki patted her arm. "Let's not get ahead of ourselves right now. You're already a full partner. Let's just see what happens with Jack before you go committing your entire nest egg to our venture."

"I agree," said Elizabeth. "Give me a few days to go through those numbers and his receipts. I'll see what I can find. Marcus, can you do a public records search? I'd like to know what his other assets are."

"Already working on it." Marcus stood. "That's all I have for you now. Make sure you give that username and password for the cloud drive to Lizzie." He turned his attention to his cousin. "I need it by the end of the week. Can you do that for me?"

"You bet. Probably even sooner."

"Good!" He clapped his hands together loudly and then rubbed them together. "This is going to be great fun! I love taking arrogant assholes down a notch or two. Pardon my French."

"Your French sounds good to me," said Aimee, now more relaxed about her prospects.

The girls left the office after saying their goodbyes to Marcus. They battled traffic on the highway on the way to the gym, Elizabeth following behind in her Buick.

"I am so relieved at his news," said Aimee. "Not only is Jack going to have to share, but I'm safe from his nonsense now."

"Damn straight," said Kiki.

"And I live in a secure neighborhood ... "

"You're dating a cop, too, don't forget that part."

"I'm dating a cop. You're right. What could go wrong?"

Kiki didn't respond to that. She knew the answer was, *'Plenty,'* but she didn't want to rain on Aimee's parade. *Let her have some days where she doesn't worry about what bad things might happen to her.*

They arrived at the gym and started with the circuit routine. Aimee and Elizabeth moved to the treadmill section while Kiki went to the free-weights. She was in the middle of the leg exercise that Brent had showed her when she heard his voice coming from behind her. She looked up and saw him in the mirror.

"I see you've decided to include my tips in your workout."

Kiki stood up straight and put the hand weights she was using for her modified lunges on the floor, grabbing her towel so she could wipe her sweaty hands and face. She didn't want to turn around and face him, but even more, she didn't want him to think she was a chicken shit.

"Hey, Brent, what's up?" She turned and was bummed to see his legs and arms were just as gorgeously formed as the rest of him. *Too bad he's a nut job.*

"Thought I'd drop by for a quick workout during my lunch hour. Feel like spotting me?" He gestured to the bench that had a barbell and a set of weights all ready to go on it. He must have been there for a little while without her noticing. *He probably thinks I was avoiding him. And I probably would have tried to avoid him if I'd known he was here.*

"Sure." *What am I going to say? No? That would be rude.*

He laid down on the bench and grabbed the bar. "I'm sorry you had to go so quickly last night. I didn't even have time to make you that popcorn."

"Yeah, that's too bad," said Kiki distractedly. She was trying not to stare at his bulging muscles as he strained to lift the bar twelve times in fairly quick succession.

When he was finished, he got up to add more weight to each side before lying back down again. "I kind of got the impression you were running away, actually." He looked at her intently for a few seconds before focusing once again on lifting the bar and starting another round of twelve reps.

"Yeah, well, I kind of did, I guess."

He put the bar back on the supports when he was done, breathing a little heavily. "You admitted it."

She shrugged. "No sense in denying it. I saw that picture in your room and figured I was about to get attacked or something, so I felt it was best to disappear rather than give you the high kick that I keep in reserve for just those occasions."

He laughed, in spite of the seriousness of her statement. "Wow. I do *not* want to see that move. At least, not used on me." He got up and added another set of weights to the bar and laid back down. Before he started lifting again he said, "I know it seems nuts. But I promise you ... I'm not a stalker or a lunatic. I just ..." He shook his head, as if he couldn't express what he was thinking. "I don't know. I can't really explain it. I saw you here, and I just felt this connection. It was weird."

"Sounds like a stalker to me." She was only half-kidding.

"I know, it really does, now that I hear it out loud. Geez, I hope I'm not a stalker." He lifted the bar, more slowly now, the additional weight and his fatigue causing him to strain a little.

"There's probably a list of questions to ask potential stalkers, and if you can answer yes to more than three of them, it means you are one," Kiki said.

"Like ... what?" he grunted out.

"Hmmm. Let's see ... okay ... have you ever tried to find out where your target lives?"

"No."

"Have you considered sneaking around to take pictures of your target?" She gave him a hard look. This one was obviously going to be hard to deny.

He put the bar up on the supports and rested his hands on his chest, breathing heavily. "Okay, I admit, I did take the picture. But it was because I'd seen you somewhere before and I wanted to try and jog my memory later about who you might be. Then the more I looked at it, the more I thought how beautiful you are. And Sebastian caught me looking at it and asked to see it. He proposed the idea of painting it for me. He said, 'Why not make it into something you can really enjoy?'"

"Wow, he's a good salesman."

"Yeah. Like I said - he's not just an artist. He's a businessman. When he was finished I was just stunned. He told me before he started that I didn't have to buy it if I didn't like it ... that it would only be a vague representation of you. But once I saw it, I knew I had to have it. It captured the mystery of you perfectly."

"So maybe I have two stalkers."

Brent smiled. "No. I never told him who you were."

"He had to have recognized me at the gallery."

"Maybe, but he's discreet. He wouldn't say anything to any-one about his subjects."

"Okay, so about that stalker list..."

Brent stood up and wiped his face. He was only a few feet away, but it felt like only two inches. His presence was over-whelming in a way that excited Kiki and made her nervous at the same time. She wasn't sure if she liked it or not, and prayed in her head that it had nothing to do with the craziness of thinking he was obsessing over her. Obsession was never a good thing, even if for a few moments it might make a girl feel desired.

"Go ahead. I'm confident in my sanity. Ask away."

"Do you have a strong desire to sneak into your target's home and take something of hers to keep and admire several times a day?"

"Like what kind of thing?" He smiled deviously. "Like panties?"

"Seriously?" she acted all miffed that he wasn't taking it seriously, but she was secretly glad he could joke about it since that made her feel like he couldn't be nuts.

He started laughing silently. "I'm sorry, I'm just joking. Okay, no. I have no desire to sneak into your house and take a memento."

"Do you get jealous when you think of other people talking to me?"

"It depends who it is."

"Stop."

"No, this one is the truth." He walked over and looked her right in the eye, talking softer now and more seriously. "I like you, Kiki. You're all full of spit and vinegar. Go out with me. I promise, I won't do anything freaky."

Kiki bit her lip, unsure of what to say. She like him, despite the fact that he'd had her painted. His explanation made sense, and she could easily verify it with Sebastian if she wanted to. Maybe Elizabeth had his number. *What the hell.* "Okay. I'll go out with you one time. But no crazy stuff. No popcorn at your house, or ... whatever."

"Oh. I was going to cook for you. Would you prefer to go to a restaurant?"

"I'd prefer neither."

He looked taken aback. "Okay. Care to fill me in on your plan?"

"No plan. I'm looking for something a little more ... creative. Anyone can do dinner at a restaurant and a movie."

He nodded his head at her appreciatively. "A challenge, eh? I like it. I can work with this."

"Good. So I'll see you around." She turned to go join her friends.

"Wait a minute, not so fast. When are we going on this mystery date? Are you available Friday?"

"No." She actually didn't have plans, but she felt like being ornery.

"Saturday?"

"Nope."

He play-frowned at her. "Sunday? Come on, Kiki. How am I going to meet your challenge if you won't fit me into your schedule?"

"Fine. Sunday. Afternoon. One o'clock."

He nodded his head. "You're on. Better bring your game face."

"Oh, I will. Trust me." She left him standing in the free-weights as she struggled to keep the smile off her face. *This is going to be fun.*

elizabeth

So, I WAS STANDING THERE, and all of a sudden Kiki says, 'I need some popcorn'."

"No she *didn't!*" gasped Aimee.

"Yes, I did," said Kiki, walking up to join them on the treadmill to Elizabeth's left. Aimee was on Elizabeth's right. "I thought I saw some sparks fly, so I decided to fan the flames a little. So what happened after I left?"

"Well, we talked for a long time about art and galleries and the business aspect of selling creative goods. Then he gave me a personal tour of the paintings in the show."

"Wow, that's cool," said Aimee.

"Yeah, but that was only the beginning," said Elizabeth, unable to keep the smile from appearing. Just thinking about it made her go warm again - this kind of heat being different than the treadmill warm she was already feeling.

"Ooooh, do tell," said Kiki, pressing buttons on her machine to get it going faster.

"Well, when he got to the end, he kind of got this crazy look in his eye and told me he wanted to paint me."

"Paint you?" said Aimee. "Oh my god, how romantic can you get?!"

"Seriously. I'm jealous," said Kiki.

"Well, at the time I wasn't sure if he was romantic or crazy, but I decided to give him the benefit of the doubt. I followed him to his warehouse, and he started painting me."

"Ohmygod, ohmygod, ohmygod," said Aimee. "What happened next? Did you guys get all crazy and cover each other in paint and make love in his studio?"

Elizabeth frowned at her playfully. "Not exactly."

Aimee pouted. "Bummer."

"What did happen? I'm betting something good," said Kiki.

"Well, I got up on this stage he has set up and laid down..."

"And ...?" asked Aimee, excited all over again.

"And I fell asleep."

"What?! What kind of story is that? You're not supposed to fall asleep at the sexy part," insisted Aimee.

"That is kinda lame," agreed Kiki, smiling.

"Well, I couldn't help it! It was warm, and I was tired ... and I had that stupid champagne."

"The perfect storm," said Kiki.

"Exactly. I woke up later with drool on my face and a cramp in my arm."

"What did Sebastian do?"

"Nothing. He painted. He wouldn't let me see it when he was done. He turned it to face the wall and told me I couldn't look until it was finished."

"Was he mad you fell asleep?" asked Aimee.

"No, I don't think so. He looked exhausted. I didn't leave until about three in the morning. He was kind of distracted, actually. He gave me a quick kiss on the cheek and told me he'd call."

"Damn. I want to see that painting," said Kiki. "He does good work."

"Me too," said Aimee. "Has he called yet?"

"No. But it's been less than a day, so I'm not worried about it."

"Do you want him to call?" asked Kiki.

• 306 •

Elizabeth didn't even have to think about it. "Yes. I do, actually. I'm a little surprised by that, but whatever. It's out of my hands. I just have to wait and see if he feels the same way."

"No, you don't, Lizzie. This is the age of women's empowerment," said Aimee. "Call him if you want to go out again."

"Well, it's not 'again' since we technically haven't gone out yet. And I know I could call him, but I kind of want him to call me. Sometimes, for me, empowerment is letting go of the power."

"I hear ya, sister," said Kiki. "I like to control my world. Letting go of that control is torture."

Elizabeth switched off her machine and walked slowly until it stopped. "I have a lot of work to do with this divorce accounting, so I'd better get going. Aimee, will you email me a link to the service and your username and password?"

"Yes. And, Elizabeth ... I really want to thank you for doing this for me. I'm going to bake you a mountain of things so I can express my gratitude, since I can't afford to pay you much."

Elizabeth waved her concerns away. "No, don't even worry about it. Feel free to bake me some things, but don't feel like you owe me. Friends help each other out when they need it. Your friendship is all the thanks I need." She smiled so Aimee would know she meant it.

"That is so sweet. I feel exactly the same way about you guys."

"Oh, I meant to ask you ... are we doing the book club meeting this Friday?" asked Elizabeth, calculating how much time she'd have to set aside to read the next book before then.

"Oh, I hope so. I have some treats planned for Betty."

"I wonder what hideous color the booties will be this week," said Kiki, getting off her treadmill and standing next to Elizabeth.

Elizabeth play-slapped her on the arm and laughed. "That's not nice. Maybe someday she'll make booties for your babies."

"*Pfft.* First of all, I'm never having any of those messy creatures, and second of all, if I did, they wouldn't be caught outside the house in anything that looked like that."

Elizabeth decided it was wiser to let Kiki's argument go than to try and convince her otherwise. The booties *were* kind of ugly, but they were the type of gift you cherished because they were made by someone special.

Elizabeth left the girls and went home. She glanced at her phone and saw that there were no messages and no missed calls. She sighed, thinking about how much it sucked to have to wait by the phone. The idea of calling Sebastian was tempting, but in the end she decided it just wasn't her style. *If he wants to see me again, he knows my number. I put it into his phone myself.*

She made herself a snack and by the time she was done eating it, an email had popped up with Aimee's username and password. Elizabeth logged in and said to her computer, "Okay, Jack the Jerk ... let's see what you've been up to behind my friend's back ..."

Six solid hours later, she stood up and swung herself side to side, cracking her back and trying to work the kinks out. The stuff she'd found would probably fill an entire legal file at her cousin's office.

Marcus had sent over a computer dossier of Jack's assets discovered during a public records search that went nationwide, along with tracers showing bank transactions not only domestically but internationally. Elizabeth didn't want to know how her cousin had gotten that information. That data plus the things she had found were going to make quite a case for Aimee.

Jack, the devious bastard, had been very, very busy behind Aimee's back. Elizabeth smiled when she thought about how her cousin was going to make mincemeat of him in court. Marcus was not going to be happy at all about what she'd found. Well, he'd be happy to have the ammo, but mad to see what Aimee had suffered without even realizing the extent of it. Marcus hated it when women were taken advantage of.

She spent the next thirty minutes on the phone with her cousin, giving him details, including the final estimate of Jack's net worth. Marcus told her to put it all together in a report for his team to look at the next day, and thanked her profusely for working so fast.

"Have I told you lately how amazing you are, Lizzie?"

"Last week."

"Well, that was entirely too long ago. You are my precious angel, and no one deserves you. No one but me."

"Well, I hope that's not true. It sounds lonely."

"Well, okay. There is a man out there somewhere for you. But he's going to be damn special, and he's going to have to work really hard to convince me he's good enough."

Elizabeth's mind wandered to visions of Sebastian, wondering if he was up to the task.

"Well, I can tell I've lost you. I have to go anyway. Duty calls. Toodles, lovie!"

"Toodles, Marky Mark."

She disconnected and then went upstairs to take a shower. She couldn't wait to tell her friend the good news and the bad news: that Jack had over two million dollars in assets, and that he'd hidden three quarters of it from his wife.

34

aimee

 IMEE SAT IN STUNNED SILENCE, listening to Marcus and Elizabeth outlining the web of deceit that Jack had woven around her life over the past several years.

"And this is what we found without serving any discovery requests on him. Once we have an order from the court, we can subpoena his partnership returns on his business, bank and brokerage account records we might not know about, and lots of other things. This is just the beginning of the nightmare," said Marcus.

"I don't know what to say," said Aimee, fighting tears. She felt like the world's biggest fool. Even Joe's earlier phone call arranging their next date for that evening wasn't making the pain go away completely.

"You don't need to say anything yet. I have a suggestion, if you're ready to hear it," said Marcus.

"Yes. Please. Go ahead," she said, sniffling a little and wiping her nose with the tissue Elizabeth had handed her.

"We know he has at least two million in hard assets we can prove right now. I'll bet when it's all said and done we'll probably find another half a mil in the business and some other assets we haven't yet uncovered ... maybe more."

"You mean besides the boat, the dock at that marina, and the condo downtown I had no idea even existed?"

"Yes. So let's assume we're dealing with two point five million in assets. You're entitled to half of that. I suggest we contact him and offer him a settlement of one million."

"He'll never say yes to that," Aimee deadpanned.

"Don't be so sure. He's stupid, but without his law license, he's not going to be able to hang on to the few assets he'll have left. So he's not *that* stupid."

"What do you mean?" whispered Aimee. She knew how much Jack valued his ability to practice law. Marcus was talking crazy now, in Jack's world.

"We have reason to believe that he's done some unethical things with some clients. Some of these assets were previously in the names of people he has listed as clients. Attorneys aren't supposed to have outside financial dealings like that. He knows it. I know it. We all know it. Not to mention the fact that his partners probably wouldn't appreciate him accepting payment in this form and putting the reputation of the firm in jeopardy."

"Do you mean ... you're going to blackmail him?" Aimee nearly squeaked at the b-word.

"No. I'm simply going to put together a package of the evidence that we've uncovered and suggest he do what's in his best interests - which is to pay you your half, or rather, less than your half. I will cite the case law and statutes for him so he can make an informed decision. He'll come to his own conclusions about what the court would think of what I found. I won't have to spell that out to him. If he's not completely insane, he'll go for it."

"Or try to kill me," said Aimee, joking.

"If you really think it's possible that he'd try to harm you, you need to tell me," said Marcus.

"No, not at all. I was only kidding."

"Okay then. With your approval, I will approach him about a settlement."

Aimee hesitated for a moment, worrying about how Jack was going to flip his lid over this approach, but in the end decided to just do it. He deserved to feel the pain of the law after all he'd done. "Go ahead. You have my consent."

"Oh, and one other thing. Jack has already stated in the documents he's filed with the court that the birth of his child must be figured into his expenses, thereby lowering your support amount. I have moved the court to order a paternity test. If he wants to claim the child, he's going to have to prove it's his."

"I'm sure it is," said Aimee sadly. He was finally having the baby he'd always wanted. Just not with her.

"Stranger things have happened. At the very least it'll get his goat. And I like to keep the other side a little off balance. Maybe we'll get lucky and he'll lose his cool in front of the judge and show his true colors."

Aimee looked at Elizabeth. "You weren't kidding. Your cousin is hardcore."

Elizabeth smiled. "That's my Marky Mark."

"Okay, you can bring your other friend in. The confidential part of this meeting is over."

Elizabeth got up to let Kiki in.

Aimee asked Marcus, "Do you really think he'll settle?"

"Yes, I really do. The evidence of his deceit is overwhelming. And you have the extraordinary good luck to have pulled Judge Halsey for your case. She does not like cheating husbands one bit. She had one of her own, once."

Aimee smiled. "Poor thing."

"Oh, don't feel sorry for her. She took half of his eighteen million dollar estate. She works for the fun of it, not because she has to."

"Were you her lawyer?"

"No, thank goodness. Otherwise, she'd have to recuse herself from the case. No, actually it was my mentor. I learned everything I know from him."

"He must be very proud of you."

"He was. Before he died."

ELLE CASEY

"Oh, I'm sorry," said Aimee, feeling bad about the pain she saw in Marcus's eyes.

"Complications of AIDS, I'm afraid. He was one of the group that had it before all these great medication cocktails came along to fight the disease."

Kiki walked over and sat down, breaking the mood and causing a distraction. "So, are we taking this guy downtown or what?"

"All the way downtown," said Marcus, smiling again. "I'm looking forward to it. I'll have this put together by the end of the day and presented to him by five o'clock. I'll keep you in the loop, of course, Aimee. I'm going to give him a five-day deadline. I don't want him sitting on it too long or coming up with any nonsense."

"What if he says no?"

"Then we go to court. And take half of *all* of his assets, not just the ones we found this week. The amount will be much higher, and he'll have to pay attorney's fees and costs too. He'd be colossally stupid not to take our offer."

"He'll counter probably," said Kiki.

"And we'll consider it when he does. I'm not inclined to accept anything he offers, but it's up to my client." Marcus nodded at Aimee.

Aimee felt powerful all of a sudden, as if for once she was going to be in the driver's seat with Jack riding in the back. It felt good.

Marcus stood. "I need to get going. If that's all, I'll show you to the door."

The girls stood and went out with him.

"Aimee, as always ... it has been a pleasure." He took her hand and kissed the back of it. He did the same for Kiki and Elizabeth as they passed by.

Out in the lobby of the building the girls regrouped to discuss the meeting.

"Wow, that was amazing, wasn't it?" asked Elizabeth. "I love Marcus."

"He's awesome. I'm so lucky he's on my side," said Aimee. "And you too, Elizabeth. You found most of that stuff. You're just brilliant!"

Elizabeth smiled. "It was my pleasure. Really."

"Your ex is a serious prick, Aimee. No offense," said Kiki.

"Believe me, none taken. He *is* a prick. I cannot believe all the stuff he hid from me. I feel like a total ... I don't know ... idiot."

"Don't feel that way," said Elizabeth. "Some of the most brilliant, wonderful women have been taken for fools by the men they loved. It just goes to show what a loving person you are ... that you forgave him all his issues and loved him anyway."

"More like it shows how blind I was. I just don't know why I let myself be so *used.*"

"Stop. I can't allow you to go back in history and beat yourself up about something you had no control over. Come on. Let's go have some drinks," said Kiki.

"Well, actually, I have a date," said Aimee, smiling her head off. She was already getting butterflies over her upcoming dinner at Joe's house. He said he cooked a mean quiche, so she was going to go see for herself that real men do, in fact, eat it. She hoped the dessert included more sexy stuff. She hadn't been able to stop thinking about it and the way it felt to have his body against hers.

"Well, excuse me," said Kiki. "Fine, go on your date with His Hotness. Lizzie and I will just go ring in the new year six months early."

"Seven," said Elizabeth.

"Who's counting? Come on."

Aimee rode back with Kiki to their place, listening to her friend sing off key, thinking about how lucky she was to have met these two girls. She had Jack to thank for that - Jack and his stupid golf clubs. She'd never been so happy about her husband's selfishness in her life. Even if he never paid her a dime, those golf clubs and her putting them on Craigslist had gotten her friendships and allowed her to benefit from circumstances that were worth way more than any settlement he'd ever agree to.

35

kiki

*K*IKI FINISHED AIMEE'S MAKEUP AND stood back, admiring her handiwork. "Done. You are gorgeous. Now go tear his clothes off and show him your stuff."

Aimee smiled. "I plan on it. Now that I know what the Big O feels like, I want more."

"Oh, boy. Does Joe know he's created a monster?"

"Yes. But I don't think he minds."

"As well he shouldn't. Go put your shoes on. I want to see the whole look."

Kiki busied herself with putting away the makeup and brushes she'd used on her friend, smiling to herself at the transformation she'd seen in her. It went way deeper than the shadows and powder she'd just put on Aimee's face. It was in her heart. She was feeling good about herself again, and Kiki was so happy to be a part of it. It made her feel all choked up a minute later when Aimee came dancing into the room, spinning around to flare her dress out, her cheeks a rosy pink.

"What do you think?"

"Amazing. Did you douche?"

"Kiki!" Aimee shrieked, giggling but acting like she was trying to stay serious. "Stop saying that!"

"Well, did you? What if he goes down on you tonight?"

Aimee's hand flew up to her mouth. "Oh my god. I've never had anyone do that to me before. Not really. He kind of did a little ... last time."

Kiki smiled, trying not to get so much pleasure out of teasing her friend. "I'm only kidding. You took a shower, you're fine."

"Maybe I should go put some perfume on it?"

"Perfume on your va jay-jay? No. Cologne does *not* taste good, so I have to assume perfume doesn't either."

"Okay, what then?"

"Nothing, goof," said Kiki, pushing Aimee out of her room and then gently down the stairs. "Let your girl just be herself. I'm sure he'll love it."

Kiki sat down at her laptop and clicked on her Skype icon.

"What are you doing?" asked Aimee, looking over her shoulder.

"I'm Skyping Lizzie."

"She'll kill you if you keep using that name."

"That's why I'm doing it."

Aimee slapped her playfully. "You're so bad."

Elizabeth picked up. "Hey, girls!" Her cheerful face was beaming on the screen.

"Why are you so happy?" asked Kiki.

"I just got a caaaallll ... " She held up her cell phone so they could see.

Aimee squinted her eyes. "You got a call from ... artist guy? Who's artist guy? Oh, wait ... oh, that's so cute! You got a call from Sebastian!"

"Yes. He wants to show me the painting."

"I'd like to see it too," said Kiki.

"Well, me first. If it's good I'll take a picture for you."

"Cool. Are you going to see it tonight?"

"Yes. In a couple hours. I'm going to take a raincheck on those drinks, if that's okay. Oh, Aimee, you look gorgeous. Are you meeting Joe?"

"Yep. Going to his house."

Kiki typed a message into the Skype screen when Aimee turned around.

Elizabeth read it and got a frown on her face for a second. Then she shrugged her shoulders and said, "Hey, Aimee?"

"Yeah?" she said, turning back to the screen.

"Did you douche?"

"Oh my *GOD*, you guys, you are so mean!"

Kiki nearly busted a gut laughing so hard.

"You told her to say that, didn't you?!"

Kiki shook her head in denial, but Elizabeth sold her out.

"Yes, she did. I'm sorry. I didn't realize she was teasing you."

"Do you think I should?"

"Should what? Douche?"

"Yes."

"God, I don't know. No? Yes?"

"Would you?"

"I don't know. It depends."

"On what? Whether you thought he was going to go down on you?"

Elizabeth barked out a laugh, nearly choking on the sip of water she'd just taken. "Uh, no. More like it would depend on what time of the month it was. You know. If some ... freshness was in order." She waved her hand back and forth. "Why are we talking about this? Don't worry about it. Just go have fun."

"But what if ..."

"No. Don't say it. Just go. Enjoy yourself. Get naked. Don't stress about it."

Kiki finally got a grip on herself when she heard the doorbell ring. "Gotta go. Prince Charming is here for his lover."

"Bye, girls!" said Elizabeth before her face disappeared with a pop.

Aimee ran to the door, and flung it open. Joe stood on the front stoop, looking as gorgeous as ever.

Kiki moved to the kitchen to give them some privacy. A minute later she was joined by Joe, who said hi and then looked around the room, checking all the counters.

"Looking for cookies?" Kiki asked.

"Yep."

"Here." She reached into the fridge and pulled out a small tupperware box. "She made you some."

He took it and frowned. "Kind of a small box."

Kiki shrugged. "You gotta earn 'em, babe."

He raised an eyebrow at her. "Mission accepted."

Kiki laughed. "Good for you."

She watched Aimee and Joe walk out the door and grinned. *Life is good.*

elizabeth

*E*LIZABETH LOOKED DOWN AT HER phone. There was a text from Aimee's number on her screen.

HAVE YOU SEEN AIMEE?

She frowned. *What the heck?* Her fingers typed out her response. *WHO IS THIS?*

Three seconds went by before the answer arrived.

JOE.

Elizabeth ran over to her laptop and flipped the lid up, clicking on the Skype button for Kiki's contact. Kiki picked up within two rings. "What's up?"

"Did you just get that text from Joe on Aimee's phone?"

"Yeah. What's the deal?"

"I have no idea. Wasn't she with him tonight? And why is he on her phone? I don't want to leave for Sebastian's until I know what's going on."

"I'm going to call him. Hold on a sec."

Elizabeth watched as Kiki dialed. She held the phone away from her ear. "I'm putting it on speaker."

The phone picked up. "Yeah, this is Joe."

"Hey, Joe, it's Kiki. What the hell, man? Is this a joke?"

"No. Unfortunately, it's not. I seem to have lost my date."

"How could you lose your date?" laughed Kiki.

Elizabeth wasn't feeling as entertained by the notion as Kiki was. Maybe because she knew her cousin had transmitted that settlement file to Jack earlier this evening and had received a furious phone call in return an hour later from a nearly incoherent Jack Parsons. The guy had been beyond angry and issued all kinds of threats. Marcus called Elizabeth and told her the gory details, mentioning offhand how it had reminded him of a guy one time who'd kidnapped his kids shortly after getting bad news from his lawyer.

Joe's voice came over the speaker phone again. "Well, we were in my car, driving over to my house, when I stopped for gas. I went in to pay for it, and when I got back, she wasn't here. She's not in the store and she's not in the bathroom. She just disappeared."

"And she left her phone?" asked Elizabeth. This was not looking good.

"Yes, in her purse."

"Oh, shit," said Kiki. "This is bad."

"My thoughts exactly. Joe, did she tell you what's going on with her divorce right now?"

"No, not really. She said she got some good news today, that's about it."

"Well, yeah, even Kiki and Aimee don't know the stuff that just happened recently, though."

"Tell us," demanded Kiki. "And make it fast. I suddenly have a very bad feeling about this."

"Well, Marcus called to discuss some of the financials with me. I learned that he presented the documents and settlement offer to Jack. Without divulging any confidential stuff, he let me know that Jack absolutely flipped out. The guy went nuts. Marcus said he was glad he wasn't anywhere near him since he seemed a little unhinged."

"And he didn't bother to tell Aimee this?" asked Joe, clearly upset.

"Well, Aimee had assured him Jack wasn't anyone to fear. And Marcus knows that she lives in a gated community and dates a cop. He probably figured the news could wait until tomorrow."

"Listen, girls, thanks for the info. Aimee mentioned she thought she had seen Jack's car outside your neighborhood when we pulled out, but I didn't see it, so we blew it off. I have to go call this in. I think we can assume for now that Jack has her somewhere. I'll call you back."

The line disconnected.

"Holy fuck," said Kiki. "I *cannot* believe this." Her voice wavered a little.

Elizabeth tried to keep the feelings of nausea from taking over. She swallowed several times in a row before saying, "Joe is going to get the cops involved. Maybe there's something we can do."

"You have the addresses of Jack's condo and townhouse in your stuff?" asked Kiki.

"Yeeessss," said Elizabeth, not sure she liked the direction Kiki's mind had gone.

"Give 'em to me. I'm going to check them out. Maybe he's brought her to one of those places."

"How about if we give them to Joe instead?"

"Fine, give them to him, too. But I want them also."

Elizabeth hesitated. She was worried about both of her friends getting into danger. One of them was bad enough.

"I'm not kidding, Lizzie. Hand them over. You can go or not, I don't care either way. But I am, even if I have to come steal the files from you."

Elizabeth couldn't help but smile at her friend's fierce determination. "Okay, on one condition."

"What?"

"I drive."

"No way."

"Why not?

"Because you drive like a granny in a granny's car."

"Kiki!"

"I'm sorry, but now is no time to spare feelings. We need a car that can kick ass and take names. A Buick just doesn't cut it. Sorry."

"Fine. But no guns."

"Fine. No guns. How about knives?"

"No! No weapons. We use our brains to get her out of this."

"I'll be over in ten."

The picture of Kiki on her screen dissolved, sending Elizabeth's screen saver into motion.

Elizabeth reached over and grabbed Aimee's file, writing down the two addresses of the properties she knew Jack had nearby. She prayed they'd find Aimee before Jack did anything stupid.

37

aimee

$\mathcal{J}$ACK'S TRUNK SMELLED LIKE SMELLY shoes and leather. Aimee was wedged up next to his second-string golf bag, her skirt tangled in her legs. She had started screaming as soon as he'd shoved her in there, but that only made him pull over and slap the crap out of her. She could feel the split in her lip with her tongue. It was still bleeding, and it stung like hell.

"Jack!" she yelled. "This is a really bad idea! You're going to get in *big* trouble!"

"Not if they don't catch me, I won't."

His answer made her blood run cold. *Is he going to kill me? What else could he possibly mean besides that?*

"If you kill me you'll lose your law license!" she yelled.

"Not if they don't catch me, I won't!" he yelled back, his insanity only made more obvious by the hysterical laughter that followed.

Ohshitohshitohshit. Isn't this just my luck? I finally have my first orgasms and then I get killed before I can have a third one.

Jack drove over something that felt like a speed bump, and it made her head hit the hard metal side of the car. "Ouch!" she yelled.

"Shut up!" he growled. "If you make another sound I'm going to come back there and smash your fucking face in."

Aimee gritted her teeth together. It took all of her strength not to tell him to go screw himself. *Man, am I glad I'm not married to this turd anymore. Even Tiffany the cheating slut doesn't deserve to be locked in a trunk and smacked around.* She amended her thought: *Well, maybe just a little.*

The car stopped and a few seconds later the door to the trunk flew open. She saw that she was in an underground parking garage of some sort, and opened her mouth to scream; but the sound was cut off by his fist smashing into her face and knocking her unconscious.

38

kiki

KIKI SQUINTED AT THE ADDRESSES on the high-rise condos that passed by her window.

"There!" yelled Elizabeth, leaning over and pointing out Kiki's side of the Camaro. "That one. With the pink marble on the front."

Kiki did a quick, illegal u-turn and pulled over, ignoring the 'No Parking' signs. "Let's go."

They jumped out of the car and went to the lobby doors. They were locked.

"Now what?" asked Elizabeth, her eyes scanning the keypad near the entrance.

"We buzz a few," said Kiki. She noticed there was a video camera above them, and hoped it was hooked up to the condo owner's security systems. "Just don't press the one that's Jack's."

"Which one is that?" asked Elizabeth, her voice going into a higher, nervous pitch. "I didn't write it down!"

"I'm not sure. But he's an ass, so let's assume he picked one of the top three floors. His ego wouldn't allow for anything lower."

"Good point. Okay, I'll start with the first floor." Elizabeth pushed a button on the directory screen.

Kiki unbuttoned the top of her blouse, making sure there was ample cleavage showing.

"Hello?" came a voice over the speaker.

"Hello, this is Tiffany. I, um, lost my key. Can you let me in?"

"I don't recognize you. Use the combination pad there," came the cranky voice.

"I forgot the code."

"Sorry," said the voice. A click told them they had been disconnected.

They tried five more numbers before they hit the jackpot. The sound of an old man's voice came over the speaker.

"Who's there?!" he shouted.

"Hard of hearing," whispered Elizabeth.

"It's Tiffany! Can you let me in? I forgot my key!"

There were a few seconds of silence before they heard a response. This time it was an old woman's voice. "Who is it, Herbert?"

"Oh, I don't know. I think it's that teenager from down the hall again."

"Just let her in, already. It's time for your medication."

The buzz sounded and Elizabeth leapt forward, grabbing the handle of the door and pulling it hard before the buzzing stopped. "Got it!"

Kiki ran over to join her in the lobby, buttoning up her blouse as she went.

"Now what?" asked Elizabeth, pressing the button for the elevator.

"We start at the top and work our way down."

"Won't we need a key or a card or something to get to the upper levels?"

"Hopefully since this is one of the older buildings, there'll be more than one condo per floor." Kiki and Elizabeth stepped into the elevator. "We'll start with number fourteen."

The door opened onto the floor and they stepped out, looking right and left. "Four doors," said Elizabeth.

"Plus that one going to the stairs. Keep it in mind, just in case."

Elizabeth looked at her with fear in her eyes. "Just in case what?" she whispered.

"Just in case we have to get the hell outta here, fast."

Kiki walked up to the first door and knocked, putting her finger over the peephole.

"Who's there?" asked a woman.

"We're looking for Jack Parsons. Is he home?"

"There's no Jack Parsons here."

"Oh, sorry. Wrong door."

They tried the other three and either got no answer or the same one - no Jack here.

"What if he's there but he's not answering?" asked Elizabeth as they took the stairs down to the twelfth floor. There was no thirteenth floor in this building. Kiki rolled her eyes at the superstitious nonsense.

They came into the foyer area of the floor and stood still for a moment. Elizabeth opened her mouth to say something, but Kiki stopped her with a raised finger, mouthing the word, 'Wait.'

Elizabeth looked at Kiki curiously but said nothing.

Kiki cocked her ear to the side. She could have sworn she heard a noise like furniture being knocked over. She knew when Elizabeth heard it too, because she jumped at the next sound. It sounded like a woman's muffled scream.

"That one!" whisper-yelled Elizabeth, pointing to the door on their right. She whipped out her phone and started furiously pushing buttons.

"What are you doing?" whispered Kiki.

"Texting Joe on Aimee's phone. I'm telling him where we are. Hopefully he'll send the cavalry."

"I don't want to wait for them. She could be dead before they get here!"

Elizabeth's fingers froze. "Are you serious?"

"Of course I'm serious! This guy is nuts! He kidnapped her!"

"Okay, you're right. But how are we going to get in there?" She finished her text and put her phone in her back pocket.

Kiki reached in her bag and pulled out her gun.

Elizabeth's eyes nearly popped out of her head. *"Kiki!* You were *not* supposed to bring weapons! We agreed!"

"Well, I'm glad I lied. Now, come on." She walked over to the door and put her ear up to it. The sounds of screaming and scuffles had ceased. She knocked, once again covering the peephole with her finger.

Elizabeth stood on the other side of the door, ready to push it open if they got the opportunity.

No one answered.

Kiki knocked again and said, "Hello? Is anyone home? This is maintenance. We're going to use our key to come in if you're not home. We're permitted to do this under section eighteen point four of the condo owners' documents."

Elizabeth looked at Kiki with her WTF expression, her hands thrown up in confusion.

Kiki put her finger over her lips, motioning Elizabeth to be quiet. She knocked one more time with the butt of the gun. "Maintenance. We're coming in!" She played with the handle a little, trying to make it sound like she had a key.

"Hey! Who's there?" came an angry male voice from within, just on the other side of the door.

Elizabeth grabbed Kiki's arm in a death grip, her face going white.

Kiki slapped her hands away. "Sorry to bother you, sir, but we're with maintenance. We're having a problem with ... a water issue, and we need to get into your place for just a few minutes. We'll be out of your hair real quick."

At first there was no response, then, "I'm not having any issues with my water. Send someone tomorrow."

"I'm sorry, sir, but we have to come in now. Like I said, this is an emergency that involves the common area space between the units. Under section eighteen point one we have the right to enter."

"I thought you said it was eighteen point four."

Elizabeth put her hand to her heart and looked like she was having a heart attack.

"Actually, sir, it's both. One covers general issues and the other, specifically water."

"Just give me a minute," he said.

Elizabeth leaned in so she was up against Kiki's ear and whispered, "Where in the hell are you getting this stuff? He's not going to open the door!"

"Shush!" said Kiki, quietly. "He is too!"

A second later they heard his footsteps near the door. "Are you covering the peephole?"

"No sir. There appears to be a film over it, though. We can write a maintenance ticket out to have that cleaned for you tomorrow during regular work hours."

Kiki heard some grumbling and then the lock sliding back. She looked at Elizabeth and whispered, *"It's go time."*

39

elizabeth

ELIZABETH DIDN'T HAVE TIME TO think. She just acted. As soon as the seal on the door was broken and it started to open, she rammed it with her shoulder, putting everything she had into it.

Jack, not expecting her WWF techniques, fell backwards, propelled into the wall behind him.

"Aimee!" screamed Kiki, the gun held out in front of her, pointed at Jack and shaking like crazy. "Go find her, Elizabeth! I'll keep him here!"

"The hell you will!" he yelled, struggling to get to his feet, murder in his eyes.

Elizabeth grabbed a crystal vase off the front table and threw it at him, managing to hit him in the chest.

A muffled, *'Oooph'* escaped his mouth before he went down a second time, thrown off balance by the attack.

Elizabeth ran into the main room. "Aimee!" she yelled. There was no response.

"Find her!" yelled Kiki.

Elizabeth didn't have to be told again. She ran into the bedroom on the left side of the living room, flinging the door open and scanning the room as quickly as she could. There was no sign of Aimee anywhere, or any clues that she had been in the room.

She ran back into the main area of the condo, a quick glance toward the front door telling her that Jack was back on his feet and Kiki had moved to put more space between them, coming a little into the living room space herself. Elizabeth wasted no more time worrying about that problem, and went into the second bedroom.

The first thing she noticed was the bed. It looked like a serious wrestling match had just occurred on it. "Aimee!" she yelled. There was still no answer.

Her heart was in her throat. She knew Aimee had to be here somewhere. She noticed a door on the far side of the room, closed up tight, but with a faint light framing the bottom where there was a space between the door and the floor.

Elizabeth raced over and pulled the door open. On the floor of the walk-in closet lay her friend, her dress up around her waist and her face beaten to a pulp.

Elizabeth got down on the floor with her, crawling over carefully, trying not to bump her. "Aimee, sweetie. Are you okay?" She started to cry, overwhelmed by the idea that Aimee was dead at the hands of her ex-husband, and that she herself might have had a hand in enraging him with the work she had done on his books. The sobs came out unbidden. "Oh, Aimee, I'm so sorry, honey, I'm so sorry!"

She reached over and put her fingers on Aimee's neck. She had no idea really where to feel for a pulse, but couldn't think of anything else to do.

Aimee's body was still warm. *That's a good sign, right? How long does it take for someone to lose body heat after they ...* She couldn't even get the thought out in her head.

Aimee's neck provided no pulse that Elizabeth could sense. She grabbed for her friend's wrist, hoping she'd have better luck there. Near Aimee's thumb, she thought she felt something. She shook Aimee's hand, strongly, suddenly energized by the idea that she might still be alive. "Aimee! Wake up! Aimee!"

Elizabeth continued to cry, but moved so she was in a better position to touch her friend. "Aimee, it's Elizabeth. I'm afraid to move you because you look pretty beat up. But I need to know if you're okay. Please answer me!" There was no response.

Elizabeth jumped up and ran out of the closet and the bedroom. They had to get Aimee to the hospital. She came out into the living room and started speaking immediately, before her brain had a chance to compute what her eyes were seeing. "She's hurt bad! I don't even know if she's alive. We have to get her to the ..."

"Sit down and shut the fuck up," said Jack, holding Kiki's gun. "That stupid bitch isn't dead. Not yet, anyway."

Kiki shrugged her shoulders at Elizabeth's look of confusion. "He got it away from me. I let him get too close."

"I told you not to bring that damn thing," admonished Elizabeth.

Kiki smiled sadly. "You just cussed."

"Shut the hell up, you stupid whore. We're getting ready to take a trip."

"Don't call me a whore, you cheating, lying piece of shit."

"Kiki," begged Elizabeth, "Please don't piss him off!"

"What did you just call me?" he said menacingly, moving closer to her.

"I called you a cheating, lying, piece of ..." Kiki didn't move in time to save herself from the strong backhand that came so quickly, Elizabeth hadn't even expected it. Kiki's head snapped back, and her hair flew over to cover her face. Kiki's hand came up slowly to move her hair out of her eyes as she brought her head back to its former position.

Elizabeth could see a dark red mark just below her friend's eye. She cringed inside at the obvious pain Kiki was in and would be in for the next few days with that injury - if she lived that long. Elizabeth decided she had to distract him from Kiki, otherwise Kiki's mouth was going to get her shot.

"Jack, Aimee's in bad shape. Why don't you let us take her to the hospital?"

"Why would I do that?" he laughed. "I hope the bitch dies. I plan on helping her on her way in a minute, once I take care of you two."

"You'd murder three women in cold blood? For what?" spat Kiki. "A piece of ass?"

"That piece of ass you're referring to is carrying my child. Something that worthless piece of garbage in there could never do." He waved the gun in the direction of the room where Aimee lay near death.

Kiki opened her mouth to speak, but Elizabeth silenced her by talking louder. "Aimee feels really bad about that, Jack. She wanted to give you a child. She told me that, several times. Why don't we sit down and talk about it? We can pop some *popcorn* or something."

Kiki's eyes perked up.

"Popcorn? What the fuck is your problem? You think I want to sit around with you cunts and chat about the fucking weather? Just shut the hell up and sit down."

Elizabeth stared at Kiki, hoping and praying she'd gotten her signal. They had one chance to make this happen, and if Kiki didn't get it, one or both of them were going to die here tonight.

Elizabeth started walking in the opposite direction of where Jack had motioned for her to go, saying with false cheer, "I'm just going to go check and see if you have any popcorn, first."

"What the ...?" he started saying, turning to follow her progress, the hand with the gun going in the same direction.

Elizabeth watched Kiki jump up out of the corner of her eye, and grab Jack's gun arm, managing to get him pointing it down at the floor.

Elizabeth sprang into action, jumping on Jack's back, putting him in a choke hold from behind.

He spun around and jerked his body back and forth, trying to shake her off. She held on for dear life, keeping visions of Aimee's limp and unresponsive body in the forefront of her mind. If she let go, Jack was going to kill them all, and everything she'd grown to love about these two other women would be snuffed out, just like that. She leaned in and bit his ear, clamping down as hard as she possibly could. His blood filled her mouth, but she didn't let go.

His screams rent the air.

Meanwhile, Kiki had turned so her back was to Jack's chest, while both of her hands held his forearm in a death grip. She was doing everything she could to keep that gun pointed away from anyone.

A shot rang out as his finger pulled the trigger. Kiki screamed, and Elizabeth heard a ringing in her ears that she was afraid would be permanent. Then the earth felt like it was tilting. The three-body tangle was going down, and she was going to be the cushion for the full force of it.

Most of her breath was knocked out when they landed. She'd managed to move herself to the side a bit so it was her ribs that took a lot of the jolt and not her spine. Her teeth lost their hold on Jack's ear, so she spat the blood that was in her mouth into his hair.

"Let go of the gun, mother ... fucker," grunted out Kiki, now sitting on top of him.

Jack continued to struggle but was seriously hampered by the monkey on his back.

"Aimee!" said Kiki, astonishment in her voice.

Elizabeth ceased her struggling and looked up to see what appeared to be a walking car accident victim stumbling toward them. Her dress was ripped to reveal one of her breasts. It was purple with bruises, as was her chest.

"He ... he ...," she sobbed, unable to get the words out.

The gun went off again, and she jumped, screaming pitifully and then crying again. Her face started to change, going from desperate to angry in seconds. "He raped me," she shriek-whispered, her voice sounding raw and brutalized. She walked in slow motion over to where the three of them were still struggling, Jack now with renewed energy.

Aimee bent down and grabbed the gun, twisting and turning it, trying to free it from his grasp. "Give that to me, you *bastard*," she growled.

"Aimee, watch out! Don't get shot!" yelled Elizabeth, nearly hysterical with worry over her friend. None of this was going to end well. None of it. He was going to shoot her, or she was going to shoot him and then she'd go to jail for murder. Her beautiful, sweet, cookie-baking friend was going to be in prison.

Aimee finally worked the gun from his grasp and stepped back with it in her hands. "Get away, girls. I have to shoot him now, and I don't want to hit you by mistake."

"Aimee, no!" shouted Kiki. "He's a prick and an idiot. He is not worth your life. Now put that down!"

"No!" she shrieked.

"Aimee, please," begged Elizabeth. "We love you, sweetie. Please don't do this to yourself. Don't do this to us. What about Desperate Measures?"

Aimee looked up, a flash of recognition moving across her face. "Desperate Measures?"

"Yes! Desperate Measures. It's our dream! Don't walk away from the dream!" encouraged Kiki.

"Desperate!" laughed Jack. "I'd say you cunts are desperate. You look ridiculous and you sound worse."

Aimee's eyes hardened. "I really wish you hadn't said that, Jack." She lifted the gun and pointed it at his chest.

"Aimee! Aimee Haggenbloom! *Put* that gun away!" yelled Elizabeth.

Aimee looked at her in confusion. "How did you ... know my maiden name?"

"From your files. Now stop being a fool and put that damn thing away before I come over there and slap you," yelled Elizabeth, now feeling like she was the one who was losing it.

"Did you just swear at me?" Aimee asked.

"Yes, she did!" said Kiki. "Look what you've done, Aimee! You've made her swear. Now put that down and help me up."

Just then a banging on the door echoed into the space. "Open up! Orlando Police Department! This is a knock and announce!"

"Break it open!" yelled Kiki. "We're in here!"

The door flew open, the frame splintering into several pieces and flying to the floor. Several uniformed and flak-jacketed officers entered with guns drawn.

Aimee threw her hands up, tears streaming down her face.

"Ma'am, put the gun down!" yelled a guy from behind a clear mask.

"I ... I ...," stuttered Aimee.

Elizabeth could see her friend was in total meltdown mode. "She's in shock! She was attacked and kidnapped. Don't you dare shoot her!"

Just then Joe's face appeared from the middle of the crowd at the door. "Aimee!" he shouted, pushing past the others. "Hold your fire. Do you hear me?! Hold your fire!"

He took four long strides into the room until he was standing just inches away from Aimee.

"Babe. I need that gun, okay?"

Aimee nodded her head, two more tears coursing down her cheeks to drop onto her battered chest.

Joe reached up and gently took the gun from her hand, gesturing to the officers behind him to come in.

Kiki untangled herself from Jack, giving him a quick, hard punch to the crotch before she stood. "That's for Aimee, asshole."

Elizabeth felt him tense up and heard the groan of pain come up from his gut. *Good one, Kiki.* She waited for the police officers to pull him off of her before she tried to stand. She felt a little bit bummed that she couldn't give him a shot to the balls herself. He deserved that and more.

"She needs to go to the hospital," said Elizabeth, limping over to join Joe and Aimee. He had enveloped her in a tender hug. Elizabeth could see tears in his eyes.

Aimee started sobbing and trying to explain to Joe, but he just petted her head and back while he tried to soothe her. "Ssshhhhh, it's okay now. You don't have to talk about it yet. Let's get you to the hospital first and then we'll sort it all out, okay?"

"Are you going to come?" she asked Joe in the most hopeful and pitiful-sounding voice Elizabeth had ever heard. Her heart was breaking over the raw emotion that was being expressed by her friend.

"I wouldn't be anywhere else. I'll stay right in the room with you, the whole time you're there. I won't even leave for a shower."

Aimee smiled as much as her split lips and bruised cheeks would let her. "That's nice."

Elizabeth moved over to stand by Kiki, who held her hand up for a high five. Elizabeth was happy to join her in that small celebration. Nothing was fixed, really, but now they had only one direction left to go - up.

40

aimee

 IMEE OPENED HER EYES, TAKING in the view around her. White walls, a white board with some writing on it that she couldn't read because her vision was blurry, and an IV bag. *An IV bag? Where am I?* She looked to her left and saw a person sleeping in a chair next to her. A big someone, with hairy arms and a short-sleeved police uniform on.

"Joe?" she croaked out.

His head flew up and he scrubbed his face a couple times real quick before focusing on her. "Hey, beautiful. You're awake!"

"Yeah," she said softly. Her throat hurt something awful. "What the heck happened? Why am I in the hospital?"

"You don't remember?"

She thought about it for a second. "A little. Bits and pieces. I remember going out with you and then stopping for gas. Then ..." She felt confused. The memories were there, they were just ... hiding.

Joe stood and came to sit on the edge of her bed, taking her hand in his. "Jack kidnapped you at that gas station. He took you to his condo and beat you up pretty bad. If Kiki and Elizabeth hadn't been there to rescue you, I'm not sure ... well, let's just say, your two friends pretty much saved your life. I owe them a huge debt of gratitude that I'm pretty sure I'll never be able to repay."

"What do you mean? It's my life they saved."

"Yeah, well, there's that. And that's important. But that's not all."

"What do you mean? Was there someone else involved?"

"Yes."

"Who? Is it someone I know?"

"Not yet."

Aimee frowned. She wasn't sure if it was the knocks to the head she'd obviously suffered or if he was deliberately playing with her.

"Joe, I'm getting a headache. Please don't play with me now."

"I'm sorry babe. I just ... don't really know how to say this right, I guess."

"Say what?"

"That your friends saved the life of the woman that I love and the life of my unborn child."

"Your unborn ... what?"

Joe sat there staring at her, tears coming to his eyes. One escaped and dripped off his cheek to land on their entwined fingers.

Understanding started to dawn. "Are you saying ...?"

Joe nodded. "Yeah, babe. You're pregnant. We're going to have a baby."

"But ... how? I'm infertile."

"The doctor said it was probably Jack, not you, who was infertile. You can't argue with the blood tests, babe."

Aimee's eyes began to tear up. "I'm so sorry," she whispered.

"Sorry? Why are you sorry? I'm not." He lifted their entwined hands and kissed her fingers.

"You're not?" She said, hope making her voice tremble.

"Heck no. You're going to be a great mom. I consider myself lucky to be sharing this miracle with you."

"But you hardly know me," she said desperately, not believing that this man could possibly be interested in sharing this kind of commitment with her.

"I'll get to know you. If you'll let me." He had to stop talking because he became too choked up to continue.

Aimee couldn't think of anything to say to that. All she knew was that her heart was so full right now, it felt like it was going to burst.

41

kiki

$\mathcal{K}$IKI ROLLED HER EYES AT Aimee's stubbornness. "Yes, it is possible, duh. Obviously."

"But how could they know I was pregnant already? It's only been a few days since we had sex!"

"Blood tests, dork! They're very accurate. Even pee tests can tell in less than a week these days."

Aimee shook her head. "But I'm infertile."

Kiki threw up her hands. "I give up. She's nuts."

Elizabeth came over to the bed. "It's true. You're pregnant. Now you have to decide what you're going to do. You have the baby to think about."

"Do? What do you mean *do?*"

"Well, are you still going to live with Kiki? Are you still going to do Desperate Measures with us?"

"Don't you want me anymore?" Aimee asked, sounding near tears.

"Of course we want you!" yelled Kiki and Elizabeth simultaneously.

Aimee smiled, wiping her tears away with the back of her bandaged hand. "Geez, okay, relax."

"So, what's it gonna be?" asked Kiki.

Aimee shook her head. "No, you're not getting rid of me. I'm totally in, one hundred percent. We've gone this far. Why would I turn back now, just when it's getting fun?"

"Good," said Elizabeth. "And I have a message for you from Marcus."

"Did you tell him I said thanks for the flowers?"

"Yes, I did. And he said, and I quote, 'Their beauty pales in comparison to yours.'"

"Oh, that is so sweet! What's his news?"

"He talked to Jack's defense lawyer, and Jack is ready to settle."

"Of course he is," said Kiki. "Ass."

"What should I do?"

"Just do it. Get him out of your life once and for all."

"He already *is* going to be out of her life," said Kiki. "In jail. For a really long time. Kidnapping? Attempted murder? The guy's a lifer. But I agree. You should take the money and run. He won't ever be working as a lawyer again."

"Poor Tiffany," said Aimee. "Now her child has to live with the fact that its father is a criminal lunatic."

"Don't worry about old Tiffany," laughed Kiki. "She contacted Marcus and told him that the baby isn't Jack's."

"What?! *Get! Out!*"

Elizabeth was smiling. "Yeah. It didn't take her long to put some serious distance between herself and Jack."

"Is she lying?"

"Marcus doesn't think so. She said she'd do an amnio ... whatever to get the baby's DNA now, instead of waiting for it to be born. She does *not* want that shit in the public record of your court documents ... saying Jack is her baby's father."

Aimee shook her head in disbelief. "I can't believe it. It really was Jack's sperm and not my lady parts that was the problem. All that time I let him make me believe there was something wrong with me."

Elizabeth patted her hand. "Let it go, babe. He's not worth it."

"What about the townhouse Tiffany is living in?"

"It's yours as part of the settlement."

"I don't want it."

"Sell it, then. Keep the money," counseled Elizabeth.

"Maybe you can move in with your baby-daddy," suggested Kiki.

Aimee's face colored. "We haven't talked about it."

"Well, I have a feeling you will be," said Elizabeth as the door opened and a large bouquet came in the door.

"Delivery for ... Aimee."

"Put it over there," Elizabeth said, motioning for the man to put it on the tables that already held several.

"Is it from Joe?" asked Kiki.

Elizabeth pulled the card off and handed it to Aimee.

Aimee opened it and teared up again. "Yes. He signed it 'Yours'."

"I told you that you hit the jackpot, didn't I?"

The door opened again and admitted a little old lady carrying a bone-white vinyl purse. "Is this Aimee's room? Oh, hey girls, how are you? I've been in five different rooms already, looking for this one. I saw two asses, one breast, and a pecker. What the heck is wrong with people these days that they can't keep their robes closed?"

Aimee started laughing, grimacing slightly at the pain it caused her face and ribs.

Betty came up to the bedside. "Hi, sweetie. It's Betty. Can you see me okay?"

"Yes, I can. Thank you for coming."

"That's a hell of a shiner you've got there. You look like you were in a fight with Muhammed Ali."

"No, just my ex-husband."

"Bastard!" she yelled. "Anywho, I have a little something for you I made the other day. I heard you were *in a certain way*, from a little bird, so here you go."

She unsnapped her vinyl bag and pulled out a pair of mustard yellow baby booties.

Aimee took them gently and turned them over, getting the full effect and trying to ignore Kiki's not very discreet snorts coming from across the room. Aimee could see Elizabeth rolling her eyes to the ceiling and tapping her foot, trying not to laugh.

"Oh, Betty, these are lovely."

"Well, the color looks like shit, I know. But I get the yarn from the bargain bin. I'm on a fixed income, you know." She turned to go out of the room. "Well, I have mah johngg in a few hours or so. I have to go prepare myself for Madge's next abomination. You know, ever since I brought your delicious cakes, she's been on a one-woman mission to bring me down. Last week she actually brought fruitcake and marshmallow kabobs. *Kabobs!* I looked at 'em and said, 'Are you kidding me?' She just gave me one of her looks. Oh, those looks. I see 'em and I just want to pop her in the kisser. Aimee, honey, you need to get better soon and make me some more tarts before I'm forced to take matters into my own hands." She waved at the girls over her shoulder on the way out. "Toodles, girls. See you at the book club meeting!"

Kiki held her stomach, laughing so hard she couldn't stop. She looked up at her friends and saw they were suffering the same as her. "Man, I love that woman."

"That's what you're going to be like when you're ninety," said Aimee, laughing and crying at the same time.

"Ninety? Try forty," said Elizabeth, peals of laughter ringing out and surrounding Kiki with echoing reminders that she was in a really good place in her life right now, even if she had just recently wrestled a mad gunman to the floor to save the life of a friend.

42

elizabeth

ELIZABETH CLOSED HER LAPTOP. "OKAY, it's all done."

"So I'm finished? I'm a free woman?" asked Aimee. She held up Elizabeth's favorite pen, having just signed her name to her divorce settlement papers.

"Well, I need to file these with the court and get the judge to sign off on them, but that shouldn't take longer than a few days," explained Marcus. "Judge Halsey is well aware of your situation and is more than happy to fast-track this for us."

"Marcus, I don't know how to thank you for everything," said Aimee.

"Oh, goodness, don't even think about it. I still feel terrible for getting Jack all riled up at you."

"That was *not* your fault, Marcus," said Kiki. "The guy's a nutter."

"Yes, well, be that as it may, I still feel responsible. Whatever you need, you say the word."

"So when is she going to get her money?" asked Kiki.

"It should be wired into her account within five days. That's the agreement."

"I'm glad you took all the cash, instead of the property," said Elizabeth. "It's going to be so much easier for you."

"Yeah, well, it's less than I could have gotten, but you're right; it beats trying to sell Tiffany's love nest."

"Hey, seven hundred grand is nothing to sneeze at," reminded Kiki.

"Oh, I know. It's my nest egg. Mine and Junior's," Aimee said, rubbing her flat abdomen.

Kiki walked up and patted Aimee's belly. "Does Junior want to go see the place?"

"Yes, I think he does. And so does his mommy."

"Excellent."

They started walking out of Marcus's office. "I can't believe we found the perfect location for Desperate Measures so quickly. Can you believe it's only been a week since the doo-doo hit the fan?" asked Aimee.

"I told you, Rich is some kind of genius, in a weird, almost creepy kind of way," said Kiki.

"Oh, he wasn't that bad," laughed Elizabeth. "He's just a little over eager."

Kiki rolled her eyes.

"And the landlord meeting us so soon and being so willing to negotiate and sign off on everything we asked for? I think we're benefitting from this terrible economy. I'm trying not to feel guilty about that," said Elizabeth, stepping into the elevator that would take them down to the lobby.

"Don't feel guilty about our happiness. We're going to help revitalize the area," said Aimee.

"You got that right," agreed Kiki. "I gave the keys to Brent yesterday, by the way. He said he wanted to drop a couple things off for us. I'm guessing flowers or something. He said he'd meet us over there after our meeting with Marcus to give me back the keys." said Kiki.

"Want me to drive?" asked Elizabeth.

"Sure. If you want," said Kiki, trying not to smile.

"I'm not going to break the speed limit, Kiki."

"And you shouldn't either. You'll have baby on board, after all."

Elizabeth narrowed her eyes at her. "You called me a granny driver."

Kiki shrugged. "It takes you fifteen minutes to drive ten blocks, Lizzie."

"Girls, girls, please. I'm getting nauseous. Stop."

"You keep using that morning sickness excuse for everything. Eventually we're not going to believe you anymore," warned Kiki.

"Well, then you will suffer the consequences," said Aimee, trying to hide her smile and look serious.

They piled into Elizabeth's car, Aimee in the center of the back seat and Kiki the front passenger. Kiki turned on the radio and started singing loudly, off key, to the worst song Elizabeth had ever heard. Elizabeth reached over twice to turn it down, but Kiki slapped her hand away. Elizabeth gave up. All Aimee could seem to do was smile. Elizabeth caught her look in the mirror and grinned back. She loved her new friends.

They pulled up to the curb in front of the future site of their business. All three girls were stunned speechless at what they saw.

Three men stood outside the commercial space, all of them wearing paint-spattered jeans and t-shirts that had seen much better days. Each was sporting beard stubble growing in thickly and hair that looked like it needed a good washing.

"What the heck?" said Aimee, distractedly. "Is that ... *Joe?*"

"And *Brent?*" said Kiki.

"And *Sebastian?*" asked Elizabeth.

Elizabeth shut off the engine while the three of them stared. A sign hung above the door that read: "The Future Home of Desperate Measures Cafe". The windows were covered in paint to block the construction that would soon commence inside. But it wasn't just regular old white paint; it was a mural, painted by Sebastian - assisted by the other two guys if the looks of their clothes were any indication. They'd obviously been painting for twenty-four hours straight - creating a gorgeous work of art that depicted the three girls together.

All of the painted women were smiling. One was holding up a plate of cookies, one was on her computer with a pen behind her ear, and one was holding a gun pointed up in the air. And all of them were wearing heels.

What to read next ...

If you enjoyed *Desperate Measures*, try *Don't Make Me Beautiful*, a standalone romantic suspense novel.

Or ...

For a more light-hearted romance, click here to read my *New York Times* bestseller *Shine Not Burn* next.

Being an independent author, I depend entirely on *you*, the reader, to get the word out about my books. If you liked this book, won't you please leave a review online and recommend it to a friend? The more you spread the word, the more books I can write, and nothing would please me more than to put a new book in your hands every single month.

I read all my reviews!

Find more Elle Casey books at the following retailers:

Amazon
iBooks
Barnes & Noble
Google Play
Kobo
Walmart
Your Local Library via the OverDrive ebook platform

Want to get an email when my next book is released?
Sign up here: www.ElleCasey.com/news

ABOUT THE AUTHOR

Elle Casey, a former attorney and teacher, is a NEW YORK TIMES, USA TODAY, *and Amazon bestselling American author who lives in France with her husband, three kids, and a number of horses, dogs, and cats. She has written more than 40 novels in less than 5 years and likes to say she offers fiction in several flavors. These flavors include romance, science fiction, urban fantasy, action adventure, suspense, and paranormal.*

A personal note from Elle …

If you enjoyed this book, please take a moment to leave a review on the site where you bought this book, Goodreads, or any book blogs you participate in, and tell your friends! I love interacting with my readers, so if you feel like shooting the breeze or talking about books or your family or pets, please visit me. You can find me at …

www.ElleCasey.com
www.Facebook.com/ellecaseytheauthor
www.Twitter.com/ellecasey
www.Instagram.com/ellecaseyauthor

Other Books by Elle Casey

CONTEMPORARY URBAN FANTASY

War of the Fae (10-book series)
Ten Things You Should Know About Dragons
(short story, The Dragon Chronicles)
My Vampire Summer
Aces High

DYSTOPIAN

Apocalypsis (4-book series)

SCIENCE FICTION

Drifters' Alliance (ongoing series)
Winner Takes All (short story prequel to Drifters' Alliance,
Dark Beyond the Stars Anthology)
The Ivory Tower (short story standalone, Beyond the Stars: A
Planet Too Far Anthology)

ROMANCE

By Degrees
Rebel Wheels (3-book series)
Just One Night (romantic serial)
Just One Week
Love in New York (3-book series)
Shine Not Burn (2-book series)
Bourbon Street Boys (4-book series)
Desperate Measures
Mismatched

ROMANTIC SUSPENSE

*All the Glory: How Jason Bradley Went from
Hero to Zero in Ten Seconds Flat*
Don't Make Me Beautiful
Wrecked (2-book series)

PARANORMAL

Duality (2-book series)
Monkey Business (short story)
Dreampath (short story standalone, The
Telepath Chronicles)
Pocket Full of Sunshine (short story & screenplay)

www.ingramcontent.com/pod-product-compliance
Lightning Source LLC
Chambersburg PA
CBHW021526250626
47154CB00006BA/1986